www.clocktowerbooks.com
Clocktower Books
Presents:

Progressive Thrillers Series

Valley of Seven Castles:
A Luxembourg Thriller

By

John T. Cullen

Valley of Seven Castles: A Luxembourg Thriller

This novel is a work of fiction. All the characters and events portrayed in this novel are fictitious and are not intended to evoke any persons living or dead.

A big acknowledgement goes to Sarah Dawson, our intrepid editor, for her diligence and skill in line editing the manuscript. Any errors remaining are the author's fault. Interested parties may contact Sarah Dawson online at **www.wordplayediting.com.**

Published by Clocktower Books
P.O. Box 600973
Grantville Station
San Diego, California 92160-0973

LUXEMBOURG: OLD OR HIGH CITY

Image Credits: Fotolia (paid), CIA World Fact Book (public domain)

Maps 1 and 2:

Luxembourg seen in Europe. Inset=closer image of Luxembourg between Belgium, France, and Germany. Luxembourg at 998 square miles (2586.4 km) is one of the world's smallest sovereign nations.

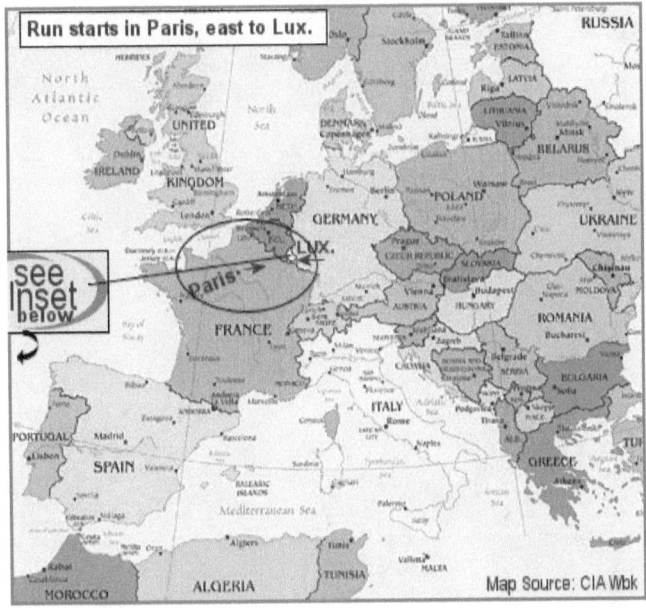

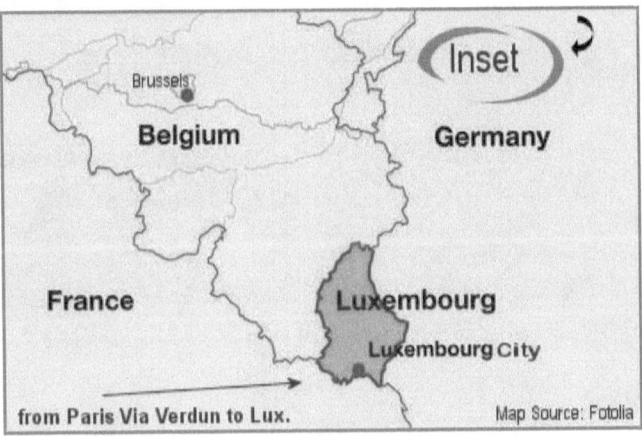

Map 3

Rick and Hannah meet in Paris, then flee for their lives eastward to Luxembourg. They leave France at Thionville in Lorraine (Chap. 3) and head to Luxembourg City.

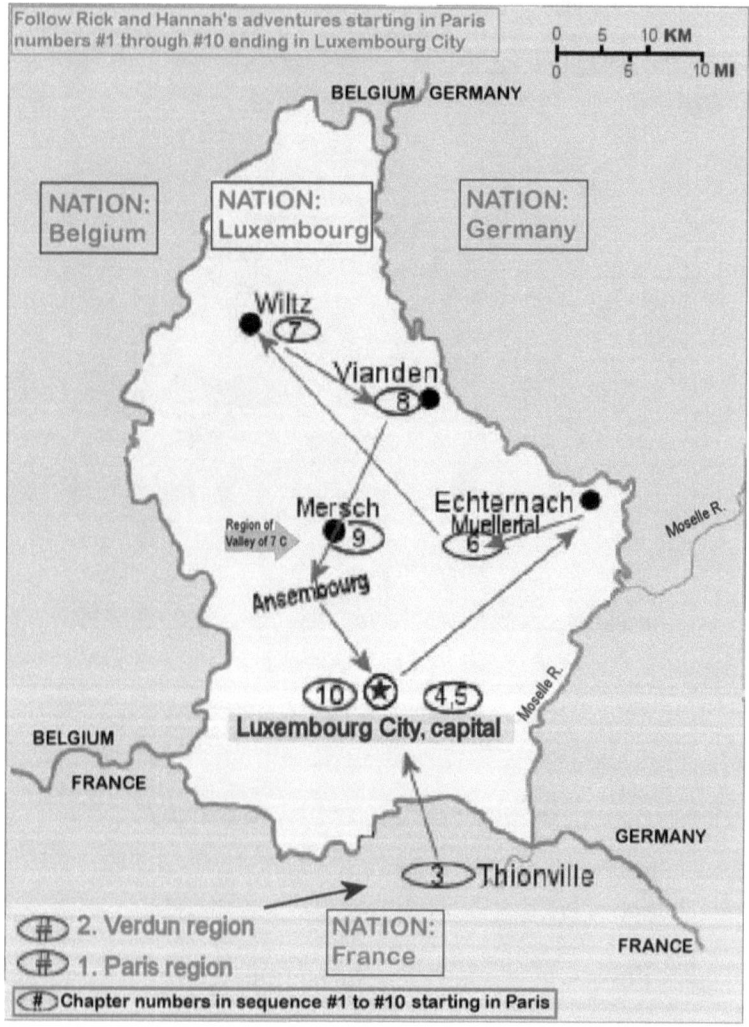

Contents

<u>Dedication</u>

For Carolyn and Andrew

Merçi

Villemol merçi to my dear Luxemburgish cousin Jean Arendt for his help with some Luxembourgeois phraseology. My *Lëtzebuergesch* is rusty after an absence of many years (of the author but not the heart), so readers will hopefully be patient with well-meaning efforts

Thanks to Sarah Dawson, my intrepid editor, for her skill and dedication in line editing the manuscript. Any remaining errors are the author's fault. Interested parties seeking editorial support my contact Sarah Dawson online at www.wordplayediting.com.

Preface

Thrillerology:

(explained herein at John T. Cullen's Thrillerologue)

Valley of Seven Castles, a Luxembourg Thriller

is the 21st Century's first

Progressive Thriller

for Our Dangerous Age*

*Combines the relentless, pounding cross-European pace of

Robert Ludlum's The Bourne Identity

With the Romantic and exotic plot points of

Alfred Hitchcock's 1959 all time great film

North by Northwest

As well as

The plot points of John Buchan's 1915

The Thirty-Nine Steps

And

Alfred Hitchcock's 1935 thriller film

The 39 Steps

Author's Note: This Preface and brief Prolog (next page) are continued at the end of the novel. See also: dedicated website at:

www.johntcullen.com/

Prologue: a Thrillerologue

Includes a Bombshell Revelation for Thriller Fans

These sections continue at Appendix: Thrillerology, starting on page 301. For more info, also visit www.johntcullen.com.

1. Welcome: a Luxembourg Thriller

This novel is the world's first Progressive Thriller—dedicated to democracy versus corporate tyranny in the United States, the West, and the greater world. It's a rousing thriller with a dark, exciting pace and passion as in the 2002 film *The Bourne Identity*. This story is also dramatically relevant to our dangerous times—exuberantly and blatantly progressive, tolerant, intelligent, positive, and humane. In this brief and cursory Thrillerology, I trace the broad outlines of thriller history as I understand it, and more generally suspense fiction.

2. World's First Progressive Thriller

If you read a 2016 news item that sixty-three (63) billionaires own more than half the entire world's wealth—not to mention power shakeups in the USA after this novel was published in early 2016—you must meet Professor Sander and the Progressive Alliance for Peace (PAX).

3. Thrillerology Historical Sketch (to 1900)

From Gilgamesh to Homer's Achilles and Odysseus, from Virgil's Aeneas to Daniel Defoe's Robinson Crusoe (1719), there is no discernible starting point. The 1800s in particular brewed an Industrial Revolution's worth of brilliant thrillers and heroes, from Mary Shelley's 1816 monster to the detectives, victims, and monsters created by writers like Edgar Allan Poe, A. Conan Doyle, Bulwer-Lytton, and H. G. Wells to name just a few.

4. Thrillerology Historical Sketch (since 1900)

My story begins with John Buchan's 1915 archetypal thriller classic The Thirty-Nine Steps, and progresses through a series of film remakes spanning a century—most interestingly not one but two films by Alfred Hitchcock.

5. Bombshell Revelation for Thriller Lovers

Detailing my path in reaching the current novel, I offer a surprising and delightful revelation about Alfred Hitchcock's plot and structure choices over a lifetime.

6. The Final Secret of Alfred Hitchcock

I'm not the only one to emulate John Buchan's 1915 story structure, which works so well because the hero is on the run from both the good guys and the bad guys. My Alfred Hitchcock revelation will surprise you. The pacing and rapid locale shifts owe much to the 2002 thriller movie The Bourne Identity, starring Matt Damon and Franka Potente, based on a 1980 Robert Ludlum thriller.

7. Gender Equality & Plot Structures A Century After Buchan

Forget "the girl" or "no girl." An author's best bet for a powerful story is to write a strong female and a strong male lead, pairing them for max effect. More info at *Appendix: Thrillerology* starting on page 301.

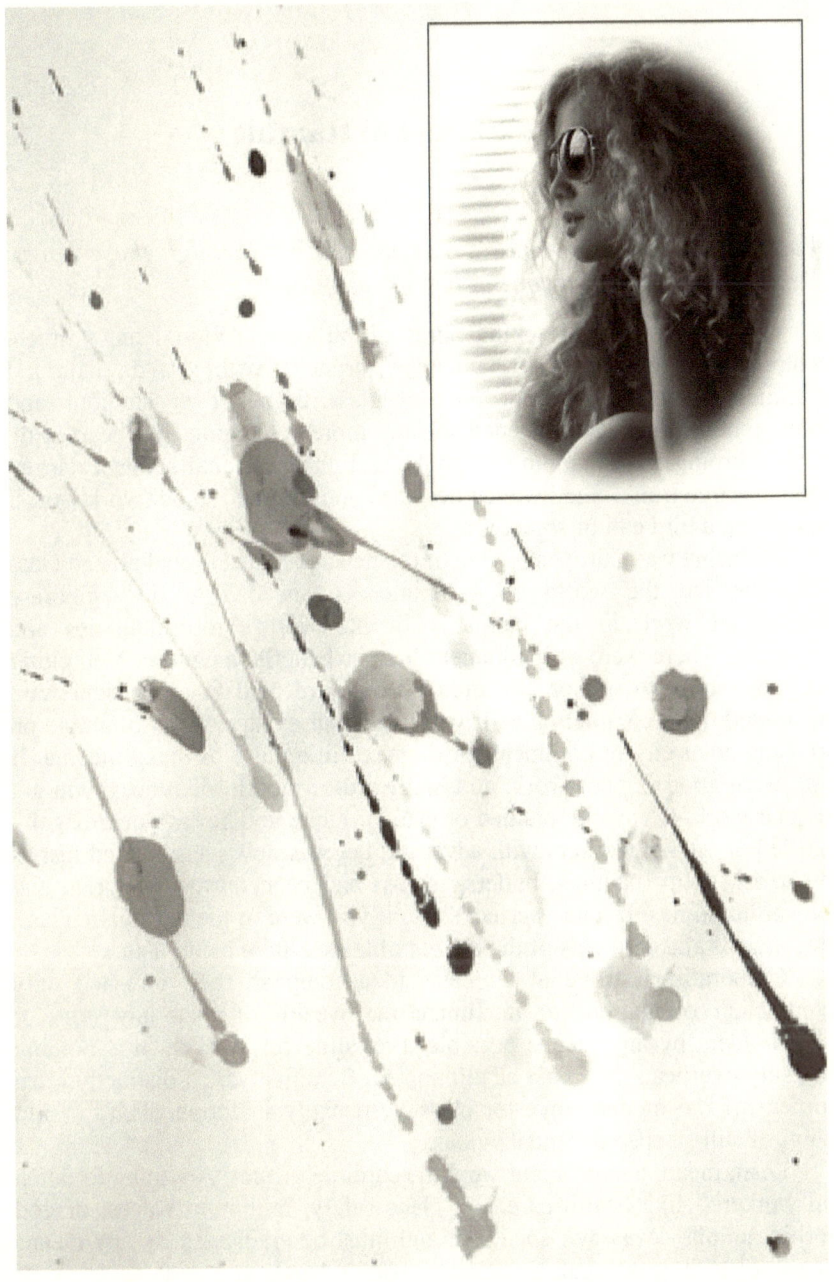

1.   Shanghai Ramble

Was that a terrified woman's scream, knifing through these balmy Shanghai pleasure gardens in broad sunshine?

On a balcony overlooking acres of billionaire Wan Hong's green, sculpted parkland estate sat a slender brunette with straight hair and feminine-looking transparent blue eyeglass frames over studious and intelligent features. She listened for any more screaming, but heard only birds chirping, carp jumping in pools, and an occasional squirrel darting around a tree trunk. She lowered her head and returned to her work—must have been a bird call or something.

Mélusine was European—one of the new, educated global artisan class who traveled the world on assignment as needed to do temporary intellectual work in the hierarchy of the world's top industries and oligarchs. There were no permanent jobs or benefits anymore. You either had something to sell or you didn't. You were paid to get it done, and dismissed upon completion as if you had never existed, only to ramble on to some other city or continent for the next little piece of lucky income. If you were good at your work, and had word-of-mouth references, you got regular work. If you complained or made trouble, you never worked again. Skilled or artisan workers with advanced degrees now were treated just as household help (nannies, butlers, maids) had been during Victorian and Edwardian times. It made perfect sense if you were of the zillionaire class, the bishops and cardinals of the church of laissez-faire capitalism.

Corporations strove at all costs to accomplish their one and only contractual obligation: to maximize the wealth of their investors or shareholders by any means possible. Providing for workers was nothing but silly overhead that must be eliminated. Benefits were a distraction that turned off the modern investor class—especially in former Third World cultures still steeped in feudal values.

Lean, mean, and efficient were the cardinal virtues. Anything to fatten up workers—like health care, job place safety, minimum wages, or god forbid, unions—was evil socialism and must be eradicated by any means possible. If it was legal, great. If it wasn't legal, you sent an army of lawyers and spent a fortune bribing the oily politicians in your pocket. Miraculously, you could thus quickly make anything legal to know, love, and serve that ultimate divine grace: profits.

Mélu fortunately had long ago learned to dance between the rain drops. She had solid references, while hiding the subversive democratic aspirations of her young life at twenty-eight.

As a light wind blew her papers, Mélu compared statistics on a computer pad about stresses on aircraft frames, and made notes in pencil on old-fashioned lined paper.

Mélu was a contract worker from Luxembourg, performing a month's worth of very specific, skilled engineering documentation for Wan Industries. She was privately also a spy for the Progressive Alliance for Peace (PAX). Hers was a subversive resistance movement growing around the world against the unimaginably powerful feudal network of corporations. The goal was to restore real democracy, not just in name but with actual meaning, so that even the wealthiest thousand families who now owned or controlled most of the world's wealth could be made part of the law, rather than above it. If the people elected a certain candidate, he or she actually took office rather than being replaced—on trumped up, unconstitutional excuses—by agents of the moneyed class who owned the media, courts, politicians, and financial structure of nations and continents.

As Mélu well knew, if Wan Industries realized her affiliation with PAX, they would have hired some obedient, quiet little corporate mouse or blathering false news addict.

The murder of Pierre Sander recently in London—during the hijacking of vital military data he was carrying to neutral NATO and U.S. hierarchies—now gave her special impetus. She was not here to damage Wan Industries in any way, but to gather intelligence. She would deliver solid engineering work to this employer, as contracted. She'd return home, unlike some of Wan's less fortunate employees—for example, the young BAN contractors who were virtual prisoners in vast pleasure mansions like this one in Shanghai, where Wan entertained his business contacts (or feudal vassals, one might say). The latest fad among impoverished youth, especially in the United States, was to sell yourself into indentured servitude, most often on a five year contract. During that time, you lived as a virtual slave—yes, boys and girls were frequently used as sex toys for foreign guests at discreet pool parties. When (and if) you satisfactorily finished your term, you retired for life on a lucrative pension.

She'd been listening for two hours to a party going on in a nearby condo unit that was attached to her own temporary guest apartment by a long, elevated walkway over trees and flower gardens. She had been trying to tune out throbbing rock music, men's and women's laughter, an occasional alcoholic shout, and crashing bottles breaking in trash cans.

A scream was something different and distracting. Mélu's eyes fluttered, and she looked up from her work.

Around her, the early summer air was hypnotic and balmy. City smog lay among distant hills and skyscrapers, but Wan Hong's estate was clean—as if he piped in mountain air. And for a man like Wan, almost anything was possible.

Almost.

Mélu's contract employer, Wan Industries, was one of the world's most powerful aircraft manufacturers. She'd met the billionaire, Wan Hong, on her first day during a presentation about the project. She would be here for thirty days at most, after completing a documentation subset for the new China Air Transport liner capable of carrying nearly 1,000 passengers. Then she'd be back home in Luxembourg, watering her roses in a tiny garden behind the tidy little white bungalow she shared with her young husband, Romain.

Hearing a woman's desperate shriek, Mélu set her tools aside and rose. She was an athletic, modest woman who regularly jogged, played tennis, bicycled, and more. Her features were pretty in a plain, healthy sort of way that made men drool—except she was happily married to a handsome young man with whom she shared love and affection. She had a level-headed air about her. She wore a black blouse and a black skirt that came to just above rounded knees, hinting at strong, rounded thighs under the garment. Her skin was caramel-tanned from the Shanghai sun. She wore simple black loafers.

She heard more noises.

Running.

Curious, she walked across her small patio and leaned her elbows on the wooden fence, overlooking the concrete walking path, hedges, and sprawling green gardens of Wan's estate.

Running toward her was a terrified looking blonde woman clutching a white, terry beach towel around herself. She was barefoot, terrified, and slapping the concrete with her feet.

"Are you all right?" Mélu asked, extending her lightly fuzzed arms over the fence so that her silver link bracelet swayed on one wrist. Her nails were bright pink. When she took a break from her work, she liked to sand her nails, touch them up, blow on them, regard them. Right now, she was regarding the blonde with concern.

"Help me," the woman cried.

She's young, Mélu thought—*maybe 25 at most, and certainly not from around here.*

"Come in," Mélu said automatically, opening the wooden gate.

The woman scrambled into the patio area, nearly collapsing on giraffe legs. She was beautiful, with blue eyes, creamy skin tinted a finer caramel shade than Mélu's, and her long golden hair done up in a bun on the back of her neck, but coming undone in an ungainly bouncing tangle.

Mélu heard the sounds of men running, yelling, and cursing. She heard the powerful, ominous pounding of their feet on concrete walks and wooden bridges. They would be here in seconds.

No time to waste.

Mélu slid open the glass door, pushed her inside, and swung her own behind around the door frame while pulling the door shut. Hiding behind industrial lace shades, Mélu watched. Her dark brown eyes were wide as she stared at three Triad or Yakuza gangsters running past. Their torsos were bare and rippled with muscle like steely cables. Each of the men had long, flowing black hair and was covered with garish tattoos: dragons, ghosts, gangsters, flowers, swords, and of course plenty of delicately drawn female skin. She heard them curse as they huffed and puffed jogging past.

Mélu locked the door, turned, and rested her back against the slider. She said in Luxembourgeois-accented English, "You are safe with me."

holding the towel around herself as best she could, for modesty, the young woman looked up through swollen, tear-reddened eyes. "Thanks."

"You sound American."

"My name," she said between sobs, "is Hannah Smith. I'm from San Diego and I don't want to be here anymore."

Mélu extended her hand. "Come, let's go to the bathroom and wash your face. I'll make some nice tea, and we can talk." Her voice was dry, authoritative, and strong, like a teacher's. "You are a BAN?"

The girl nodded emphatically, with a sob. "It's considered so hip. People are intrigued about BDSM and sex slaves. They think it's cool somehow. The money is really appealing because we all live in so much poverty these days. But it's just sex trafficking by another name. Once you get in with these animals, you never get out."

The young woman sounded intelligent, Mélu thought. She wouldn't ask about college, because there was no chance the girl had any advanced education. The U.S. corporate universities scam had collapsed after driving millions of hopeful young people into phony education programs, with zillions of dollars in student loan debt that only enriched the zillionaire class more, and no hope of ever paying the debt off because all the jobs had been outsourced to cheaper markets—including the contract artisan class who were educated programmers, accountants, and other intellectual workers hired strictly as temps. Talk about indentured servitude, Mélu thought as she prepared some nice tea and cookies for the two of them. *Poor girl.*

Hannah Smith was a bit taller than Mélu, and walked on long, slender legs as pale as ivory. You could see tiny traces of blue capillaries, so fine was her skin. Mélu got the picture totally. This woman from California was a BAN—the new kind of indentured servant or contract slave, euphemistically called Butlers And Nannies. In reality, when Asian, African, and South American billionaires bought themselves the pick of these snowy, desperate flowers from the decaying, collapsing West, they had other things in mind. And sometimes they shared their property with their footmen and killers. It was like tossing a bone to your dogs in the baronial manor.

Hannah tied her towel around her waist, revealing a long, slender back that same fine color like art paper, wanting to be painted on or made love to. She actually seemed a tall, gangly surfer type, with strong arms and golden fuzz on the forearms. She had small breasts, cupped in an expensive silk merlot bikini top probably made by one of Wan's Paris couture houses. Or maybe his fashion division was in London, or New York City, or L.A., or all of the above. Men like Wan could afford anything they wanted, including dozens of BANs both male and female. He would share his prizes with anyone he happened to be partying with, the way a person might pass around a roach to toke, or a thousand-dollar bottle of rare wine to share once and throw away empty. Young people were just something pretty to be sucked on once or twice and disposed of like trash.

Mélu gathered a nice tray of snacks from the fridge, while Hannah washed her face and gathered her composure. "You are far from home," Mélu said cautiously, not wanting to hurt her feelings more.

"It's a long story," Hannah said as she combed her long hair and wound it back up into a tight, orderly bun. Her shoulders were too narrow to be a swimmer's, but they rippled with sparse muscles under that nougat-white skin that stayed real (like the most precious diamonds or sapphires) by its imperfections. These included a sprinkling of faint orange freckles, some tiny chocolate moles, and small, fading childhood scars. She also had a large, angry bruise on one shoulder blade—a storm cloud shape of black, dark green, roiling blue, and spreading mustard yellow.

"He must have hit you hard," Mélu said.

"I punched him in the face and ran," Hannah said with surprising courage. She held a small comb in her perfect teeth while binding her hair up. Her blue eyes looked defiant. "He fell over on his ass, but these guys are Triads, the Chinese version of Yakuza. A woman hits one, they take turns raping her and maybe kill her. I have to hide until they leave."

"Which will be?"

"In a day or so."

"You can stay here with me."

"That is so nice of you. I promise not to be a bother."

Mélu shrugged. "I have a couch. Help yourself to the food and drink. I need to keep working. I'm on contract."

"Where are you from?" Hannah asked as she pulled out a chair at the table in the small kitchen.

"Luxembourg. You can tell I have an accent?"

Hannah smiled. She looked really lovely. "I sort of noticed."

Mélu said, "Are you hungry?"

"A little. They are having a feast over there, the tattoo crowd—wine, song, women, and all the chow mein you can chopstick. They don't think about letting the BANs have any."

"Whew." Mélu exhaled hard. "Stay indoors. You can watch videos. I hope you don't get too bored."

Hannah shook her head. "I'm just glad to be safe."

"You're safe with me," Mélu said.

They stood facing each other.

"Thank you, thank you," Hannah said.

"My pleasure. Don't worry, I am not gay. My husband is just now in Europe on another job."

"I'm not either," Hannah said. "I wouldn't care if you were. I'll just sleep on the couch. But thank you, thank you." She wrapped her long arms around Mélu's strong brown shoulders and pulled her close.

They hugged in a brief, stiff little embrace, keeping apart except that they pressed their cheeks together in a warm gesture of comradely affection.

"I have to get back to work," Mélu said.

"Your name?"

"Mélusine."

"That's so pretty."

"I am named after a famous river mermaid."

"You're not."

"I am. Mélusina was a river nymph who married the founder of Luxembourg, Count Sigefroi of the Ardennes, in the 960s A.D. He had no idea she was anything but an ordinary woman. She was very beautiful and nice. She did not tell him she was actually a river maid, sort of a sea-maid or mer-maid like the Lorelei on the Rhine River, or the Sirens in the Odyssey. She had one request. On Saturday mornings she must be alone in her bath. He must never disturb her. But men being men, he got nosy and one day went tip-toeing down the hall of the castle—*Lucilin Burhuc*, Small Castle in ancient Mosel-Frankish. He peeked into the keyhole."

"Yes? And?"

Mélu smiled mysteriously. "They were both shocked. He was shocked because he was looking at his wife, who turned into a river nymph once a week, with her big fins and flosses hanging out of the tub. She was shocked that he would betray her so."

Hannah laughed. "Men always fuck up, don't they?"

"Oh, they do sometimes." Mélu thought of Romain, her husband back home in Belair. "But they are nice sometimes also."

"I dream of finding a nice one," Hannah said with good humor. Her voice was both musical and a little throaty. "I can't wait to get back home and find Mr. Right. Or at least Mr. Good Enough. Nothing but bummers out here. So what happened to Mélusina?"

"She was bound by mermaid or river maid law and had to leave him. So she jumped from the tub and threw herself out the window. She fell down the famous cliffs of the old city and landed by a miracle in the Petrusse River—down in the valley with a big splash, and he never saw her again. But people may sometimes see her apparition around the old city of Luxembourg. Sometimes she comes as a beautiful woman, and other times as a snake with a key in its mouth."

"Sounds very dangerous," Hannah said. She laughed. "Like, these days you take any job you can get."

"You might get work carrying a key in your mouth."

"It would beat being a sex toy."

Mélu gave her a grieving look. "How did you get into this predicament?"

Hannah's face lost its forced, surfacy cheer. "I was trying to get the money to pay for my mom's cancer care. I was extra cute, and got brokered to a few different zillionaires, and ended up with Wan." She shrugged. "I've seen worse, but I wouldn't recommend him. Anyway, they let my mom die in a cheap rental back in San Diego after they took her house, her savings, and her pension. She died broke after they cut off her treatments. And I wasn't there with her. I had no idea. I thought they were taking care of her, while I was out here getting raped and abused. But they saved money and let her die. Health insurance—what a joke. Call it what it is—a Health Denial Industry."

Mélusine regarded her darkly. "We always wonder why you Americans can't figure it out. Everyone else has universal health care. We can afford it, it's cheaper, no health denial Mafia are stealing a trillion dollars every year, nobody loses their home or pension, and health care is a basic human right, not something you can traffic away like slaves."

Hannah shrugged lightly. "That's how it is over there. They lie to us, and we believe it."

Mélu resisted the urge to lecture the poor thing. "You Americans are so much better and smarter than everyone. You cannot learn from anyone else because you are god's chosen people. You didn't need to deny reality and try to reinvent fire or the wheel. You could have learned from over a hundred countries that have universal health care."

Hannah shook her head. "Corporations own all the media, so we don't know any better. We're told by all these corporate nazis and fake preachers that Jesus wants it that way. I tried to tell my mom to move to Canada, but she didn't want to leave her home and friends after my dad died. So she stayed and lost everything and died."

Mélu said, "I have to get back outside and work. But I'll tell you what. Maybe you will be interested in helping our underground network called PAX—the Progressive Alliance for Peace. We are working to reduce corporate power and restore democracy in your country, and around the world."

Hannah nodded. "I'm ready for anything. They killed my mom, abused me, and took everything."

Mélu said, "*C'est bien.* Before you leave here, I will give you some information. Particularly, be on the lookout because your friend Wan has a new toy."

"Oh?" Hannah looked uncertain, but willing.

"Yes. I am working on some of the documents. It is a new technology for aircraft and missiles called Intelligent Fuselage Skin, or IFS. It is very powerful and effective. It makes all existing aircraft and missiles obsolete—including military ones. His killers murdered a friend of mine in London to steal it."

Hannah looked her directly in the eyes—frankly, honestly, and without fear.

Mélu pressed, "If you see him with it, could you let us know? Could you steal it for us?"

Mélu nearly choked when the girl nodded without batting an eyelash. *Too good to be true.*

"You have direct, daily access to Wan," Mélu said. "I only have a tiny segment of the overall plan—not enough to mean much. I hear that Wan carries the main data around with him."

"Why?" Hannah asked brightly, carrying the tray of tea and cookies to the kitchen table for Mélu.

Mélu said, "There will be a world wide parliament of CEOs in Luxembourg this summer. It's the Confederacy, or CEOC. He will use IFS technology as one of his tools to intimidate the CEOs. This guy doesn't just use simple persuasion."

Hannah said, "Yes, I know. He uses intimidation. Fear. I've seen it."

Mélu said, "This IFS technology—they killed my friend for it. If PAX could get back those data, it would help fix the balance of power."

Hannah shrugged bravely. "I'll see what I can do."

Too good to be true—but this poor kid has nothing lose. She's for real. It's all she's got.

Mélu leaned close. "Hannah, PAX is working with a very important man in Luxembourg—Professor Sander, who proposes to challenge Wan for the presidency of CEOC when the world's CEO class have their parliament at the Chateau Ansembourg in the Valley of Seven Castles on the Eisch River. Wan wants to make himself the next Attila or Napoleon to rule the world through this tangle of corporations. Sander wants to help bring back a strong democracy with division of powers and balances, so that everyone will get a fair share and an equal voice."

"Count me in," the California blonde said with a startlingly angry, powerful look in her blue eyes.

Mélu said softly, "It could be very dangerous, Hannah."

"I have absolutely nothing to lose."

Mélu found a pencil, and wrote down her name and contact information in Luxembourg. She pushed the scrap of envelope paper across the table to her new friend. "Whatever happens, you can always reach me at home in Belair, a neighborhood in Luxembourg City. If you get any information about the IFS, we can contact Professor Sander." She patted Hannah's hand. "And in the meantime, maybe we can help you get back home to California, away from this horrible mess."

Hannah sipped her steaming tea, wincing both at the heat and at her predicament. "I don't have my papers. The first thing these pricks do is to take your passport away."

Mélu winked, with a little grin. "We can get papers for you. No worry. Whatever it takes."

Mélu returned to the balcony outside to keep working for the Wan Industries project as if nothing happened. The Triad goons came trooping past, and presently the party resumed with more shrieking amid loud music and sounds of shattering bottles.

Two days later, Hannah hugged Mélu goodbye and returned to the now-silent wreckage of the Yakuza-Triad party. The apartment where she and several other women had been molested was now empty—and stank of booze, smoke, and sex. She returned to the main house, where she had a temporary room at the convenience of Wan Hong nearby.

A week later, Mélu wrapped up her job and took a plane home from Shanghai Pudong International Airport to DeGaulle at Roissy just northeast of Paris, and then to Luxembourg City on a connecting flight. She all but forgot about Hannah Smith—her blonde surfer friend, Wan's contract BAN or slave.

2.   News Clips of the Day

Unidentified Air Assault

ANN (Europe)—Free Western news agencies are reporting rumors of a mysterious, fast-maneuvering aircraft that shot down a NATO military jet over a Belgian forest near the Luxembourg border. Observers claim the attacker was unmarked and unidentifiable.

ANN has received no official reports of casualties, although a Belgian driver and his wife—a couple who own a bakery in the Bastogne area— reported seeing the fireball and no parachutes over the small Belgian town of Houffalize, north of Bastogne.

Official Belgian and NATO sources continue to deny the incident ever happened. Unspecified police, fire, and civil aviation authorities in the region have reported receiving civilian phone calls about an exceptionally fast-maneuvering jet, which civilians described as being like a small UFO. The unknown aircraft had no markings and might be of a radar-stealthy variety despite its shiny skin. It allegedly tangled with the military jet over a forest near a sensitive Belgian air force base.

The aircraft, described by witnesses as a kind of golden, glowing UFO or perhaps a top-secret drone, was allegedly able to penetrate the base's defenses, coming from the direction of Germany and Luxembourg to the east. It evaded a missile fired at it, and stayed long enough to shoot down a Belgian air force jet before disappearing into cloud cover eastward. This is denied by government sources in Belgium and neighboring Luxembourg.

(continued)

(continued)

A corporate CEOC attaché in Brussels, who declined to be named, states semi-privately that the reports were a rumor based on a viral Internet video based on a computer game played by hackers. Nevertheless, ANN has independently verified from reporters on the ground that Belgian and Luxembourg military and police units have sealed off an area at the border, and rescue/recovery units have been seen entering the area with a mobile command post and other

equipment. A Belgian army ambulance was seen leaving the area without sirens or flashing lights, indicating there would be no survivors in the ambulance requiring emergency transport.

There have been unconfirmed reports of NATO military aircraft and ground units on high alert, sweeping the skies and mountainous Ardennes region in search of an unknown craft, which unnamed but reliable sources have described as being constructed with a so-called Intelligent Fuselage Skin, or IFS. This revolutionary new IFS technology allegedly enables a missile or aircraft to fly intelligently and faster, eluding attackers, while calculating optimal trajectories to home in on a target. Official NATO sources, responding to ANN inquiries, have denied the existence of any such technology—which, again, officials attribute to cartoonish pranking by elusive civilian gamers and hackers. ANN and ANN-EUR will keep you updated on all further breaking news.

News Clip: U. S. Army Deserter

ANN (Europe)—NATO and Interpol agencies across Europe have issued an alert for civil and military authorities to be on the lookout for a dangerous deserter, identified as infantry Sergeant Richard Buchan of the U.S. Army, who escaped from military judicial custody at a stockade in Mannheim, Germany. Buchan allegedly murdered a local police official in Huilongistan. He is also accused of perpetrating negligent and derelict acts resulting in the criminal loss of a combined military and corporate contractor unit while serving in NATO's last remaining Eastern war zone. He was being bound over for trial in a Staff Judge Advocate court in Kaiserslautern, Germany before his escape, facing multiple felony charges under the Uniform Code of Military Justice (UCMJ).

Buchan is reportedly on the run, alone, and dangerous. He may be suffering from psychological trauma resulting from head wounds sustained in an explosion on a highway in the oil-rich region of Huilongistan. He is said to have caused the deaths of ten fellow U.S. Army troops and contractors (or mercenaries) under his supervision, then covered up his crimes by shooting a local police official. He was captured on the run in Western Asia and brought to Germany for trial, but escaped from a high-security U.S. Army prison and was last seen heading west toward Luxembourg in a series of misadventures involving stolen cars, hitch hiking, and jumping trains under false identity papers.

Warrants circulating through Interpol state he is wanted in connection with negligence, malfeasance, and murder in connection with the shooting of a police official loyal to the Huilongistan regime, a

(continued)

(continued)

close ally of global corporations, including former U.S. oil companies now part of global CEOC interests. Buchan's unit is one of the last former U.S. Army elements in the region, and being rapidly replaced by private contractor armies directly employed by global energy interests.

Our reporters, who filed this report, have been denied any information or interviews with corporate officials in Huilong, capital of the dictatorship, as well as corporate headquarters in Shanghai, Delhi, London, Paris, and Washington, D.C.

A brief statement of "No Comment" has been issued by the U.S. State Department in response to press inquiries.

A semi-official spokesman for the Corporate Republican Party in power stated at their liaison offices in CEOC's Paris office complex, "We are following the case with interest. Obviously, if Sergeant Buchan were not guilty, he would not be charged."

When asked if this contravened the moribund U.S. Constitution, whose language long required that a defendant be "innocent unless or until found guilty beyond a shadow of a doubt," the CRP spokesperson said, "You cannot always be literal minded. Sometimes you have to run with the spirit of the law, rather than the letter of the law. Our Supreme Court justices travel back in time and consult the Founding Fathers about what the words really mean, not what the antiquated language appears to say. We know what's best for the American people, and let nothing stand in our way to get done what must be done. That is why millions of citizens always rally at every event where our Leader speaks with passion and logic to their souls."

When asked who determines the spirit, if not the literally written words, the spokesman smiled but offered no further comment while slamming the door in a reporter's face. Attempts to contact the Supreme Court offices for comment went unanswered as well, except for a recorded commercial about the objective and unwavering scalias of justice.

3.   Rick Buchan

The young American man appeared to be traveling alone through France, which in itself could be taken by any insightful observer as a sign of alarming possibilities.

From police reports later compiled from witnesses, he appeared to be haunted by pains and troubles deep and secret at the core of his soul. So thought his various fellow passengers in the cabin over the hundreds of kilometers and half dozen travel hours from Germany into the Île-de-France, where he lost himself in the sprawl of glorious Paris.

Handsome but unshaven and dark-natured, he kept to himself—a sturdy young man of average height. He sat collapsed into a corner near the window, facing backward in the direction of north or northwest as cities of night poured by like a spilled and slowly passing river of stars. Traveling in Europe by night one has the impression of being near a beach on a vast sea, if only because the lights of cities and towns seem to hover and stand still in the cold distance while the train moves through arteries of time freighted with the tragedies of unending wars and conspiracies.

It was early summer, but a steady drizzle streaked the dusty windows without cleaning them. The cabin was well-lit and warm, as the coach rumbled and clattered through eternity.

The young man's fellow passengers included a trio of German school girls who got out at the border by Saarlouis; a French provincial couple in sturdy travel suits heading home to the city of Metz from a shopping trip in Homburg; then a quiet North African man wearing a dark blue suit, who kept to himself in a corner; and finally two French university students returning to their apartment in the Latin Quarter. Soon enough, Metropolitan police and Interpol would track them all down and interview them about the mysterious young American man.

His name, it would be established soon enough, was Rick Buchan, age twenty-five, a sergeant in the U.S. Army stationed at a major headquarters in Kaiserslautern—and a deserter on the run from various police and military agencies in the European Union. Though he appeared young, strong, and handsome, Buchan was reportedly talking to himself with a vacant, otherworldly gaze.

Though his observers had no idea he was wanted, they uniformly reported that he seemed in trouble of some sort—serious trouble. His face, reflected in the night time windows of the train, looked pale as if he were sick or in shock. He wore the standard American jeans, sheathing powerful thighs. The tail of some sort of outlandish purple T-shirt hung from under a thick gray pullover with crew neck, like those worn by sailors on stormy seas. Beside him on the seat rested a compact backpack, strategically placed as if to shield him from intrusive company. Only the Algerian man, who owned a restaurant in Nancy, sat on that side, jammed into the corner by the door. The other fellow travelers all sat on the bench opposite Buchan, feeling uncomfortable and glad to change cabins or get out.

The conductor, a M. Serlain from Verdun, stopped in twice to check tickets, and remembered the American passenger well enough. He said it appeared there was a vision of terror in the man's eyes, and a pained expression on his young face. Nobody asked questions, which would have been impolite. The American never made eye contact that any of the police interviewees could recall.

New World Order: Contractual Slavery

ANN (Europe)—U.S. State Department officials have decried the recent surge in cases of U.S. nationals being held in virtual slavery overseas, particularly in China, India, and other Asian countries belonging to the self-declared CEOC, or Corporate Executive Officials Confederacy. CEOC, whose governing parliament is about to meet at the Chateau Ansembourg in the Valley of Seven Castles in Luxembourg, represents the world's 900 wealthiest families from all parts of the world, representing half the world's wealth.

The entrapment situation results from voluntary contracts into which desperate young people from depression-wracked U.S.A. put themselves for an average of five years, typically expecting their freedom and a pension for life after completing their term. This fad is all the rage in the West, especially in the United States. Because the United States is still today the only major nation without universal health care, some victims sell themselves to gain medical care for a loved one, and to avoid having all their savings and property seized by predatory so-called health insurance companies.

Horror stories about enslavement were once a problem faced mainly by domestics from the Philippines and other Third World countries working for private families in the world's wealthiest oil exporting nations, particularly in the Middle East.

The so-called nanny and butler contacts being marketed to U.S. teens over eighteen, and twenty-somethings, are currently a serious fad. Under a type of indentured servitude contract, attractive young U.S. women—and some men—sell themselves into virtual slavery for periods typically of three to five years. During that time, they serve their owners in any manner required, under the misleading concept of BAN (Butlers And Nannies). Services include—it is unofficially alleged—sex slavery. In return, these

(continued)

(continued)

young people's contracts guarantee, upon satisfactory completion of the full term, a lifetime pension equivalent to those of the lucky few in the United States who currently have full time jobs with benefits and some modicum of health care.

According to State Department sources, dozens of these modern indentured slaves have petitioned for release from their contract and return home under safe conduct, citing abuses including rape, torture, sexual slavery, and even murder. Governments of the newly wealthier nations around the world have been notably unwilling or unable to assist the U.S. in seeking extradition of U.S. and European nationals, citing the legality of the contracts and the unparalleled global power of international corporations. These corporations are often wealthier and more powerful than nation-states. Instead of making war, they deploy armies of top lawyers to stymie all human rights efforts on behalf of the so-called BANs, who in no way resemble their namesakes of previous centuries.

Reports of further abuses have surfaced, including allegations that BANs are forbidden any contact with the outside world, to prevent them from escaping or appealing for help. Several of these captive U.S. women have allegedly tried to run for their lives, only to disappear in the underworld and brothels of major cities like Shanghai and Delhi, never to be seen again.

The internationally corporate-controlled U.S. Congress has refused to move forward any legislation to investigate or remedy proposed by the Labor and Middle Class movements. In the absence of a free press—with U.S. media 99% under corporate control for the past century or more—and with the investor base now global rather than U.S. based, there appears to be little interest in finding remedies for U.S. workers' grievances in what the corporate media dismiss as 'socialist and communist agitation by illegal foreign elements undermining our Constitutional rights.

4.   Hannah Smith

A private, corporate jet with discreet markings arrived from the direction of Asia and coasted toward a landing in drizzle and fog on the outskirts of Le Bourget, Paris. This was not the common airport for international travelers (Charles de Gaulle, at Roissy) but a hub for cargo jets—as well as corporate executive jets requiring extra privacy and security.

With flashing flight lights and glaring headlamps, the fourteen-seat Embraer Legacy twin engine jet, with two pilots and two flight attendants, touched down at an exclusive and discreet corporate air terminal.

Inside the plush, wheat-themed interior were several passengers, including the fleet's owner, a billionaire named Wan from Shanghai whose industries sprawled across the globe without loyalty to any particular nation. Most of the world's wealth was concentrated in about one thousand families like Wan's, fairly evenly divided between Capitalist China, India, the so-called Islamic Belt, and the remaining West. The West, by mid-twenty-first century, was a shadow of its former self in the previous five centuries, when they had been world's Eurocentric-Christiancentric rulers. The billionaire manipulators of Western cultures, particularly in the laissez-faire U.S.A., had created a global oligarchy whose families and retainers now stepped across the corpses of their former colonial masters, and picked as they wished on the carcasses of former empires from Europe to North America.

Wan—one of the richest men in the world—was a slender, graying man with a deceptively pleasant expression on relatively youthful features, behind which lurked hungry, cold eyes that glistened like dark fruit. He was in Paris to set the ground for his run for the presidency of CEOC, whose parliament of global Chief Executive Officers was due to meet in Luxembourg this month. CEOC had rented the Chateau Ansembourg, lately owned by a secretive Japanese religious cult, in the touristy Valley of the Seven Castles. Wan even contemplated making an offer to these Japanese cultists—the chateau sounded like a useful little toy to own, where you could entertain guests without getting hassled by cops or do-gooders.

As the Embraer came to a landing, the billionaire kept one hand on a slim black leather case on the seat beside him. The little briefcase was important enough to merit a window seat, while its owner occupied the aisle seat beside it.

The four-seat configuration surrounded a compact conference table at the center of the fuselage. With him in conversation, sitting across the table, was his French corporate *demi-roi*, Armand Pascal, who chaired ten corporate boards under the feudal domain of Wan, and was one of his principal Caucasian faces.

Pascal and his ilk were useful. Using Caucasian shills tended to calm the racist fools. The European and U.S. press were calmed when they saw white faces selling out the works. Good for jobs, they told their fools. When Wan thought about how the British in particular, along with the Germans, French, and other colonial powers, had crippled China in past centuries; how the West had poured thousands of tons of opium into China, ruining millions of lives while an ineffectual native emperor and bureaucracy sort of helped and sort of hindered without much effect—why should anyone care what happened to these European and U.S. swine? The capitalist, industrial class had been the true rulers of the English and other hegemonies during the industrial revolution, so why should things be any different now?

Wan had viceroys similar to Pascal in Germany, England, Canada, and the United States. He owned lesser fiefdoms in Russia, Brazil, Egypt, and Nigeria, and worked tirelessly to increase his world clout. All the zillionaires did this as an unstoppable prerogative of their DNA.

Moving about the plane's passenger space were two tall, slender cabin attendants—blonde Swedish women in sky-blue uniforms and high heels. Wan liked to surround himself with tall blondes. Being one of the wealthiest men in the world, he could afford whatever his heart desired. Women like this were just toys—pets, like owning a nice dog or cat. His own wife was of good Chinese Mandarin stock, discreetly living with their two natural-born children in a fortified compound, on a breezy and temperate plateau inland of Zhuhai on the South China Sea coast. His wife and family were well provided for, he visited them often, and she made no demands on him as he busied himself with his world conquests.

Wan's two chief enforcers were never far—one female, the other male. The woman was a former Olympic gymnast and Judo champion named Savia. She was Cuban-German and had glossy black hair tightly bound into a bun at the back of the head for maximum range of vision and unencumbered fighting motion. Her strong physique had not an ounce of fat, and was usually clad in dowdy, unremarkable earth-tone skirts or pants, sensible shoes, a modest blouse and vest, that sort of thing. She had café-au-lait skin and a certain exotic, brutal beauty including dark, almond-shaped eyes, a strong but feminine nose, and a wide, thin-lipped mouth enhanced with slashes of cherry-red lipstick.

The other chief bodyguard and knight was Yoichi, a gladiator raised in the Tokyo and Macao gambling worlds. Yoichi was of Japanese ancestry. Overcoming prejudice, he had proven his prowess in private arenas of

Bangkok and Okinawa, where desperate men fought to the death in duels the police would never know about, or were bribed not to know by men and women of Wan's class. Yoichi was armed with those opposite dragons, a yin and yang of brains and power, plus an amazing speed to combine the two for fast, blurry victories in the ring or in private demonstrations favored by Wan. Where feasible (legal or not), Yoichi carried firearms and knives according to his personal discretion. Whatever other bodyguards Wan kept about, he preferred close and personal associates like Savia and Yoichi, who were prepared to lay down their lives for their owner if need be. In return, they lived lives of incomparable power, luxury, and gratification.

Savia and Yoichi hired their own specialized and discreet agents—spies, assassins, enforcers—as needed. Wan kept close to them, received regular reports while maintaining a legally safe distance, and otherwise did not interfere in how they carried out his orders. The unsaid reality was that they, like anyone else, were disposable and could be replaced at a moment's notice. He knew what they were doing at all times, but rarely ever interfered.

Finally, seated and sulking on a three-seat couch in the rear, opposite Yoichi, was a Caucasian woman named Hannah Smith. She was young, with long blonde (of course) hair swept up in a classic *chignon* on the back of the head. Her eyes had a hurt, almost tearful weather in them today, which Wan indulgently ignored. Hannah wore an Asian-style garment that might be mistaken for a Chinese *cheongsam* skirt of deep, lustrously dark blue silk. It was, in fact, a creation by Wan's Paris House of Style, modeled on the Vietnamese *ao dai*. This was a long, graceful one-piece garment with a tight-fitting top that split down both sides from the waist, reaching almost to the ankles in a light, wind-blown configuration of dance-like elegance. When they stepped out together, Wan required that she wear a Vietnamese-style straw sun hat and walk fifteen paces behind him with the luggage and slaves. Hannah and her class were of course slaves in all but name. She was a so-called Nanny, a female Butler in effect, contracted to Wan because owning blonde U.S. girls of the California surfing type was a status symbol for the oligarch class, of which Wan was a leader. Much of this was also very discreet and under-reported, since Wan's class owned the major global media, whose reporting pretended to be very open when in fact it was very closed—at least, on sensitive topics like the BAN class of indentured servants.

The Swedish flight attendants wore frozen smiles and sparkling, sky-blue eyes as they towered over the table on royal-blue leather high heels. They served hot tea, Viennese tortes, and lingonberry ice cream in round scoops floating in frost-hulled silver goblets. Wan's plane carried a fully stocked bar and wine room, and on occasion a five-star chef as needed.

The flight had stopped in Austria to pick up Pascal from a conference of the military guns industry. Wan was eager to learn the latest opportunities in this area, since his weapons design and manufacturing firms constituted a major part of his multifaceted enterprise.

"Who is the sultry blossom in the rear?" asked Monsieur Pascal as he prepared to dip a silver spoon into his ice cream.

"Oh, that is my American girl," said Wan. "She's a private property I bought through one of my North American brokers a few months ago."

"She looks like—" Pascal hesitated, trying to remember the name of a famous Nordic movie actress, and not quite delivering the syllables mixed with a slurry of bluish-red ice cream on the tip of his tongue. "She is beautiful," he concluded lamely.

"Yes," Wan said. "She is a rare find, if she is temperamental. I enjoy those little small-town treasures that are so innocent in their village sort of way. I believe she even prays each day. I've never asked, since I pray for nothing and take what I want. She is clean—"

"—You mean—?" Pascal interjected helpfully.

"—Yes, no drugs or diseases. I wouldn't have that. She offered a fair deal. Herself, for her mother's health."

"The Americans are so stupid about health care," Pascal said with a cold laugh.

Wan shrugged. "Their loss is our gain. They are made to believe health care is some form of evil, and they must not have any of it. It's a religious thing to them." He shrugged. "They are peasants."

"Exceptionalism," Pascal said. He glanced toward the blonde woman and asked, daring to favor his master with a sarcastic snicker, "Why does she seem so sulky?"

"Oh, she's had a little disappointment," Wan said. "The corporation that brokered her contract decided to let her mother die."

"Of what?"

"Breast cancer." Wan sipped his tea without caring much. He emitted a little shrug. "If I had been told, I would have paid for the surgery. Maybe she did say something, and I didn't listen." He shrugged. "It would have been a trifle for me. So now I have to put up with her temperamental outbursts. She cries at any strange moment."

"Maybe you need to trade her in for a better one."

"Maybe," Wan said. "But I am still intrigued with her for now, so I will keep her. With these village idiots, it's like this. They are like zoo animals. You toss them some oranges and candies and other treats, and pretty soon they forget. Their preachers, magicians, and television clowns have had them in thrall for generations."

"We all must die some time," Pascal contributed hopefully.

"Of course," Wan said. "I will offer her a lot of money, and maybe a little chalet in Switzerland—whatever her little childish heart desires—and she'll get over it. I'll tell her Jesus wills it, and that's all they need to hear. They'll eat poison to make Jesus happy, and of course their owners laugh all they way to the bank."

"I wish the Europeans were quite so docile," Pascal said, probably thinking of temperamental French, Italian, and Spanish women. Pascal eyed Hannah Smith desirously. "What are you going to do with her?" He eyed her boldly, making it obvious he was interested if Wan tired of her and sought another plaything.

Wan bristled a bit. "Good slaves are hard to find, Pascal. Do you need a toy of your own? Do I not reward you with enough money and perks?"

Pascal blushed and looked down, knowing he had pushed his limit with this master of the modern world. "Of course, my Lord. I'm sorry." Truth was, Pascal had his own exotic tastes, which ran to orgies with a mix of teenage boys and girls recruited in big Arabian or Brazilian cities where nothing could be traced to him, and human life meant less than a snatch of pretty song, lasting a few minutes and then forever evaporating into thin air. As they said in U.S. chicken restaurants, he preferred dark meat, but sometimes something a little different, like a taste of white breast meat. Not to eat, of course. He grinned inwardly. He was not as crazy as some other lieutenants of industry—just a modest bit perverted. An orgasm was an orgasm—the more exotic, the longer and better. It was addictive, and his mouth watered at the thought.

The engines powered down with a long, drawn-out double sigh filled with tired strength, as if they were prize athletes from one of Mr. Wan's Olympia-style stables around the world. As Wan and Pascal spoke, the aircraft rolled to a stop at a miniaturized docking port. Near-silence filled the air.

"Hello, Pascal," Wan said.

Pascal shook his head, coming out of his reverie. "Sorry, boss."

Wan took a look back toward Hannah and Yoichi. The young woman lay on one side, as if asleep or crying. Across from her sat Savia on a chair, and Yoichi on the opposite couch. Wan had lately asked them to keep a closer eye than usual on his girl.

Wan exchanged looks with Yoichi, who rose obediently—as did Savia.

Wan told Pascal, "Come, let's go to the lobby of the terminal. It's time to meet with my executives. I have some interesting and exciting news for you all before we travel to Luxembourg for the summit." As he spoke, Wan picked up the precious leather case at his side. "In this case are the data from Pierre Sander' experiments with the Intelligent Fuselage Skin experiments."

Pascal chuckled secretively. "You mean like the experiment that shot down the Belgian air force plane last week?"

Wan, who normally was so secretive that he seemed cryptic even to his top lieuteants, allowed himself a hard grin. "Proof of concept. When I address the CEOC chiefs, I will impress them with my power and determination.

Pascal lowered his eyes. The boss at times seemed to have ambition for becoming the world's next Attila the Hun or Napoleon Bonaparte.

"With this technology," he told Pascal, "I will be able to revolutionize aviation and space technologies. I will create a lighter, stronger, semi-intelligent air skin that can interpret its way through the air. That means more efficient fuel usage, weather-adapted flying, and so forth." He smiled mysteriously. "I'll brief you people all at once when I have you assembled in the board room here in the airport." So saying, he opened an overhead compartment, placed the precious briefcase inside, and closed it. He flipped the lock idly, never noticing it did not completely catch.

Hannah Smith's sullen, vengeful eyes did not miss a thing from halfway down the fuselage tube on her couch, where she reclined like a stylish and beautiful ornament.

Wan and Pascal, accompanied by Yoichi and Savia, walked toward the Embraer Legacy's main fuselage door. There, the ever-cheerful Swedish women bowed slightly, in the Asian manner, as the three men and Savia passed through en route to the docking tunnel and thus to the reception hall. There, a conference room specially chartered by Wan Industries awaited a key group of corporate executives—the new world order's *daimyo* or feudal lords.

The pilot and copilot—Asian men in elegant black uniforms—stepped out of the cockpit and flirtrf with the Swedish women. The captain wore the traditional four circles on his sleeves, while the copilot wore three. Each Swedish women wore one gold ring around her slender sleeves. On larger flights, there'd be a chief steward with two rings.

Hannah was just as glad that Wan disdained to even tell her to stay, or wish her good day, or anything. She was property, like a ceramic dog or a bowl of fresh fruit. That was what she'd signed up for. But she had not signed up to be traded around and abused, as she had been; and letting her mother die in a cheap Los Angeles apartment had not been part of the bargain.

From her seat, alone on the couch about twenty feet back, in the rear section of the cabin, Hannah wiped her tear-swollen eyes and felt an intense wave of rage welling up inside. The pilots and the flight attendants chatted and laughed together as the captain led his three companions into the cockpit for a more intimate conversation.

Hannah seized the opportunity—this might never again come.

She did not care what happened to her.

Rising from the couch in a blur of motion—only half tracking consciously what she herself might be doing or thinking—she raced toward the table. Leaning one hand on the table, she reached up with her other hand and tried the latch. Wan's casual flick had not pushed it fully shut. Down came the metal hatch flap, and there lay the leather case, which was the size of a shaving kit. Hannah clicked a little suitcase latch open and, standing on tiptoes, held the case open with both hands without removing it from the hatch.

Inside were papers—and a wine-colored object containing the secret of Wan's future rulership of world industry, as emperor (in all but name) of

CEOC. The data were stored on an ALEC drive like she'd seen advertised on TVideo, thick as her index finger, round, could fit in her palm, and no heavier than a chocolate bar. She held it up for an instant. It gleamed dark merlot in the light—very pretty, and worth a billion dollars at least. It was a jewel worth a king's ransom, and it was now hers.

She stuffed it into a pocket under the *ao doi*, and strode down the ramp into the tunnel. Rather than continue around the bend into the main lounge, where Wan or Yoichi might spot her, she opened a service door.

She blinked as wet, windy air ruffled her bangs in front.

Am I free yet? Or is this an illusion?

It was a long drop down.

I'm ready to die for my freedom, but I'm not crazy. I want to live.

But a metal ladder extended—from beside the door in the ramp—down to the tarmac.

Living well is the best revenge, and I plan to hand him payback.

Quickly, she clambered onto the ladder.

Now or never.

She pushed the door shut, hoping to gain a few minutes before anyone figured out that she was gone, or where she'd gone. She placed the leather case back into its compartment and latched the door tightly as Wan had done. She'd buy some time before he discovered he'd been robbed of the crown jewels—and eventually figured out who had done it.

The steel rungs felt cold, wet, and slippery. If she fell now, she'd lie in a crippled heap on the ground almost twenty feet below. Determined, she gripped the rungs tightly and went as fast as she could, hand under hand, swinging her slender body with her monkey-like motions, until ten seconds later she felt hard ground under her rubber soles.

Luckily, the shoes they'd given her in wardrobe were like sneakers—practical, comfortable, and elegant without sacrificing flexibility. She could dance before her owner, kneel, perform on him as he wished.

Now they were made for running.

And run she did—through the rain, loosening the dark blue silk *ao doi* top as she went. She discarded it among some parked orange steel baggage carts. From another cart she lifted a man's dark, dirty work jacket and put it on. There was even a badge, in case she needed to get through locked doors. Hannah was on the run with Wan's irreplaceable plan for the future of aviation, and his next zillion or so yuan.

Presently, she was gone.

The airport loomed at its glacial mountainous maximum, swimming in lights and rain, drowning in mist and stray voices, snatches of music amid the steady roar of the vast city that lay beyond—Paris, City of Light, place where you could hope to lose yourself and make deals with the devil and get away with murder and mayhem.

Chapter Two: Paris

5.   Napoleonic and Homeric Dreams

Richard Buchan, 25, was rushing nowhere—not toward, but away from. He dimly understood that, but walked all the faster and harder. As an infantryman, this was the one thing that came most naturally to him. He was better at it than at almost anything else, including thinking, shooting, or making love—walking. And walk—or march—he did, endlessly and blindly—along the sidewalks and boulevards, beyond the tourist districts, and into the real gritty but attractive, everyday Paris.

Rick Buchan had been to Paris numerous times before, during his four years of duty in Europe with the last U.S. Army NATO units (not to mention his disastrous combat deployment to western Asia).

He'd seen happier days, read history books, even studied a little French. Funny thing now was, he remembered some of his reading, the memories of which sat on the shelves of his mind like dusty but orderly books. He just had trouble focusing on the messy present.

He'd seen all the tourist magnets during earlier visits—Eiffel Tower, Arc de Triomphe, Louvre, and many more—including the magnificent Haussmann avenues designed in the 1850s-60s by Napoleon III's Prefect of Paris. A hidden agenda behind the wide, light modern avenues had allegedly been to offer a clear field of fire for artillery—the late Uncle Napoleon I's military specialty—to quickly clear the streets of any unwelcome protesters by means of steel chain or grape shot. Napoleon III, like all tyrants, had never stopped fearing the deadly street battles—which, ironically, helped him into power as the Second Republic turned into the Second Empire. *(*Endnotes #1)*

Rick knew the history and classics, yet he did not know where his next meal or piss break was coming from. He couldn't remember when he'd missed the last hour to take his pills and be sane again; but he could remember history—the endless, repetitive tapestry of human folly. Maybe that was because his life was like a fast-moving car in heavy traffic, while the river of time and events moved in slow motion, giving the appearance of standing still.

He dreamed a typical Homeric aside into this skein: A wide, strong river glows red-hot like liquid metal in late sunlight, and appears to stand still when Ocean's tide rises at its mouth. The river roils as if burning or in pain, and seems to flow backward; but this is an illusion like life itself, which can only flow forward to a man's dark and violent destiny as the Fate-spinners beckon.

★★★ ▮▮ ═ ▮▮ ▰ ꙮ ★★★

Rick Buchan hurried along, lost in thought. He kept his chin pulled in, his head down, and his hands jammed in his pockets. There were no rioters on Paris streets these days—just lots of scurrying, impoverished people, many of them from various worse-off places around the world.

The poetic river of which he'd fantasized was really a roiling current of car roofs glowing in a melancholy last evening light. Countless little people rushed home from work to pick up their children at school, to go home, light the cooking stoves, fill the air with smells of roasting meat and sautéed onions, smells of baking bread and sweet chocolate puddings. Then it was story time for the children, an hour of stolen kisses and weary news for the parents, and precious hours of dark safety through the night.

Rick had once heard the old German folk tale of a beggar who walks into a tavern at night, going from table to table asking for coins until the innkeeper takes notice. The beggar is given a coin by one, a crust of bread by another. He goes to the fire, where a rack of meat is turning on the spit. He holds the crust over the meat to absorb its aromas. The innkeeper challenges him to either pay, or get out. The beggar then wisely says, Since I am asked to pay for the aroma of this meat, I will pay you with the sound of my coin. So saying, he drops his coin on the table, making a clattering sound, and puts the coin away, leaving the innkeeper speechless.

In that same spirit, it seemed to Rick that Paris in rush hour filled him with the sounds and smells of life, but gave him none of it for his own nourishment. He might as well rattle a few Euro notes on a street corner, put them back in his pocket, and call it even. It would be like paying for the illusion of joy with the illusion of money. There was no joy in it for him—he'd left that behind on a bloody road in Huilongistan, and in a suffocating military jail cell in Mannheim.

★★★ ▮▮ ═ ▮▮ ▰ ꙮ ★★★

Crossing wide streets, Rick had no concern with history—past, ongoing, or yet to come.

Preoccupied with his unchanging predicament—locked into an eternal present of guilt, dread, and impending doom—he walked for hours with his hands jammed deeply in his pockets. He saw his reflection passing on plate glass—a troubled look on his face, seen rippling past in smoky shop windows. In his own life, his personal clock had stopped and might never start again.

Looking over his shoulder from time to time, he got on and off the metro system at many stations, trying to shake possible pursuers. He had just under sixty Euros in his sock, stolen in Bad Homburg from a shifty Russian sidewalk carpet seller, who was illegally working outside the VAT and deserved to get burned. Then too, the Siberian still had the carpet, so he wasn't out much. Probably pissed. But he was alive. Rick hadn't had to break his neck for him to get away.

At a kiosk near the Louvre, Rick bought a cheap throw-away cell phone with ten hours of talk time. He stood for a few minutes, contemplating heavy traffic flowing around the square near the main entrance of the great art museum. Should he risk calling Major Kendra Walsh at the Judge Advocate General (JAG) office in Kaiserslautern (K-Town in G.I. jargon) and see how bad things looked for his upcoming court case—assuming he ever showed up alive again? After looking at the burner for several agonizing minutes, he shook his head, stuffed the phone into his backpack, and resumed walking.

He kept a couple of loose Euro bills in the black leather wallet in the left hip pocket of his jeans in case he were robbed on the street. For all the African and Middle Eastern looking faces that drifted by, nobody bothered him as he exited the Gallieni station on the metro in Bagnolet and wandered along desolate suburban boulevards. He felt dead already—a ghost, at one with the dark people and their dark lives passing in smoky gloom, on streets smelling of strange foods and distant, deadly homelands.

Night fell among the few drab, same-same glassy high-rise buildings. Torn sheets of cloud rippled over tree tops, reflected in greenish, underwater-looking plate-glass windows. The world seemed to be drowning in tears—swimming in dreams. Rick talked with his old buddy Charley Hafford, who tagged along some distance behind him and never seemed to catch up any more. Sometimes it seemed that Charley had died in the sands of Huilongistan—on a sun-baked asphalt road torn by an improvised mine. At other times it was not true—Charley definitely was along with Rick, as only a best friend could be. Much of the time, Rick was alone and pounding down as much mileage as he could to stay ahead of his pursuers.

With only sixty Euro on him, Rick knew he could end this at any time. In his pocket was the business card of Major Kendra Walsh, the JAG officer who was tasked with his defense before a court martial in K-Town. Kendra's boss was a big, ugly old black infantry colonel with flinty eyes, who hated Rick and made no bones about sending him to the slammer for life. Desertion was the least of it. According to the articles of accusation, Rick had led his convoy into an ambush through negligence. Under a quarter moon in a sky like dark blue ink, three explosions in a row had taken out the vehicles. Only Rick had lived because he had halted and stepped out to take a leak in a safe, quiet area that turned out to be anything but that. Six men had lost their lives, plus another six contractors. Each had been a joke, a smile, a conversation, a few moments of comradeship in a hostile, alien world stuck a thousand years back in time, where modern people might as well be an outer space invasion fleet—especially soldiers from far away, some of whom were women—it all meant the devil's work to these Neolithic people, who were of course manipulated for money and power by dour mullahs and ayatollahs from the bloody Middle Ages.

What are we doing here? was the frequent question. Oh yeah, invade to beat their fucking brains in, kill their kids, destroy their fields and goats, defile their women, and get the oil—it's a corporate crusade to bring them slogans of alleged freedom they cannot comprehend; and in the process get our dicks shot off, our faces ripped off our skulls, and our legs blown off since they strangely don't want us here. Should have stayed in good old Freedom Fries, Rick often thought. By their fruits ye shall know them.

There was other stuff in the story about events in Huilongistan, which Rick could not remember. Or he did not know if he remembered remembering anything—it was all very confusing. Luckily, he would die with his genitalia and face still attached. He'd die with the memories of six soldiers' and six contractors' brains and meat scattered on a gravel road surface, and he was accused of negligence in putting them in danger.

The concussions had left Rick muddled and wandering about until an MP patrol found him and called in a Medevac. It was all a mess, and Rick months later was still wandering around in shock. Sometimes he felt very clear, like this morning when he'd walked purposefully along busy, trafficky-loud boulevards in Paris as if he were not in his old life but this new life that he so desperately preferred to his own. Other times it was like swimming in deep, dark water.

Talking to himself and to Charley and sometimes Major Kendra Walsh, Rick walked and walked and walked. Sometimes it seemed as if he could walk around the globe from city to city, continent to continent as the line of day swept across the earth the way a clock's hands sweep over its face. You could keep marching or doing the ranger shuffle from traffic light to traffic light, city block by luminous brooding city block, all that gorgeous hewn stone sometimes carved in gryphons or gargoyles and choked with moss and ivy, at other times smooth and achingly bare in the finest modern traditions. Strangely, exhilaratingly, people in every city were the same. You could circle the globe in this dream state, melancholy in its truthfulness, visit a thousand cities—and it was all just Paris again and again. Or Keokuk, or Bangkok, or Calicut, or Ankara, or sipping *kvetch* in Ukraine. It was people, human lives, over and over again. Everywhere the same. Kind of bright and sort of melancholy all at once in a truthful way.

Rick took metro line 3 toward Bagnolet. The area had its own magic, Rick remembered—away from the tourism of central Paris, and more like a normal city with glass skyscrapers, industrial blocks, apartment jungles, and heavy traffic pouring like hot, glowing lead around the peripheral highway. Buried just one or two metro stops on line 3 west of here lay Père

Lachaise Cemetery, a city of memories and mausoleum, where world famous names of politics, the arts, and other cultural lights lie in final rest—including Edith Piaf, Colette, Maria Callas, Oscar Wilde, Ahmet Kaya, Marcel Proust, Frederic Chopin, and more.

When evening fell, the time Rick dreaded most, he was walking along a very old street. Under crumbling asphalt he could see green-fuzzed paving blocks from centuries ago. Ghosts walked here, dead people who lived long ago, crisscrossing before him and all around him, as he sought the refuge of a sign whole loopy red neon letters spelled out *Bar-39* (subhead in smaller green neon: *étape trente-neuf*) within a pale blue neon rectangle almost as blue-gray as cigarette smoke. The corner was sandstone, with laughter spilling from an open door. Rick stopped, swaying lightly, and smelled steak.

Now that's a homey aromey.

He smelled fresh beer, or at least the foam maybe swirling along copper bar surfaces, quickly wiped away by a firm, bare hand while a barmaid's strong voice barked at a joke told by a patron. People were in there, talking and laughing as if all the problems of Arabia and Persia and the Indus Valley and the Afghan mountain ranges either did not exist—or could be solved here.

"Go in there and get something to eat," Charley said. "Have a beer for me." He was a disembodied humanoid figure like a shadow in the night, or a rippling reflection dimly caught in a passing bus window. Turn around, and he was gone. But he was always there. Just sometimes he wasn't visible much.

"I think I will," Rick said. "I am feeling faint with hunger. That's why I'm seeing you, Charley."

6.   Hannah on the Run

In her purse, Hannah had a hundred Euros, which Wan had thrown on the carpeted floor for her, in a Vienna mansion owned by an Arab prince whose cousin had raped her months earlier.

Now free and in Paris, Hannah walked briskly. She felt empty and scared, but free. In her purse she also kept the red drive with Wan's industrial magic in it.

As she strode through random crowds in the night, she felt the loss of her mom, the loss of trust, the loss of everything. She let soft colors along wet streets bathe her in a drizzle of light. Green, blue, red, orange was neon, plus the dry white blaze of headlights and the red afterglow of taillights. She walked as if in a dream—free but empty. Scared but defiant. For the first time, she could see how much her life had been shattered, and how it would take a long time to rebuild.

She stopped at a kiosk to buy a *crêpe* wrapped in wax paper, sprinkled with powdered sugar and a splash of sweet, tart, red *framboise*. She ate hungrily, not enjoying it as much as she had expected. At another stand, she bought a short flute bread with ham, cheese, and butter. That she devoured, and felt a bit nourished.

She sat on a park bench, keeping in plain view of the sidewalk and the rushing traffic so nobody would bother her. Plenty of passing men eyeballed her balled her with their eyes—and she turned away to display an offended cheekbone, a pouty mouth, violently angry eyes.

Eventually, as the night wore on, she pawed around in her purse and found the slip of paper her Luxemburgish friend Mélusine had given her in Shanghai. This pretty brunette from Luxembourg, who was in Shanghai on a legitimate work contract for Wan Industries, had saved her from those horrible, abusive men, and hidden her for a whole day. They had talked a great deal, with Hannah often in tears—and sometimes the European woman in tears of sympathy. Eventually, Mélusine had given her some phone numbers to call if she made it to this city or that. Some were numbers for the Progressive Alliance for Peace (PAX). Others were people who got things done with local political parties in various countries. All were working to restore democracy and laws that kept the big, beautiful dogs called corporations on the same leash of justice and order that private citizens had to observe. Now, Hannah found the name of one such person—a fixer of sorts named Mr. Fincoff, a lawyer with a ratty office in one part of town, and a ratty apartment in another arrondissement.

She called Fincoff and they agreed to meet. She took the metro to his apartment, and they talked for a bit. He did not seem to be interested in her for sex, which was a welcome change. He was older, and repulsive, with chalky white spittle stuck in the corners of his mouth, and wrinkles on his face. He seemed to have been born in that cheap brown suit that hugged his emaciated frame. She thought he smelled a bit of mothballs. But he was all business. Yes, he would talk to PAX about the data she had stolen from Wan. That was the moment when she realized there was a mission for her in Europe before she figured out how to get back to California and forget all this as if it had never happened.

Fincoff's apartment smelled of old man—of mothballs, of rotting apples in a basket near a window, of spoiled milk in a drain, of stale clothing piled on a bedroom chair.

Hannah waited around while he sat in a small office and talked endlessly on the phone.

Meanwhile, Hannah did her own research, studying notes Mélusine had given her, scribbled in pencil on torn pages from a small journal. She'd given Hannah directions on how to find her home in the Luxembourg City section of Belair. That sounded so romantic and pretty, almost wistful— Beautiful Air, Pretty Air, Nice Air. As if people could lose themselves in a place like that on the horizon of wishes and dreams, where bad things did not happen and your parents did not die but stayed to love you and care for you, maybe guide you a little better than you could figure things out for yourself. Mélusine drew a map for Hannah in that same blurry pencil. Names like Gare, Avenue de la Liberté, Pont Adolphe lay scrawled across a net of hastily drawn lines. And then, written beneath in capitals and underlined three times was the name of a Professor Hilaire Sander, Ph. D., and a note that he taught Economics and Political Science at the Uni Lux or University of Luxembourg. In parentheses after his name were three letters, also underlined with force: PAX—Progressive Alliance for Peace, from the initials P and A, and the X sort of rounded it off to the Latin word *pax*, meaning peace.

Fincoff reassured her that he had made contact with the right people— PAX, in Paris—and they would come to receive the materials she had taken from Wan. It was all in the cause of peace, he said, and she believed him. He stood before her in his brown suit, with a yellowing white shirt and blue tie whose stripes made it look more like a nylon sock than a necktie. He shook her hand with his smooth, clay skin and strangely cold eyes. He told her to wait at the apartment while he went to Bagnolet to meet with some contacts from the democracy movement.

After Fincoff left, she noted some information he had scribbled on a pad beside the phone. It was phantom information, a palimpsest, because he had taken the scrap of note paper with him. But he had written so firmly that the pen made a ghost image on the next sheet. She was able to decipher: *Bar-39*, Bagnolet, on the line 3 of the etro past Père Lachaise Cemetery toward the Galieni Station. She'd been in Paris with Wan several times, and had played tourist with two pretty young Hungarian brunettes who served Wan at his villas in Shanghai, Honolulu, and San Francisco. Hannah had carried with her a paper place mat from an ice cream parlor in the Quartier Latin, on which was printed a sort of fun, cartoonish map of the city's highlights. From there she'd invested in a metro map, and together the two documents had given her a sense of how to get around the city. Each metro line was designated by its two end points. She lost Fincoff in the crowd as the afternoon aged toward evening, but she understood that she must take line 3 past Gambetta, past the Porte de Bagnolet, under the peripheral highway, and get off at the Gallieni terminus. There, off the Rue de Lenin, on a side street, he was to meet these PAX people to negotiate the turning over of the stolen data.

Something in his eyes had not rung true, which made her wonder about Mélusine—the kind girl on Song Lu in Shanghai. She wondered all the more about this shifty old man, though. He'd tried to get her to turn over the McGuffin, but she'd been crafty enough to refuse. It was hidden first in a stairwell in his building. Then, after he'd left, she'd hidden it on top of the water tank under the ceiling in his toilet. Now she wanted to get a glimpse for herself, secretively, of these PAX freedom fighters and democrats he was supposed to meet. Before she turned it over, she must be absolutely sure it was not going to fall into the wrong hands. If someone in the underworld got that experimental data record of the IFS, it would end up getting sold to Wan. That was the last thing she wanted.

7.   Bagnolet: La 39me Etape

Rick's friend Charley did not answer. Rick stepped across the worn sandstone threshold into the folksy bowels of the Bar-39. He plunged into a crowd of mostly young men and women. Most seemed well dressed. Many were somber-skinned, some with kinky African hair, others with dark eyes in which the moon of Morocco or Mauretania still glowed.

As he did so, he stumbled and brushed against a strong, pretty young woman with caramel face, beautiful sea-blue eyes, and a wide African nose. Looked a lot like Kendra Walsh but wasn't her. This woman stood wearing a beige business getup, nursing a wine cooler with both hands to her breast, and passing time. "*Allô*," she remonstrated in a melodious accent, *vous êtes saoul déjà?*—which basically meant, "Hey, you're staggering in here drunk already?" She was obviously hunting for a suitable man, and this staggering salop did not meet her criteria.

Rick dodged some angry men, raising his hands in apology, and slid behind an open table. It was good—a safe corner, a nook, away from everyone, almost hidden behind a wall of people's backs turned to him, wearing coats. Someone had left a half-eaten dinner, waiting to be cleaned up, and Rick looked about furtively before scooping the best remnants under his arm: a half-eaten piece of buttered bread, a few slivers of ham and gristle, a splatter of tomato with Parmesan cheese and basil, an olive-drab stick of army-issue asparagus. They'd left a glass with a splash of wine in it, which he drained. There was a thick white paper napkin with a woman's mauve lipstick print on it. Rick scooped the food into the napkin and pulled it into his lap under the table. Someone somewhere might have made a sound of disgust, but it was distant, like a young woman's voice. Her voice was lost as if across a street of fleeting traffic elsewhere and elsewhen. Bodies crowded all around, and Rick had a whitewashed wall solidly at his back. He felt safe for the moment.

An Algerian looking waiter in a white shirt, sleeves rolled up, and black vest and pants pulled the plate and glass away. "Monsieur? How are you this evening?" If he saw the scavenge hidden in Rick's lap, he did not let on.

"I'm fine," Rick said. "Can you bring me a beer?"

"*Oui, bien, Monsieur.* And what else? Something to eat?"

"Yeah," Rick said, remembering his lunch hours ago. "*Un sandwich au jambon avec fromage, peut-être.*"

"*D'accord, et vite,*" said the waiter grandiosely as he swept the remaining table debris into a little bucket, and ran a black-haired brush across the surface. "*Avec plaisir.*"

The waiter disappeared, and Rick ravenously ate the scavenge from the napkin in his lap. Looking furtively about, he reached down and fingered his sock, digging out a ten Euro note. His money was depleting fast, and he'd have to figure something out or starve to death or become a robber. How fucking sick was that? And he had money, lots of it, waiting in his bank account at American Express back at Vogelweh. But that was a lifetime away, an ocean of circumstances and aching difficulty to cross. Maybe he would find himself a guitar and sit around playing on the sidewalk. No, the French police would nab him sooner or later without a proper license, and there he'd be again. He was running out of time. There was no way out.

The ham and cheese sandwich came—a wonderful baguette warm from the toaster—along with a cool Stella Artois in a mug. The mug had the distinctive Belgian logo on it—*Stella Artois*, in white letters on a red field, surrounded with gilded leaves folding on themselves. The dot over the *i* was missing.

He gorged himself, looking around with starving eyes. As he did so, he became aware of a man sliding into the bench beside him from the other direction. The man was older, graying, with a pelt of unkempt whatever, like a mullet, down the back of his neck going into a too-big shirt collar. The man looked French enough, Caucasian, with big black bristly eyebrows, fleshy lips, wrinkled face. The mouth had a hard-bitten quality to it, and the eyes were incisive like a rat's, darting about with hard looks, taking everything in. Rick backed away a few inches from the man's intrusive presence. The man wore a dark maroon blazer, open-collared shirt with a loud wallpaper pattern (at least in a sort of matching merlot). He had pasty, pale hands that looked more like gloves, with loose black pig bristle hair. Looking around, the man briefly nodded to Rick—just a perfunctory look as if to say you're here, I'm here, now fuck off, I am busy with more important thoughts. They dismissed each other simultaneously. The man looked one way, and Rick—seeing the other's inattention—looked away.

What to do? The ham sandwich was finished. The beer was getting low. Must order another. Buy time, try to think, plan something.

At the other end of the table, a different waiter sidled close and placed a fresh beer before Mr. Mystery or Monsieur Mullet, whichever. Rick tried to get the waiter's attention to order a fresh beer, but without success. Frustrated, he drained his glass and pushed it away; then raised it slightly and slapped it down so it made a clapping sound on the table. Through the surrounding blur of coats and the surf-like roar of voices, he could not get a glimpse of his waiter from before. So he waited.

As he waited, he absently reached down and raised his beer glass. Ah, so the waiter had come and gone, maybe through the wall behind him. How else? But there it was, a fresh beer, and he drank thirstily. Feeling a bit giddy, he looked to his right and saw—wait a minute—the other man had an empty beer glass in front of him now. It was Rick' glass, with the missing dot on the *i* in *Artois*.

"Wait a minute, what's going on here?" Rick said.

The man slipped out of the booth and disappeared into the crowd, leaving Rick alone on the bench. Rick' hand remained protestingly and questioningly in the air a moment. He felt very, very drunk. He was getting woozier by the second.

Oh god gonna pass out...

Rick pushed himself out of the bench and erect, swaying slightly. Remembering his clumsy entrance, he resolved to make his exit as little noticed (or awkward) as possible.

As he started in search of the door—feeling blind—he stumbled backward and fell on his ass amid a chorus of disgusted and laughing voices, both male and female. People said things in French and in Arabic—he could not make out what. Strong hands lifted him by the elbows and half propelled, half carried him gently but firmly somewhere.

The back door.

Easy, dear fellow, a student voice said in broken English. *We won't let the staff call police on you. We'll help you out the back—you sleep it off in the alley.*

Fresh air flowed welcome around his face. It would have been wonderful, except he felt terrible. Something in the beer. The guy had switched drinks. Why? The waiter bringing the guy's drink had seemed threatening. The man sitting beside Rick had reacted with fear and finesse—a shifty tactician...

Rick landed face down on a pile of trash, mostly soggy cardboard smelling of rain water and glue. Old refrigerator transport box, it seemed like. For a few minutes, Rick lay helplessly sprawled on the soft cardboard. His palms were splayed on either side of his head, facing downward. His stomach was wet. His legs felt paralyzed.

He heard voices behind him—angry, frightened, then desperate. A man's voice sounded a scream of terror.

He heard something that clicked like the safety on a pistol.

8.   Execution in an Alley

Rick barfed out some foul-tasting liquid that almost seemed steamy as it spiraled out of his open mouth and hurled in an arc, splattering on cobblestones. He seemed energized, almost electric, with wide eyes and a focused gaze. It was all like a dream, kind of. There went the ham, the cheese, the bread he had just eaten, all in little soggy puffs frothy with Stella Artois. His entire body arced, again and again, hurling the foul poison through the air. Anything—*just please let me get away*—emptying himself out. Sobbing at the evil and the injustice of it, he tried to get on his knees. If not on his feet, then at least up as far as his knees, to try and get some control over this. "Charley, where are you? I need you." But nobody came to help him.

Rick managed to raise himself up in a genuflecting position, and just as quickly fell. He tried to brace his fall with his right hand, landed on his right elbow.

He had been thinking this was about him—about his flight from the Army, his wanted status as a deserter and an alleged war criminal— charges he might be able to fight, because truth was on his side, but he didn't know if he had the heart to defend himself. Maybe it was easier just to run—or die. Now he realized that the craziness going on around him was about something entirely different, foreign, almost alien. This had nothing to do with him. He was just an accidental bystander. The stranger beside him hadswitched drinks with him—why?

Rick could see—clearly, for an instant, a snapshot, before confusion set in again—that he was in an alley behind the bar. He remembered the bar, foggily. Laughter and voices sounded distant. From somewhere, cigarette smoke drifted in a raggy haze across his nose, making him want to sneeze. Drizzle out on the brightly lit street seemed to cleanse the air. The asphalt had a nightlight quality, tranquil, burnished, almost affectionate in its gentleness. Rick felt himself pulled down to the asphalt, face forward, helpless and against his instinct to brace his fall. Rick also knew, at that moment, that they had not seen him—and he was afraid any second now they would notice him and turn in his direction. Then he too would be doomed—and he had no idea why.

Four persons—a woman and two standing men; plus a broken, pitiful man on the ground—were at the other end of the alley, which opened onto the next street with its own shine and its lights.

The man who had sat beside Rick in the bar now lay on the cobblestones in the alley, pleading for his life. Rick could see his face clearly. He recognized the grooves, the yellow tortured flesh, graying mussy hair, the rat eyes and anguished brows. The man's hands were upraised as he half lay, half sat propped against a pile of empty grocery boxes—the kind stores discard after stacking the contents on their retail shelves.

Standing over the doomed man were two men and a woman. Squinting, Rick tried to focus and figure out what this meant. Who were they? What were they? What was going on here?

The standing man was a tall, very dark-skinned man who looked African judging by his facial features and short, kinky hair. He wore a brown silky suit, white shirt, dark necktie.

The other guy was shorter, slim, dressed all in black including a beret. He had tattoos and looked Asian—maybe Japanese.

The woman was hard, of medium height, with shoulder-length black, almost glossy hair—judging from her skin tone, perhaps Mediterranean, which could mean anything from Spanish to Arab or Turkish to Berber and a hundred things in between, but definitely Caucasian. She looked firm and athletic, almost mannish, rather than stylish. Her face was handsome rather than pretty, but she had a certain verve or polish, from the beautiful, thick hair pulled tightly into a bun on the back of the head; to her dark, animated eyes and red-colored, expressive mouth. She wore a sort of drab military field jacket over a plain red skirt, nylons, and pragmatic black half-heels.

The three killers would never have attracted notice in a metro train or walking amid the crowds along a Paris boulevard. Neither seemed cruel, but more like this was business. They were here on a job. They wanted something, the pleading man wouldn't or couldn't give it up, and they were not so much angry nor even frustrated but simply running out of time. That was Rick's instant take. He felt paralyzed by the drugs and his own ignorance, unable to help the man who was about to die. Did any man deserve this wet, chilly, anonymous end in an alley smelling of mold?

Am I next?

The doomed man's fleshy lips were open, exposing large, yellowish-brown teeth and a curl of raw meat—his tongue—before the tall African shot him with a silenced automatic pistol.

Rick slipped and lay totally flat, just maybe twisted a little to that side. He saw two muzzle flashes and heard popping noises.

One *pop*, accompanied by a flash.

The victim fell back. His arm dropped, no longer pleading.

A second *pop*, another flash.

Finished. Or not quite.

The Asian simply bent forward slightly to look, without any wasted energy.

The woman was more thorough. She folded her knees slightly to lean closer. She put a third round into the man's head. The body jerked briefly, lifelessly, with the impact.

The woman and the African pocketed their guns. The three killers did not look happy or fulfilled. If anything, they looked more frustrated. They had not gotten what they'd come after.

The former man was now meat lying in the rain.

Rick woozily swayed where he lay, hoping they could not hear him breathing from twenty or thirty meters away. Why had the dead man switched glasses with Rick inside the bar?

The two shooters turned to walk away on that other street. The little Asian walked between them.

At that moment, Rick felt a hand over his mouth, silencing him. A woman's voice whispered in one ear, "If you want to live, shut up." Rick's eyes widened. His gaze roamed up and back. He saw that she was young, blonde with a chignon, attractive, wearing some sort of airport worker's jacket over silk pants and ballet-like shoes. She put the finger of her free hand over his lips. "Shh!"

Rick had emptied his stomach, which felt as if it had been scoured with acid. His guts burned.

"You need me more than I need you right now," the young woman whispered.

Rick shook his head to clear it. His eyes felt like prisms. His vision was swimming.

He felt a convulsion, and hurled again.

"Shut up!" the girl said, shaking him.

He noisily vomited.

At the other end of the alley, the killers turned.

The woman waited, with her hands in her pockets, one hand on her gun. The man walked cautiously a few steps back into the alley. He listened attentively, having heard a sound.

Rick and the girl were in shadows.

Out came the gun. The African advanced carefully, slowly, and deliberately.

"Come on," the girl said. She pulled on Rick' elbow.

Rick had been in combat. This time he was unarmed. How crazy was that? Panicking, he shoved himself erect. He must survive to fight again.

The girl pulled on his arm, and he followed her. He ran, stumbling, but kept up with her.

Pop.

Pop.

Two shots in quick succession as the African man saw them.

Each shot took flakes of brick from a nearby wall at eye level.

Spatters and slivers of stone nicked Rick's cheeks.

They rounded the corner and emerged on the street under the neon sign: *Bar-39*.

Had he walked past here an hour ago, none of this would be happening.

They were on a busy street in Bagnolet.

He looked back at the alley, but the killers were gone.

"They'll find us," she said as she towed Rick along by his hand. "It's just a matter of time."

He shook his head, wishing he could lie down and sleep.

Drowsy, he let her tow him through crowds. They probably seemed like a young couple out on a date, and he'd had too much to drink, and she was guiding him home.

Home. Where the hell was home?

After what seemed like a nightmare of moving, vomiting, staggering, bouncing off walls, hearing strangers laugh or make cruel and cutting remarks in French and in Vietnamese and even U.S. English, Rick felt himself being shown into a safe place. He heard the rattle of a key, the creak of a door, the click of a light switch.

"We're safe here for the time being," said the young woman.

It was the last thing Rick heard before death-like sleep took him into its deep well of darkness.

9. Gaston Mendé

Wan Hong was furious.

General Mendé was philosophical. "With your resources, Mr. Wan, you will recover the data in no time. I am sure of it."

Wan made a fist, so that his knuckles whitened. He trembled with rage. "When I get her back, I will punish her. Oh yes, she will pray on her hands and knees for my mercy."

They sat in Wan's plane, which was still parked at the airport in Paris.

"I was supposed to be in Luxembourg by now," the industrialist said. He looked every bit the image of graying fury with his short hair, fox-sharp features, and blazing eyes. "Do you suppose it's PAX getting even for the Pierre Sander exchange in Paris?"

The other shrugged. "I have agents in the field, tracking Miss Smith. We already have her located in an apartment in a shabby area of Paris. Don't worry."

At that, Wan reluctantly backed off from his trembling anger, though he remained furious.

Mendé had dealt with many men and situations over the years. He had faced death as a young officer in the field, and had dealt with dictators and vindictive generals. This man reminded him of a cross-section of several frightening characters he had diplomatically caressed and soothed in dire situations. And yet, Mendé recognized, this man was in a class all by himself. Mendé did not let Wan's rage take him off focus. If anything, he most provide the focus that Wan seemed to be blurring. At the same time, he knew that Wan had survived many situations in his day, and always emerged the winner by any means possible. That was why Mendé was throwing his lot in with this Chinese zillionaire.

"Mr. Wan, look on the bright side. We will recover the Sander data that Miss Smith stole. We will create a corporate military like nothing the world has ever seen before. You will be the new Augustus Caesar of this wonderful new empire on which the sun never sets. There will be world peace, and you will be remembered in the history books for a thousand years."

Wan seemed to regain his perspective as Mendé massaged Wan's ego and his fears. "Like a thousand-year Reich," he said in a sudden burst of humor. "Without all the goose stepping and Sieg Heiling and the big rallies."

Mendé nodded. "Money operates like water, not fire. Money puts out fire and trumps the other elements. Money seeps into the cracks and finds its own level. Quietly and quickly, it drowns fire and air and earth; then glows like hell. There will be no more marching armies or flags or cheering crowds or millions of fools to march off and die for their magicians or their owners. We will control the air, the land, and the sea."

As Mendé spoke, Wan grew visibly calmer—colder, calculating, far-seeing as he looked across the horizon of possibilities and searched for the running figure of Hannah Smith.

Wan said, "You're right. She can't get far. I have Savia and Yuichi and Yolo after her. I can put more troops in the field to find her."

"Please, leave that to me," said his security chief, who grinned. "After all, that's what I get paid to do, so you can be free to concentrate on your important mission."

"Right," Wan said with a new light of calm in his eyes. "I have to continue preparing my speech for the CEOC parliament in the Valley of Seven Castles."

Mendé knew when to pour on the salve. "You will be at your amazing best, more than ever. We will find the girl, tear her to shreds, and get the data back as soon as possible. You concentrate on more important things. You will take the CEOC parliament by storm, and become their new president."

"Right," Wan said with a thousand calculations rolling through the casino of his eyes. "I will make myself their president for life. They cannot imagine what plans I have for the organization."

Mendé reached over and patted his boss' hand. "You cannot allow trivial matters to distract you. That is why you have the best people working for you."

10.   Post Office

A drizzly, gray morning dawned over the narrow streets of a suburb on the northern edge of Paris. The air was already heavy with smells of African and Middle Eastern cooking. Laughter and conversation in a dozen languages other than French floated in the air. The streets were crowded with women in face veils and men talking animatedly together while kneading prayer beads.

From a chipped wooden doorway emerged a young blonde woman who looked too preoccupied to care about the stares, whistles, and rude comments from immigrant men.

The young California woman named Hannah Smith wore her vanilla-golden hair wrapped in a chignon at the back of her head, and a silken, pretty kerchief in citron and absinthe shades draped over that to fit in better with the largely Muslim neighborhood, and to hide her blondeness better. She carried a small, clay-blue leather purse. Her clothing included a kind of blue work coat like those worn by airport workers or baggage handlers at rail stations, plus wrinkled wheat-colored, silken pants that had seen better days, and soft shoes resembling those of a ballet dancer. She kept both hands tightly on a rectangular object inside a torn, white plastic grocery sack that had been meant to be used once and thrown away.

The young woman spoke halting French as she asked directions to the nearest post office. With some effort—ignoring general rudeness, especially feral grins and hateful looks from jobless, aimless young men who looked down on non-Muslim women as whores—she found the small postal station on a shady, quaint little side street from another age.

She pushed open the heavy wooden door and entered, smelling familiar aromas of paper, ink, and rubber as befitted any post office in the world. For an instant, it was like being home—but achingly not, as she remembered just as quickly. Soon, though; soon she would be home in California, back to normalcy, where she understood the rules and knew the daily game of living. She was a free woman at last, though still in great danger. But she was in charge of her destiny now. Just not to blow it, that was the challenge. She had been around the world, courtesy Wan, and had come to trust her instincts

The small lobby was shady and empty at this hour. Her business at the wooden counter with its antique metal grill took just a few minutes. The heavyset, dark-skinned woman in postal uniform behind the bars was efficient and pleasant. She helped Hannah wrap her package in the appropriate postal envelope for express delivery to an address in Luxembourg-ville, Luxembourg. The package should arrive within a day or two.

That done, the blonde woman clutched her receipt and hurried back outside. Her path took her the way she had come, to the apartment of the man whose murder she had witnessed not far from the Gallieni station in Bagnolet in the hours of darkness not long ago. Tucking the receipt into the small, strapless purse, Hannah made her way back to Fincoff's apartment—and some intriguing, unfinished business awaiting her there.

She stopped along the way to buy two ham and cheese baguettes wrapped in wax paper, along with a glass bottle of mineral water with an ornate label.

11. Paris Apartment 1

Rick had more of his usual terrifying dreams.

He was running down a dark road while a *muezzin* droned out the call to prayer from invisible minarets under a full moon. The terrifying, droning voice was amplified and echoed by a million loudspeakers. In the dream, Rick was being chased by an armored vehicle that was going to explode any second.

He came to a place in the road where, in full moonlight, his old buddy Charley stood. Charley had his arm out, to stop Rick. *You're okay, man,* Charley said.

Charley, that car is going to blow up and kill us.

I can't be killed twice.

You mean you're dead.

It was a question, posed in a blind panic. Rick's heart beat in his ears.

Charley shrugged.

Am I?

Charley shook his head. *You're going to be okay, and we'll see each other again soon.*

The armored vehicle caught up with him and exploded in a blinding flash of black smoky oil and orange-yellow flame filled with terrifying grimaces and hooked claws reaching out to impale Rick.

He fell out of bed, screaming, and landed on the floor.

"Are you okay?" that same angel cried out, shaking him gently.

Rick could not speak, but lay in her embrace gasping for air and making jerky, panicky hand movements.

The girl holding him across her lap, like Mary holding Jesus in the *Pietà*, patted his cheek gently while her other arm curved protectively around his back. She sat on the floor, where he had fallen and then crawled and she had intercepted him to calm him down.

"You were having a dream."

"Charley..."

"Who?"

He licked his lips and paused to think. "It was a dream."

She nodded, slowly letting go so he could sit up on his own facing her on the wooden floor.

"Charley was a friend of mine. Never mind." He lowered his forehead onto his hands, resting his elbows on his knees with crossed legs. "Huilongistan..."

"That war is long behind you," the girl said. "We have a new one going on. This is Paris."

"Paris," he echoed stupidly.

"France," she said. She was pretty. No, beautiful.

His head felt as if a car had run over it.

She rose and yanked a window shade up and open.

Oh no...

A beam of light shone into his eyes, blinding him and baking his face.

"Mistake," she said. He saw her as a floating form made of dark green and brown and violet and maroon blobs. His eyes suffered as if there had been an explosion. He rubbed his eyeballs with his knuckles while groaning and writhing.

A pretty hand swept through the air, ripping a shade down, and the light turned dark. It wasn't death, but gentle shadow. Sunlight swayed into the room as the ugly dark-green shade swung where it had been let go over a dingy white wooden windowsill.

The young woman approached, offering something. "Here, drink some water," she said. Her voice had a nice quality, tinged with fear, frustration, and hurt. "Your name is Richard?"

Rick inched up into a sitting position with his back against the wall.

"Rick," he croaked. "Call me Rick. And you?"

He was on a rumpled, unmade bed whose dirty quilt had a fetid smell. He accepted the nicked, cloudy glass with both hands and sipped yellowish tap water. He drank it down—cold, vaguely tasting of cisterns and rain.

"More?" she asked.

He nodded.

She was slender and pretty, maybe still just a bit of teen softness about her as she padded barefoot across a dirty wooden floor with a faded, threadbare oval rug near its center.

She finally answered, "My name is Hannah Smith."

He felt a warm thrill inside. "You're American." It was a question.

"Bigger than pancakes."

A touch of home.

"Aw geez," he said, "I love you already."

"I'm not that easy," she said in a funny tone.

"What the hell is going on?"

She returned with a newly refilled glass, and held a handful of pills. "I found these in your backpack. It says you are supposed to take these pills three times a day."

He looked into her pink palm with its pretty, curling fingers. Almost baby fingers, with neatly trimmed nails under red polish.

He took her open hand in both of his, and held it to his lips as if it were a plate. The pills rolled onto his tongue. She followed with the other hand, driving the glass to his lips. He took it, swallowing more of the tepid gutter water (or so it seemed) to make the pills wash down.

"Thank you." He regarded her. "I wasn't going to take them anymore."

She sat on the bed beside him, folding pale arms between soft thighs. She sat half-sideways, not yet ready to fully face him. "What a mess."

"You tell me. What is going on?"

"You first." She regarded him with a pale, worried face. She had blonde hair, blue eyes, and that sort of creamy complexion that spelled Middle USA and could come from a lot of things. He touched himself on the cheek, self-consciously, and realized he had not shaved in about three days.

Rick regarded her back at the same time. "I saw a man murdered."

She nodded, and tears welled up on her lower lids. Tears dropped, one by one, onto her lap. Her lips fluttered in a sob. "I'm sorry. You were not supposed to be there."

"Yeah." He sidled into a more comfortable position. As the medications took hold, he felt more relaxed, and his thinking swam into focus. "What did you give me?"

"The stuff in your prescription bottles. I found them in your backpack, Rick Buchan."

"My wallet." It was a question.

"I took it out of your jeans and put it in your backpack. All your money is still there. Forty Euros. I counted."

He reached out and took her hand. She let him pull it toward him, onto his lap. They sat holding hands. Their fingers closed together in a gentle, desperate squeeze. "You must be an angel."

"Hardly." She wiped tears away with her free hand, and sniffled. Her blue eyes were rimmed with pink, swollen—she must have cried during the night.

"That bullshit in the bar cost me twenty Euros for nothing." He laughed bitterly, thinking of how he'd been poisoned, how it had felt as if a tiny alien was cutting its way out of his solar plexus with a dull wooden blade.

She squeezed his hand a little extra. "You're okay now. I found some tummy medicine and some headache medicine for you, plus the stuff in your pill bottles. Got anxiety disorder?"

"PTSD. Long story."

"You and me both." She scrunched her shoulders in a brief shrug. "Life goes on."

"Why are you here? Why are we here?"

She pulled her hand away, folded her arms straitjacket style, took a deep breath, and nodded as if putting a sheet of paper in a typewriter to start a very long story. "I am here..." she started, and stopped.

He thought she was going to start crying again. He reached out to offer his arms in an embrace, but she was strong and pulled away.

"I'm going to tell you the whole thing so you understand. Right now, Rick, you are all I've got. You didn't have anything incriminating in your pants or your backpack, so I want to trust you." She squinted at him suspiciously. "You're not a drug dealer or a—?"

"A what? I'm a law-abiding guy. I'm also a deserter on the run from Uncle Sam for something I didn't do."

"I believe you."

"So does my lawyer, I think."

"You have a lawyer?"

"Yeah, nice lady. JAG officer. I'm just not sure that the Army can accuse you and defend you at the same time."

"That doesn't seem logical."

"To the Army it does."

"What's the nutshell?"

"I was in the war, and lost my squad. I was squad leader. A dozen guys died in an IED explosion on a road we should not have been sent down. I got blamed, and I take full responsibility. They sent me back to Germany, and patched me up at Landstuhl. That's the big U.S. Army hospital. Then want to hold a General Court Martial. Only I don't think I'm guilty of any crime. Just losing my buddies. I'll carry that in my soul forever. Can you see the difference?"

She stared at him with large, luminous blue sky-eyes, shaking her head *no*, she didn't get it, but *yes*, she wanted to. She placed both her paws on his lap, and he held them as if they were playthings. He longed to hold them to his cheeks, because they were soft and feminine, but she'd have razor burn, and besides that he didn't like himself too much.

She said, "So you stopped taking your meds. You wanted to die."

"Yeah." It was an uncertain word. "I wanted to run away. You know, it was so sweet to feel the rain and cold air, like I was starting life all over again. I knew it was bullshit. You can't just run away and leave your skin behind."

She laughed suddenly. "What a silly idea. Stepping out of your skin and walking away."

He caught her emotion and laughed too.

She said, "You'd look very funny without your skin, Rick. Like—" her expression clouded, at a morbid vision best left unspoken.

He shook her hands as if they were little stuffed toys. "That's my story, Hannah. I'm wanted for desertion because I went out the window of an MP van while my guards stopped for bratwurst with mustard and sauerkraut at a street stand. I was handcuffed to a rail, but wriggled forward and snagged the master key from the glove compartment. I lost so much weight over there in the desert and then the hospital that I just slipped out the window of the cop car and down the street. I went in my plain old civvies. They didn't even have me in an orange jail suit yet."

"Lucky." She blew her nose on a paper napkin she'd gotten from somewhere. Collecting herself, she said, "Sounds like a fashion statement."

"Yeah. I had my backpack along, with all my stuff in it. So what about you?"

She kneaded the napkin in her hands, between folded legs, with those ridiculous pajamas. "I was a sex slave."

"Oh my god."

"Yeah." Her voice was dry and matter of fact. "I was desperate. My dad died some years ago. He was an Air Force guy. I was actually born in Germany myself, so I know Europe a little bit. We moved back to California when Dad got out. We lived near San Diego, where I went to school in Chula Vista. Dad died in a car crash that wasn't his fault, but Mom didn't get much of a settlement. We did manage to pay off the mortgage. I was in college at San Diego State when Mom told me she had cancer. She was getting treatments at the University hospital, and was doing okay for a while, but the insurance motherfuckers put a lien on the house. We were going to lose everything, which hurt especially bad because it was everything my parents worked for all their lives. So my so-called boyfriend, Ronny Shit Head, he got this offer. He knew some people. Well, he was a shady character anyway. There were these people, outside the so-called health insurance system. The health care denial industry. If I went to work for this agency in L.A., they would pay my mother's hospital bills, as long as I did whatever they wanted me to. It's a long story, Rick, but I was like a call girl for a while, got traded around between some oil zillionaire Arabs, and then somebody brokered me off to this Chinese zillionaire who has a taste for chewy blue-eyed blondes. So I became his property until I just ran away the other day."

Rick felt his stomach churning. "Poor baby. I thought I had a shitty deal."

"We both do, it seems." She looked away to one side, as if eyeballing a whole stack of crappy options and facts in the matter. "I did try to get Mom to move with me to Canada after Dad died. They have universal health care, like everyone else outside the United States. She wanted to stay in California because of the weather, her friends, and my dad's ashes being in a cemetery there. So we stayed, she got cancer, and we lost everything."

"Wow," Rick said with a huge sigh. He took one of her hands in both of his, and she let him hold it. "What about this Chinese geek? Didn't he have the money to pay for your Mom's health care?"

Hannah's features twisted into a wry look. "Wan just wanted sex. We never talked much. I think I amused him. He has about a hundred girls like me planted all around his mansions from Paris to Tokyo, from Rio to New York City. I was just one of his harem slaves. And then—"

Rick squeezed her hand, seeing that the next thing was coming out with difficulty.

This was where she really started bawling in a keening, high, heart-broken voice. "I found out that they let my mom die anyway. They denied her the care she needed because of some fucked up technical reason, like she had a cold once so it was a preexisting condition or whatever. I wasn't even there while she died. I was getting fucked by this rich animal, this wealthy predator, and my mom died all alone, asking for me, in a cheap rental unit after they took her house away. That was the house my parents bought together when they were young and full of hope, and it must have broken her heart worse than dying. That and never seeing me again."

Rick held her as she lay against him, wracked with tears and broken sobbing.

"That's really my main regret," she said as she regained her composure and washed her face at a small corner sink. "I wish I could have held my Mom's hand as she was dying. When I found out what happened, I started to really hate Wan and the brokerage that gave me to him, and the creep back home who put me into this mess—I will never mention his name again. And the corporations that do this to us day in and day out. And nobody seems to get it. We don't have to live like that, but they tell us it's the American Way. Apple pie, with rat poison."

"American roulette," Rick said as he rose and stretched, yawning. "I have to confess—it's something you don't think about in the U.S. It's always going to happen to someone else. Until the trigger clicks, the bullet goes off, and you lose the lottery."

"And nobody wants to talk about it," Hannah said as she toweled her face dry. "Like somehow you were bad and it's your fault. I don't know if I ever want to go back."

He changed the subject. "This your place?"

She shook her head. "Fincoff was his name. The guy you saw murdered."

"Fink off?"

"Yeah, something like that. I swiped Wan's most priceless treasure—the chemical formula for a new kind of aircraft fuselage, rocket skin, whatever. I overheard him talking with one of his Paris CEOs. He had it locked in a compartment. They were going to meet some big shots and present the idea to them. I grabbed it and ran."

"And here you are." So the execution of Fincoff had something to do with her theft of this criminal's deadly weapon.

"Yeah. Well, I thought it would go better. See, I made a few friends during the months that Wan kept me as his harem girl."

Rick couldn't get over it. "How in the hell—?"

She brushed it off with a shrug. "It's the latest thing. You can sell yourself for three to five years, usually—like, you can become an indentured servant, kind of. It's totally legal. Foreign zillionaires love owning Western people—it's status, prestige, and sometimes good sex, they figure. Stupid people in our country think it's hip, erotic, sexy, whatever. Lot of poverty. It's the new lottery."

He echoed, "Pot of gold at the end of that rainbow. I can see if you're desperate, you'd play. I'm sorry about your mom."

"Thanks." She brushed her fingers against his face. "You're nice. Anyway, if you do it, the story on the street is you can walk away set for life. Money means nothing to these rich people. It's like we're living in a new Middle Ages."

"Feudal times," Rick echoed. "I read history. Someone else wrote that it's like a new Gilded Age, but global."

"I've had plenty of time to read," she said. "Here, I brought some lunch for us."

12.   Paris Apartment 2 Phone JAG

Rick heard her go into the kitchen. As he waited, he pulled a cellphone from his backpack. He'd bought it near the Louvre, but decided not to use it late that afternoon. He'd boarded the metro at the Louvre-Rivoli station and resumed his aimless wandering—before his misfortune at the Bar-39 in Bagnolet. Now he dialed the number he'd gotten to know by heart.

In Germany, a telephone rang, and a young specialist started to say, "Office of the Staff Judge Advocate..."

"This is Sergeant Richard Buchan."

The young woman fell silent. Rick could hear her swallow hard.

"I want to talk with Major Kendra Walsh."

"Just a moment, Sergeant."

After being on hold for about twenty seconds, he heard the familiar voice of his JAG lawyer. "This is Kendra. Rick, where are you?"

"Never mind. What's the latest?"

"I know you were framed. I believe you...still putting it all together."

"How's it look?" He was desperate, and had no idea what he wanted to do—or how he really felt, other than betrayed and on the run.

"It'd go easier if you'd turn yourself in, and testify under oath in a deposition. We can't get past square one if I don't know where you are."

"We?"

"We are a team, Rick. The SJA here in Kaiserslautern. Defense team; and we're both Army."

"I'll think about it, Kendra. Keep pushing."

"I'm doing the best I can, my friend. You've gotta help me. Help yourself."

"I'll check back with you."

He rang off. He rose, walked to the toilet, and dropped the phone into the bowl. It sank, gurgling, into the brown neck of the toilet bowl. If there was a water tank in these European *klos*, or toilets, it was buried in the wall. No access. This would have to do until he bought his next phone.

He walked back into the bedroom and plopped on the bed.

What to do? What the hell to do?

13.   Paris Apartment 3 Death Knocking

Hannah poked her head in, just as he rocked up and down after returning from the bathroom. "You okay?"

"Yeah. Just talking to myself."

"Talk to me. I need it more."

"So come out here and sit with me."

"Hold on. I'm going to feed us first."

"Let's get married." It was a joke.

"You are insane." She looked pleased.

"Bad joke. But I like you."

"I can take a joke. Even a bad one sometimes."

At least he could joke with her. She'd saved his life, and she was a good sport besides. Then he felt an icy fist contracting in his gut—what if she got hurt because of him?

Then again, he'd almost been killed because of her.

He heard the refrigerator open. There was a rustling of paper, and the clink of a bottle.

"There's, like, one clean plate in this dump," he heard her say.

Then he heard a crash, and a clatter. "Oh shit."

"You okay?"

"One plate and I dropped it."

He heard scraping, clattering noises.

A moment later, she emerged with a pleased look holding the food. She waved some cold sandwiches and a bottle of Vichy water at him. "Bought these on the way back from the post office."

"Very thoughtful," Rick said. "I'm starving."

They sat at a small round table by the open window. A damp, fresh breeze blew in, along with traffic noise and distant voices. Aircraft thundered overhead in the clouds.

"Thanks."

"Don't mention it."

He chewed, or rather, they faced each other and had a funny-faces chewing contest, so much that they almost burst out laughing and nearly choked to death. She had a high, pretty voice like a bell when she laughed, even with a mouth full of food.

"I hope my situation doesn't get you hurt," he said.

"I can't be any more worried about your situation than I am about my own," she said.

"Fair enough," he said. "Your situation almost got me nuked. But you saved me."

"It was the only decent thing to do."

They ate quietly, nodding and chewing and swallowing.

"Good stuff," he said.

"Mm-MM-mh," she echoed with her cheeks blown up like a monkey's, and her eyes big.

"It's good to be alive," Rick said.

"You're telling me."

They ate hungrily, each thinking of the horror they had witnessed the night before.

"How are you feeling?" she asked soberly.

"Better. Lots better." In his mind's eye, he replayed a *pop-pop-pop* of shots in the dark alley. He froze, jammed up between here, now, and memory. He saw other things, like exploding military vehicles on a gloomy desert road bathed in moonlight and stars, surrounded by bone-white mountain ridges.

"You need to take your medicine."

He nodded. The explosion had rattled his brain, not to mention seeing bloody boots, helmets, body parts, and glistening caviar splats of gray-pink brain lying around. His thoughts slammed shut like a dark door. He froze. He pushed his food away and sat leaning forward with his head down and his arms out in defense.

"Eat," she urged. She rubbed his arms briskly with her soft hands.

He rose like a drowning swimmer, raising his head out of the abyss. For a moment, he'd forgotten how to breathe, or didn't want to. He took a deep breath and exhaled. He wanted to live. He almost wished he had that phone again to call JAG. He pictured Kendra Walsh—beautiful, with a ball of dark hair and a sweet, wide face. He knew from her eyes that she had something for him, even if her boss was that gigantic linebacker with a face like a wood-chopping stump with an axe in it.

She pushed a plastic bottle into his face. "Rick, here. Drink, man, drink. Get over it."

He took a swig of spritzy, cool water and wished it was whiskey. "Yeah."

"Snap out of it," she said. "Stay with me."

He wiped his forearm across his mouth, took a deep breath to brace himself, and repeated, "Yeah."

She continued her story about the McGuffin or MacFluffin she'd stolen from Wan, "So I knew I had something of great value there. I knew Wan had stolen it, or got his goons to steal it, from some PAX people at a university, who had no wish for it to fall into the wrong hands."

Rick understood the score. Most people didn't see it, but the world was spinning into a war between large corporations and their owners, to controlled all the wealth and money. It wasn't about nations anymore. It was about a new global order in which wars were fought with lawyers, and corporations were becoming more powerful than nation-states. By PAX she meant the Popular Alliance, a group of intellectuals and union activists trying to turn the clock back to the vanishing notion of popular democracies. The opposition were CEOC, for Corporate Executive Officers' Confederacy. It meant a growing alliance of convenience by oligarchs in various nations, like Wan, without any sense of national belonging or obligation. They increasingly owned and operated the world. All else was pretense by now, including sham democratic voting, while the propaganda grew more shrill than ever. Sheep believed all the lies, which were usually couched in the lingo of *faux* patriotism or religion.

"I had a friend in Shanghai," Hannah continued, "named Mélusine, from Luxembourg. Doesn't wear a bag over her head to prove she is men's obedient property. She's married to a nice Catholic boy from Luxembourg. That's where she lives now. They both teach at the university in the capital city. Mélusine taught me a lot about the world that I didn't realize. Like how my mom would have lived if we were anyplace else in the industrialized world except the U.S., which never had universal health care. We are the only place where they kill you if you don't have cash-and-carry for medical care, or as I call it Medieval Care; the most expensive so-called care in the world, and you still get nothing for it. Well, anyway." She sighed deeply and tearfully, thinking of her mother and her lost property now owned by the health denial industry's banks and so-called insurance jokes.

She took a break from her bitterness to chew the excellent *jambon et fromage* on a *pain normal*, just ordinary French bread that Rick found wild, chewy, and wonderful.

She continued, "Once I ran off with the McGuffin, I made the mistake of contacting PAX through this creature Fincoff. I thought I could trust him because Mélusine gave me his name originally as a contact in Paris. He supposedly was teaching at the Sorbonne for a time. Actually, they never heard of him. So much for trusting people. By then it was too late. By contacting him I contacted PAX but come to find out—too late—he got in touch with CEOC and offered to sell the McGuffin back to Wan for a million Euros."

Rick began to see the light. "Don't tell me. The hand-off was supposed to happen at the *Bar-39*."

She gave him a wry look. "Yeah. And you walked into the middle of it."

"I should have kept walking."

"What's done is done," she said. "Fincoff was sort of naïve. He didn't realize what an evil person Wan is. There was no way Wan was going to hand him a fortune in return for the McGuffin. When Fincoff was in the bar—I was watching; I saw you; I saw the whole thing go down—Wan's two goons tried to slip a knock-out drug into Fincoff's beer."

"Ah," Rick said. "That is why he switched drinks with me."

She nodded. "And why you were loaded to the gills. They wanted to drug Fincoff, take him into the alley, get the McGuffin from him, and leave him there."

"Instead," Rick said, "Fincoff let me take the drugs. He knew he was getting screwed, so he tried to duck out another door."

"Yes," she said, "but they caught him in the alley. They tried to get the package from him, but of course he didn't have it—I did. I didn't even have it with me."

"Who's they?"

"Yolo is the big Nigerian guy. Savia is Cuban. They are some of the goons who work for Yoichi, who is Wan's chief executioner at the moment."

"At the moment?" Rick echoed.

"Yeah. People like Wan change their favorites the way you change your underwear—hopefully from day to day in your case."

Rick found it humorous but did not laugh. Neither did she.

"Like he was getting ready to sell me to the next customer," she said. "I knew he was tired of me. When my mother died, I wanted to kill him. I hated myself for becoming a whore. I hated myself for selling myself to the corporations. With all their lies, I still had no guarantee of a payout at the end. No five year deal, pension, nothing. I just wanted to save my mom, and when they let her die to save a few dollars, I hated them, him, and everyone connected with health denial, laughingly called health insurance. No other country on earth has a corrupt system like that—"

He interrupted her. He agreed, and had heard it before. Health care was communism and evil socialism, we can't afford it, every man for himself, Jesus loves capitalism, we are all fucked and stupid. "So, Hannah, you were smart enough not to let Fincoff have the package."

"I was. Give me credit for at least that much. I hid it under the bed here in Fincoff's apartment. My plan was to play him and play them, because somehow I smelled a rat. I never did really trust Fincoff, even though Mélusine gave me his name. He didn't have it on him. He was obviously all bullshit. So they tried to beat it out of him, and when that didn't work, they killed him."

"And I was lying there at the other end of the alley, puking."

"You and me both, partner."

"You could have left me there."

She gave him a fair and square look. "Not my style. I got you into it, and I figured it was my duty to help you get out of there."

"Thanks," he said ironically, meaning both thanks for saving him, and no thanks for creating the situation in the first place.

"I needed a friend," she said. "I knew you were American."

"From California," he added.

"No way."

"Way."

"Where?"

"Santa Barbara area."

"Up the coast a ways. How cool."

"Neither of us has a friend in the world right now except each other."

She regarded him hungrily. "I'd give anything if you'd be my buddy."

He stared at her, wanted to gush out that he already loved her as a friend. He thought about the dead men standing all around him, especially Charley, and said nothing. He couldn't speak.

"You poor guy," she said. They had stopped eating and sat staring at each other. "You're wondering if you'll ever have another friend in the world."

He nodded. "I want—so much—" he started to say, and then nothing more came out.

She sighed deeply and bit into her ham and cheese bread. "Eat, Rick. We are going to be lucky to have each other."

He started to eat again, savoring the fresh food, and being alive. "I suppose you'll want to go home."

She nodded. "I want to go back to the States. Someplace where Wan will not be able to find me. Those huge internationals, they are all in it together, even when they are fighting each other tooth and nail for profit share. I'll have to go down deep somewhere, maybe even in Canada, change my name. And you?"

He did not have to think long. He'd never stopped thinking about it. "I ran away, and there are warrants out for my arrest as a deserter. NATO, the EU, the U.S., you name it. Everyone is looking for me. I just bought myself a little time to be free before they catch me."

"You stopped taking your medicine."

"Yeah. Well, maybe it was a way of committing slow suicide. I was half whacked out most of the time, talking to myself, seeing little men— seeing ghosts, like my buddy Charley, who died out there on that road in Fuckmestan. But I could still enjoy how it feels to walk in the rain, to feel fresh air that's scented with trees and grass. Even little things like the smell of wet asphalt."

She nodded. "That's all part of how it feels to be alive. You don't want to leave before your time is really up. Do you?"

He shook his head. "Honestly, no. And I wish I could go home to the World with you. But I'll never make it. They will catch me, and ship me back to Mannheim for my trial. Then I'll face years at hard labor. Yeah, I'll see the USA again—in plain, ragged old prison fatigues at Fort Leavenworth. When I was in basic, we used to call them ghosts—the old men who were doing life for some reason in the Army system. If they weren't doing hard labor anymore, they'd be on light duty, like policing spent brass on firing ranges. They wore fatigues, but no insignia. They weren't allowed to salute or be saluted. They couldn't talk to anyone. They didn't have much to say to each other. I think most of them smoked cigarettes all day, hoping to get sick and die to escape their life."

Hannah shook her head. "Geez, Rick, get over it. You'll never end up like that."

He felt sick inside. More than anything, he wanted to stay with her, forever maybe. And he knew it could never happen. There was one hope—a JAG officer named Kendra Walsh. As the medicine coursed through his blood stream, he felt his thoughts getting less depressed, less jumbled. He could see her before him—African American, attractive, with a ball of black glistening hair, dangling silver earring loops, and sympathetic plum-colored eyes. Her skin was milk chocolate; she had a wide, pretty nose, and full pink lips. He smiled at the memory of her—the one person who had shown an interest in him, who might have trusted him after all that went down. When Kendra Walsh smiled, her teeth showed, and she had the most infectious, wry way of smiling that made you want to laugh with her. Her boss was a big old Infantry colonel, 85% cacao, and gnarly as shoe leather, with whom Rick had locked eyes once.

He told Hannah about Kendra—Major Walsh, Staff Judge Advocate's Office. "The worst part of it is that I feel guilty about her too, like everything else. Like why drag her into this mess I'm in? She can't save me from the people who want to flush me down the toilet."

"You are too hard on yourself," Hannah said. "Finish your sandwich. We need to get going."

"Going?"

"Yeah," Hannah said. "Didn't I mention it? We are going to leave for Luxembourg as soon as we finish eating. I want to make sure Mélusine gets the package. There is a Professor Hilaire Sander who teaches political science at the Uni Lux. He is going to make sure the package reaches the right people in PAX this time—not a sleazy middleman and opportunistic bottom-feeder like Fincoff."

At that moment, there was a knock on the door.

Hannah and Rick stopped chewing and looked at each other, wide-eyed.

Hannah gripped Rick' wrist in terror while she stared toward the door.

The knocking grew more persistent, so much that the door rattled.

14.   Paris Apartment 4 Savia and Yolo

"Open up in there," called a man's powerful voice without any humor in it. The door rocked with several fist blows, for good measure.

"It's Yolo, the Nigerian," said Hannah. "That means Yoichi and Savia can't be far."

Rick assessed the situation quickly. Yolo was at the only door, and the two windows in the room overlooked a steep drop down mossy, stained stucco of about three stories into a cobblestone courtyard.

Several more pounding noises shook the door. He must be tapping his automatic against it—the very gun that had killed a man less than ten hours ago.

"Hold on," Hannah said. She wrapped herself in a sheet and strode to the door. "We have no choice," she said over her shoulder. "Yes!" she called. "I am coming."

Rick sat on the edge of the bed, unarmed and helpless. He kept his hands in sight and hoped the man would not start shooting.

Yolo crashed through the entry, shoving Hannah and the door out of his way. He was huge, holding the cannon before him with both massive hands wrapped around the grip. He reached with one hand, took Hannah by the scruff, and hurled her so she went flying toward the bed. She landed in a heap at Rick' feet.

"Don't move," Yolo said in a heavy, mellifluous voice. Nigerians generally spoke a good English that sounded a bit Caribbean. "I want the package you stole from Mr. Wan."

At that moment, the Cuban woman entered, also pointing a black automatic before her. "No tricks!"

Rick raised his hands and shook his head. "No tricks. We are unarmed."

Savia stuck her gun under her jacket, into her belt behind her back where it would not be seen. "I'll go tell Yoichi we've got them." Her English was fluent, with a Hispanic accent.

"We don't got nothing until we got the package," Yolo boomed. "Hurry."

Savia paused, as if to tell him not to give her orders. Her eyes blazed briefly. Then she whirled, went back out into the rickety hallway in the cheap hotel, and disappeared clattering down a flight of steps.

Yolo backed up, and shoved the door shut with one heavy black shoe. He almost grinned. Rick saw that his face was shiny-black and scarred around the chin. "We don't want curious neighbors looking in," Yolo said. "Okay, now, let's get the business done. You want to live today, you hand over the package."

Hannah was still sitting half on her knees, awkwardly, on the floor. She looked at Rick with scared, desperate eyes. She'd mailed the package, so there was no way out of this.

Yolo said, "The deal still stands, per orders of Mr. Wan. You hand over the package, we pay you the 200,000 Euros that Fincoff tried to extort, and you go free. If you don't hand over the package, this is your last hour on this earth, right here in this shabby rat hole."

Rick made a face, pretending to agree. Inwardly, he felt cold terror rising up his spine.

Hannah looked at him with a face distorted with fear.

Rick nodded. "It's in the trash can."

"Where?" Yolo demanded, pivoting powerfully while swinging the gun this way and that.

"Kitchen," Rick said. "In the garbage."

Yolo made a face. "You show me." He pointed the gun at Rick' head. "No tricks."

Rick rose slowly, keeping his hands elevated in submission.

Yolo tracked Rick, who walked in small, submissive steps, crouching slightly with his hands up, toward the kitchen. Rick felt his knees shaking—partly with fear, partly with adrenaline energy. He didn't care what happened to him. He desperately wanted Hannah to get out of here alive and in one piece so she could make it home.

Rick and Yolo moved in one unit, step by careful step, toward the small kitchen off to one side. The kitchen contained a ratty-looking sink with fifty-year-old linoleum for a counter, and Fincoff's last several meals' worth of dirty, crusty dishes piled amid circling flies. There was a smell of decay in the air. Yolo made a face, but never took the gun off Rick's temple.

"Slow now. Go slow," Yolo intoned.

Rick studied the powerful purplish hand, the massive fingers curled around the stock, the other hand sailing slowly in free motion as if Yolo were doing slow ballet in mid-air.

The plastic trash can stood where Rick had seen it before, next to the sink, almost under the one narrow window with its flaking, grimy wooden architecture the color of rotting bananas.

"It's in there," Rick said, pointing.

"Get it out for me," Yolo said.

Rick leaned forward over the trash can. He felt the gun boring into his back. He squirmed with pain as the muzzle lay rough on his vertebrae. "Take it easy."

The gun eased off. "No tricks."

"It's cool," Rick said as he began to dig with both hands in the trash. Fincoff's last meals lay rotting in the bottom. Flies rose.

"Gross," said Yolo. He stepped back a pace.

Rick pushed his hands down, feeling rancid, liquid garbage, crumpled papers, and other debris. "Maybe we can make a deal."

Yolo laughed. "Go figure. I knew you'd have some shaky plan."

"We split the money half and half."

"No dice, man. I split you half and half."

"Okay, it was a nice try. You win." Rick lifted a shapeless mass of paper slowly and carefully, turning toward Yolo as he did so.

The Nigerian kept the gun on Rick with his right hand. His eyes opened eagerly, and his tongue appeared pink between pearly white teeth. He reached with his big left hand to grasp the package.

In one smooth motion, Rick let the covering paper fall away.

In each hand, he held a shard of broken pottery—the plate Hannah had dropped.

With his right hand, he slashed the hand reaching toward him. He caught Yolo where he wanted—across the wrist.

Yolo made a horrified face as arterial blood—bright red, translucent as ruby—twirled in the air. It was illumined by sharp daylight slamming through the dirty window.

Squirt, squirt, squirt went the severed artery in Yolo's wrist. Thin streams of dark, rich blood pulsed across the room. Yolo's eyes widened with terror as he tracked his impending death.

Horrified, the man held his wrist up to look at it, forgetting the gun in his other hand.

Yolo's blood splattered in powerful hosing motions across his face, dripping from his nose and lips, blinding his eyes. His mouth hung open in mortal terror.

In a second smooth motion, Rick slashed with the other hand, cutting across the side of the hand holding the gun. The razor-sharp edge of broken pottery cut across the fingertip in the trigger guard and slashed deeply into the thumb coming around the side of the grip. The artery in the thumb began to squirt thin streams of blood.

The gun fell to the floor. Yolo stood clutching his hands across his chest, trying without hope to stanch the blood flying out of his hands. His eyes, blinded by spattered blood, started to glaze over with shock. He was visibly weakening and fading as he sank to his knees.

Rick snatched up a heavy cast-iron skilled and beat Yolo over the head again and again, driving him down to the linoleum floor. Yolo landed, face into the corner, by the trash can. Rick's emotions were somewhere else as he mechanically moved through what he must do to survive and save Hannah's life.

Kill or be killed—this was not my choice. You dealt me in, and picked your cards, and lost.

"Hannah!" Rick wasted no time, but dropped the frying pan, pushed the trash can over on the dying man, and quickly washed blood spatters off himself at the sink.

She came running—saw the body sprawled like a fallen Goliath across the kitchen floor—and grabbed Rick by a handful of sweater. "We might just make it. Quick!"

Rick recovered the gun. He checked the clip—it was full. Thick little copper bullet heads protruded in a row like deadly teeth. Safety off, he followed Hannah into the bedroom. She grabbed a plastic grocery bag with her meager possessions. She tossed him his backpack.

Together they hurried to the door, which was not entirely closed.

Rick pulled the door open with his heel, holding the gun ready. Hannah hovered behind him.

The hallway was quiet. Dust motes danced peacefully in a beam of sunlight, making a shaft of light that fell down the center of the flight of stairs.

"Let's go," they said in unison.

Rick remembered to pull the door shut and lock it, which would gain them a minute or two before their pursuers broke in and discovered Yolo's body.

Rick and Hannah circled a third floor landing—whose empty center that dropped dizzyingly into darkness—each clutching stray possessions. Rick held the gun ready. He was in combat mode. He'd kill anyone who got in their way. Then he'd be sick forever after.

Voices rose through the hollow center of the stairwell, where dust motes continued to dance peacefully in a broad beam of diffuse, sleepy sunlight.

Hannah grabbed Rick by the jacket and pulled him to a stop, so that she collided with him.

They listened. Rick felt his heart pounding in his throat.

The unmistakable voices of Savia and Yoichi rose up to their ears, along with the pounding of soft rubber soles as Wan's goons came running up the stairs to join Yolo—not knowing that their accomplice was already dead.

"There," Rick said, pointing with the gun. He'd spied a slightly ajar door along the many closed doors lining the gloomy hallway. The hotel was a flop for the poorest of pensioners. Luckily, none had arisen from drunken or drugged torpor to look outside their door to see what the commotion was.

Rick took Hannah's hand and pulled her along.

They crashed into a shared laundry room, with a battered washer and an equally decrepit dryer. The dominant color was somewhere between mustard green and olive drab. Blackened, rotting wood planks showed under the eroding linoleum, which in itself must be half a century old and covered with slop and stains.

"There," Rick said. A black steel fire escape beckoned outside the room's flaking, chocolate-painted window. He let Hannah go over the window sill first. He pulled the door shut while she made her way out on the sill. "Hurry!" she called out softly.

Rick pulled the door shut and locked it with a primitive sliding bolt of hardware store brass, installed for unknown reasons—maybe to offer a person doing laundry safety from prowling predators. They launched out onto steel steps and rattled down a fire escape.

They were in an alley with tall brick and wood buildings moldering all around them.

Rick hid the gun in his pocket, holding it surreptitiously as they ran down the alley.

They ran over moist soil covered with moss and bearded grass, inset with rubble and broken bricks.

Coming out onto the sidewalk, they spotted a dark Mercedes sedan parked askew before the hotel's steps. "That is Yoichi's. Let's grab it and go," Hannah said.

Together, they ran to the car, got in on opposite sides of the front, and pulled their door shut.

"Go, go!" Hannah urged.

Rick needed no invitation. He reached under the dashboard, ripped the wires his trained fingers sought, and touched them together. They sparked and bypassed the key circuit. The starter roared into life, as if he'd inserted and turned the key. So far so good.

A few random, dark-complexioned pedestrians innocently walked on either side of the street—a man in a suit, smoking a cigarette and glancing at a folded newspaper as he walked; an attractive thirtyish housewife lugging grocery sacks; a teen couple with linked forearms, lost in each other; and more.

Rick pulled the car out from the curb, where it had blocked a loading zone. He pulled into the street, amid sparse traffic.

He glanced out the window and upward. No sign that Savia and Yoichi and whoever else was with them knew they were about to get their getaway car hijacked.

Hannah draped herself over his shoulder, touching the gun in his pocket in case it needed to be taken out and fired. She stared past his head, upward, at the doors and windows of Fincoff's seedy hotel.

"We're outta here," Rick said.

"All right." Hannah relaxed, sat back, took her hand from his pocket.

"You know how to use a gun?"

She shrugged. "Necessity is the mother of invention."

"You wanted to head out of town."

"Take the Boulevard Périphérique."

"Okay." That would be the circumferential highway that skirts Paris' twenty districts or *arrondissements*. "Good plan."

"Look for signs. I think it's the A4 we want."

Rick glanced into the rear view mirror. "We're in luck. So far, anyway. No sign of anyone following us."

"They'll be after us soon enough, if I know Wan. He wants his package, and nothing will stop him. That's how he got to be a zillionaire." She added with a wounded, angry look in her eyes, "And a rapist."

15.   London Three Months Ago

A young college professor at London School of Economics walked through the antique, wrought iron glories of Victoria Station in the City of Westminster, London, England. Pierre Sander was in his early thirties—a handsome man, tall and dark-haired with an air of self-assurance. He was well-dressed in a charcoal business suit with a salt and pepper overcoat (more pepper than salt). He carried a briefcase in his right hand, and a cell phone in his left.

The red brick and otherwise ornate ninetheenth century façade of Victoria Station loomed behind him as he left the station and strode on long legs toward the Vauxhall Bridge Road. As he walked, he kept looking over his shoulder to spot an available taxi. He jostled among crowds on the sidewalk, and at the same time ordered the phone to connect him with a phone number on the Continent. It was a number in the small town of Echternach, Luxembourg, and the house in which he had lived as a child twenty-five years earlier.

A familiar voice answered curtly. "*Bonjour.*"

Papa, ech sin et, de Pierre. "Papa, it's me, Pierre."

Ah, mai leiwe Pierre. wéi geet et dir? "Ah, my dear Pierre. How are you?"

Alles an der Rei. Ech hun dei Daten. "Everything is okay. I have the data."

Wonnerbar. Da maache mer elo Schluss. "Great. Let's finish this."

Ech wärt maar de Muren zu Letzebuerg sinn. "I'll be in Luxembourg tomorrow."

Also bis dann, mei leiwe Jong. "Until then, my dear boy."

Pierre strode along the major road. He had just come from his office at the college, where he had been teaching five classes. The winter break afforded him a chance to bring his test results to his father—Professor Hilaire Sander—who was seriously considering making a run for the CEOC parliament in June. While it was pretty much obligatory for a seasoned CEO of a major conglomerate to run for the presidency, any competent newcomer could challenge the election if he or she offered a compelling case to improve the global status of the Chief Executive Officers' Confederacy (CEOC). Certainly, his dad—being an economics professor with extensive practical business experience in computer systems development—was qualified.

A black London taxi slowed, pacing Pierre at the curb.

Pierre had not hailed the cab just now. He'd given up a few minutes ago, but planned to try again in a moment. Why not? Now or never. He stepped off the curb, pulled the back door open, and climbed in with his briefcase. With a jerking motion that threw him back in the seat, the cab sped away in to traffic.

Pierre immediately knew something was seriously wrong.

The driver was an enormous African man with short, woolly, mussy hair. In the taxi were two other persons beside the driver. A handsome, dark-skinned woman, with black hair and eyes, sat in the front seat. From what Pierre could see at this angle, she wore a butterscotch leather coat, fastened with a belt. A forest-green silk scarf at her neck was tucked into the coat's collar. Most significantly, she held a small black automatic pistol, which was aimed at Pierre's head.

In the back seat sat a smallish, slim Asian man with short-cropped hair and a certain crazy laugh in his features. He too held a gun, which had a silencer on the muzzle. "Hello, Professor."

"Who are you?" Pierre said heatedly. The data must not fall into anyone else's hands.

"We are a data transport company," said the Hispanic-looking woman in the front passenger seat.

Beside Pierre sat the slender Asian man with short, ragged black hair. He wore dark pants and a black T-shirt. His bare arms were covered with lurid, colorful tattoos. His face bore a crazed, anything-goes expression as if he were silently laughing. He seemed to be enjoying himself.

The Asian man said, "Open the briefcase."

Pierre froze, hugging the precious leather case to his chest. He realized with sickening finality that these people were not taxi drivers but criminals. Murderers, no doubt. And they were after the data carrier in the briefcase, which could tip the balance of airpower around the world. He understood who they were working for—not PAX, but the other side.

"We can double whatever CEOC is paying you," Pierre said in English.

The women in the front seat spoke with a Latina accent—probably South American or close. "You would never want to pay us for what we do. We get paid by your enemies. That is who we are."

The driver chimed in with a Nigerian accent, "We know on which side our bread is buttered."

"You don't have the bread," the Asian quipped in a double entendre that made his companions snicker. "For the last time, open the briefcase."

Pierre recognized that the woman was the smartest. "Please," said to her, "we can make a deal."

She shook her head matter-of-factly. "We don't need a deal, Dr. Sander."

The Asian reached over and roughly grasped the briefcase. Pierre tried to resist, but felt his hand being cruelly twisted in a martial arts hold. He could not maintain his grip.

The Asian took the briefcase, used a knife to pry off the locks, and looked inside. "Appears to be what we want." He snapped the briefcase shut. "With regrets, Dr. Sander. We must say goodbye."

"Wait," Pierre said, "let's talk about this."

The woman smiled thinly. "We have the data, and you are now the problem. If we let you walk away, you can duplicate your work in a matter of weeks. Without you, it will take two years for NATO or the U.S. to figure out all the twists and turns."

Pierre felt a cold wave of shock and realization flood him, as if he'd been tossed into the North Sea on a freezing night. His Titanic had hit its iceberg—and he just understood this now. His last thoughts were of his widowed father, and how this would create unbearable agony. He was all the old man had left in life.

"Goodbye, Dr. Sander," the Asian said.

The Hispanic woman pulled the trigger.

Her finger, pulling the trigger—the rounded little first joint of her finger out from the knuckle of her trigger finger—soft and lovely as cocoa butter—was the second last thing Pierre Sander saw. He meditated on its feminine beauty and gracefulness.

He closed his eyes and let his mind to drift to find a memory of his father's face, gazing at him lovingly, framed in wind-blown white hair. It was a weathered, reddish face, with lines of worry and bitter experience etched into it, but the eyes remained alight with hope. With him was his dear mother, smiling again as she had in life, proudly—loving her only child…

Fade to nothing.

16.   Mélusine Three Months Ago

The house phone began to ring about one in the afternoon in a small white bungalow in the pleasant Luxembourg City quartier of Belair. Romain and Mélusine Poncelet were both home, enjoying a day of rest. They were an attractive, athletic couple, thirty-something and enjoying life while working hard at their professional careers.

Romain sat in their little study, playing computer games in his underwear with a hot cup of coffee at his elbow. It was homey and relaxing in the semi-dark room among their books, papers, knick-knacks, and electronic gadgets.

She was in the garden, watering her roses with a green rubber hose. If he looked up, he could see her white top, her bright red shorts, and the white band holding her plain, straight brown hair. She wore tapioca-yellow leather gardening gloves.

Mélu rapped on the window with her knuckles. *Romi, den Telefon schellt bis op de Plafong.* "Romi, the telephone is ringing to the ceiling."

"I hear it," he said reluctantly, swinging his rear out of the seat while leaning forward and continuing with the keyboard and mouse to run down corridors shooting alien invaders. He forced himself to tear away, and picked up the old-fashioned white plastic receiver.

"Allo."

Visible out in the garden, Mélu held the hose with one gloved hand, and wiped sweat off her brow with the back of her other wrist.

It was a PAX contact calling from London. The young woman was native to Longwy, France, not far from the Luxembourg border. The contact had gone to Uni Lux with Mélu and Romain. Professor Sander had been their faculty advisor, and remained their ideological leader as a major intellect of the Progressive Alliance. The woman spoke in French.

Romain's face went gray as he heard the news. While listening on the phone, Romain walked to the window and rapped to get Mélu's attention.

Mélu turned innocently, saw his expression, and opened her mouth in shock and anticipation. She knew immediately that something horrifying had occurred.

Romain made frantic circling motions with one hand to make her come inside.

Mélu dropped the hose. She turned off the water, peeled off her gloves, kicked off her muddy shoes on the doormat in the rear, and rushed inside.

Romain hung up and faced her. "Pierre has been murdered in London."

"No." Mélu froze with a shocked face and open mouth.

"He was shot and left in the back seat of a stolen and abandoned taxi found in Wapping. Police cannot find any fingerprints or leads. It's undoubtedly the work of CEOC hardliners because—get this—his empty briefcase was turned in as lost and found at a bus station near Wapping. Police made a positive I.D. that it belonged to Pierre. When PAX heard the news, they figured out he must have been carrying vital defense data when they robbed and murdered him."

"Oh god. And the data?"

"Gone."

"Does Dr. Sander know?"

Romain shook his head. "I don't think so. We have to drive to Echternach immediately to see him. Whether he knows the news already or not, he will need our support as friends. He will be devastated."

"I would rather be the first to tell him, much as it hurts me," Mélu said.

Pierre had been a drinking buddy of Romain at Uni Lux. Mélu had sometimes gone along with the two men to this tavern or that in Grond or Knuedler. Pierre was single, a handsome and flirtatious bachelor, who always had the prettiest girl by his arm. It was impossible to comprehend that he was dead.

"Why?" Mélu cried as she washed up at the kitchen sink. She paused to lower her face between her elbows, bowing her head. She shook with sobs. Romain rose to comfort her.

Romain shook his head. "There are rumors that he was developing some special aviation technology for a NATO consortium. I think it is called Intelligent Fuselage Skin (IFS)."

Mélu was all the more shocked. "Strange. I have an upcoming contract job for a month in Shanghai, working for Wan Industries. As far as I know, the assignment has something to do with airframes and fuselage components. Nobody mentioned IFS, though."

"Probably top, top secret," Romain said. "The rumors speak of it as the McGuffin."

"Like some sort of code name." She nodded, and stepped into the shower.

She emerged five minutes later naked and toweling herself. "Let's hurry. The poor, poor man."

"Maybe it's a coincidence," Romain said as they hurried in the foyer, gathering street clothes for a quick run of twenty minutes to the Luxembourg town of Echternach near the German border.

"I will find out soon enough," Mélu said.

They walked out to the car and got in. Romain started the engine and backed out of their little driveway onto a narrow, quiet residential street.

Within ten minutes they were on the E29 heading east toward Echternach, Luxembourg's oldest town, famous for its ancient monastery and shrine. It was also famous across the region for its annual *Sprangprozessioun* or Jumping Procession in honor of St. Willibrord, an English missionary to the Frankish people, who had miraculously cured some local people of St. Vitus' Dance in the early Dark Ages.

Along the way, Mélu called the Professor's house from her cell phone.

Of all possible phone calls in her life, this was the call she least ever wanted to make. She felt a pit of devastation in her stomach as it rang and the professor's housekeeper picked up.

17. Professor Sander Three Months Ago

The phone in a shady hallway rang, and the housekeeper came from the kitchen to answer.

It was one of the professor's many admirers and former students.

The girl actually sounded as if she were weeping, but would not say why and insisted on speaking with *den Häar Professer*.

Frowning with puzzled concern, the middle-aged woman set the receiver down and hurried into the garden in back to inform Professor Sander that he had a call, and it sounded important.

The elderly man was at the moment chipping away with a masonry pick at a flat piece of stone to be laid into the property's far back wall. His white hair fluttered in a wind-blown shock over his pink skull. He dripped with sweat, frowned with concentration, and looked very robust for a man of his age. He wore the dark blue overalls of a common laborer, and looked like a guy who'd stop anonymously into a tavern for a beer when he was done with his labors.

As she called his name, her womanly instinct told her the weeping girl on the phone meant this was a life-changing telephone call.

"Telefon!" she called out, full of concern, as she stood on tiptoes with hands folded together over her black housework dress

★ ★ ★ ▮ ▮ ═ ▮ ▮ ▰ ✳ ★ ★ ★

Hilaire Sander heard a voice calling him, and looked up from his labors among greenery and flowers in the yard. Nearby sat a wheelbarrow, a bag of mortar, a pail of water, a trowel, and a semi-neat of broken stone. He used the wheelbarrow for mixing mortar. He would hose it clean later. The air around him had a biting cement smell, tempered by flower and greenery freshness.

Sander was a robust man in his seventies. He'd made a new life for himself after his wife had died of cancer ten years ago. His joys in life now revolved around his son, his books, his gardening, some teaching, and his growing passion for the Progressive Alliance for Peace (PAX).

Over the years, he had been offered many civil and academic honors, and he had refused most of them. He did not want to be co-opted by the establishment. It was enough to carry the titles Ph.D. and Professor. It was the greatest honor of all to have his articles published in peer-reviewed journals to the approval and pertinent but respectful critique of his peers. He had been offered knighthoods by several European monarchies, and had politely refused. The independent, rigorous academic scholar in him tended more toward an ascetic, simple honesty of facts and analysis. He was forever, as the Spanish might say, *Forastero*—outsider. As a Belgian journalist had once quipped in writing: "Sander the Outsider is so out that he is more in than most of the in-crowd." That had made Hilaire laugh. It was years ago, when he was still a brash disciple of Bloch and Braudel to lead new generations of the *Annales* school of understanding human history. He liked to call his broad interest macro-history. He saw it as a parallel way of segmenting history into micro (detail) and macro (abstraction), compared with micro-economics and macro-economics, between which the first dealt in numbers and names, the second in variables and abstractions.

He greatest pride lay in seeing the growing professional success of his son, Pierre, a professor of engineering in London. Pierre was tall, handsome, an unmarried man still playing the field with adoring women friends, a promising intellect of good income and connections, and an only child who would carry on the Sander family name.

Professor Hilaire Sander, having retired from his long teaching and research career in economics and business, now worked when he pleased. He was a professor emeritus at several universities in rotation, from Trier to Louvain to Paris and other places depending on his interests and their needs. He sometimes did a stint in Luxembourg, but was more interested now in savoring distant cities and new faces.

When he wasn't home writing or gardening, his time was increasingly taken up with the PAX movement. The power of global corporations had passed critical thresholds in the twenty-first century. Many corporations were wealthier and more powerful than some nations—many certainly had more clout than Luxembourg, for example.

With ground swell support in many nations, the Progressive Alliance was a peaceful, moderate movement of students, workers, and small business interests around the world. It was a moderate-center ideology to regain ground lost by labor unions and municipal governments. It was gaining support from many smaller national governments who recalled the larger powers, where democracy had become a sham because of relentless bribery and lobbying by armies of lawyers and insidious persuaders pushing a million different business agendas at the cost of the common good. Sander wanted a revolution, not in blood and violence, but at the ballot box—before things could get out of hand. If people became desperate enough, they would resort to arms to overthrow politicians and justices who were in the pocket of Big Money. Something had to be done before it came to that, and increasingly this took more of Hilaire Sander's time than his teaching.

Aside from his thoughts of Pierre, and his hopes for PAX, the anchor of his life was the little residential property southwest of Echternach, not far from the large park and recreational lake. His small cottage nestled in a tangled, English-style quarter acre of flowers and shrubbery, trees, and even a bubbling fountain. The garden was what the English had once called an ambage, from the Latin *ambulare*, to walk. The property's outer boundaries were defined by a low masonry wall that the professor himself kept repaired with mortar, loose stones, and sweat as he wore leather gloves and old clothes like a worker. He liked to get dirty once in a while, dressed in blue overalls like a railroad baggage porter or a truck mechanic. He identified with working class people as much as he enjoyed being an intellectual with a home library of over a thousand old-fashioned print books in addition to all the world's resources online. His economics and political science scholarship was respected and published in peer-reviewed journals around the world.

The housekeeper, a middle-aged woman, came to the back door. "*Monsieur le Professeur*," she said in typical *Letzebuergesch* with a sprinkling of French words and phrases, "there is a telephone call."

"Thank you. I'll take it at the side door. Don't want to get the hallway dirty."

Wiping sweat from his brow, he ambled along the garden path and came to a little flagstone walk behind the house. He stopped a moment to run a brass faucet and clean at least some of the soil and dirt from his hands.

The receiver lay off the hook on the mail table in the little back hall. Hilaire picked it up and happily said, "*Bonjour?*"

"Professor, this is Mélusine Poncelet."

Her voice sounded tragic. He frowned. "Yes, dear?"

"I am afraid I have terrible news for you."

He knew, right then. Tears started to flow from his eyes before she said it. His knees grew weak, and he slumped into a wooden chair with hard arm rests.

Pierre.

A big part of his life ended for him at that moment; he felt as if he had been shot, along with his beloved only child, who had brought so much joy into his life. To lose that child was unthinkable.

As Mélu Poncelet spoke—quavering, in tears, but bravely, trying to be strong for him—he felt as if the same bullets had pierced his own body. He saw himself becoming a smoky shade, a living ghost, walking into the ante-chamber of a gray afterlife. He thought of the wavering ghosts who had come to visit Goethe's *Faust*, or the shades of deceased warriors visited by Ulysses in the *Odyssey*; not to mention Aeneas' descent into Avernus in the middle book of the Virgil's Roman epic; or Dante's story of a descent into the *Inferno*. All the literature he had ever read now made his new reality out of those dramatic and crushing visions of the gray afterworld.

"Romain and I are rushing to see you," Mélu said.

"Bless you. Thank you," he whispered. He sat by himself, all alone in the world now, and wept brokenly with his hands over his face. Hot tears flowed between his fingers. He cried more than he had when Marie had passed away. That was cancer, and Marie had lived a full life. He had thought to himself, standing by the urn of her ashes in the cemetery in town, that she was fortunate—she would not live to bury her husband. Now he envied her all the more, because she would not have to bury her only child. Or had she gone to her reward, knowing in the afterlife what was to come? Hilaire Sander cried despairingly.

At the same time, a tiny flame of rage leapt to life deep in his soul. It was a flame that would nurture itself and grow stronger as he rededicated his life and old age to the one thing that mattered now—the cause of equality, liberty, and happiness for all people, not just the greedy, cruel medieval overlords who arose in every age and on every stage as part of the Human Condition.

Weeks passed by.

Kind, sweet Mélu and Romain stayed with him for a few days, as did other students from past years. Finally, he was alone again in privacy and suffering and grief. That had to be so, he understood; and now he must reshape the few remaining years of his life to a crystalline new cause.

The little flame growing at the center of his new dedication was the knowledge that Pierre had not died by accident. It was clear the boy had been murdered. He'd promised to bring two years' of research data on a new Intelligent Fuselage Skin technology to Echternach for release to responsible, neutral NATO and European Union officials in the service of the common good.

Hilaire's professional networks included clandestine services working around the world, as nation-states were weakened and global corporations became the new feudal manors. He knew the names of some of the dangerous ones.

Among the most prominent was General Gaston Mendé, the short, portly, but hard-faced and iron-fisted retired Danish flag officer who was lobbying to be the new world order's Goering or Agrippa.

Mendé was not demagogue material, nor was he a political leader. He was an infighter, a military back-bencher, a ruthless and relentless organizer. He was a *daimyo*, a feudal lord, who best served a charismatic overlord of the type exemplified in history by a Caesar or a Hitler. Today, the most prominent candidate for that position was the Chinese billionaire Wan Hong, already one of the world's wealthiest men. A man like Wan Hong did not need to be a populist rabble rouser. He would have the entire global corporate media at his disposal to shape his image in countless films and commercials once his campaign really got going. That campaign was about to start at the parliament of the world's Chief Executive Officers' Confederacy (CEOC) to be held in the Valley of Seven Castles in Luxembourg.

What more appropriate place for a giant step back into the Dark Ages than in a valley of castles dating to European medieval centuries—when barbarian citadels on rocks, with dirt paths and forest trails connecting them, replaced the lost cities and highways of the great Roman empire in the West?

According to PAX intelligence—which included subversive, resistance elements among lower-level NATO and U.S. military and intelligence ranks—Wan Hong had made it clear he wanted to run for the position of Plenary Chief Executive Officer of CEOC, the world's parliament of the thousand wealthiest families.

Hilaire understood quite well that Wan's plans only began with the leading position of CEOC. Wan would turn CEOC into an all-powerful capitalist empire founded on false, hijacked religion and oppressive tyranny.

Sander had only one thing left to live for. It wasn't so much revenge for Pierre. It was to serve the cause that Pierre would want. Let Pierre's life not have been thrown away for nothing. Not for the greed and venality of a Wan. Not for the brutality and selfishness of a Mendé.

Not for the criminal insanity and megalomania of a Milosevic or a Pol Pot or a Mussolini, and a thousand demagogues like them yet to come, who would lead entire nations into death and rubble as Hitler and the Germans had done to themselves in a mass suicide of evil and foolishness.

Even as he suffered in terrible grief that could never be healed, Sander resolved that he would continue the fight for Pierre and the world's children and future generations. Pierre would never have a wife and children now, but the world's children would be his descendants if Hilaire and PAX could prevail. If nothing else, there should one day be a memorial somewhere in a great square, maybe in London or in Paris, and certainly in Luxembourg City, to Pierre Sander. That was worth living for.

By the time his young former students Mélu and Romain drove up, Sander had composed himself oddly—on the surface, at least, betraying none of the volcanic pain deep inside.

18. North by Northeast

Rick Buchan and his new friend Hannah Smith drove away from Paris. Rick drove past the peripheral highway system that circles Paris, and headed north by northeast toward Luxembourg.

The more Rick steered the car into heavy traffic, and the farther they got from all that had happened, the more secure he felt. It was a sense of relief—although he still had the matter of JAG and his trial hanging over him. No matter where he ran, eventually Uncle Sam's forces or NATO or Interpol would find him.

Hannah sidled close to him. She laid her left arm over his shoulder, and clutched his jacket with her right hand. "Thank you."

"For what?"

"Being you."

Busily steering amid roaring trucks, buses emitting black diesel smoke, and darting cars, Rick managed a wry face. "If I had time, I'd return the emotion."

He threaded his way through city traffic, until he reached the A4 auto route at Charenton-le-Pont.

"We'll have time."

"At least for a while."

"Think positive."

"You should talk."

"I'm fine."

He favored her with a long look. "Are you?"

He could now lie low in the middle lane. It was all straight traffic, without a lot of weaving and jockeying, on the A4 as he headed north by northeast.

She nodded. "I'm getting there." She patted his thigh lightly. "I have you."

He patted her hand, squeezed it. "You're cool."

She rested her head against his shoulder.

As he drove, Rick felt a contentment he had forgotten was possible. His demons and terrors lurked at the periphery and would not go away—but here was a warm, live woman from his homeland beside him. They'd have much in common. He dared not think it any further through.

"We'll make it somehow," she said softly, snuggling.

He laughed softly, feeling a refreshing draft. "This is better than having a cat."

She punched his arm gently. "I can bite and I can scratch, too."

"I'll be careful."

"You better be." She snuggled all the harder, pressing against him with her arms folded together and her legs pulled up. "I didn't get much sleep last night."

"I was zonked."

She spoke with her eyes closed. "I'm not surprised. They gave you enough drugs to knock out King Kong."

"Why were you awake—were you scared?"

"Yes. We saw a man get killed, rotten as he was." She paused. "I was more worried about you. I lay there looking at you."

"If I'd known, I would have pulled you closer."

"I was afraid to get close."

"But no more?"

She shook her head. "I trust you, Rick Buchan."

"Even if I fall out of bed screaming?"

"It means you are human. I can touch you and you won't bite."

"I liked it when you held me after I fell on the floor."

"I should have been a nurse. Maybe I'll go to nursing school if we live through this."

He wanted to say that he hoped they would be friends if they lived through it, but didn't want to push the warm feelings he was having for her. He thought of Kendra Walsh, his JAG contact. That made two good women in his life now. Must be a good sign.

While Hannah dozed against his shoulder, Rick drove steadily in a silvery drizzle. Sometimes he had to keep the windshield wipers of the Mercedes going. It was a late model car, though not the latest or the top of the line. He supposed that Wan's henchmen could not all be driving luxury cars. Probably best to stay unobtrusive this way. It was a nice car to drive, in any case.

A few times, he leaned close just to sniff her hair. She had a warm, clean smell, hard to describe. Kind of like a fuzzy kitten.

As he drove, Rick thought about how special she was, and became a little more nervous. Was there any way that Wan's people could track the two of them? Surely their escape could not be this easy. Especially since he'd now killed a man—not in battle, not an enemy combatant officially, but a civilian. At a minimum, if he were investigating a case like that, he'd want to haul himself in for questioning. He realized with a sinking feeling that he'd probably left fingerprints on the broken pottery in the kitchen. Not to mention that he and Hannah had left their traces all over Fincoff's apartment. He must expect the worst, therefore—it was just a matter of time. Could he manage another two or three hours and reach Luxembourg unbothered? And what then? He had no plan, and doubted that Hannah did, short of visiting her friend Mélusine.

As signs for Reims started coming into view, Rick noticed at least two police cars—probably random, but seeing the white and blue cruisers with their red-white-blue light bars on top made him nervous. Having the gun in the car might get him arrested, in itself. He placed it in the glove compartment and stacked papers on top to hide it as best possible.

They were nearly halfway to Luxembourg now. Cruising along, even staying within reasonable speeds to avoid being noticed, the run from Paris to Luxembourg would take between three and four hours. There were a few tolls along the way, which he paid from his cash in the automated turnstiles.

About an hour later, as they approached Verdun (an hour or so from Luxembourg), Hannah rose and stretched. She yawned. "Are we almost there?"

"About an hour, maybe. Hey, I have an idea."

She sat back, looking sleepy, and rubbed his right shoulder with her left hand. "Oh?"

"We need to dump this car."

"And walk, sweetheart?"

"One thing at a time."

"What's the plan?"

"I've been thinking..."

19. Verdun

Hannah rested in her seat, with her head back and eyes closed.

Rick steered among wan yellowish street lights along rainy roads. The houses looked civilized and somehow sadly pretty. They were passing near the ancient city of Verdun in the Lorraine region.

Wan's people would be unlikely to report either Yolo's killing or the car theft. The less they involved the police, the less likely they could be connected to Fincoff's killing in Bagnolet, and much other messy stuff.

On the other hand, it would be careless to underestimate Wan's reach. He no doubt had a network of contacts and operatives all over Europe, not to mention the world. As he considered the options, Rick was less worried about legitimate police than about private agents.

Rick began to feel nervousthat Wan might have a Global Positioning System on board all of his cars, and might be tracking them—to the package. What a thought.

"We are going to change cars," he told Hannah.

"Whatever you say." She yawned tiredly, and stretched.

As she moved about, he looked at her hands from the corners of his eyes and wondered. What would it be like to have a woman like her? What would it be like to live a normal, peaceful existence without killing or running or fear? He took her nearer hand and squeezed it gently.

She looked at him in surprise. She laid her other hand over their two entwined hands and gave him a quick peck on the right cheek. Then she purred like a cat, snuggled, and fell asleep facing toward him.

He thought again how impossible this was. One of them would get both of them killed.

As they drove through the region south of Verdun on the *Autoroute de l'Est*, Rick noticed a regional airport. He followed the signs toward the airport. It was starting to rain again, and cars passed in either direction on the road with their wipers on. The road was pleasantly decorated with green, leafy trees on both sides. Overhead, small planes took off, landed, or buzzed between clouds.

"The rain will cover us a bit," Hannah said hopefully.

"Maybe." He leaned over the steering wheel, craning his neck. "There."

"What?"

He pointed to a multistory parking garage of wet concrete, ornamented with blue on white signs: *Parking. Airport.*

The next building along the road was a rental car service. "Okay," Rick said. "I'm already probably wanted for murder." He said it in a macabre, sardonic tone, not really believing it—though it might be true. With his luck, maybe he was already wanted for Yolo's killing—never mind that he'd had to save himself and Hannah. He thought of his JAG protectress. That would heap one more serving of misery on her plate.

Rick pulled off the road, followed a driveway, and went down into the parking structure. Evidently, you could park your car here for days or weeks while you flew away on business or vacation. He drove matter-of-factly down a ramp, and stopped at a ticket machine to remove a date-time stamp for theoretically paying when he left the garage; maybe in a thousand years, if the world still existed.

He tossed the ticket on the floor and drove as deep into the bowels of the garage as he could.

She spoke gently, tentatively. "I hope you know what you're doing."

He shrugged. "We've got to ditch the car. Too risky. I could steal some plates and swap, but I'm just really paranoid that maybe there is a GPS transponder in this crate."

She nodded. It was clear—they could not allow Wan's people to track them to the package, which would not only mean potentially losing the fuselage formula, but their own lives, and the lives of Mélusine and others in the PAX movement.

Deep in a dark corner of the garage, two stories underground, Rick pulled into a remote corner. Hidden behind a massive concrete pillar, it was beyond the reach of anemic overhead fluorescent light bars.

"Grab your stuff and let's go."

They climbed out.

Rick popped the trunk lid. "Let's have a quick look."

"I'm half expecting to see Fincoff's body," Hannah said.

"Nothing that drastic," Rick said as he leaned into the ample trunk. In the gloom, he made out two boxy objects. "Look there." He pulled the objects close.

"Careful," Hannah said, half hiding behind him and gripping his torso with both hands.

He liked the touch of her small, busy hands, except she gripped him hard enough to bruise ribs. "Easy, baby. My bones. We'll need them."

"Sorry." She eased her embrace from behind and pressed her cheek against his back.

The two objects were small leather valises, almost like camera cases. He unzipped one of them—and whistled. "Wow, look at that. Money."

Packed into the valise were bundled stacks of ten and twenty Euro notes.

"Those liars," he said. "Yolo was talking about 200,000 Euros. This is at best twenty grand."

"It's all we need." Hannah started to take some of the bundles. "Wan is nothing but lies. Everything he touches is dishonest."

Rick laid his hand over hers to stop her. "Just grab the valise."

"What about GPS?"

"Good point. Okay, Plan B—put the bundles in my backpack. We'll leave the valises here. Take what you can, and we'll leave the rest."

She was already at work with both hands, leaning into the trunk. She took stacks of money out. She checked each bundle to make sure there was no electronic tracking gadget.

Rick opened the other valise.

He whistled softly and said, "More money—except—" He lifted some of the bills, and found underneath them some empty shoe boxes. "What's that all about?"

"Plan X and Plan Z," she said.

"Enlighten me."

She waggled a finger thoughtfully. "They had two options. One was to pay us some money, which is the stacks I'm putting in your backpack."

"Wan is desperate enough," Rick agreed.

"Or they hand us the fake valise with money on top and empty boxes underneath."

"Bastards."

Hannah laughed. "We faked them out. Serves Wan right. We got the car, and the money."

"And we got our lives."

"Right. Let's go."

They unloaded as much cash as they could into the backpack. Rick resisted the temptation to set the car on fire. It would draw unwanted attention. He slammed the trunk lid shut. They started walking back the way they'd come. Within ten minutes, they had reached ground level and exited the garage.

Rick and Hannah stood in a light rain, eyeballing the car rental center. Several leading companies—including two or three they knew from the U.S.—provided rental cars to travelers. They backed under the overhang of a parking ramp and watched. After a while, the pattern became clear. Passenger walks into the lounge and talks with a clerk. The clerk processes the traveler's credit card, and while waiting for the payment to clear, talks on a phone with a garage attendant—a young man or woman in a plain uniform with dark pants and white shirt, who jogs away someplace and returns five minutes later driving a car. Attendant leaves the car in a row in the driveway outside the rental agency. Traveler picks up approved receipt, thanks the clerk behind the counter, and walks outside. Traveler enters car and drives away. Meanwhile, the attendants fetch the next car so that there always is a lead car ready to go. It's a well-oiled machine, very routine, fueled with yawns.

20.   Econoligne

"I need to go in there," Hannah said, taking Rick's hand.

He looked surprised, but went along with her. What was it now? Tampons? Some female thing?

They entered a cramped little mass-produced convenience store—the type you found at gas stations around the world—and sidled down the narrow aisles. A heavyset woman with greasy looking black hair and thick glasses looked utterly bored, almost annoyed, as she rang up purchases for two black teens, an Asian girl with a pink umbrella and braces and a simpering smile, and a middle-aged, graying white businessman of military bearing and no-nonsense expression.

Rick followed her, holding a black rubbery-looking hand basket with a flip-up handle.

One by one, Hannah piled her purchases in Rick's basket: hair color, scissors, canned cola drinks, cellophane-wrapped sandwiches with sausage and pickle slices hanging out the sides, a map.

"*Quarante-sept*," (forty-seven) said the woman at the counter, punching her computer cash register with pudgy fingers. She took the Euros while she gave them a single raking, sidelong glance with dark, heavy-lashed eyes behind those bottle-bottom lenses.

Rick spotted a cheap burner-phone, which he added to the stack.

The woman made an exasperated gesture, signaling for Hannah to bag her own purchases from a rack of plain white plastic bags with the Econoligne store logo in black lettering, growing larger from left to right as if climbing out of a sack.

As he glanced up, Rick felt an icy shower in his guts. He saw the display screen of a small surveillance camera. In grayscale, he saw himself and he saw Hannah, two pale faces in bedraggled clothes, with soggy hair. Rick wondered if it made them look like two vagrants, and if that made the checkout clerk extra surly.

Moments later, they stepped outside of the Econoligne convenience store. They were back outside on the wet sidewalk, in the fresh air and rain, enveloped by the omnipresent, mixed aroma of green trees and oddly scented diesel fuel.

"You're going to freshen up," Rick said sarcastically. "Like we have time."

"We're going to change our hair and appearance," she said.

Oh. "I knew that."

She made a punk face. "You need me."

"I do," he agreed. He wanted to add, jokingly, "like a hole in the head," but he felt like hugging her instead. Only there wasn't time, or it wasn't the right time, or something. His feelings were all up in a blender again, but this time sort of a nice one.

She did not reply but went out of her way to bump her shoulder against his torso.

"We were being recorded on a surveillance camera," he told her.

"I noticed."

"Smart move going in there, huh?"

"Don't be so paranoid."

"We've got to get serious," he said.

"Go on," she said. "I'll follow."

"Okay. Here goes. Stick with me."

"I'm all glue, all over me."

"A sticky chick," he agreed.

21.   Cosmetics

Shortly after, Rick and Hannah walked past the rental office. As if on patrol, they walked some distance, and then turned around in the rain on the sidewalk. They headed back the way they'd come.

They stood for a few minutes outside the rental office's big plate glass window, waiting for an opportune moment. They watched the glacial pace of nearly nonexistent operations. Two or three people entered, paid, waited, and left to pick up their rental cars at a driveway under a rain shelter beside the little rental office. A row of cars stood in the waiting lane, extending backward into the dark bowels of a two-story parking garage behind the office. Two attendants in dark trousers and white shirts, wearing dark gray chauffeur caps, kept the line of cars moving.

Rick waited for just the right moment, when both attendants took off—one to get the next car, the other maybe to step into the restroom.

"Come on," Rick said.

Hannah and Rick walked at a brisk but controlled pace as if they'd just come out of the office. If anyone noticed them, the game would be up. But nobody did.

They got in and closed the doors. The key dangled in the ignition. Rick released the emergency brake, started the car, and immediately drove away. If anyone noticed, there was no sign. Behind them lay a blur of rain and watery neon.

"I'm hoping it will take them a while to sort things out," Rick said. He glanced in the rear view mirror several times—on impulse, but with futility, because the rear window was fogged up.

"All we need is about an hour. We'll be at the Luxembourg border. Then we'll dump this car and get something else."

"How about a pair of train tickets?"

He snapped his finger. "That's a great idea. Got that map?"

"Here." She unfolded the map she'd bought at Econoligne.

Neither of them had a working cellphone with apps, so they had no access to online services. Which was probably good—one less way to be hacked or tracked.

"I think we can get to Thionville pretty quickly," she said, rattling the large paper as she unfolded its sixteen or so sections over the dashboard. Rick helpfully gripped a corner to hold it open. "Thionville is a city in

France, south of Luxembourg, and we should be able to hop on a train to Luxembourg-Ville, the capital of Luxembourg."

"You got it," he said. "Watch for road signs."

She laughed. "Can you believe this?"

"Huh?"

"The nearest city is Yutz."

"You're yutzing me."

"You wish." She pealed with laughter. "You'd love to be yutzed."

"I'm not so sure."

"By me."

"Now I'm really scared."

She punched him playfully on the arm. "Look here. It's a small, picturesque city," she read, "with 41,000 inhabitants, parks, hotels, yadda-yadda."

"Ba-da-bing, ba-da-boom. Is there a train station?"

"Bigger than Stuttgart," she said, using an old G.I. expression. She pointed to a spot off the south side of the Meuse River, which wound through the city. "That big letter G."

"Stands for Goofy."

"Stands for *Gare*."

"Train station." He glanced aside while driving. "I see the lovely acronym SNCF."

"Yup. *Société Nationale des Chemins de Fer Français*. National Railroad Corporation. And look next to it: *CFL*."

"Can Figs Love?" He could figure it out, but preferred to lighten the moment.

"*Chemins de Fer Luxembourgeois*," she said. "Iron Roads of Luxembourg."

"Ah. That's what I was hoping. There is a Luxembourg train connection from Thionville."

"Half hour, and we're breathing free air."

"We should be there soon," Rick said.

"So far, so good."

He wasn't so sure. "We've got to keep our eyes open."

She pointed to a passing road sign. "About an hour now we'll be in Thionville."

"Go back to sleep."

"*Avec plaisir*." She turned her face to the window, where beads of water arced and tore away.

Rick drove in silence, as much through tunnels of rain as through his own jumble of thoughts.

After a while, he saw a cluster of buildings off to the right side. Taking the exit ramp, he came to a local road in a small town.

Hannah woke up, confused. "Where are we?"

"Nowhere. Time to become other people."

She sat up, watching alertly as he steered into a large parking lot. Surrounding the hundreds of obediently lined up, parked cars was a shopping area that included a gas station at one end, with a motel near it. At least, it would be called a motel in the U.S. Here it was a Zavotel or something—obviously a chain, therefore probably not overrun with roaches or pickpockets or whatever.

He left the car in the larger parking lot, rather than park behind the hotel.

They walked together, entering a small lobby with dingy carpeting and a good smell—something with lots of onions and garlic.

"Mmm," she said, "sheep eyes."

"No, roasted mountain oysters."

"This isn't Appalachia."

"Might as well be."

The man on duty was small, portly, and old. He wore a slouch hat over a presumably bald head. The thick glasses and black-colored mustache might have come from a Halloween trick kit.

Hannah nudged Rick, looking at him and then up to the right. There again was a surveillance camera. They saw their own pale, shocked faces looking up at the camera.

"Don't be paranoid," he said softly, echoing her earlier instruction to him.

She raised two fingers. *Une chambre pour la nuit.* "A room for the night."

"*Deux personnes?*" The man matter-of-factly threw open a large, flat book—a guest register.

"*Vous avez des papiers?*"

He was asking for papers, Rick understood. Everything here was under police control as a normal matter of civic procedure. "*Les papiers sont dans l'auto. Ça suffit?*" He fanned out a three twenty Euro notes. He leaned forward. *C'est une affaire du coeur, entendez?* "It's one of those matters of the heart, do you follow?" In other words: *We are having an affair and we'd like to keep it discreet.*

The man shrugged, took the notes, and disrespectfully shoved the book at them. He held up a pen to sign their names, addresses, that sort of information, which he expected would be phony.

Rick obliged, making up some names that sounded French: *Roger et Michelle Belville.* He added a made-up address in Metz—*39 Rue des Marchés.* He tried to write as indecipherably as possible, in case anyone cared to follow up. He held up another forty Euros just to make the point. The man would get these later if he let them be.

The man slapped a room key on an absurdly large, bell-shaped plastic handle on the counter.

"*Merci bien,*" Hannah and Rick both said as the clerk was distracted by a shrill ringing sound.

They got only a grunt and a dirty look in return, as the man turned away to attend to a telephone call.

"Two-one-one," Rick read from the dangling key plate. "Room 211."

"Let's get it over with quickly," Hannah said.

They could not unlock the door fast enough. Together, they pressed into the room and pushed the door shut. Rick tossed his backpack on the bed, while Hannah dumped the Econoligne sack on the bed. Shaking it, she emptied out the hair coloring and other cosmetic objects.

"He might call the police," she said.

"I hope not. I tempted him with some more Euros."

Hannah filled the sink in the bathroom with warm water. "I can't read French well enough, but I have a general idea how to color hair."

"Women do a lot of that."

"Not blondes. We don't need to." She loosened her chignon, so that her thick golden hair fell around her shoulders.

"Excuse me," said Rick, whose hair was a nondescript very dark brown.

"You don't need to either," she said, stroking his head with her pretty hands. An electric feeling went through him.

"Oh, do that some more."

"No time," she said. "Sit and I'll cut. We don't want to leave any traces of what we did here."

She quickly trimmed his hair a bit around the ears and neck. "You have a military cut, so there's not much to fix. Wish I could put a long hair wig on you."

"Blond," he quipped.

She held up an end of her hair. "I wish."

"Shame to do this."

"We have to." She offered the scissors. "Want to make yourself useful?"

"I have never cut hair in my life, much less a woman's."

"First time for everything."

She sat in a plain, upright red plastic chair with chrome tubing—a cheap imitation of a 1950s style statement. "Cut, baby, cut."

He tore a sheet from the bed and spread it around her feet as she sat in the chair. "Can't leave any stray hair." He approached her as if she were going to melt. "What do I do?"

"Use your imagination. Just cut it short, like a boy's. Hurry."

So he began clipping. "This is kind of fun. I feel like an artist."

"You don't have any magazines to read."

"Our shop is fresh out," he said, "and the TV is off because we didn't pay the power bill."

"You're doing fine." She eyeballed herself in the mirror.

As he cut her hair, it fell onto the sheet—gorgeous gilded ropes and strands of it.

"You're actually starting to look sort of cute," he said.

"The *gamine* look," she said, eyeballing herself.

"Ah yes." Rick understood the clever French double-entendre. *Gamine* was a made-up word suggesting a female who looked like a boy (*gamin*). "There is definitely something exotic about this. Weirdly sexy. Like I'm giving you a sex change. Like Garden of Eden, the novel by Hemingway."

"Published decades after his suicide," she said. "I know. I've read it. We're not weird, bored, or exotic, *mon ami*. We are desperate."

"Of course, mademoiselle. You are always right."

"And don't you forget it." She was just about to settle back, when she jumped. "Hey, don't cut my fucking ear off!"

"Sorry, a little slip, mademoiselle," he said in his best fake accent. "As an apology, I will give you zis 'aircut for free."

She pretended to pout. "I should make you pay me for the haircut, you bozo."

"Ah, you will be grateful when this is over."

"You're telling me." She squeezed his upper arm in a soft, nervy spot that made him squirm. "But I'm taking you with me after it's all over."

"I think I would take you up on that offer." He didn't explain how gladly.

Within twenty minutes, they were done. She had colored his hair to look slightly blonder, while her own hair had become a short, ragged punky clip that could best be described as dark oxblood red. She used mascara to darken her golden-brown eyebrow hair. And she applied a brownish lipstick that made her small, full mouth look bigger.

"You look different," he said, standing before her.

"No shit, Sherlock." She started to gather the wet, dripping comb, scissors, empty bottles, and other debris.

Rick scoured the sink to remove as much of the hair coloring evidence as possible. "This is going to be impossible."

"Yes, but it'll take time for forensic analysis if it comes down to it."

He felt a sense of relief. "You're right. It's just a dirty old man at the desk. Screw him."

"Better not."

"No, I'll just leave the money for him. We have plenty to burn."

Rick strewed about sixty Euros across the torn, mangled bed.

"Looks like we had that affair," she said, glancing at the bed.

"I'll bet it was fun. A passionate affair."

She made a little gurgling laugh deep down, without comment, and gave him a familiar little shove. She went into the bathroom and closed the door. "I'll be out in a minute." She went into the facility.

Rick dug the burner phone from his backpack and redialed.

A man answered, babbling some nonsense about being Private Wucknut at the JAG office, blah blah blah.

"Sergeant Buchan. Let me talk to Major Walsh."

Kendra was on the phone in half a yadda. "Richard, where are you?"

"Running."

"You've got to come in."

"I'm scared. Any change?"

"Not yet. I can get the case against you frozen if not thrown out. I'm trying to locate the witness I need to corroborate that you were where you needed to be when your team was killed."

"Good luck."

"Rick—"

He hung up.

Hannah came out of the toilet.

Rick sidled past her. He tossed the phone into the *Klo*, which was the German word for Kloset (or something) meaning porcelain throne. This time he flushed, and a whole mass of yellowish water like piss vinegar swelled up and burbled before whooshing away into the mystery plumbing of Thionville. The drowned phone almost went along, but stayed stuck, just peeking out from the brown calcified bottom of the saxophone neck. "No wonder this town doesn't draw more tourists," he said. The phone jumped slightly in the water, fizzing and bubbling as its innards committed electronic suicide.

"Hurry, I'm getting really nervous," she said.

"But you just peed."

"You'll make me go again."

"It's all my fault."

Kidding turned into tears. Her cheeks dribbled miserably as she gathered the stuff to be left behind into a trash bag she'd found in a drawer. Rick stuffed his backpack with stuff they were going to keep. Loaded up, they eased carefully into the dingy, carpeted hallway outside.

Not a soul in sight.

They looked at each other, silently, nodding with wide eyes. Pulling the door shut, they hurried down the hall. Rick carried the backpack, and Hannah the trash bag. The weather-door at the end of the hall took them out onto a balcony whose floor had been treated with no-slip, good-grip rubberized paint. Rick dropped the key into the dark arms of a pine tree, where it fell from the second floor down to the first and landed on pine needles under the tree. They walked down a zigzag stairway and emerged on a back street. They followed the sidewalk to the end of the building, where a side street *avec* driveway led back to the main parking lot.

Walking as fast as they dared, so as not to attract undue attention, they made a wide circle around, avoiding being seen by the dirty little old man in the motel lobby. Minutes later, the garbage bag was in the trunk of the stolen car, the backpack in the back seat, and Rick pulled out into traffic, while Hannah kept watch all around for anything out of the ordinary.

"We are on our way to Thionville," Rick said to the dark, short-haired stranger sitting beside him with the dark eyebrows and punky brown lipstick. She sat with her arms crossed, looking distressed, and stared straight ahead.

22.   Thionville

A little over half an hour east of their personality changes, they turned north onto the A31 highway and in another half hour—by two p.m.—they were in Thionville, France.

The Gare de Thionville was a long, low, rather plain building east of the Moselle River.

Rick parked the car on a side street by the river, hiding the keys under the mat. "Some meter maid will eventually find it."

"Let's wipe off our fingerprints." She produced an open, half-gone roll of paper towels that had lain in the back seat.

"Oh yes, good idea."

They spent the next ten minutes wiping down any surfaces they might have touched.

It was drizzling as they walked across the main street toward the railway station.

Across the Chemin des Bains from the Moselle riverside docks was a big rail complex. It seemed huge for a small city.

Thionville was a smallish industrial city with 41,000 inhabitants, which to Rick's eyes resembled a forest-choked town of comparable size in New England and many similar locations. It was a major rail head in the northern part of France, in Lorraine, which had historically been a pawn between the German and French powers. The Allies had dropped a whole lot of bombs here during World War II, Rick had read.

Today, there was a tall building of about fifteen stories, dedicated to the national railway service (SNCF) while the city train station was a one-story building whose divergent tracks connected Metz with Luxembourg, and Thionville with Trier (in Germany).

Things went smoothly for once. They walked into the train station, bought tickets, and picked up coffees in paper cups before strolling out onto the passenger platform. They sat in the shelter, or rather slumped a bit, after all that had befallen them during the day—including the murder of Fincoff last night, and Rick's killing of Yolo that morning.

"You feel okay?" she asked.

"Yeah," he lied. He was hyperventilating.

"Pills."

"I'm okay."

"No you're not."

He felt spacey. She rummaged in his backpack and pulled out more of his PTSD medicine. "You also have Prozac here if you want."

"No," he said sharply. "I hate all that crap."

"I know, dear, but you have to take this stuff in the small bottle. Come on."

He let her put two pills in his mouth and lift a water bottle to his lips. He gulped the water, more because of dry mouth than the pills. In fifteen minutes he'd be feeling more level, he knew. He tried not to think about Yolo. Why did people like that have to threaten you with guns? Why was there violence in the world? Why, why, why? He wished he could retire to someplace with no guns, no hate, no anger, no violence.

"You've had some heavy duty training in the military," Hannah said gently.

"Yeah." He drew deep breaths, as the shrinks had shown him. He held the air in, counting slowly, while playing happier videos in his head.

"You have nightmares, don't you?"

"By day and by night," he admitted. "I want to go home. I'm no good to the Army anymore. I just want to go live in as small a town as far from everything as I can possibly find."

She laid her hands over his. Her touch felt warm. He closed his eyes and let her energy soothe him. He wished he'd told JAG he was on the run now for real. *Send help.* But would they? Probably send the French police.

"Here is our train," Hannah said, rising.

"Great," he said. He was tired of being in France. Maybe crossing the border would change things.

He lugged his backpack, and she kept her hand under his shaky forearm as they boarded the Thionville train bound for Luxembourg-Ville—Luxembourg City—the capital of Luxembourg.

"Let's go up top," she said.

"Sure." He followed her fine, jeans-clad figure up a flight of stairs on the double-decker train. This took them into a clean, modern coach, whose plush upholstery smelled of a gentle, almost vanilla-ginger carpet cleaner. It was not crowded. Only a few persons of varying ages and appearances dotted the seats.

Rick and Hannah found a pair of facing benches all to themselves, and sat by the window. He landed facing in the direction the train was about to move. She, with a slight girlish excitement, switched from the opposite window seat to sit beside him. She sat leaning against him, as if they were on a date, and looked eagerly out the window at the wrought iron steel posts holding up the aging platform in the station. Rick rose, gestured for her to take his window seat. She slid over, and now he sat where she had. He was bigger, and put his arm around her. She leaned against him, looking pleased.

The train gave a little jerk as the air brakes released. It started gliding as if in free fall. Then it moved more definitively forward.

Without preamble, their hands slid together, interlocked, and hung over the seat edge between them.

Outside, slowly, green countryside moved past. It seemed as if everything were getting brighter.

"Is it me," Rick said, "or is the sun coming out?"

She snuggled closer. "You are hallucinating. It's nighttime."

"You light my fire," he said, echoing the famous Jim Morrison song (who lies buried in Père Lachaise Cemetery, at the outskirts of Bagnolet in Paris).

"You are stoking my embers pretty well too," she said in a low, husky voice.

"I have been wanting to hold your hand ever since I met you."

"You can hold my hand all you want."

She looked up at him in that straight forward way people have when they first really look into each other's hearts. Her pretty face floated glowing beneath his, and her blue eyes spoke to him of her hunger for him. He moved his own head, just those few inches, and her mouth was ready for his. She pressed firmly up against him, surprising him. His tongue sought hers, and found it. She was eager to taste him, and he groaned as he pulled her close. She pressed herself into his embrace, a perfect and more than willing fit.

They were alone together in a universe all their own.

After a while, he just hugged her close to him, and she snuggled in his embrace.

"I think this is the nicest train ride I have ever had," she said softly.

"Yeah," was all he could say. "My sentiments also."

She rested her cheek against his chest. "I need."

"You need what, baby?"

"I need to heal. I had no idea what I was getting into. I have been raped, used, and left for dead. I have lost my mother, the house, everything. I lost my trust in people until I met you."

"I will not let you down."

"I know that from the depths of my heart." Her eyes rolled upward, regarding him with that blue sky full of light that played in her irises. "I trust you totally, Richard Buchan."

He touched her soft, rosy cheek with his fingertips. "I would give anything for you, Hannah Smith."

"You need a nice girl in your life, Richard."

"I have one."

"I don't know if I'm so nice. I'm damaged material."

"So am I, baby. Where would I be without you and the pills?"

"Dead, or in Germany getting your name cleared."

"I can't get the circus out of my head."

"Neither can I." She looked up at him imploringly. "It's a lot to ask, but I wish you would just hold me and help me feel better inside."

"I am holding you, sweetheart, and I will not let you go."

"Please." She raised fists under chin, assuming a fetal position.

"Please what, baby?"

"Tell me that every day—once a day for as long as we are together."

"I promise. And I think we'll be together for a long time."

"You think?"

"I know."

She nodded, closed her eyes, and seemed to sleep. He held her close to him, all the way into the greenery of Luxembourg and then the tiny capital with its green-roofed main *Gare* (train station). They sat together as still as a statue of two people, almost sort of a Pietà in reverse, with the *he* holding the *she*. The thought amused him. It brightened his emotions as he watched lush green hills and thick forests roll past without hurry. A few times, he raised his hand from her shoulder to gently touch her hair.

As the train came to a stop under the overhangs in Luxembourg, she stirred on his lap. She opened her eyes and sat up. She was not yawning, nor did she look as if she'd been asleep.

"You were awake the whole time," he observed.

"I was in heaven." She gave him one adoring look, then regarded the busy platform outside.

"You know," he said, "I was right." He stroked her hair as if she were a pet.

"What's that?" she asked, looking suddenly at him, and eager for his every word.

"It is brighter and sunnier here in Luxembourg."

"Oh, that's just because you're here."

"With you."

"Oh."

23. Spy at Gare

An East Asian man wearing a dark raincoat and dark hat stood in the Luxembourg City train station, the Gare, watching crowds of people swirl around him. He was in his mid to late twenties, with brown-rimmed eyeglasses still sprinkled with rain drops from outside. He stood watching the flashing announcements of arrivals and departures on the *tabelles* overhead.

His name was Shen, and he was a spy. On the surface a young history professor in the making, he carried a snub-nosed Beretta under his coat and was prepared to kill anyone who stood in his way. He was devoted to the cause, and willing to die for it, although with complex, qualifying layers and nuances. Beyond such things, he had a pleasant demeanor and a nice sense of humor. One day he would retire and teach history someplace, like in the newly tamed and fractured states of North America, or (he dreamed even more fervently) on a ranch amid kangaroos in Australia. For now, the pay was far better than an academic's salary, and the cause was right.

Built in the Moselle Baroque Revival style in the decade before World War I, the station suggested the outlines of a basilica. Its central hall had a rounded ceiling in recent years painted with playful comic strip sun, moon, and stars. In front was a tower with a dark metal knob on top, and over the main entrance, with its mythological figures in stone, was a large clear glass window of ogive shape. At the opposite end of the main hall, overlooking a small number of platforms and tracks, was a similar window—with a brooding stained glass view of the city, including the Petrusse bridge, the tall narrow roof-towers of the national cathedral, and the stockier tower of the old savings bank. *(*Endnotes #2)*

Shen was a man of the twenty-first century, caught in new global struggles no less dangerous or deadly than those of the past—just the players now were different. Somewhere in this station were his enemies, and he kept a wary eye out for them. He understood their danger and ruthlessness all too well.

Unobtrusively, he reached into his pocket and produced a tiny phone, which he raised to his lips. To the casual observer, he might have seemed to be picking at a shaving nick over his lip. He spoke very softly, barely moving his mouth—knowing that surveillance by the enemy was everywhere. "The train from Metz-Thionville is due in ten minutes. I will move along and observe. No bogeys in sight, but I am careful at all times."

He slid his hand back into his pocket, and sauntered among a crowd of well-dressed men and women toward the stairs leading underground, from where the passenger platforms could be accessed. He studied the train lines carefully. The Lorraine Region Train Express Régional (TER) Line 1 from Metz, leaving Thionville in France at mid-afternoon, had already crossed the border into Luxembourg, picking up CFL Line 80. At Bettembourg, it switched to CFL Line 60, which would shortly bring it into the main train station in Luxembourg.

Shen took the escalator down into the minor labyrinth of tunnels under the platforms. He must be sure of his targets, lest they hurry past him and be lost to him. If he missed them, it would be painful to report upstream, and his superiors would have to switch gears to find the two in the city. Shen walked down the echoing, tiled underground tunnel and climbed up the middle flight of stone stairs. The wide stairs took him up on the platform. The train from Bettembourg would arrive any time.

He carefully positioned himself at the center of the platform, with his back to the stairs leading down into the tunnel. Standing with his hands in his pockets, he tried to look as unobtrusive as possible. He felt the ground rumble as the sleek double-decker train rolled in, with a powerful diesel locomotive at its head. The loco was marked RTE—the French regional express on Lorraine's Line 1.

As the train drew to a halt, a woman's voice began sing-songing information. It was a charming tone, almost a whisper, and quite undecipherable unless you listened closely and were not mesmerized by the musicality of her *Letzebuergesch*, the national language. Its tonality lay somewhere between French, German, and Flemish to Shen's ear.

Passengers about to board waited impatiently on the platform, in knots, as the train doors opened. Passengers from points south—mostly France, with a few Luxembourg locals like university students and commuting workers—poured out.

Shen stiffened involuntarily—he had only seconds now. Where were they? He almost stood on tiptoes, anxiously scanning the onrushing travelers. He saw an older professional man in a blue scarf and long gray coat, trundling a brown briefcase. The man hurried, bent double, with a pained expression as if he were late for a meeting. Three tall, giggling, pretty teenage school girls in short skirts, colorful hose, and high-heeled boots passed, carrying armfuls of school books. A heavyset middle-aged woman in a headscarf, probably a grandmother, led two toddling little kids by the hands, scolding and fussing. A young professional woman, looking darkly elegant and insular, walked by with her purse slung over her shoulder and her hands in her jacket pockets. A punky-looking couple in their twenties walked arm-in-arm, the young man carrying a backpack, while the young woman affected a rock 'n rollish pout with short reddish-dyed hair cut raggedly short.

Wait.

As he gave them a glance that was a microsecond too long, the young woman's eyes met his. She glared at him. He had an impression of dark slash lipstick, a pale soft face, and very blue eyes swimming amid too much mascara. The young man, in whose arm hers was draped, looked tough. That must be the two. No other couple came from the train.

Shen raised his phone to his lips. "I made them. They're going down the stairs. They'll be in the main hall any second. She has dark, short hair and chocolate lipstick, blue eyes, a dark blue jacket. He is brown-haired, unshaven, with a rough look. Both are wearing jeans and under them boots. He has a backpack. She has only a small shoulder purse. I think she saw me. No idea what she thought." He rang off, and bounded down the now-empty stairs. In the tunnel, he saw them again—the man's lean, wiry shape, and the woman's softer, shapely figure. They disappeared, climbing the stairs to the main hall of the Gare. In minutes they'd emerge outside in the transit square of buses, trolleys, and taxis. That would put them in reach of the next person in Mr. Wan's chain of observation.

24. Arrive Luxembourg-Gare

Hannah felt shaken. "That man was looking at me."

"You are dreaming," Rick said—without looking too sure.

"No really," she said, "he looked Chinese, and his eyes looked right into me as if he recognized me. I've never seen him before. He is probably one of Wan's creepy goons."

"Oh god let's hope not." Rick squeezed her arm close to him, and she pressed against him. "What now?"

They stood overlooking a major transit hub, consisting of a relatively wide avenue with a row of hotels and restaurants opposite. On the nearer side were ample islands for buses, taxis, parked limos, and even a trolley turn-around.

Hannah made a quick phone call on her low-end cell. It reminded Rick he wanted to buy another burner, thinking he'd break down and call JAG again. She spoke briefly, and put the phone away. "That was Mélusine. She says she is working but will be home this evening. She and her husband, Romain, are going to dinner after work. She said she'll leave a key under the mat for us. Just make ourselves at home. It's only a half hour walk from here in a part of town called Belair. So, we'll walk there to kill some time. But we have urgent business first."

He had been here a few times on weekend passes, but never on business. Never with anything more than the next tavern and beer in mind before taking a taxi to a decent hotel outside town, where the rates were cheaper.

"I was here as a child," she said. "I don't remember too much, but I did a lot of research on the Internet before I ran away from Wan, so that's mainly what I know. Look." She pointed across the street with her free hand. "That's the post office where we need to go." She looked back. "Nobody following us, as far as I can see."

Together, they hurried across the Place de la Gare, to the Gare-related main post office. It was little more than a busy storefront, but very efficient and official looking, almost like a bank.

The weather had cleared, leaving the air breezy and fresh. The sidewalk was busy with pedestrian traffic. Rick looked back, and saw nobody.

Hannah, holding his arm, towed him into the post office lobby. There, a few people milled about doing various things related to mailing letters and packages, plus checking mail boxes.

Several service desks sat behind thick, bullet proof glass, two of them staffed at the moment. Hannah approached an older, gray-haired man who wore a white shirt and a blue sleeveless sweater. "*Bonjour,*" she said.

"*Bonjour,*" he replied. *Wéi kann ech haut behelleflech sin?* "How can I be helpful today?"

Hannah switched to English. "I am expecting a package today."

"Your identification please," the man said in lightly accented English without breaking stride. People in Luxembourg particularly were used to switching among several languages—Letzebuergesch, German, French, English, and several Romance languages. Grand Duchess Maria Theresa was of Cuban extraction, for one thing; and a third of the population were native to Portugal, Italy, and other points far away.

Hannah produced an international driver's license for Europe, which she had obtained while property of Wan—as a hedge, when she began to think about running away to be with her mother, before the entire dark situation went down.

The lean, bright-eyed clerk compared her I.D. picture with her present appearance. "You play in a rock band now?"

"Yes. It's all a lot of fun."

"When I was young," he said, "I played guitar in a disco."

"That must have been very exciting."

"I don't know. We were all too drunk to know if we were coming or going. Today, I limit myself to two cups of hot tea and some biscuits."

"You'll live longer."

"But you have all the fun." He winked at her. "Here you go." He pushed across the package she had mailed to herself, general delivery.

"I need to forward it to a friend," she told him.

"Of course. No problem. Fill this out." He pushed a pen and a form across the counter.

Rick pressed close behind her as she leaned against the counter, writing while the clerk busied himself about other matters.

"I'm going to forward it to myself at the professor's office," she said. "With an online notice of delivery."

"And then what?"

"I'll tell you." She put a finger over her lips to signal he should be quiet.

The man behind the counter told her, "That will be five Euros, please."

"Very good," she said, and turned her hand upside down, palm up, behind her. Rick slipped a five Euro note onto her hand. She crinkled it up and laid it on the counter.

"Thanks." The clerk took the money, did the usual dance of banking red ink-stamps down to make everything official. He slipped a piece of paper back across. "You can check the online code against the Luxembourg postal service website to see when your package arrives."

"Thank you," Hannah said.

She turned to Rick. "Come on, let's go sightseeing."

She took him by the hand, and towed him outside.

"See anybody?"

Rick looked carefully up and down the broad avenue and the transit square. "Not a bogey in sight." He saw buses and taxis coming and going, pedestrians hurrying across the wide avenue in a brisk wind, pigeons fluttering among the eaves and statues around the greenish-metallic roofing of the train station with its tower—just no bad guys. At least, not the ones from Paris.

"It's light out pretty late this time of year," she said. "Let's take a stroll."

Rick gladly took her hand. "I was hoping you'd say something fun for a change."

25.   Wan in Rage

"Have you found them yet?" asked the angry zillionaire to his technical lead, Nirmala, a pleasantly dowdy-looking young Indian woman, thirty years old, from Kolkata. She looked a bit plump in her *sari* and heavy eyeglasses. She wore her black hair in a bob over her forehead, pulled tight under a dark-plum headband above the *sindoor* (a dark-red spot of *kumkum* powder) on her brow.

"Yessir," Nirmala said. She had light caramel skin and fine white teeth. Wan, who evaluated every female for her sexual potential, found her just unattractive enough to prevent diverting his attention from the urgent business at hand. He found her nose too long and protrusive, her cheeks too round, her mouth just a little pinkish slit that looked even thinner when pursed in anxious concentration.

He had over a dozen major corporate executives waiting for him in Paris—surprised that he could not deliver the design project he had been pushing with such glowing salesmanship the past few weeks. They would not wait long. His plan had been to fly some of them to Luxembourg, as he made his speeches in a bid for presidency of the world CEOC. The IFS technology was vital to his presentation.

It was galling, to say nothing of mortifying. When Wan wanted something done, it got done. He was not used to having an American airhead run off on him with secrets and plans that could change the world balance of power, doubling his fortune in the meantime. His credibility had already taken a hit—and was totally on the line now. If he could not control his subordinates, why would anyone trust him? The Irish called it blarney. He called it positioning—the ability to project confidence and competence, whiel caring about the other person whose money he wanted.

Wan, Nirmala, and a half dozen network technicians sat in a semi-dark cool room deep in the refurbished bowels of a 19th Century building in Metz, France. He had flown here on one of his private jets to be close to the action.

"I want that package back at any cost. I don't care what it takes."

"We are narrowing it down," Nirmala said. "Look."

She pointed to a screen on the wall.

Wan looked closer.

"There they are," Wan said. "Where are they?"

"In an Econoligne convenience store near Verdun earlier today, sir."

"Can you make it color?"

"It is grayscale," she said, "but I can colorize it for you." She typed something. The image took on color, as if fresh pixels were pouring into a clear liquid. "The display is painting for us."

"Good," he said absently, focusing on the blonde with blue eyes and the tough-eyed young man with the set jaw beside her, holding a basket full of things they were about to purchase.

"What is all that stuff?"

Nirmala blew the picture up, enhancing it one push at a time, until it became too blurry. "I'd say they have some food, and some stuff to drink, and if I am not mistaken, that is hair coloring. A comb. Scissors."

"So they are going to change their appearance," he said. "That was this morning."

"I have something else," Nirmala said.

"Yes?"

"She was in a post office in Paris very early today. We managed to hack into the local surveillance feed on a commercial bypass, because the postal location is too cheap to use encryption, so they are in a local shopping network. The servers are shared around the strip mall." As she spoke, she brought into focus another image, this time of Hannah Smith alone. It was grayscale, again, what most people would mistakenly call black and white.

"What is she doing?"

"Mailing a package. Is that about the size of what she stole from you?"

Wan almost fell out of his seat. "Oh god yes. I'm sure of it. Where is it going?"

"Luxembourg, from the looks of it."

Wan sat back, steepling his fingers in deep concentration. "So you were able to track Yolo's car until you lost it near Verdun. But right near there, you found some footage of these two buying hair color in a convenience store. If I am not mistaken, there are train lines running from Lorraine into Luxembourg."

"Yessir. They stole a car right in that same little town. We also have footage a little later of them checking into a motel in this little place."

The screenshot changed to a scene of a parking lot, a motel front overlooking a large row of middle-income store fronts, and then the lobby of the motel. "The lobby clerk called police to check the license plate. He saw them get out of the car, and went outside to look while I assume they were in a room cutting and dyeing their hair. By the time a patrol motorcycle arrived, they had left." The screen switched to showing a police motorcycle, and a uniformed cop in helmet, boots, and leather jacket getting off. He removed his heavy driving gloves as the motel clerk came out. Then the screen went blank.

Nirmala continued. "We have three other things. One, a police car ticketed the stolen car in Thionville near the main train station. Two, we hacked into surveillance footage from the Thionville train station. There they are."

"They look like hell," Wan said with grim humor. Just then, the door to the computer lab opened, and Yoichi entered, with the competent and grim-looking Savia right behind them. Wan said rather loudly, "You two. While you are asleep, we are tracking the two who murdered Yolo."

"Good, sir," they both said, looking nonplussed.

"They are in Luxembourg by now," Wan said.

"Confirming," said Nirmala. "We were able to track the delivery number on the package she mailed in Paris. It is in Luxembourg at the Poste de la Gare office."

She showed a dim image of the interior of a store front, presumably the post office in Luxembourg.

"We can fly into Luxembourg and be there within the hour," Yoichi said. The loss of Yolo was a personal blow to his pride. Savia's grimly handsome face reflected a new, unstoppable determination.

"Get me my plans back," Wan shouted, waving his fists in the air. He was normally a tightly controlled man, but this was outside the bounds.

"Yessir," Yoichi said.

Savia had a cell phone in hand. "I am calling for a chopper on deck as we speak. We'll be there as fast as the man can fly."

"There is a heliport near the train station, from what I remember," Yoichi said.

"Good," Wan grimly interjected. "Kill them if you have to."

"The girl?"

"I don't care," he said. "She is nothing to me now. I just want back my property. Not her—the plans."

"Very good, sir," Yoichi said.

"Here is this also," Nirmala said. The screen resolved to show a young Asian man in a coat, unobtrusively standing in the train station.

"Who is that?" Savia asked.

They watched as Nirmala zoomed in and out, losing and regaining focus as the hacked train station servers divulged their secrets.

First, they showed the Asian man standing at the top of a platform behind the train station. Then they resolved to a shot of the couple walking hand in hand through the train station.

"They've become cozy," Savia said venomously.

Yoichi scoffed. "That will be a weakness. And the guy?"

"His name is Shen," Nirmala said. "He works for different agencies, doing a little of this and a little of that."

"Does he work for us?" Yoichi demanded.

"Sometimes," Nirmala said. "Look, here they are again."

The screen showed Hannah Smith and Richard Buchan in the lobby of the Gare post office in Luxembourg City.

Looking through the surveillance camera over her shoulder, Wan could just make out that she was handling that package again.

She handed it back to the clerk.

She'd mail it to herself somewhere else. All they'd have to do is track the two, and they would lead Wan's people directly to the missing documents.

"Track every move," said the angry zillionaire. "You two get going!"

"We have people in Luxembourg," Yoichi assured him. "We'll get them on the case with a phone call."

"So what are you waiting for?" Wan shrilled in anger and frustration.

26. Luxembourg City Walk

It was still bright daylight in late afternoon when Hannah and Rick strolled up the Avenue de la Liberté toward the Ville Haute (high city, in practice also upper city, old city). They passed expensive and stylish stores on either side of the street, with the finest name brand watches, clothes, shoes, and other accessories from the world's leading capitals.

Rick stopped in a corner convenience store and bought another cheap burner phone, which he slipped into his backpack. He bought Hannah a lollypop. "Purple grape, the color of your hair."

"Grape is great." She sucked on it and got purple lips. She let him lick it, laughing. "Now you have grape lips too."

He held her close, enjoying the rhythm of her body, and the way her clothes slid easily over her firm, smooth waist under his touch, and the sway of her long, slender body against his.

"Thank you," she said (post-lollypop) as they swung clasped hands between them. The raggedly cut purplish hair did not diminish her youth and beauty. *Or am I just falling like a ton of bricks?* Rick thought.

"For what?"

"I need this."

"So do I."

"I know. We are good for each other."

"Can I do this?" He stopped, swung her around, and held her in both arms so that she arched back and looked up into his eyes. Her figure felt slender and smooth to his touch.

"You can do what you want."

"I would like to..."

"What?" She coyly kneaded his jacket in both hands, looking down at his chest, awaiting what clever he thing was going to say that would thrill her to the core.

He struggled to find the exact way of expressing that he wanted to make love to her, right then and there, on the street, without going so far as to say so.

"Well?"

"I wish you were ice cream."

She giggled. "That's original."

"Yes."

"What flavor?"

"Doesn't matter. Vanilla, the color of your skin. Blueberry, the color of your eyes. Pink bubblegum, the color of your lips. Then I would lick you."

"But then nothing would be left."

"We'd start all over again."

"I will give you all my ice cream," she said. She threw herself at him in an explosive hug. "You can lick my ice cream, and I'll lick yours."

"All over."

"Yes, all over." She pulled away and took him by the hand. "Come on, we have places to go."

"Of course we do. That's been the story of my life since I left K-Town."

"Aren't you exhausted? I am."

They'd been on the run in a carousel of death, danger, and love. Sounded like a bad joke, but unfortunately it was a grim reality for both of them.

"Yeah, I'm exhausted. Who wouldn't be? Actually, I am so used to being wrung out that this is sort of like being on drugs or something. You know. Pleasant, dreamy—can this be for real?"

"Am I your dream?"

He laughed. "You're not my nightmare."

She pretended *ouch*. "That's not a very romantic thing to say."

"Oh, so you want me to be romantic."

"Yes. You already are romantic, in your rough way. I'd like you to keep on the gentle side, just hold me and whisper nice things in my ear, make me feel all mushy inside, and hold me like you'll never let me go."

Like in the song. Coming from a woman, that kind of honesty and directness meant all her defenses were down. All of her systems were down, like in the Pointer Sisters song *Automatic* that his mom used to like to listen to on the back patio in California while she was still alive.

They strolled up the avenue, and soon came to a smallish, oddly shaped square with trees and benches. He pulled her down with him to sit on a park bench. She willingly sat by him as he put his arm around her back. The little square was called Place de Paris. Like everything in Luxembourg, it had a miniature quality about it. Several major streets raced around the square, suggesting a circle without being one—where over a century ago had been some of Europe's mightiest fortifications. Place de Paris was an oddly situated pair of round-cornered triangles with bands of differently shaded concrete radiating from a central feature on each side of the street—on one side, a tiny garden with flowers and bushes; on the other side, an odd little reddish fountain.

They had eyes only for each other. She rested her cheek on his shoulder. "Please, let this dream not end too soon."

"You don't need to ask me. I am having the time of my life."

"Are you?"

"Yeah. Look, I'm with this beautiful girl who seems to like me, maybe a lot. I've got a backpack full of money. I don't have to go drive around in some wasted country where everyone hates us and we have no idea why we are there, except they have oil. So here I am in this little dream country that's like one giant doll house, and I'm with a doll."

"Keep talking." She smiled, without raising her head. With one hand folded in her lap, she kept her other hand on his belly and rubbed gently as if he were a pet. Her eyes were closed, and she had a dreamy expression.

He didn't want to say the crazy things rushing like traffic through his mind. Was it time for pills again? He didn't want to joke about waking up from a dream and finding himself shot and dying in a squalid alley behind a bar in Bagnolet. He didn't want to joke about her waking up in some harem of Mr. Zillionare Bucks and Zero Human Concept.

"I feel like I'm back in high school or college and we are on a date."

"Like on campus," she said.

"Yeah. Were you taking classes?"

"I was before my mom got sick."

"My mom died of cancer."

"I'm so sorry."

"Yeah. And my dad left us when I was pretty young. I don't remember much about him."

"Do you miss him?"

"Not really. Nothing to miss. He was never there for me or for her. A jerk, I guess. What about you?"

"My dad died in a motorcycle accident at thirty-five. I was still small. My mom and I made life work together, just the two of us."

"And then—"

"Yeah. Cancer. So there is this fad going around in the USA. Since the whole country is now practically owned by foreigners, and we're like serfs on our own turf, it's kind of hard to make ends meet. Particularly since we never had universal health care like the Canadians and every other civilized country. We could afford trillions of dollars for worthless wars so the rich could get richer, but we couldn't afford medical care for our loved ones. This fad is like the way people get tattoos and other crazy gotta-have-its. The fad is that you sell yourself into slavery for a set number of years, basically, only they don't call it that. It started with butlers and nannies, and became what they call BANs."

"Allegedly, for polite purposes, you get hired as a chaperone, I guess, or a, what's the term? You are a—"

"—au pair?"

"Something like that. Well, the catch is, in my case I was an attractive blue-eyed blonde with an English-sounding name. I let someone talk me into contracting with this agency that promised that whoever purchased my five years would pay the extortion fees of my mom's doctor bills. And all those thieving so-called insurance assholes, bunch of middlemen who do nothing but rake in money for doing nothing—and people are brainwashed into believing it's like Jesus wants us to live that way. So naturally, I ended up getting sold, I mean my contract got sold is how they officially say it, but in reality you're a slave and someone sells you to someone else. I got raped by an animal in Riyadh who sold me to an animal in Delhi who sold me to this animal in Shanghai. They all despise Western women, and they want to have a good animal fuck with us because we're suddenly serfs and they own the world. Flipped it around. They treat us the way we treated them."

"You never treated anyone. I never did," he corrected.

She shrugged. "Whatever. We did it to ourselves. We let the corporations sell us down the drain. I wanted out so bad I cried every night. I did it because they said they were going to pay my mom's health denial extortion fees. I would have preferred to just go there and let her die in my arms. Instead, I'm in China getting banged by this foul asshole, and she gets her health care denied on some technicality—after they took away the house, which is all she had—and she died alone anyway, in a dirty little apartment of all things, and the apartment block is owned by a New Delhi mutual investment fund, to complete the global picture." Her lips quivered, and her eyes teared up. "I would break down crying for the millionth time, but I am so fucking cried out I could just die."

He petted her gently, but she stayed frozen in her horror and misery.

"Come on," he said, "let's walk some more."

Slowly, she rose and joined him, dusting herself off, not so much of dust but of bad memories. They strolled some more on the Avenue de la Liberté, until they came to a much larger park. This was called the Little Rose Garden (Rousegärtchen). It was one side of the street only, facing a palatial old building across the street.

"I'm sorry," she said, getting behind him and putting her arms over his shoulders as if she meant for him to carry her. It was a metaphor for her broken life.

"You don't need to be sorry," he said, squirming so that he faced her. He put his arms around her, welcoming the smooth curves of her body—her long, slender waist, her spare but soft and sufficient rear end and hips. "You're my medicine. I didn't know you before last night, but already I feel like we've been, you know—soul to soul—for a million years."

She made a wise, sorry, wistful face. "I know. We fell in the same ditch together from different directions. I've been betrayed, ripped off, lied to, raped, and kicked around. I should never trust anyone again, but I want to just—" She lips got that quiver again.

"Now, now," he said, touching her eyelids with his fingertips, very gently, and regarding the big pearls of salty water that came away. "Let's leave the past where it is—dead and gone."

She wrapped her arms around him, firmly. "You have an appointment with the devil back in Germany."

"Yeah, that. My lawyer says they figured out it was all a mixup and she's going to get me off."

"Was it?"

"Damned if I can remember. It's all a blur. We were driving in a convoy and hit a couple of IEDs that were spaced just right and set off by some murdering idiots waiting behind a bridge. That much I remember. After that, my head feels like it was inside a huge bell that never stopped ringing."

"Your pills," she said pragmatically. "I'm getting you all worked up and you need to take your pills. What happens when you run out?"

He couldn't answer. He could not imagine. But he'd have to face that moment soon, when it came.

As they sat on a bench, he let her rummage through his backpack. She found a half-empty plastic water bottle and a couple of pill bottles. "You know what, Rick? I'm going to stop feeling sorry for myself and start taking care of you."

After taking the medicine, as she put things away and tidied up the backpack, he rubbed her back. "I feel like I want to take care of you."

"We should take care of each other."

"That sounds like the best deal yet."

"I have nobody and nothing except you. Right now, you are my world."

He kissed her sweetly and slowly on her cheeks, which were soft and flushed.

"Let's be on a date."

"Okay," she said. "You be the guy." She laughed. He laughed. "You are the guy. I mean, you lead and I'll follow. Please, I want to be your girl."

He took both of her hands in his. "You are all I have in this world. I love you like crazy, okay?"

"I love you too, Rick. Richard. Isn't that insane? I didn't know you before today, basically. Well, you've already saved my life at least once—when that big guy came storming in Fincoff's apartment waving a gun."

He held her hands between his as they sat on the bench. "Yeah, but you got there first. Whatever made you rescue me from the same goon the evening before? Why didn't you just leave me there and run?"

Her blue eyes darkened slightly, like a cloud passing over a perfect Southern California sky. "I think we were meant for each other. I don't know. I couldn't just leave you there. Well, and—"

"Yes?"

She looked down, ashamed. "I was in a real nasty place in my head. I was on the run from this billionaire monster who would throw his own mother out of a plane if he thought it would fly faster. Seriously. A total sociopath. I mean, how else do you become that rich? Anyway, I think in some tiny little corner of my mind you looked like a big strong guy—and a very decent one, I might add—and I thought it would be, well, what's the right word, useful to have you help me. I saved you because I needed you, the way I'd need a horse to get through the desert."

"I don't mind being your horse. I think you saved me because it was the decent thing to do."

"I don't mind being your concubine. Seriously. I sold my soul already, Rick. Being with you is like being born all over again. You make me feel like—a girl."

"You are a girl." He shook her. "You are an angel."

She patted his chest with her palm, feeling the steel in his muscles. "I would love it if you could just hold me like a little hamster and let me slowly heal and get better. I would be your friend, your buddy, your soul mate, your slave, your angel—anything you want, anything you need."

He shook her upper arms gently. "Hannah. Look at me."

Shamed, she slowly turned her gaze up to him.

"I don't want a slave or a concubine or a—whatever. I do need a woman in my life, and I've never met anyone as beautiful or as nice as you. You are my angel already, okay? If you stay with me, I'll stay with you forever. I already know that in my soul. I've been near death a bunch of times. I've seen people blown into rags of bloody shit. I've seen stuff I don't want to remember and I'll never tell you about. I've been to the edge of hell and back. I need you more than I need those friggin' pills."

"Okay," she said. "Okay." It was total surrender this time, not just kids on a date. She gave herself to him, resting her cheek against his chest and surrounding him with her embrace. He surrounded her embrace with his. He held her for a long time, kissing her exposed neck gently. She was all he had, and he was all she had. It was totally clear between them. The rest was academic. Nothing else mattered; not even close.

27. Belair: Mélusine's Place

They continued walking up the Avenue de la Liberté, soon reaching the Petrusse (River) Valley.

"Wow, that's scenic," she said as they came out to the Place de Metz, an opposite book end from the Place de Paris—at the other end of the avenue—where they had sat for a while after leaving the train station. From the twin small park circles of the Place de Metz, one had a panoramic view of the High City across the valley. Here, on this side, was the century-old, iconic tower of the *Spuerkees*, Savings Bank. The edges of the valley were lined with mansions, including those of ambassadors and millionaires. There was the tragic memorial of Villa Pauly, owned by a Jewish doctor who had been deported to a concentration camp by the occupying Germans in World War II. Dr. Pauly's offices had become Luxembourg Gestapo headquarters, with torture chambers conveniently in the former patient examination rooms, and the railroad administration across the street.

Across the valley from Place de Metz maybe two hundred meters or so rose sheer cliffs out of the Petrusse River valley, huge granite walls buttressed long ago with fitted stone blocks to create Luxembourg's formidable fortifications. The three slender turret peaks of the national cathedral, which they'd seen in the stained glass mural in the Gare, were visible across the valley.

Holding hands, Rick and Hannah ambled tiredly across the old, narrow *Adolphe* bridge, named for a nineteenth century Grand Duke of the still-ruling Nassau dynasties, related to earlier Bourbon-Parma royalty by complex interlocking hereditary titles and marriages.

A lovely, calm sort of evening, almost a faint haze like the beginning of a fog, lay over the deep valley. The Petrusse was filled with greenery, and trees, and a mix of ruins and rooftops. The Petrusse River flowed like a silver ribbon in its concrete canal along the bottom.

Rick and Hannah emerged in the High City—the oldest part of the city, though most buildings along the Boulevard Royal leading away from the *Pont Adolphe* were modern. Much of the city's vibrant economic health flowed through these corridors, building up to the almost metropolitan appearance of the glass and concrete Kirchberg colony of miniature skyscrapers beyond Belair.

Hannah and Rick walked across the *Pont Adolphe* to the *Place de Bruxelles* (Brussels Plaza), where they walked left along the edge of the Petrusse Valley on major roads, coming into the commune of Belair within a kilometer or so. It was a pleasant, leafy walk along a series of busy avenues named for long-ago royalty.

Passing the Parc Belair with its playgrounds, they passed by avenues named for historical cities and generals like Verdun and Marechal Foch.

"There is something haunting about this place Belair," Rick said.

"I know, I feel it too. It's in the air. Like a time capsule."

"This whole country is a time capsule," he said.

She made a dream face. "Belair means Pretty Air. I'll bet it was really sweet here centuries ago when this was probably mostly forest."

"The whole world was probably sweeter then, although life was harder in other ways."

"Aren't we the philosphers?"

"Yes we are. Do you have the exact address?"

She nodded. "You know, it's coming back to me now. When my parents were still young and together, and my dad was in the Air Force stationed in Germany, they had friends who lived here in Belair. That's what it was. They were nice people. I have no idea what ever happened to them. I just remember we came here a few times from Germany on weekends to visit, and it was always so nice and dreamy. Oh god, look at these quaint little streets."

They walked deeper into the neat, semi-modern quarter of Belair. Leaving the chateaux and mansions along the edge of the Petrusse, they came to quintessential, miniature Luxemburgish neighborhoods that possessed the sort of Germanic tidiness mixed with French softness that one found in Lorraine and Alsace.

"We are here together in Belair, a bit of magic from my childhood," she said. She squeezed his hand for emphasis. He returned the sentiment, thinking there was indeed a haze of otherwordliness hanging around here.

They found a narrow street with whitewashed houses on either side. Each house seemed to have a neat little driveway, and an ornate wooden door, and a livingroom picture window with a flower trellis hanging under it.

"Mélusine and Romain's house should be right along here soon," Hannah said as they walked along a sidewalk of small concrete puzzle-piece stones—everything laid out with agonizing neatness. She added, "Their main meal is lunch here. They take a long lunch. During the noon time, you can smell beef or pork dishes cooking from house to house, along with things like Sauerkraut, steamed beets, and all sorts of vegetable things and of course the potato, for which they are famous."

"And a little wine to help things along," Rick added. "Moselle River valley wine."

"There are farms and cows across most of the country too," she added. "Look, here we are."

The sign by the steel mailbox, set on a brick post amid whitewash, read *Poncelet*.

Hannah pointed. "We're here. That is her husband's name—Romain Poncelet. He is an architect, and she works as a technical librarian. I met her in Shanghai where she was on contract for one of Wan's industries. We sort of hit it off, because she was staying in a guest house where I was also staying—or being kept, I should say, along with two or three other girls, one from Canada, the other from Ecuador. I broke down and cried and told her what happened to me, and she said I should visit her when I became free. Now here I am. Back in the garden of my childhood."

"That's kind of ironic."

"Kind of. You tell me." She leaned down by the steps leading up to the little front door, and found a house key under a heavy black rubber mat. "Here's our key to adventure."

"I can't wait to get some sleep," Rick said.

They stepped inside, gingerly, aware of intruding in other people's home. Hannah said, "Mélusine said we should make ourselves at home. Romain knows we are coming. She says her husband is very sympathetic. He's a big PAX supporter."

Rick had long been sympathetic to PAX's global efforts toward a movement for democracy, labor unions, universal health care, tolerance, and all the other issues of quality of life for working and middle class families that were being tossed overboard by the global corporate-republican movement. *(*Endnotes #3)*

"Mélusine does technical docs for corporations," Hannah explained as they made themselves comfortable, and Rick examined bookshelves and photographs. "Romain teaches at Uni Lux. Luxembourg is one of the world's tiniest nations, but one of the wealthiest. They keep dancing between the raindrops. At one time they were one of the top seven steel producers, but they sold the national industry to the Indian billionaire Lakshmi Mittal, who has not been kind to workers and unions while owning half the world's steel production."

"That's why they are zillionaires?" Rick said. "Like J. Paul Getty once said, if you know how much money you own, you're not really wealthy."

"Luxembourg became a banking and tax haven like Switzerland."

"With rich friends in high places around the world," Rick echoed.

"Whatever. There's good and there's bad. Not all zillionaires are bad; I was owned by one of the worst. It's a mix. So Luxembourg started making connections with China—smart, but dangerous—like a flea sitting on an elephant, drinking lots of nice blood until you get squished."

"It's over our pay grade," Rick concluded. "We have so much else to worry about, like survival." He liked to voraciously read popular history books. He wanted to understand more about where humans had been and where they were going. He hoped to gain admission one day, somehow, into a university, gain his degrees, and teach. That all seemed a long way off right now.

They explored the small house of Romain and Mélusine. From photos decorating the living room, Rick noted that she was an attractive, pale-skinned young woman. Romain was the darker-haired and café-aut-lait colored of the couple, a handsome young man with a determined expression and intelligent dark eyes in the photos. Hopefully, he was an ally in this crazy venture.

"She said to take the guest bedroom," Hannah told Rick.

The walls inside the house were white plaster, like the whitewash outside. This was offset with dark wood wainscoting and crown molding that gave it a kind of Bavarian look (so Rick thought of it). The living room was cozy, with a plush faux-bear skin rug on a plank floor. Book cases brimmed with old-fashioned print books, and a million knick-knacks (marble statuettes, stone vases, glass photo frames, and more). Against one wall stood an extra-large video screen set in a media center with the latest sound speakers.

The kitchen was modern and sleek—small but tidy, and functional.

The bathrooms were clean and fragrant.

They did not venture upstairs, where Mélu and Romain had their large bedroom and bath.

Downstairs by the rear entrance was the smaller guest suite, consisting of a little bedroom with double bed, and a bathroom with shower but no tub. The floors downstairs were set in glossy, brick-colored Spanish pavers, covered with throw rugs. There were more bookcases, photos, and knick-knacks.

"We have to shower," Hannah told him.

Rick threw his backpack on the bed. "With my last ounce of strength. You go first."

She giggled. "Want to shower with me?"

"Oh my lord. You'll see me naked, and my flag has been at full mast all day long around you."

"I will lower your flag after I raise it," she promised. "I will blow the bugle and give you taps."

They wandered into the bathroom in the guest suite. It was a square room with sink and shower, and a separate little toilet off to one side, up a step, with a door for privacy.

"I need to find the laundry," Hannah said as she peeled his clothes off for him.

He obliged, unbuttoning and unzipping and peeling hers as well.

In a few moments, they stood adoring each other in the pink.

"I don't even want to touch you," she said, "not because you are dirty and smell like a bear in the forest, but if I start I won't stop."

"Licking each other's ice cream," he finished her sentence. He thought of the abuse she had been through, and was glad she retained a healthy interest in life, sex, and ice cream.

"Man-flavored ice cream," he said suggestively as they stood in the glass shower cubicle, surrounded by steam, and lathering up with Mélusine's lemony-scented herbal soap.

She cupped his privates and pressed them to his body with an eager hand. "Oh baby, I didn't know you would feel so nice." She leaned into him and gave him a long, tonguey kiss.

He took her naked form, wet and soapy, into his hands as he responded tongue-on-tongue.

They showered long and hard, soaping and scrubbing each other.

"We deserve this," he said.

"We worked hard for it," she agreed. She tossed an arm over his neck, pulling his head close to her small, pink-nippled breasts. "Try some woman-flavored ice cream."

He mouthed her firm boobs, one after the other, and made happy sounds. At the same time, his hand explored the fur on her Venus mound, and the moist, yielding cleft that melted open as he touched down there. She stood slightly up and apart on the balls of her feet as she let him touch her where he wanted (and she wanted). She steadied herself with her hands on his shoulders. "I am going to fall over in ecstasy," she whispered. "Oh yes. There. And there. That's right."

They toweled dry quickly and marched hand-in-hand to the bed.

Crawling under the covers, they entwined like one body. The feeling of her skin on his, her bones and muscles against his, her blood throbbing against his, her breath going in and out in ragged gasps like his own, made him crazy with desire. She clawed at him with her small, delicate, but surprisingly strong and determined hands. "Take me," she whispered. "Oh god Richard take me I am yours every bit of me my heart and soul, baby, do me now all the way. Put that rod inside of me and make me come. Oh god oh god oh god how I need you. And I love you, I do."

"I love you, baby," he said, sliding into her and thrusting. He pressed her willing thighs apart. Her lower legs dangled in the air over either side of his head. He found the soft wonder at her center, which she gave to him with all of her heart, using her fingers to hold her lips apart and guide his blundering head into the softness where he found bliss like nothing else on earth. His entire body ran electric with shivers that pulsed up and down his spine. They trembled together with the crazy overwhelming force of their desire for each other. His hard body slapped repeatedly against her softness and her yielding desire. "I just want you—you—you—you," he repeated with each pounding thrust. He could hear the slapping of his flesh on hers. The more he rammed her, the more she beat him on the back with her fists and cried for more—animal cries, roars and grunts, as she pawed him and hit him and bit his neck and sucked in the purity of his love and sex while exorcising the devils that had defiled her humanity. He wasn't sure if she was bawling or crying for more sex. She was loud, and it didn't matter. He bore down on her with pile driver thrusts, slamming her into the bed, and she wrapped her strong legs around him, yelling for more. She thrust her legs over his shoulders, pressing his head between her knees, until his strength overcame her hunger and she went limp again, letting him bang her noisily and with lovely rage in the darkness swirling all around them.

She wrapped her arms around his neck, choking him, and bit his ear. "I want you to fuck my ass." When he moved too slowly, she kept her arms around his neck, and headlocked him, flipping him off her. She turned onto her belly, and spread her long legs so he could easily part her round, upthrust buttocks. "Take me," she growled. "Take me, man." She was breathing hard and talking fast, like a woman possessed. "You know what? I want you do do everything to me that they did. That way we can erase the filth of them touching me. Go on. Fuck me. Fuck me with love and destroy how they fucked me with hate. Stick it in my ass. It is nice and tight for you."

He gazed at the violet pucker at the center of her wish. It was her most intimate spot, a dark secret full of nerve endings tied by a million flashing, hammering synapses to the highways leading to her brain, her identity, who she was, whom they had violated.

He did not mount her as she demanded, but gently laid his cheek against the twin mounds of her buttocks. He stroked her buttocks very delicately and softly. He closed his eyes and basked in the warmth of her firm body. She was slick with sweat from both him and her. He touched the dark pucker with his finger tip, and she groaned. He heard her distantly, "Take me."

"I already have you, sweetheart." He kissed each of her taut, café-au-lait orbs. "One of these days, we'll play with it. We'll eat all the ice cream. Nothing will be secret. I love your beautiful ass."

He blew on those smooth planetary curves, rubbed them with his fingertips until her disappointment dissolved in laughter. "That tickles, Richard. You are so mean and cruel to me." She curled up laughing, and then bounced around like a kid. "Don't stop!"

He chased her on the bed, and they scampered like puppies. They played and played, rolling together, licking and sucking each other's precious wet secret parts, getting each other all wet until they were slippery and made sucking and slapping sounds when they touched. They stuck together and came apart. "Pet my ass some more," she said.

"I'll pet your ass all day long." He held her tightly, so she almost couldn't breathe, and cupped her ass in both hands while gazing up at her as if she were the full moon, shedding light on his world. "I'll bet every man on the street, and half the women, turn to look after this when you go by."

"A girl learns to ignore all that," she whispered shyly. Then she became bold and aggressive. She reached down with both arms to cup his cock and balls in her hands, owning them; and simultaneously speared his mouth with her tongue as if her tongue were a cock, fucking him fast and furious.

It was a healing, he knew. She was desperate, finding herself again. He wanted to be there with her. He kneaded the tight spheres of her ass as her lower half labored like a man screwing a woman, shoving against him, in rhythm with her upper half. His hard shaft slid inside her and she gasped at the renewed entry. This time it was she who did the thrusting, made the slapping sounds, though the slapping sounds were still mostly her womanly softness against his steely male hardness, as it should be, a beautiful music.

He eagerly sought her thrusting tongue with his mouth. His groans sounded hungry in the darkness, to his ears. Her groans seemed frantic as she puked forth in reverse what evil strangers had done to her. He rubbed his hands up and down the fine, delicate straits of her back, pulling her toward him, urging her on, pulling it out of her. She slid up and down on him, dripping wet and horny.

He let her take him in the mouth with her tongue. Still inside her, he also had three or four fingers of both hands up her cunt hole and held her wonderfully apart while she savaged his mouth with her passion. Her fervor softened from anger and violence into love and sweetness. She gripped his head in both fists while she power-drilled him with her rage and energy.

At some point, her teeth struck his teeth in a jarring, agonizing collision that made them both cry out in pain and back away quickly as if stung.

He and she eased off (just for a second) amid the stunning pain. She touched her mouth with her hands as if something had bitten her.

Rick felt throbbing pain and saw floating colors.

Each felt their teeth to make sure nothing was broken, and then started up again.

No amount of sex was enough to sate their starvation right now. She had blood on her mouth from the teeth collision and he tasted it—like raw liver. He licked blood off her mouth. She spat blood all over his face, deliberately, angrily, again and again. He licked her face until there was less and less blood and then only spit—gobs of it. They rolled over and over, drinking each other's spit. It was like eating raw, bloody meat, tartare. They were animals, rolling on the jungle floor. Spit never tasted so good, he thought as he possessed her and she gave herself to him from the dark caves of her soul, her need, her desire, her want, her hole.

Slowly, the fury of their sex and the madness of their love gave way to exhaustion.

They had seen death twice. They had run for their lives and now found shelter for whatever short time. It had been one insane day of terror, horror, unreasoning madness. Here, they had found intense, growing passion and redemption. At some point, in the darkness, when she lay under him—they were soaked with sweat and come and fluids—she threw her arms out and went limp. "Baby, I can't anymore right now." She laughed. "Get off me—you are heavy as a truck."

"I want more." He rolled over onto his back, taking her with him so that she lay straddling him. She looked down into his face with shining delight. She cupped his face in her palms and kissed him on the nose, on the lips, on the forehead, on the chin, on the mouth, all the while laughing and snuffling happily. They were mammals, grooming. It was all natural, healing, good.

"You have blood all over your head." She laughed at the funniness of it.

He laughed too. "Blood-flavored ice cream."

She growled like a long shoreman. "Lick me, baby, lick me."

"I am too fucking tired. Save some of that for later."

"There is lots more where this came from."

They laughed and laughed.

He hugged her roughly and kissed her, crushing her head and neck against him. She clutched him tightly, pulling herself into him as she wrapped her strong legs around him for a tight seal. He whispered in her ear, "My cock hound is baying for you."

She laughed. "My full moon is gazing on your dog."

They laughed as the metaphors ran dry.

It was his turn to throw his arms back over his shoulders in surrender. She could do with him whatever she wanted to. "I'm—powerless—to—resist," he panted in gasps. "You wore me out. Eat me quick, baby bear. Don't be cruel."

She licked his cheeks, bit his ear, kissed his forehead. "You're mine. All mine. I will take my time, drag you back to my lair, and slowly devour you one delicious pickle slice at a time, my sweet little hamburger meat."

"I am the hot dog. You are the bun," he informed her. "And you are mine," he whispered. He hugged her naked body close to his, enjoying the solid feel of her back against his wrists. He ran his palms over the curves of her buttocks, felt the heft of her thighs, pulled her as close to his flesh as possible. She pressed against him. It was their mutual desire and delight and passion and crazy love to want to squeeze together and become one person.

"Next time," she whispered sweatily, dripping onto his face, and he licked the salt of her sweat from his lips where it fell. "Next time, I am going to really suck your pickle, buster."

He pulled her close with his left arm and held her bouncing breast with his right hand. "I am going to lick that ice cream right off of your lips, bitch."

"Talk dirty to me."

"Both sets of your delicious little floppy lips."

"I will hold them open for you, prince. Talk more, sexy prince."

And talk he did, while she pressed herself onto him and shuddered with joy—until they passed out from exhaustion a few heartbeats later.

They made love again in the gray of dawn.

Then they passed out again and woke around eight a.m. when a woman knocked to see if they were alive and well.

Rick and Hannah both shrieked in shock until Mélusine fully poked her face in to show herself, to check if all was well, and to make sure they were who she thought they were.

They all laughed, Romain in the background included.

Hannah said to Mélusine, who hovered in the slightly open door, afraid to intrude, "You had me terrified there for a minute. I thought we might be in the wrong house."

"Would that not be a gas?" Mélu said in her melodious train station announcer voice, while she nearly collapsed laughing. Rick threw himself back on the bed holding his head and roaring. He heard Romain (whom he had met only in photographs so far) guffawing out in the hallway. So they were off to a good (roaring, literally) start, Rick thought.

Mélusine said as she pulled the door shut to give them privacy, "Come, I have some breakfast ready. Coffee. You like coffee, yes?"

"We'll be there as soon as we can!" Hannah yelled to the closing door.

"Yes," Rick said wryly when he got his breath and his strength back. "Yes. Please. I need some stimulus."

Hannah twisted his semi-limp pecker—gently.

He groaned. "Ow. I'm sore."

"I'm sorry."

"You did this. Now fix…"

She put her head under the sheets and surrounded him with the healing wetness and warmth of her mouth.

He lay back and moaned blissfully, "That's right. Just like that. Oh yeah."

She made a popping noise and emerged with a muzzy expression of delight. "Is that better?"

"Paradise."

"You want to keep me?"

"Forever."

"Promise?"

28. Belair—Breakfast and Decisions

After a refreshing shower, Rick and Hannah sat in the pleasant light of a wide picture window. They were in the living room of the Poncelets' compact house. The Luxembourgeois couple really made the best of every square meter. "I can see you are an architect," Hannah said to Romain as she stirred her coffee.

"What do you mean?" He was a pleasant, easy-going man of thirty, with intense, intelligent dark eyes, wavy black hair combed back over the ears and falling to his shoulders. Rick assessed him as an avid sportsman, probably *Fussball*, cycling, all those European things. He imagined that a woman would find Romain intriguing.

As they four sat together, Rick and Hannah sat thigh-to-thigh on a love seat overlooking a coffee table. A chill window overlooked greenery—trees, shrubs, some roses outside. As usual, it was drizzling lightly, though it was early summer. Hannah kept a hand on Rick's thigh, as if guarding him and holding him and possessing him. Unable to resist passion, he put his arm around her. He kissed her passionately during a moment when Romain went to the kitchen and Mélusine ran to the *klo* for a tinkle. Hannah whispered, "I'm going to take you home with me to California when we're done with all this crazy stuff."

"I'm ready," he whispered. "We'll get it done."

"Operative word is we," she said. "I'll stick by you no matter what happens."

He choked on the words he wanted to say, *me too, forever*.

Shortly, they were all four together again, buttering rolls, pouring steaming black coffee, scraping the bottom of a glass orange marmalade jar, all the homey things that were so little and yet so important.

"Thank you," Hannah said.

"*Gär geschitt*," Mélusine said. *Glad to be there for you.*

Rick added, "We are so grateful."

Romain nodded and gave him a light man-punch on the upper arm. "It's okay, dude," he said in a comical imitation U.S. accent. He and Rick man-laughed together, deep and throaty.

Hannah put her arm possessively over Rick's back as she said to Mélusine, "I was such a lost soul in Shanghai."

Mélusine was a pretty brunette with darker blue eyes than Hannah. Hers was the sort of athletic tennis player face with broad cheek bones and a tapering lower jaw that Rick associated with sports news. Mélusine's voice, too, had a full, strong quality like someone who was used to competing and probably winning. A glance at Romain told Rick that Mélu's husband was perfectly in tune with that. Mélu was one of those women who moved in a somewhat side-to-side sportsy way, a real gamine, a buddy girl. Hannah was grateful she and Hannah had hit it off during Hannah's servitude and Mélusine's contract work for Wan Industries in Shanghai.

"Tell me again how did you two meet?" Romain asked.

Rick savored sliced, German-style salami on brownish Luxembourg farm bread with butter. This went with strong black coffee like sports and beer. Mélu moved her head in quick little sideways motions that made tiny muscles in her neck ripple. "It was pretty scary, actually."

"Oh god," Hannah said at the memory, rolling her eyes. She wrapped herself around Rick, pulling tightly. He patted her hands.

Mélu said, "One day, I was sitting on the patio of this condo place I was sharing with three other women. We were all engineering workers with Wan Industrial. I heard this shrieking of women and I thought what can that be all about? There were trees and bushes all around, in the middle of Shanghai in this park owned by Wan with his palace in the middle. Next thing I know, this Caucasian girl comes running, dressed only in a white robe and looking terrified. Well, as one woman to another woman, I didn't ask questions. I let her in and closed the sliding glass door."

Hannah added, "I found a closet and hid inside."

Mélu continued, "Next thing, I hear these slapping feet and I see two guys running by who looked like pirates or Cossacks or something. They were young men, with long hair, with scars and tattoos all over. They had mean, brutal faces and vicious eyes."

"They were Triad from Macao," Hannah said. "Las Vegas times ten. Money laundering for Chinese zillionaires who otherwise aren't allowed to gamble and do a whole lot of other things legally, but in Macao anything goes."

Rick shook his head. He was just getting to know this woman he had pledged his heart and soul to. "What—?"

Hannah made a serious face and patted his hands, explaining in as few words as possible. "They had four of us, all Western women. Wan gave us to them as a present. They were raping us. So I ran."

Mélu nodded in her gamine, athletic way. "So I hid her for two days in my room."

Hannah said, "It blew over. These aren't normal people. They live like wolves. One minute they are nuzzling each other at the nose, the next minute sniffing each other's assholes, the next minute ripping each other piece by piece in bloody chunks."

Romain added his bit; "It's a world run by predators. Eating, fucking, killing—they do it without thinking. Like animals, they don't remember. It means nothing from one moment to the next. Human life has no value. We have them in the West. They have them in the East. It's all the same."

Mélu nodded. "People are the same everywhere. I have good Chinese and Indian friends who are like us, not like that. They are victims also."

Romain stirred his coffee. "Which is why PAX seeks to unite the good people of the world to resist the rabble and their owners, the zillionaires. People against animals, smart people over ignorant rabble."

"PAX, Progressive Alliance," Mélu said. "We're still legal. Democracy isn't dead, but going fast. We have to act smart."

Hannah made a startled face. "Then—do you know—?"

Mélu nodded matter of factly. "Of course. You stole Wan's toy, which he stole from a Luxembourg scientist his people murdered. Pierre Sander intended it for peaceful purposes."

"That is the Doctor Sander I mailed the McGuffin to."

"And now you understand," Mélu said. "I never expected you would create such a wonderful coup!"

"Wan must be beside himself," Romain said.

Rick felt overwhelmed. "I just stopped for a beer in a Paris bar."

They all laughed. Hannah patted his shoulder. "Are you sorry, my dear?" She eyeballed him frankly.

He passionately looked into her eyes. "I am in love with you."

She softened, as if he'd been about to kill her but spared her life. "I love you too, Richard."

He looked around the table in the silence and said, "I have this dream."

"We have a dream," Hannah said, wrapping herself around him again. "We want to go home to California and live our lives together in peace and quiet. We've had enough commotion to last us a lifetime."

Mélu's eyes twinkled, amid a nod that radiated understanding.

Romain made a wry face, saying, "We would love to escape also. We are here in the middle of things. Two world wars plus Napoleon I and III started near here, not to mention a thousand wars of Dark Ages dukes and pukes. But we are stuck here. This is our homeland."

Romain and Mélu in turn linked arms and sat close together, almost defiantly.

"Maybe we can make this work for all of us," Rick said. "I have no idea how."

"I mailed the package to Professor Sander," Hannah said. "What else could I do? We were being watched by a Chinese agent in the Luxembourg Gare."

Mélu and Romain looked at each other, then at Hannah. "That might be Shen."

"Who is Shen?" Rick said.

Romain explained, treading through apparently difficult mine fields, not sure how much to say and what not to say. "Shen is known to us. He is a kind of dangerous guy. He plays both sides, but really I think he is sympathetic to PAX. We have evidence to think that."

"From two previous actions involving him," Mélu said.

Rick shook his head in amazement. "You guys lead active lives."

"We are trying to save the world," Mélu said. "The corporations have all but destroyed the environment and with it the climate. They have used the power of common mobs to destroy democracy since at least Reagan's election in the US, which was the big turning point."

Romain added, "Even the ancient Greek philosophers talked about the violent power of ignorant mobs over twenty-five centuries ago. It's the fundamental problem of democracy—when power of the people turns into rioting mobs led by demagogues."

Mélu said, "Like in those old Frankenstein movies, when the villagers march on the castle at night carrying torches. That is what the Germans became when they followed Hitler. The Italians with Mussolini, the Serbians with Milosevic. It's the Human Condition."

Rick sighed. "Look, no offense, but I have a life to live. I'm in over my ears as it is."

"We understand that," Mélu said.

Hannah patted his thigh. "Rick, listen, I have just one thing to do and then I will go anywhere you want me to. I need to get that package into the hands of the right people."

"PAX," Rick said, and again it was a question.

Hannah replied by lowering her eyelids, *yes*.

"Okay," he said. "Give me an hour to let this all sink in. You mean—yesterday, Fincoff..."

Hannah explained, "Fincoff was the best I could do."

"I wish you had called me first," Mélu chided gently.

"I had no idea you would be there to help."

"I gave you my Luxembourg phone number in Shanghai, dear."

Hannah said, "You were recruiting me for PAX." It was a realization.

Mélu and Romain exchanged sphinx-like glances, and each shrugged.

Hannah explained, "I stole this thing from Wan because he stole it, he screwed me over, and I was just plain pissed off and ready to run. It was my opportunity to stick it to him. That's all I thought about. I had no idea that people everywhere are watching each other, like animals in the woods, waiting for someone to make a mistake so they can kill each other. There must be fifty different enemies watching every move Wan makes."

Romain nodded. "That is the sort of world powerful people like that have always lived in. It is the world of Macbeth, of King Lear, of Hamlet. Terror, conspiracy, always knives and blood in the dark."

"It is their natural element," Mélu said. "Many of them are sociopaths. You have to be."

Hannah said, "So I had this thing I stole, and I was on the run. Somebody knew what I did, who I was, and what I had. Next thing I know,

I'm sitting in a Metro station in the Marais, wondering what to do next with what little money I had, and this man walks up to me."

"Fincoff," Rick said. It was a question.

"Yes. He said if I let him broker the package, he would get a million Euros and split it with me. I didn't believe him, of course. I had the package hidden in a locker in the Clignancourt metro station, and nobody but me knew where it was. So I had a leg up on everyone."

"And Fincoff still tried to screw you," Rick said.

"Yup. Only I had the McGuffin and as long as only I knew where it was, I was more valuable alive than dead. So Fincoff tried to arrange a meeting with PAX, but CEOC got wind of it. They showed up at the bar in Bagnolet and tried to drug Fincoff. They must have thought he had the package with him."

Rick brightened. "I get it. I come staggering in, full of my own woes, not knowing a thing about all this, and Fincoff switches drinks with me. I get zonked and go staggering out into the alley…"

Hannah finished, "I was watching from a distance, because I didn't trust Fincoff. I wanted to see who was who in the zoo before I handed over the locker key—and got my money."

Mélu said, "You didn't know what the package was."

Hannah shook her head. "Not really. I just wanted to hurt Wan back for letting my mom die, and doing bad things to me and other victims."

Romain said, "With the new fuselage skin, it makes all existing aircraft and missiles obsolete. A flying object with that skin can outfly, out-think and kill anything it wants to. So you get the drift now. We want someone other than Wan and his clique to control CEOC."

Rick said, "You think there is hope for CEOC?"

Romain gave him a cagey look. "We think CEOC can be defanged. Not all zillionaires and corporations are evil and heartless. PAX is a global union of students, workers, intelligent middle class, the artisan class—not the rabble who blindly follow demagogues and do the dirty work while the Hitlers and Wans count their money laughing all the way to the bank."

Rick bit his lip. "I'm a soldier, serving the United States Army."

Romain had difficulty hiding his contempt. "Your mission is long obsolete. Your country is obsolete. You were fighting in the last gasp of the oil and coal wars. The CEOC people have moved beyond dirty fossil fuels and are onto solar, wind, tidal, geothermal, even just plain gravity. As long as they control the energy that drives the world, they own you, me, the governments, the fake politicians, the fraudulent insurance companies, you name it."

Mélu added, "You walked up the Avenue de la Liberté, right?

Hannah nodded.

"You stopped at the nice park?"

Hannah and Rick's expressions said *yes*.

"That palace across the street," Romain said, "was once ARBED, our national steel industry headquarters. We were one of the top seven steel producers in the world. It was the major source of Luxembourg's wealth, with powerful labor unions, worker safety, pensions, and all that. Then an Indian bought it, along with half the world's steel production."

Mélu added, "It's not that they're Indian, or even that family. It's the general cast of characters that Wan represents and wants to lead. Those zillionaire owners—whether Indian, Chinese, French, German, or U.S.-- are not going to care about our country, our workers, our people. There is no patriotism among corporations."

"Just the profit motive," Hannah said. "It's all falling into place now."

"And no religion," Romain added, "no matter how they tell the rabble that Jesus wants it or that Mohammed speaks through whatever idiot the corporations have illegally placed in power."

"Money is the only religion for them," Mélu said, concluding in German, "*Profit über alles.*"

Romain added, "*Nichts ausser Profit.*" Profit and nothing else.

"Back to Bagnolet and the Bar-39," Hannah said. "I watched two goons I knew worked for Wan—Yolo and Savia—attack Fincoff when he knew they were trying to drug him, and he tried to escape."

"So that's what I stumbled into," Rick said. "I've been in ambushes before. Just not in Paris or New York or anything—more like some desolate stretch in the oil countries where people don't use their left hand to eat, and women have to wear bags over their heads to show they are some man's property."

"It was an ambush," Hannah agreed. She pulled on his arm. "I fell in love with you even though you were half out of it. I just had to save you. And I admit—you'd be useful to me. All that's changed."

"Let me process this," Rick said, suddenly thinking of JAG and what he needed to do before he ran out of time, pills, and sanity. His companions fell silent around the table, eating quietly and marinating in their own thoughts. He was committing himself to this woman and they'd talked about all this already. Nothing changed. He still had the burner in his backpack. "I have to go to the bathroom."

He rose, and strode from the room. He went downstairs, rummaged through the backpack, and found the throw-away phone. He took it into the guest bathroom, locked himself in, and called JAG in K-Town.

"Blah blah blah," said some private first class.

"Let me talk to Major Walsh. This is Rick Buchan."

Kendra got on the line. "Richard. I was hoping you would call."

"Progress." It was a question.

"Working on it."

"How long?"

"Not clear. Don't hang up, please."

"You have ten seconds. Talk." The call must not be traced. He plugged the sink and started water running.

"I can get you off. I am talking to Dennis Prager. You remember him?"

"He died in the explosion."

"No, he is the only one who lived. He says you were framed by Lieutenant Sherwin."

"Who?" Even as he asked, he held his head and felt memories flooding in. *Yes...*

"Lieutenant Sherwin was the FOD—Field Officer of the Day. He was in charge of operations. He had instructions to keep you guys out of that area."

"But he sent us anyway."

"Yes. He had his reasons—wrong reasons, bad reasons, stupid reasons. I'm getting the goods on him. Look, Buchan, all you need is reasonable doubt. I can get you a General Discharge."

"I want Honorable."

"We'll work on an upgrade. Six months after separation, we can petition the Pentagon."

"Not good enough, but keep working on it."

"Buchan, wait—"

"Please, Kendra. I'm scared. I need time to think." He rang off and dropped the phone into the full sink. It fell in, sizzling, bobbing, twisting in circles, as its battery fried in a massive watery short circuit.

Sounded like there was light at the end of the tunnel. He needed Hannah in on the plan. Unlocking and opening the door, he realized what he was doing. He was committing to this PAX thing. He loved Hannah and would go to hell and back with her and for her. He'd been fool enough to soldier for the foreign corporations who owned the media *(*Endnotes #4)*

...Time to serve a better cause. He went back up the stairs.

Hannah, Romain, and Mélu sat looking at him expectantly.

"I'm in," he said. It was not a question.

"Then it's settled," said Mélu, rising. She gathered their dishes, with Hannah helping. The two women went off on their own, deep in some conspiratorial conversation. Romain lingered over his coffee.

Rick went into the bathroom. He took the dead phone out of the water, let the sink drain, and dropped the phone into a little trash can by the sink. Soon, he'd get another burner phone. Hopefully, that would be the last time he'd need to call Kendra before turning himself in and hoping for a clean break with the Army and his past. He'd done his part. It was time to move on. He'd found his future. Her name was Hannah Smith.

Romain took Rick aside. "You're sure?"

The two men drifted into Romain's study, a smaller area full of books off to one side of the living room. In the study was a large glass-topped desk, with two office chairs of brown leather, plus a drafting table with waxy-looking yards of drawing paper spread out on an angle amid triangles, compasses, and an assortment of drawing pencils.

"Never more sure," Rick said. He thought about his fellow soldiers who had died on that desert road, all because of an incompetent officer who screwed up and then mercilessly shifted blame; to begin with, in a cause without purpose. "I am totally sure."

"Good." Romain was about Rick's height, an athlete for sure—photos of him and Mélu hung on the walls, in tennis gear, cycling, swimming— along with medals from university and sporting events. "It's not difficult. We go to Echternach—that's a Luxembourg town on the German border, where Professor Sander lives. Hannah mailed the package to him."

"We?"

"You, me, Hannah," Romain said. "Mélu has to work, and she can coordinate with our PAX contacts if it becomes necessary. We have a disinterlinked organization, like during World War II. Nobody knows who is in the movement outside of one's individual cell, if that much. It's safer that way. We drive to Echternach, which is maybe a half hour from here. We go to the post office, pick up the package, and deliver it."

"Where to?"

"Mélu will call Sander for instructions."

"This could all be over in an hour, if it works right."

Romain clapped him on the back. "See? It's solid, my friend. *Solit*, as we say. And then you and your beautiful friend can be on your way to California."

Rick nodded. "We have a stop to make in Germany first, but yes, I cannot wait to get this over with. How soon?"

"We leave around noon. As soon as Mélu contacts the professor."

"And this Sander invented the technology?"

"No, his son did—Pierre Sander. Wan's people murdered him, as we said. Pierre was a top engineering professor and researcher at Birmingham in England. The former U.K., before it broke up. His invention was stolen from him."

"He knew too much?"

"Yes, he could have reproduced the calculations for someone else."

"Who is this someone else PAX is working with?"

"The former West," Romain said. "Even though our governments are owned by conglomerates, along with the media and the courts, there are rival zillionaires who want to restore the West, at least to parity. It was their power base, after all. The Asians have at least two power bases— India and China. Brazil and the Spanish speaking countries of South America have another. There are at least two loci in Africa. So the logical thing is for the former West, including Europe, North America, and Australia-New Zealand, plus Japan and some other outliers, to form a counter-balance. There are very powerful players involved, including generals in your army and so forth. PAX will help them if they help PAX."

"Why would the corporations that destroyed democracy help PAX?"

Romain made a wry face. "The enemy of my enemy is my friend."

"Ah." It was the old formula of the former Middle East, today a totally rearranged set of Titanic deck chairs that would be unrecognizable from the post-Ottoman world.

"Okay," Rick said, "I'm in. Let's go."

They returned to the living room, where Hannah and Mélu stood near the window in conversation. Each looked attractive in her own way—Mélu in dark green corduroy pants that muted her wide, powerful haunches and legs made for running and jumping; Hannah the more slender, and now wearing some clean new clothing that hung too loosely on her.

Seeing Rick's expression, Romain said, "I could try loaning you some of my clothes. We are running yours through the washer and dryer as we speak."

"Looks like Mélu already fixed Hannah up."

"Women are quicker about social things. More coffee?"

"No thanks. It looks almost sunny out there."

Romain looked at the clock. "You and Hannah should talk a walk. Kill some time while you wait. It's just after nine a.m. I can drop you off at the old part of the city for a few hours. Get some fresh air and relax."

Hannah looked at Rick, having overheard the two men talking.

"Want to go for a stroll?" Rick asked.

She nodded.

"There is a lot to see," Mélu said, "but the city is not so large. You should at least see the *Knuedler*—that is the *Place Guillaume*—and the palace, the cathedral, and the old fish market area."

"I can't wait," Hannah said. She walked to Rick and pressed herself against him.

He embraced her.

29.   High City

"This will give you a little flavor of our city. It will keep you away from us and out of danger for a few hours," Romain said as he steered his compact but powerful late model white Audi with gray interior along the Avenue Foch, back along the Boulevard Marie-Thérèse that they had walked on, and onto the Boulevard Royal. At the intersection near the Adolphe Bridge on their right loomed the famous Savings Bank tower across the Petrusse Valley. On this side, among more modern buildings, the thin spires of the Cathedral of Our Lady, Consoler of the Suffering, hovered directly ahead.

Hannah sat in the passenger seat, and Rick in the rear with his backpack.

"The Romans had a fort here about two thousand years ago, and before them the Celtic people, and before that there were people living here since Stone Age times," Romain explained. "A gunpowder explosion in 1554 leveled the old city hall. Two huge cannon bombardments during two sieges in the 1600s and 1700s leveled parts of the Haute-Ville or High City. Therefore, you see very little older than the 1600s, and that is the period to which the cathedral dates. Most of the fortifications around the entire city, extending as far out as the Gare, were demolished by a peace treaty in 1867 when the Prussian army pulled out. They had been there since Napoleon's defeat at Waterloo in 1815."

He regaled them with some more historical information as they crept along the narrow street between stone and stucco walls.

"I am driving on the Rue de Notre Dame," Romain said. "I will let you out in front of the Cathedral, and you can walk around the center of the Haute Ville or High City, the oldest part of the city. I'll phone you in about two hours and pick you up back where I left you off, and we'll head straight to Echternach to get our business done."

Within ten minutes, Rick and Hannah stood alone together, holding hands. Like any two tourists, they hurried along to peek into the cathedral. In the gloom, which was lit inside by sunlight leaking through brilliant red and yellow and blue stainless glass, there lay a faint aroma of incense from a recent service. In the vestibule was a shrine filled with symbolic crutches and other metaphors for suffering that the afflicted had left here as an offering over the generations—cured or relieved of sufferings.

Rick and Hannah crossed the narrow street—everything here was narrow and tight—old but tidy.

They strolled always holding each other. Every minute, he fell more in love with her. Sometimes they stopped to embrace and kiss. Nobody much cared as people streamed around them. One or two other young people were doing the same. The atmosphere reminded Hannah a bit of Paris, where affection was as freely expressed as the annoyance of waiters, the impatience of metro conductors, and the sheepish trudging of first-time tourists.

They climbed a mossy old flight of stone stairs and emerged onto the Place Guillaume, dedicated to a long-ago Grand Duke William. His statue, complete with duke sitting on horse, stood on a pedestal. This was the true postcard square with shops and cafés all around. They took a walk around the square, promising themselves one day to return for a leisurely *café-au-lait* or ice cream. They made some quick detours through cobblestoned pedestrian alleys of stylish shops.

Their walk took them to the grand-ducal palace with its patrolling soldier in dress-green uniform. Past the palace, they walked under a little overpass into a very old area (Fish Market) with cobblestone alleys winding about. They took a quick look at MUDAM, the Museum d'Art Moderne, without entering the glassy front with its current exhibit—a wild expo of wavy paintbrush colors on neo-surrealist canvases.

Back in the Place Guillaume, they passed a modern McDonald's at the corner of a side alley leading yet higher into the old city.

Mélu had advised Hannah on some other interesting points. Hannah towed Rick along by the hand. They crossed the Rue du Curé, walked a block, and entered the Place d'Armes. A few blocks further, in a pedestrian zone on the corner of the Rue Beaumont and the Rue des Capucins, was the Patisserie Namur, the oldest and most elegant surviving tea rooms of earlier centuries. The store name in large gold script was displayed above the heavy wooden entry way on a background of glossy royal blue. Signs above the plate glass windows read *Confiseur* and *Patissier*.

"Rick, look," Hannah said, pointing to a sign on an easel just inside one of the the the tea room's display windows. "Isn't that amazing?"

"I can't believe it." Rick leaned close to read. The owner had gotten his start, of all places, in 1850s Sacramento, California! *(*Endnotes #5)*

"I wish I had some appetite left," Hannah said. "Looks yummy."

He took her hand. "Tell you what. Let's just step inside and smell the chocolate."

"What a great idea. Low-calorie pastries."

They stepped through the elegant wood and glass swinging doors and entered into an atmosphere that smelled of coffees, chocolates, pastries, and fillings.

"*Oh-my-gawd*," Hannah said. "Let's get out of here before I gain twenty pounds from just smelling the air."

They started their walk back down to the Rue de Notre Dame.

Over an hour had passed.

Rick stopped into a little corner shop and bought a burner phone. He bought Hannah a small cloth flower and pinned it on her jacket lapel while she stood beaming.

Arm in arm, they sauntered across the Place Guillaume.

"Let's sit for a few minutes, just you and me," she said. She pulled him to a bench in the shade of a small, leafy tree near some vegetable sellers.

He obliged, and sat with her. He hovered by her side, facing her while she sat with her hands folded in her lap. He put his arm around her back, and laid his free hand over hers. "Any regrets?"

"Not a bit." She looked at him frankly. "You?"

He shook his head. "We're having a crush."

She said with some certainty, "I'd know a crush when I feel it. I've had crushes before."

"Yeah, I know. Me too. This is love, I think. Are you scared?"

"Uh-uh." She shook her head. "I have nothing to lose. You have nothing to lose. We have nothing. Just each other. And—."

"Yes?"

"When we were together last night, I felt good inside for the first time in a long time. I felt all dark and angry until I was with you on the train. I already started feeling this balmy, goofy warm..." She ran out of words and looked into his eyes questioningly, to see if he knew.

He gave her hands a squeeze, feeling a certain luxury of time and place. The minutes and seconds were moving more slowly, as on a watch dipped in honey, whose works slowed down. It was a time warp, a love warp, an emotional playground within a fence that kept the world out.

He said, "I am filled with smoke and explosions and screaming and bloody things to look at. I don't remember everything. I took a hit in the head. Lucky I was wearing a helmet. I woke up with two U.S. Army MPs giving me CPR on the side of the road. Pitch black. Panic. I tried to sit up, ask about my squad, but they shook their heads. All dead. I was the only survivor. They want to string me up in K-Town, cover it up, send me to Fort Leavenworth busted to buck nobody for fifty years, but I am innocent. I'm sure I am. I just don't know that I am. I mean, I don't know how. But that's not my style. Someone sent us there that shouldn't have, and they are covering it up."

She patted his hands. "See, we need each other, Mr. Buchan. Rick. I don't think of you as Mr. Army or Mr. Soldier or Sergeant Buchan. I think of you as a handsome, nice man I'd like to lie on a towel with on a sunny day in Monterey or Half Moon Bay, and just watch the Pacific Ocean curling quietly on the warm California sand."

"You left out the palm trees." He smiled.

"Who thinks about palm trees when you've always lived there? That's for tourists."

"Let's be tourists there."

"No, let's live there."

"You mean that, Hannah? You and me?"

She nodded fervently.

He said, "You are the dream of my life now. Only—"

"I know. Kaiserslautern. It's not only, Richard. I am with you. Whatever happens, wherever you go, there I will be beside you."

"And we only just met."

"It seems like ages."

"I know." It was wonderful. He sighed. "I have someone there who says she is working to help me. Nice lady. JAG officer named Kendra Walsh. Major Walsh. I think she is an honest, brainy woman who cannot stand to see a good guy get the shaft to help a rotten apple."

"That's an equation I can agree with," Hannah said. "Thank you for last night." She embraced him tightly, squeezing the breath out of him. "Thank you, baby. I'll never forget you and Belair."

"Why talk about forgetting?" He teased, "Want to lose *us* so soon?"

She shook her head. There was a distant something on the horizon in her eyes. "You have Kaiserslautern. I have PAX."

"Yeah, we'll handle that together. I'll be with you all the way."

"That's so nice, for a change. Oh god I need you." She bobbed impatiently to her feet, changing the conversation. "Come on, my prince. Let's saunter. Destiny awaits."

"Isn't that a laundry detergent?" He rose, gently patting her butt.

"Skin cream," she said over her shoulder with a pert squint.

The air was filled with the tinkling of the cathedral's chimes, wafting their delicate way through a melody of sacred music.

They walked hand in hand to the mossy stone stairway, with its greenish balustrade, that overlooked the Rue de Notre Dame about twenty feet below.

They stopped for a moment, leaning on the stone bannister. They looked down toward the cathedral entrance across the street, and to see if Romain's car had perchance cruised to a stop at the curb there.

Rick was just about to gaze over the tiny square, hemmed in by buildings, that led from the street to the main cathedral entrance. His eyes had not yet focused when she jabbed him sharply in the ribs with her elbow.

"No." Hannah pulled on his sleeve. "Stop."

"What?"

She was pale as if she'd seen a ghost and come away even more drained of blood. Her mouth hung open in distress.

Rick saw immediately what she meant. Standing near the curb was Savia, the Cuban woman in Wan's employ—the female killer from behind the *Bar-39* in Bagnolet, Paris.

Rick and Hannah whirled and walked quickly from the balustrade back into the square. Sacred music continued tinkling around them like ice in a glass. "Do you think she saw us?"

"I'm not sure," Hannah said, "but does it matter?"

Rick nodded darkly. "If she's here, that means they're actively hunting us and the package that Wan wants at any cost. Yoichi can't be far, and Wan is probably in the city by now also."

Just then, Hannah's phone chirped.

"It's Romain," she whispered to Rick. Then, into the phone, "Are you coming?"

Romain said something.

"No," Hannah said, "swing around and we'll meet you at the other end. I see one of Wan's people in front of the cathedral."

She rang off, took Rick's elbow, and pulled him along. "We're supposed to meet Romain on the Boulevard Royal. That's going to be a snappy ten minute walk. We need to get to Echternach and finish this before Wan finishes us, and it, and everything."

Rick sighed as she towed him along. "I guess the tour is over."

"Back to business," she said with a shudder of dread in her voice.

30.   On The Run Again

On the run again, Rick and Hannah hurried across the square, among the outdoor cafes and umbrellas, past the official Luxembourg Tourist Office, and into a very old, ornately formed sandstone gallery that formed a passageway between the square and the next street up—Rue du Curé, where they had walked earlier.

The ornate, brightly lit shops on either side of the gallery were tempting, but their hearts were pounding as they hurried. They did not want to go too fast, for fear of attracting attention.

They emerged in the pedestrian street facing an old, ornate government building.

"Looks familiar," she said.

"We were just here. There's the Place d'Armes again."

This was a smaller square than the Guillaume, also with umbrellas and chairs for outdoor lounging, people watching over coffee or beer with a little something sweet for the palate.

The pedestrian zone continued through colorful, fun shopping blocks under the name Avenue Monterey. This narrow venue was jammed with people and stores of all types, for several blocks, emerging finally on the Boulevard Royal.

There was Romain in the white Audi, waiting for them with the engine running. He looked nervous, being illegally parked with two wheels up on the curb at the intersecting Rue Aldringen. They were at a large bus *rondel* opening from the pedestrian zone of the *Haute-Ville* (Upper City) onto the Boulevard Royal. Avenue Monterey changed from pedestrian zone to traffic across the road, but it was one-way coming toward them.

"Did they see you?" were Romain's first words as they jumped in— Hannah in front as before, Rick in the rear with his pack.

"Maybe not," Hannah said.

Romain steered into the intersection, left on the Boulevard Royal, and right along the Petrusse Valley frontage road in the direction of Belair.

"It was the woman, Savia," Rick explained.

"Where there is one, there will be others," Romain said grimly.

Minutes later, they pulled a bit too fast into his street and into the driveway.

Mélu was shocked at the news. She had a small green backpack ready for Hannah. Inside were their freshly laundered clothes, plus a few snack items in plastic bags.

Romain said, "We'll leave immediately."

Mélu had been busy. She handed over two small paper folders with the logo of Luxair on them. "Your Luxair tickets for when you are ready to fly home to the U.S.A. In the meantime—"

"—In the meantime," Romain said, "I will gladly drive you to Kaiserslautern when it's done."

"Oh my god, that's so out of your way," Rick said.

Romain said, "It's a two hour drive from Echternach into the Rhineland-Palatinate on a good German *Autobahn*. The Prussians invented them, right? That's what old-timers here call the Germans, not so fondly. We're all pretty much over it now—too many new problems. I'll gladly take you, as thanks for helping us. But let's get this done, yes?"

Mélu said, "I spoke with Professor Sander. He will meet you near the post office in Echternach. You sent the package by general delivery, right?"

"Yes," Hannah said. "I didn't have his address."

"This is him, my old professor at Uni Lux." Mélu showed them a picture of an aging but strong looking man with round, horn-rimmed glasses. "He looks like a distinguished author from the 1930s."

Rick examined the photo, which appeared to be a snapshot from a long-ago university picnic. Sander was bald on top, with longish white hair around the ears and down to his collar. He had a reddish, beaky face with a long nose; prominent eyebrows over deeply set, brooding eyes.

Mélu looked bitter. "The man who harmed you, Hannah, stole the fuselage secret from the Professor's son in London, Pierre Sander, and they murdered him to prevent duplication of the secrets."

Hannah looked pained, thinking of what Wan had done to her—and might yet do if he caught her.

Rick studied the photo. This man had lost his only son so terribly and senselessly. It was no surprise he did not look like a happy man. His thin lips had a pained expression, again no surprise; he probably had much to think about at night. How well Rick understood.

31. Arrive in Echternach

On the way to Echternach, Hannah and Rick got something of a breather—they could do nothing but sit, and wait, as Romain drove toward Luxembourg's oldest city—Echternach, over 1,400 years old, and dating to the chaos of the early European Middle Ages just after the fall of the Western half of the ancient Roman empire.

Hannah asked, "I'm curious about two things."

Romain grinned. "I know what they are. Everyone who comes here has the same two questions, and then a million others, but the first two answer most of them."

Hannah said, "Okay. Fair enough. Why is there an independent country as tiny as Luxembourg? Why a grand duke?"... *(*Endnotes #6)*

..."Like put up your dukes," Rick said.

"That's a nice joke," Romain said. "Actually, that expression comes from the guy who wrote the rules for modern boxing, the Marquess of Queensbury, who was a duke."

Hannah sighed. "As if we need more conflict."

The car interior became silent for a time.

Romain drove fast on the road from Luxembourg City toward the Luxemburgish city of Echternach on the German border. They drove in a northeasterly direction mostly on the E29 (European Highway 29) approaching Echternach in about half an hour.

Romain wore a black leather jacket, like a motorcyclist's, over a button down shirt with small greenish stripes; dark slacks; and black loafers. He looked a bit as if he'd dressed for work, but gotten diverted by a motorcycle club. His thick waves of black, shiny hair accentuated his youthful good looks, complete with pale visage and sprinkled beard shadow.

Rick and Hannah looked punkish but clean, thanks to Mélu's laundry efforts.

Just out of Luxembourg City, they drove past the international airport of Findel on the northeast outskirts of Luxembourg. Romain explained proudly and somewhat emotionally that, at the Luxembourg American Cemetery and Memorial near Findel, thousands of U.S. soldiers of the Third U.S. Army from World War II lay buried including their wartime leader, General George S. Patton. The grateful nation of Luxembourg in

1951 dedicated the fifty acres in the cemetery to the United States for perpetuity—in effect making it practically a part of the United States, administered by the U.S. Battle Monuments Commission in Arlington, Virginia. "So you see," Romain said, "your country and my country are very special friends and always will be, no matter what happens in the world." He pointed off to the horizon. "There, in Sandweiler, are buried over ten thousand German soldiers from the same war, who died all over Luxembourg during the Bulge and other battles. Their bodies were respectfully brought here and interred."

"You know how to make peace," Rick said.

"We live next door to them," Romain said. "Many of us have German ancestry as well as French and Belgian, and Mediterranean. We are one of the world's most diverse nations."

"Can't be much more diverse than Paris," Hannah remarked. Her sharp tone drew glances—of quiet understanding.

Walking wounded every generation, Rick thought to himself.

"You'll see a lot of German sounding place names as we get near the border," Romain said.

Past Findel airport, they drove through a mix of quaint little nestling villages, meadows with leisurely grazing cows, and dense green forest.

Rick and Hannah read the rectangular white signs that flew past: Graulinster, Wolper...

"What is Geyershaff?" Hannah asked with idle curiosity.

Romain grinned. "A *Geier* in German is a vulture. A Haff in Luxemburgish is the same as the German Hof, which can mean a lot of things, from a noble court (*cour*) to a farm yard. So literally it means Vulture's Yard or Vulture's Court."

"You're kidding," Rick said (a question).

"Well," Romain said with a laugh, "there was probably some Prussian sounding baron or something named Geyer, and that was the family seat." He waved his free arm about. "Look at the fields and the cows. Aside from trees and little villages, that is really what my country is all about. More cows than people."

He added, "It's not a superhighway like in the States or other big countries. It's more like a wide country road in Germany or Belgium." The road was in some places just two lanes across, marked like a small highway, and in other places wider depending on local traffic.

They flew past trucks, buses, passenger cars, and the occasional red-white-blue patrol car of the Grand-Ducal Police. Some of the cops were women, like in Germany or elsewhere, Rick noted—often athletic, pretty, with a standard pony tail hanging from a jaunty royal-blue uniform hat not unlike a U.S. baseball cap.

Within a short time, Romain began slowing as traffic grew heavier. "We're almost in Echternach."

"That was quick."

"We just crossed about a fifth of the nation," Romain said.

Hannah shook her head. "That's almost like going shopping back in the U.S."

Romain shrugged. "You have a saying. Good things come in small packages, *n'est ce pas*?" Like all Luxembourgers, he frequently mixed French and German words into the local *patois*. They said *Gudde Muergen* (Good Morning) almost like Germans or Flemish, but *Bon Soir* (Good Evening) in almost perfect French accents. Alternatively for Good Evening, you could just as well say *Gudden Owend*, similar to the German *Guten Abend*.

"Size is not everything," Hannah agreed with a very pretty blue-eyed smile, still with oxblood raggedy hair and slash chocolate punk lipstick.

Rick thought maybe he'd get used to her look and even grow his own hair long—once he got the Army out of his hair, so to speak. They could be retro hippies—or maybe flippies (with the dolphins)—together at the Monterey Aquarium by the Pacific Ocean in California. That all seemed a long way off.

They were now driving through neat little neighborhoods on the outskirts of Echternach. Along either side of the painstakingly marked, two-lane Route de Luxembourg were the same sorts of perfect little white or gray stuccoed doll houses that one found in Lorraine and in Belgium. The typical house here had a bluish-gray slate roof with a steep pitch to repel rain or snow in season.

"I have to warn you," Romain said. "It's June, and we are here just in time for the famous dancing procession." He explained, "Echternach is a famous pilgrimage town with a great abbey and church. *(*Endnotes #7)* They make their way, jumping together while holding white handkerchiefs between them, to the abbey church for a Mass, as if they were being cured of St. Vitus' Dance by Saint Willibrord. That is basically the story, and we are just in time to get stuck in traffic as the downtown area gets shut down for hours."

"Oh great," Rick said.

"I love it when you are so sarcastic," Hannah said, pecking a kiss on his cheek. "And when you say things that are supposed to be a question but it's a sarcastic statement."

"Like now," Rick said. "You know where we are going."

"Right?" She laughed, imitating him. She stuck her arm through his and gave him an affectionate yank.

He responded with a squeeze and a weird face that made her laugh. Then he kissed her by the ear.

"I know basically my way," Romain said with a toss of his long, wavy hair. Sometimes his accent was more pronounced than at other times. "Oops, there we are. It is late in the day, and it should be coming to a close, but I think there are many thousands of pilgrims this year so it's running late into the afternoon."

Ahead was a barrier, staffed by several Grand Ducal police in white kepis, orange vests, and dark blue uniforms. They were armed like any cop in the United States, including holstered automatic sidearm on a black belt, plus handcuffs, spare rounds, and other equipment. Most wore a small communications device on their shoulder, close to the mouth for ease of access in an emergency. Several police cars with flashing red, blue, and white lights were parked in the way as well. A cute, tall brunette policewoman in leather jacket stepped forth on long legs clad in black motorcycle boots and riding trousers, to waggle a finger at them and point toward a parking area off to one side.

"We're stuck," Romain said. "Rather than get a ticket or be detained, let me just park this thing and we'll walk. It's not a very big city—just 5,000 people normally; now probably 15,000 with all the pilgrims."

Romain drove slowly in a tortuous row of cars, into a crowded parking lot near the River Sauer (Sûre). Straggling, uniformed band members with instruments sauntered past, as did nuns, priests, and other participants. Some carried signs to show their origins in Belgium, France, and Germany as well as Luxemburgish towns. Rick noticed names like Trier in Germany, Bastogne in Belgium, Thionville where they had been in France, and Gasperech in Luxembourg.

The music was played by dozens of marching bands from all over— always the same sort of jiggy, jumpy tune that repeated itself endlessly. They stood at the steel police barricades for a few moments and watched as hundreds and hundreds of pilgrims came jumping by. They held white handkerchiefs between them as they hopped from side to side in a rhythmic swaying motion to the music.

"Here begins also the Müllertal, or the Little Switzerland," Romain said. "There are some Roman ruins and a great Museum of Prehistory. Stone Age people lived here thousands of years ago during the last Ice Age. This is actually the oldest city in Luxembourg, predating Luxembourg City by several centuries. Like much of the region it was damaged in many wars, like Napoleon's in the early 1800s, and almost destroyed by the Germans during the Battle of the Bulge, but always rebuilt on the old model. We also just missed the well-known Echternach Music Festival, which every year features jazz and classical stars in the main square. And this is not too far from Trier across the border in Germany, which was a capital city of the Roman Empire—*Augusta Treverorum*. This whole area was a key part of the Roman Empire, and it has been a crossroad of civilization for a long time."

Hannah asked, "And why exactly is this called Little Switzerland?"

Romain shrugged. "A little bit of tourist marketing. Müllertal actually means Millers' Valley, probably because of the rapids on which they could use water wheels to grind corn; what you in English call maize? Or wheat I think? We don't have high mountains like the Swiss, just little ones. But you go climbing around there, up and down steep hills and terraces in the woods, and you must be a solid, experienced hiker or you'll be worn out in no time. The scenery is first-rate, with lots of steep cliffs and dark forests. It is actually a bit like hiking in the high Swiss meadows. For example, there is the Gorge du Loup, or Wolf Gorge, which is dark and mysterious. There used to be wolves around here over a century ago, by the way. Then there is the *Schiessentümpel*, or Shooting Pond, with a small triple waterfall shooting down amid dense green forest—and lots of interesting old castle ruins."

"Wow, so fascinating," Hannah said. "Where is the post office?"

Romain walked over to consult with the police, and returned in a few moments. "Right in the middle of town, I am afraid, on the Rue du Marché, or Market Street. It is closed until at least two in the afternoon."

"We should try Professor Sander's house," Hannah suggested.

"Good idea," Romain said.

★ ★ ★ ▮ ▮ ▬ ▮ ▮ ▬ ▒▒ ★ ★ ★

They walked a brisk, pleasant twenty minutes from town toward a large lake surrounded by trees and villas. A few fishermen stood on the shore, under umbrellas, with poles out over the water. Little sailboats cruised back and forth on the blue water. It was a sunny, pleasant day. Rick and Hannah held hands. She whispered in his ear, "One day, we can come here and relax and enjoy all this."

He gave her hand a tug. "If I can be alone with you anywhere, I'll relax and enjoy myself."

"Ice cream," she said secretively with a very naughty look.

He tugged her hand in return.

Romain got the address from neighbors as they strolled past the lake. Following a long road further south, they came to a miniature castle of sorts—a gray bastion of concrete and stucco, shaped into turrets and ramparts with the typical black slate roofing.

"It's a little mansion," Hannah said. "Look, there are rose gardens all around." She waved to an elderly woman who was tending the gardens, wearing a babushka and black-and-white cotton dress. "Bonjour!"

"Bonjour," the woman replied. She had sun-reddened skin on her face and arms as she held a cutting instrument in one hand and a sheaf of grass and weeds in the other.

Romain spoke with her in Luxemburgish, then to his companions. "She says the Professor went into town earlier today for some shopping and errands, including something waiting for him at the post office."

"Now what?" Rick said.

The woman waved energetically for them to go into the house. When they appeared hesitant, not wanting to intrude, she waved all the more.

"She suggests we get some coffee in the kitchen and come sit a while to rest."

"We could take a quick peek inside," Hannah said. "I want to make absolutely sure he doesn't have the package on this kitchen table or something. Then we'll hustle back to town. I'm getting an uneasy feeling."

"Yeah, I'd hate to see the Cuban woman again, much less Wan himself," Rick said.

"Or Yoichi," Hannah said. "He's the martial arts guy who breaks people's necks with his bare hands."

They stepped into the picturesque little house, which was more of a cottage inside. "He lives alone," Romain said. "He is a widower, and now his only son is dead. Poor man."

"So he'd have nothing to lose in this McGuffin matter," Rick said. "I hate to do this."

"Go on," Hannah said.

Romain nodded in agreement, "We must track down the package before Wan's people do."

"Okay." Feeling intrusive and creepy, Rick stepped into the Professor's little study. It was a cozy little room, walled in with books, and illumined by a partially leaded glass, partially stained glass window (almost a miniature of the famous stained glass in the Gare in Luxembourg City).

"Look here." He saw it immediately, on top of piled papers and manuscripts stacked on Sander' huge wooden desk with glass top. He held up a yellow slip. "It's a notice from the post office. There is a package waiting for him."

"Do you think he knows?" Hannah said. She examined the small rectangular form, but could not make sense of the scrawled penmanship of some clerk.

"The housekeeper says he is out on errands, and she mentioned stopping at the post office in Echternach," Romain said. "It must be his daily walk—maybe his routine. Whether he knows about the notice or not, he'll stop in the post office when it opens, and they'll tell him the package is there."

"Makes sense," Rick said. "It would only take a day to get there, direct from the post office at the Gare to the post office thirty minutes away in Echternach."

Romain shouted, "Come on! Let's go." He dashed out the door, followed by Hannah and Rick.

They ignored the housekeeper's pleasant, innocently puzzled question from where she waved in the rose garden.

The three jogged along the lake road, then took the Route des Romains (Roman Road), into the city. In all, it was about a kilometer, and left them puffing for air despite being in good shape.

32.   Dancing Procession

The sound of marching bands grew louder, always repeating that same hypnotic melody—combination jig, anthem, and hymn.

Romain, an athlete, almost laughed if it weren't so serious. "It's not so much I am out of shape—it was so unexpected to have to suddenly run like that."

For a moment, Rick and Hannah stood doubled over with their hands on the knees, huffing.

"Come on," she said, and hurried on ahead.

Dozens of bands played the hypnotic music like a St. Vitus Dance. The narrow streets were clogged with thousands of pilgrims of all ages, races, genders, and nationalities. The babble of languages among crowds of watchers was indeed as diverse as anything Rick had ever heard all in one small place. People hung from windows with folded arms, watching. They leaned over balconies, crowded together. A few people threw confetti that twirled in colorful dots like snow.

The legion of pilgrims kept coming around the corners from the river bridge—hopping, holding white hankies between them, rocking from side to side.

The din was almost overwhelming, as was the sheer atmosphere of so many people jammed into the narrow streets and small cobblestone squares on the way to the great monastery and basilica dating originally to the early European Middle Ages, just after the collapse of the Western Roman Empire.

Romain told his two visitors much local history in bits and snatches on their drive to Echternach, and on their walk to and from the Professor's house on the lake just beyond the city's long ago tumbled medieval fortress walls from another age. *(Endnotes #8)*

The police of the Grand Duchy had cordoned off the center of Echternach for the annual springing or jumping procession. Coming from any direction, one had to cross through steel barricades staffed by white-kepi police in orange vests and blue uniforms. One saw many police cars with slowly—almost festively or even respectfully—flashing dome lights. There were also police Land Rovers as well as motorcycles, whose riders wore riding pants tucked into black boots.

Romain, Rick, and Hannah pushed into the crowds.

Up and down, left and right, swayed the pilgrims with their white handkerchiefs, while that obsessive music played on and on, over and over again.

It was that type of music German psychologists had long ago dubbed *Ohrwurm* (ear worm) because it was a type of melody that got into your brain and stayed there, playing itself over and over again.

Rick almost wanted to hold his ears. The sound obsessively echoed and re-echoed in every alley, every street, pumped out by tubas, drums, trumpets, all the brass and percussion of a U.S. football game halftime performance. There must be at least a thousand musicians walking or hopping around, including violinists, accordionists, and children with kazoos. It was maddening, but that was the intended hypnosis for which the pilgrims metaphorically sought a cure inside the basilica of St. Willibrord.

Romain gesticulated. He was speaking, but his words were drowned out.

Rick, trying to listen to Romain, was jostled by dancers.

For a while, Rick managed to keep a hold on Hannah's hand, until they had to separate and duck down low as dancers swept over them—one row after another.

Romain waved and pointed wildly. "I have seen the Professor down the street." Rick could easily make out the slow, deliberately formed words.

Romain took off running. He disappeared into the crowd, almost vaulting over the shoulders of spectators and passing dancers alike.

In the deafening din, he turned and found that Hannah had disappeared.

He took a few hesitant steps, thinking he would locate her easily—but there was no sign of her.

Rick's heart began to beat faster, and his chest contracted in terror. He had a sudden, terrifying, ominous premonition that it was the last time he'd see her. But it wasn't—not quite.

Starting to panic, Rick pushed his way into the Place des Marchés. He found the post office around a corner—a smallish store front with the Luxembourg flag over the doorway. This little post office was set a meter or so above street level. Surrounded by telephone booths sporting a picture of a green receiver on a yellow background was a stairway up to a landing with a metal railing on the outside. The post office called attention to itself by a standard yellow metal sign with a post-horn on it, and the letters P & T which could be deciphered as meaning Post and Telephone. There were four windows and a glass door.

As Rick approached, pushing and ducking his way among pilgrims, the next events happened all at once. Romain was nowhere to be seen—

probably looking for Professor Sander elsewhere, maybe in the adjacent triangular market square.

The smallish door was an electronic slider, meaning it had no handle. To its left was an ATM with night lighting above. It all seemed cramped and small, like everything else in this country. The man half lying, half sitting in the half-open doorway could only be Professor Sander. Blood streamed from a wound not quite on top of his head.

His bald head, surrounded by a wild gauze of white, wavy cotton-like hair, was unmistakable as was his tanned, long face with prominent nose and piercing dark eyes. His expression was shocked, dazed, and pleading.

Already, shocked bystanders began to shout and scream.

He sort of half sat, half lay toward his left side, propping himself on his left hand, and raising his right hand defensively.

Hovering over him was Hannah, taking the package—Rick recognized it from the post office in Luxembourg City.

Rick froze, unable to make sense of what he saw.

Hannah saw him. Her eyes were wide—like those of an animal caught in the headlights on a country road at night. She shook her head several times—side to side—a vision of her that Rick would carry in his mind forever. Denial. But of what? Of the fact that she was grabbing the package, and Sander lay bloody at her feet? Or of the apparent fact that she had attacked him? Nothing made sense.

Rick raised his arms as if to welcome her to him. They would run together.

But she shook her head, no, with terrified eyes, while in that half-crouched position above the pleading man. He still had his hand upraised and was saying something.

"Hannah!" Rick shouted.

She looked left, right, like a hunted animal at a crouch—then bolted.

She swung over the railing, down onto the cobblestone ground, and ducked through a row of telephone booths.

A man stepped in the way, on the street, to intercept her, but she palmed him in the face. He went down backward, sitting as Sander was on the landing. Hannah ran like a startled deer, with the package in hand, and vanished down the narrow cobblestone alley beside the post office. Rick ran after her, but stopped when he saw that the alley bent into another alley—it would be folly to try and run after her. Already a crowd congealed around him at the post office steps.

Two uniformed clerks came out to help Sander to his feet. A policewoman came running with a metal first aid box. They took the Professor into the post office. As Rick bolted up the stairs, someone locked the door in his face. A sign turned from *Ouvert* to *Fermé*.

Stunned, Rick held the railing as he stumbled down the stairs. His entire world had just turned upside down. What the hell was going on? He had the sickening gut-punch realization that nothing was going to be the same after this. He'd been living in a fool's paradise. Nothing was ever as it seemed.

His head began swimming, as if he were drunk. He needed his medicine, but that was in the backpack in the car—and he could not find it in this murky condition, much less walk there.

He staggered—not the only one who looked drunk on the periphery of the noisy, laughing, singing crowd amid that crazy music—from corner to corner, seeking a place to sit down. People made way for him, perhaps afraid he was a drunk who might puke on them or become violent.

When he gained some semblance of consciousness, it was Romain who slapped his face and shook him by the shoulders. "Rick! I have your medicine here. But where is Hannah? What happened?"

Rick swayed as he sat on the lower steps of a small monument in the Market Square. The monument was the Justice Cross, made of stone, on top of a column about four meters high.

A police SUV with flashing lights slowly made its way past, through the crowds, and around the corner to the post office. It was followed by a yellowish ambulance van with fire department markings, also with flashing emergency lights.

People paraded all around, waving banners and blowing horns. A kind woman passing by offered a plastic water bottle, for which Romain thanked her and held out two Euros, but the woman shook her head and melted into the crowd.

"Here," Romain said, "drink this and wash your pills down."

With shaky fingers, Rick fumbled through the pill bottles—nearly dropping them—but he got the required prescription into his mouth, and washed it down with water. "Is the Professor okay?"

"What do you mean?"

Rick described what happened. Romain's face grew ashen. "Stay here," he said and darted away to take a look by the post office, around the corner on the Rue de Luxembourg.

Rick sat with his head down, grieving. He thought of Hannah, and wondered what had just happened. Was she a victim somehow, or was she a perpetrator?

When his head began to clear, Rick rose and walked to the post office. He found the two emergency vehicles blocking the entrance, and the Closed sign still on the door. Romain stood at the foot of the steps with a grim look, telephoning—probably Mélu in Luxembourg City.

Just then, emergency medical technicians in yellow slickers descended from the post office, carrying a stretcher. Rick recognized the wave of white hair peering from under a sheet, along with a mass of white bandages smeared red.

"*Il reste en vie,*" a woman doctor in a white jacket and businesslike skirt with sensible brown loafers said in a tone of authority, while twirling a stethoscope. "He is alive." She added in French, "It is a trauma to the head, requiring emergency care and observation."

On the landing above, the post office sign flipped again, from closed to open.

Within a minute or two, the ambulance pulled away, guided by the police cruiser. Their top lights twirled, and several times—because of the crowds both passing and rubbernecking—the drivers had to activate their piercing *tah-too, tah-too* Martin's Horn sirens that echoed among the tightly spaced buildings.

Romain regarded Rick with a dazed, furious look. "What has happened?"

Rick shook his head. "No sign of Savia and Yoichi.

"Something happened—did she hit Sander over the head?"

"I have no idea," Rick said sadly.

Romain got in his face. Rick understood the rage. "Did you know?"

Rick shook his head. He could sympathize with the other man's confusion and anger.

"So she didn't say anything to you?"

"Not a hint. I can't believe it."

"It seems impossible—but she could be playing both sides. In this game, you never know who betrays his best friend, his wife, his boss. Her boss. Whatever."

"Let's keep our cool."

"They are taking Sander to a local hospital," Romain said. "There is nothing we can do then." He gripped Rick's arm with sudden sympathy. He looked devastated, mirroring Rick's feelings. Dispiritedly, they walked rapidly to the river, on the other side of the small city, to the car.

The dancing was over. Hundreds of pilgrims were at a Mass in the Basilica. The streets were thinning out of crowds. Police were already dismantling some barriers—in preparation to evacuating the thousands who had parked their cars and now hoped to get off the crowded roads around Echternach on their way home to all points of the compass. People were streaming out of the city—on foot, in buses, in cars.

"Mélu trusted Hannah," Romain said. "She counted on Hannah to help us get the package and get it to the professor—not knock him over the head and run away with the package."

Rick kept playing his last sight of her over and over again in his head, like that ear-worm music that would not stop tormenting a person. He kept studying her face in his memory—shaking her head, telling him *No* but about what? Did she mean *it's not what you think* or did she mean *I'm sorry but I must betray you* or simply *don't follow—save yourself—our lives are in danger*?

They got in the car, which Romain was easily able to maneuver out of the parking lot. Without speaking much, they rolled slowly in traffic. It was still bright daylight, though late in the afternoon. Police patrols directed the cars on to smooth passage at every corner.

As they came to the area around the lake, Romain's telephone warbled. He raised it to his ear. "*Jo, Mélu, jo...*" Romain spoke briefly and put the phone away. "That was Mélu calling from Luxembourg City. Our organization reports a sighting of Savia and Yoichi going into the Müllertal. We may have something to go on."

"The organization?"

"PAX."

"Oh yeah." He felt numb, and had nearly forgotten in the fog of hurt. He convinced himself right then, and there, that she was doing the right thing, whatever it was, and he must trust her completely.

As Romain maneuvered the steering wheel laboriously among slowly moving cars to change directions, Rick asked, "Like what?"

"Hopefully, they are chasing Hannah. If so, we'll chase them. A bit obvious and brutal—no longer subtle—but we have nothing to lose."

The phone warbled again and Romain picked up. "*Jo?*" He listened for a minute and said, "*D'accord.*" Then he told Rick, "We have people following Savia and Yoichi. They are heading very fast into the Müllertal near Bersdorf. We'll follow and hope to catch Hannah before they do."

Romain drove a short distance back along the E29 on whose four lanes they had come from Luxembourg City earlier in the day. Soon, however, he swung north onto a smaller country road, marked CR118. This was a narrow, two-lane street running among tall trees. The foliage was a mix of conifers and deciduous, fully in lush, early summer foliage. A gentle mist hung among the tree crowns. Dreamy sunlight full of this mix of dust and fog hung over the road wherever sunlight could stab downward among the trees.

"We are in the Little Switzerland or Mill Valley," Romain told him in a frosty manner. This is one of those areas in the country that has castles and beautiful greenery in a wild setting. There is another area like it in the center and west of the country, called the Valley of Seven Castles. Maybe if we get through all this you will visit there."

"I'd love to," Rick said. "If you think you and Mélu feel bad about this thing with Hannah, you can't imagine how I feel. I have a crater inside."

Romain relented. "*D'accord*—I believe you. You look honestly destroyed. I'm sorry."

"Thanks. I'm sorry about everything in the universe. I'd like for my mind to just go blank and forget everything that happened in the last year or two. I'd love to be sitting in some nameless little tavern in a small town in California, wearing a cowboy hat and slouched over a beer listening to the jukebox and watching clouds go by outside the window. I am so sick and tired of the Army, of Europe, of conspiracies and pissed-off people—I could puke in my hat if I had one."

"Maybe I'll buy you that beer in a small tavern in some nameless little hook in the road in the Ardennes forest."

"With my luck," Rick groused, "the Battle of the Bulge would start up again—that's how crappy my luck has been."

"There is still hope," Romain said. "It looks like Savia & Co don't have the gadget (yet). It looks like Hannah is still alive and running on those long, beautiful legs. We don't know if she is a traitor or just a girl trying to do the right thing the hard way, which seems to be how she does everything in life anyway."

"Yeah, well, her mother's cancer wasn't her fault."

"No, but you stupid people over there should have universal health care like the rest of the world. What is the matter with you? You can never learn from anyone? You have to reinvent the wheel because you are too superior to listen to a hundred other countries that have better living standards and certainly more humane health care? You can afford it—just don't let the middlemen steal trillions of dollars in fake insurance fees. If you stood up to the corporations, they would not have sold your country out to China and India, not to mention Europe and anyone else who would buy. Your young people would not be selling themselves on slave labor contracts like Hannah did."

"Thanks for the lecture. Can we go now?"

"Sorry, I am driving as fast as I can. There are over 100 kilometers of little scenic roads like this deep in these magic forests. It's a bit like your Northwest—I have seen pictures of the Olympic Peninsula, which is however more flat, I think."

"In parts," Rick allowed. Nice of Romain to say a kind word about the land of the free—or the land of the fee, whichever shoe fit better.

Their journey took them on endlessly winding twists and turns through pine forest and beech and other deciduous trees. Here and there, one saw a little waterfall deep in the forest.

"Looks like magic," Rick said.

"The old people believed in magic," Romain said. "You have to imagine Paleolithic hunters here, chasing after animals that became extinct ten or fifteen thousand years ago, right here in these hills and valleys. We have caves from that time, like the Hohlay cavern. I always think how amazing that people like us walked here eons ago, thinking about life and death."

Rick added, "And probably they were pissed off that the wealthy cave owners controlled the traffic in flint stones and spear tips."

"Nothing ever changes."

The phone warbled, and Romain spoke softly, so that Rick did not quite hear. He said, "That was Mélu. She is in Belair, but tracking with our people up here in the Müllertal. Hannah was sighted in Consdorf, driving a stolen BMW into the direction where we are headed. She is being pursued by Savia and Yoichi in a maroon Mercedes, so we are all going to have a nice reunion soon."

"Amazing," Rick said bitterly. "I believed her. I didn't know she had any of it in her."

Romain said, "*Emmer mat Gedold, Jengelchen* (Patience at all times, little guy). We don't know who stole the car. But the license plate is of a German car missing since yesterday in Trier."

"Well then she didn't steal the damn thing, because we were in Belair."

"Right. So keep your pants on."

"You mean, keep my shirt on. The pants was yesterday." He was thinking of his passionate night with Hannah.

"You people invented the blue jeans. The rest of us put our pants on one pocket at a time."

"One leg, you Luxemburger Wurst."

"You mean Luxemburger Wort, our national newspaper, in German; in English the Luxemburgish Word." Romain added, "We have to be careful now. Stop telling jokes or I may drive into a tree from laughing too hard."

They came within sight of a small settlement—the usual neat, tidy little houses on a street that looked as if someone with an anal fixation had painted it with crayons and a ruler while biting the tip of his tongue. This stretch of CR118, called Route d'Echternach, was unmarked through the settlement, and looked suspiciously like a single lane but well-paved as if made from concrete.

"You can see some old farms that have been converted to modern use, like a pension."

"You mean bed and breakfast."

They cruised on through Larochette toward Consdorf. The double lanes in white markings resumed. In many places, the forest gave way to open fields—many of them closely shorn with tractor-drawn hair trimmers by some crazed neatnik. The next sign indicated a crossroads coming up— Berdorf to the right, Luxembourg City to the left, and Larochette straight ahead.

Romain reached under the seat and pulled out an automatic pistol in a blonde, clean holster. "I have two of them. Want one?"

Rick shook his head. "Tempting as it is, I don't want to get arrested on weapons charges here. I'm in enough trouble already. You got a license for that thing?"

Romain laughed. "Are you falling from a Christmas tree? This is more illegal in Luxembourg than you are. I just think it's a good idea right now, like in your nutty gun culture that makes the corporations wealthier while your children die by the thousands. You guys are really a nation of crazy people."

"We are just original," Rick said. "Stop the commentary and watch where you are driving."

Romain made a wry face and gripped the wheel with both hands. "Soon we may either be dead or we may have some answers. I am as tired of this McGuffin chasing as you are, Cowboy."

As they drove through a bend in the road, deep in a shadowy area in the forest, Rick saw a sight that almost made his heart stop.

He gripped Romain's right wrist, on the steering wheel, with his left hand. "Stop."

Romain made a perplexed sound but pulled over onto the soft shoulder, which was strewn with pine needles and leaves. The car was half on, half off the narrow road.

"Oh my god," they both said.

Off on their right was the white BMW in which Hannah had been seen by the PAX agents in the area. It could only be—the Trier license plates and the color gave it away.

Someone had driven the car off the road, leaving deep dark tracks in the soft forest floor. There was an air of desertion about the scene—water had already seeped into some of the tire gougings.

Rick tore open the door and ran as fast as he could. "Hannah!" he cried.

When he reached the white car—nothing.

She—or someone—had driven it about a hundred meters off the road, winding among slender tree trunks, until the car went nose-first into a small ditch in which a stream flowed. The front doors were both wide open and leaning toward the earth's center of gravity. Nobody was in the car. The inside was clean—no objects on the front or back seats, nor on the floor.

"No sign of violence or struggle," Romain said.

"But there were two people," Rick said. "Otherwise why would both doors be open?"

"And why run? Or whatever this is all about. She had the package with her—and it's not in the car." Romain searched the glove compartment—nothing. He popped the trunk, but found nothing except a spare wheel, and the standard tools for changing tires.

Rick searched around the car for footsteps. He found two sets of tracks. One was Hannah's, coming from the passenger side. He recognized her smaller, softer boots. The other was a man's large shoe size, with heavy sole tread like hiking boots.

Rick squatted down, recalling military field intelligence training. "Whoever he was, there was a man driving. The steps are even, so they were moving in tandem. They were moving fast, because the fronts of the feet are digging in—almost like a run."

"Run from what?" Romain asked, standing behind Rick. "Run toward what?"

"Wish I knew." Rick rose. "Look, we have to split up. I'm going after her. I need the backpack."

They walked back to the car. Rick shouldered the backpack, which contained the Euros he and Hannah had lifted from the dead Yolo's car near Verdun.

Romain handed him the pistol. "I think you'll need this more than I will."

"Thanks." Rick accepted the gun, holster and all, and dropped it into the backpack. "I'll have it if I need it." If he encountered police, he could always drop it by the wayside. The gun culture existed here, but not anywhere as strenuously as back home.

There was only one cellphone in the car, and he didn't suggest Romain give that up.

He shook hands with Romain. "Good luck."

Romain said, "I will drive forward to Larochette. That's on the CR118. I advise you to stay close to the road. Depending on what I find there, if anything, I'll slowly head back toward you."

"Good. Maybe we'll meet somewhere in between. My greatest hope is to have Hannah with me safe and sound."

Romain made a face. "I will keep an open mind about her. Meanwhile, my biggest hope is to have the package. I will keep in touch with PAX and see if they can meet me. We'll need all the help we can get." He handed Rick a plastic water bottle. "You'll need this. And this." He added a small white store sack with candy bars, nut bars, and a few packaged sweet rolls."

"Okay—*Eddi*." It was a Luxemburgish endearment—a cute, shorter way of saying the French *adieu*—literally, 'go toward God,' as in the Spanish *adios*.

They shook hands once more. Rick started off in the direction of Hannah's abandoned car.

Behind him, Romain gunned the Audi and took off on the CR118 in the direction of the small towns of Breidweiler, Chrisnach, and Larochette.

Rick took a last look at the white car. He hoped to find any clues he might have overlooked before. Out of luck, he closed the two doors one by one, walking around the car. No sense letting the elements trash it.

As he walked around the back, something caught his eye on the ground. He squatted down and pushed leaves and debris out of the way. There, in the wet black soil where it had fallen, was a key with a tag on it. The key itself was a small brass one—nothing unusual. Looked like a locker key, if anything. Attached to it by a plastic halter—like a police handcuff—was a round plastic token. Rick examined it closely. The token promised fun and sex at the Klub Kolibri in Wiltz. Looking more closely at the key, he found a tiny number punched into it by an engraving machine in an art deco-like script: *39*.

Why Wiltz? What could that possibly have to do with Hannah and the invisible hand of global corporations?

Wiltz was a town in northwestern Luxembourg, quite far from here. He vaguely recalled the name from a book about the Battle of the Bulge, fought across Luxembourg during the bitterly cold winter of 1944-5 as Hitler made his last effort to throw the Allies back to the Atlantic—for no discernible reason other than just what it was—a final, roaring, violent death struggle of a primordial monster called Nazi Germany. It was through the tortured greenery of the Ardennes mountains and forests that Hitler's tanks had struck in lightning-quick arcs to outflank France's Maginot line further east, thus opening a titanic world war; and it was in the Ardennes Forest to the west of here, around Bastogne and Wiltz, that the Hooked Cross staged its Wagnerian, desperate finale amid operatic death music. In fact, the titanic struggles of Napoleon I around 1800, of Bismarck and Kaiser Wilhelm I against France's Emperor Napoleon III in

1871, and then World War I early in the Twentieth Century, had all seen their armies winding through these deep, tortured canyons. People had been killing people here since before history was written. Here we go again, Rick thought.

The stream banks were mossy in dark lush green glistening with moisture. The scene was not much changed since the glaciers melted ten thousand years ago. In places like this, fierce cave bears hunted the great-antlered aurochs in these regions, and humans found safety in caverns while saber tooth cats prowled after trundling mammoths—all extinct except for the humans, who now hunted each other in cars, with books and guns.

Sunlight filtered down from cliffs high above, reaching a dusty kind of twilight. Beyond the car, at the very bottom of a fissure in the volcanic earth dating eons back, a stream of water ran—green, cold, buzzing with insects. The water crisscrossed and spattered among moss-covered rocks.

Across the stream, Rick spotted a footprint—a woman's, dug into the soft black mud after she'd jumped over mossy rocks in the gurgling, tumbling stream and landed on the opposite bank.

33.   Wolf Gorge

Rick followed the female footprint in the direction it pointed—northward up a series of ancient, weathered hills choked with ferns and underbrush under lush tree canopies.

Birds chittered loudly. Their sweet warbling echoed in the wilderness all around. This was really a sort of spooky, otherworldly place.

It was late in the day, and he supposed a reasonable person would have waited until dawn before hunting across this unknown landscape. Sometimes, though, you ran with the plan. Fate had gotten between himself and Hannah. If nothing else, he wanted a sure answer. Whose side was she on? If he had only that—either way, he could return to his country and begin a new life, feeling a sense of closure.

As he hiked up and down twisting ribbons of soil—among prehistoric boulders the size of houses, amid echoing bird calls and small, scampering animals—he reflected that at least there would be no IEDs here, nor unpredictably hostile people of a different time and mindset. At the same time, dark forces swam silently like underwater icebergs among the money oceans of the world. In those seas of wealth and power, toothy paleo-sharks could suddenly appear like primordial submarines, striking and killing without warning from below. Worse yet were the pilot fish and moray eels they paid to do their dirty work, from tattooed Yakuza and Triads to Western Mafiosi and other nacre killers. Those were the enemy soldiers when push came to shove, Rick thought. He regretted ever raising his hand in that recruiting office in Los Angeles and promising to be a warrior for the money and the power. His employers had a noose hanging from a ceiling in Kaiserslautern, waiting to sacrifice him to the green gods of cash.

The air still carried warmth from the day's sunlight. Rick was soon sweating as he reached high meadows and half walked, half jogged through alternating tree shade and sunny meadows. In the evening, all the world's insects came out to drink from puddles and ponds. Small animals stirred in shadowy spots as they sought water and security. Europe had been much tamed over recent centuries, but he'd seen news stories that wolves were making a comeback. Foxes abounded. Squirrels zipped about, froze to look at you, and darted behind trees. Some U.S. military troops garrisoned in Europe had even released North American mammals like raccoons and skunks that thrived in the temperate climate.

Rick laughingly almost expected a troop of Roman infantry, or a procession of Celtic Druids, or a band of Medieval hunters to cross his path. Could Robin Hood and his Merry Men (or their Ardennes equivalent) be far at a moment like this?

He was fundamentally an infantry guy—and, as such, specialized in walking. You kept going—climbing, falling, running, jogging, rolling, getting up again. It didn't matter, as long as you kept moving. Sailors could sink miles to the abyssal plains in the sea, where no light ever reached. Airmen could fall miles from the sky and land in an explosion on land or sea. Infantry guys were stuck to the land like ants to a sidewalk. They were concerned with bunions on their feet, sweat and crap between their toes, chafing underpants, a twisted backpack strap or jock strap—or a misstep that twisted an ankle or reminded you just how many delicate little bones and muscles you had in each foot. You concentrated on walking at a steady clip, carefully moving your feet ahead, one after the other, staying level so that if you tripped or slipped, nothing got broken or sprained. That was the idea, anyway.

Rick did not stop to rest. He kept an even pace, not too fast and not too slow. He had a lot of energy left, and planned to rest only when the last light failed. He wasn't sure if it was a full moon—he could keep moving on high ground if need be, carefully. He had the nine millimeter NATO standard automatic in his backpack. Along the way, he found a nearly perfectly straight tree branch. He stopped briefly—oh, if only he had a good bush knife—to strip the branch. It would be his pole for beating the bushes ahead of him and for support. It could be a probe, a crutch, and a weapon if need be.

Carrying the pole like a spear, he jogged along a network of hard-packed trails. Most of this land was national park, so there were few farms except near the towns. There were hiking trails and a few tractor trails.

The path took him past a stunningly beautiful old castle ruin, whose empty windows and deserted battlements spoke eloquently of battles maybe a thousand years ago.

After a few miles, he stopped on a high hill and assessed his situation. He could see for miles around—tree tops as dense as any jungle, on a series of hills and cliffs rising over deep crevices. This was, indeed, Luxembourg's Little Switzerland. He wiped sweat from his forehead. He felt tension in his legs from climbing and walking. And he was starting to be a little out of breath. This wasn't easy going.

He had totally lost track of where Hannah might have gone. At this point, he was simply going in as straight a line westward as he could, following the orange sun that grew lower on the horizon. He listened intently. His only hope now was to hear some noise she or her unknown companion might make. He saw a few distant rooftops of the usual regional black slate. Smoke curled from a chimney deep in the forest.

A small idea formed in his mind. What, in this enigmatic silence, could he make of her actions? Whether she was an enemy agent, or a friendly victim in the wrong place at the worst moment, she must be going someplace—assuming she did not lie dead, face down in some cold green stream among deadly rocks dressed in moss.

If she was meant to be dead, her assailants would have killed her after they got the package from her.

That meant she was (or they were) going somewhere. To do that, they needed transportation. That meant either land or air. So the key was to find a road—preferably a town with a telephone maybe. It was his only hope.

He passed through a beautiful gorge in which three small waterfalls poured over rocks and brush to land in a miller's pond and then flow away in a stream strong and loud enough to drive the mill wheels of past centuries.

Hiking on, he walked through stony gorges clad in dark green.

Here it was, as the sign proclaimed, *Gorge du Loup*, or Wolf Gorge.

He trekked between two high cliffs so close together he almost had to go sideways. The walls were fuzzy with moss and lichens. A rough-hewn flight of stairs—of wood and packed earth—led up to a fabulous lookout place. In previous centuries, hunters had pursued the wolves here during dire winters, and shot some, while others got away to prey on livestock and children. Those had been tough times.

In some places, the same overgrown, ivied sort of landscape suggested long-ago construction of castles or walls or buried towers, but it was an illusory and elusive blending of nature and human making. In this otherworldly atmosphere, it was unclear where the fairy world of dragons and elves, of little people and fairies, gave way to the silent passage of scheming humans and predatory animals hunting for prey.

At one point, he thought he saw human figures in the shadows ahead. Darkness was growing in the hidden crevices, and his eyes played tricks on him. Was that Hannah's slender figure way ahead? Did she turn to look at him with a pale face and terrified eyes, before whirling and running out of sight?

Or was he hallucinating?

He stopped to listen, not once but many times, and heard only bird song, gurgling water, and wind sighing above in high branches.

Twenty or so minutes after passing the Schiessentümpel, he followed the twisting forest paths upward to high ground.

He saw the tightly gathered rooftops of a small settlement in the distance. Could he make it before total darkness set in? If he didn't, he'd have to stop. Maybe she would be stopped somewhere as well, waiting for daybreak.

He had nothing else to go on. As they had said to each other, "It's all we've got." Meaning each other. But now, just the memory of each other. He felt grief welling up as he hurried forward. He stifled a sob, and stamped his feet angrily. How was it possible that everything could go so wrong? Fuck all, he was going to march through thick and thin until he got answers. And march he did.

It was a pleasant walk. Up he went, climbing to the left or to the right among boulders hidden in forest. Everything was green and mossy, or covered with green-yellow lichens with traces of rusty red. Luckily this happened to be a sunny day without the usual drizzle coming eastward from far away on the English Channel—that same Atlantic Ocean prevailing wind known as a Western Maritime—which brought regular downpours of rain in London and across the British Isles.

Then, at some point, he heard Hannah's voice. It was just a snatch of conversation on the wind, but the tone and quality of it were unmistakably Hannah's.

He froze, with his heart beating in his neck. He was terrified of the truth. As much as he wanted to see her and talk to her and beg her to tell him what was going on—the idea of what she might tell him frightened him more than anything. Only the thought of her coming to harm was even more scary, so he followed the sound of her voice.

He could not make out the words, but she yelled something. He could not even tell whether she was scared or happy or what. Probably not happy. Not likely.

He heard a man's voice—a yell—then silence.

Rick held his stick before him like a spear or rifle as he advanced. For thousands of years, under various circumstances—war or hunting—men of different cultures and times had walked in this region just as he now was. He patted the backpack to feel the heavy gun there. Then he raised the stick onto one shoulder, ready to use as a quarter staff in a fight.

As he rounded the fern-shrouded corner, he came upon a breath-taking sight. A valley lay before him, spreading in a panorama. He glimpsed a road passing below—maybe the CR118, having made a long curve.

A row of figures trudged on the shoulder of the road. He could not make out who or what they might be.

A long driveway ran between the CR118 and the backyard of this farm below, right below the farm house windows and through piled rose bushes and bougainvillea, a sea of colors leading to the muddy abandon, standing puddles, and high weeds of the farm yard. Along the edges of the farm yard were rusting vehicles and harvesting equipment. The place looked dark and abandoned—generations ago. The wooden shutters had fallen down, the glass windows were broken, and bushes grew directly out of the house's interior.

Along the road a few hundred meters below were some walls. There was a row of farm structures, maybe old white-washed stone barns beginning to decay so that the gray stone below peered through.

His path led downhill, winding into the old farm yard.

Behind the farm houses that fronted on the road—closer to Rick—was a red and silver helicopter. Its rotors were turning. As Rick came into line of sight, his ears picked up the powerful sound of rotors idling but ready to kick into power mode any second. The chopper was ready to lift off.

Running toward it were two figures—Hannah, and the Chinese man they had seen in the Luxembourg railroad station.

The engine noise picked up intensely.

The chopper began to lighten on the ground.

Dust whirled all around the two running figures in the back farm yard.

"Hannah!" Rick shouted. He cupped his hands around his mouth. "Hannah!"

She could not hear him.

At that moment, Romain's Audi came down the CR118, turned right in a welter of rocks and dust, and raced into the farm yard.

Romain produced a gun and began firing at the Audi.

A copilot leaned out, aimed a flare gun, and shot directly at the Audi.

The Audi turned—Romain must be hit, Rick thought—and struck a tree with a loud jangle of broken glass and a screeching sound of bent, tearing metal.

A second later, the flare hit. The Audi went up in a bright welter of flames.

Against the exploding flames, the Chinese man and Hannah ran to the chopper.

The co-pilot pulled Hannah up into the chopper.

The Chinese man followed.

Rick stopped helplessly, waved both arms in desperation, and yelled for them to stop—to no avail. There went Hannah, and he could not stop her from being kidnapped.

The rotor noise reached deafening pitch. The farm yard filled with whirling dust. The chopper lifted off.

Rick had one last glimpse of its dimly visible occupants. It was not a military or police aircraft. Rick caught sight of its markings, which meant nothing to him. There was a logo, LX-AREF and ELNT, followed by some numbers and then the image of a bird. Since birds had been emblems of aviation, that meant nothing to Rick—except for a nagging idea at the back of his mind. What was it?

The chopper heeled, leaned, and roared away toward the red ball of the sun that lay bleeding and dying on the forested horizon.

He ran down as fast as he could to the burning car.

Romain had managed to open the door and fall outside.

Rick reached him just in time to pull the man's broken, burning body away—seconds before the car exploded with a loud bang followed by a hot draft of air that smelled of gasoline, oil, and upholstery.

Rick kneeled over Romain, scared at the sight—hair burned away, scalp an angry, welted pink, face mauled and blistered. Romain's clothing smoldered as he lay limp before Rick.

Rick felt for a pulse in the neck—and detected maybe something there.

As he struggled, he heard voices and looked up.

Figures he'd seen trudging on the road resolved into a running group of frantic young men and women in scouting uniforms, colored clay-gray, with campaign hats and walking sticks. Ten of them probably—too much of a blur to count—they came flying to do what they were trained to do.

Several threw themselves around Romain's body, checking his pulse, tearing his jacket open, starting CPR. They were probably late teens, Rick estimated, as he stood by in shock and let them take over.

Two older leaders conferred while speaking on cellphones. The younger ones acted in a professional manner that would have made any infantry unit proud. These were not just kids roasting wieners and singing songs in the woods. *(*Endnotes #9)*

"*Bonjour*," said a twenty-something brunette with a tennis player's figure, tanned strong face, and blue eyes, who she hurried to take Rick's arm.

Some of the scouts were young women, others young men; at least one was Asian, another African, and other distinctively Mediterranean—maybe Arab. Hard to say, in this diverse country.

"English," Rick said pleaded. He stared helplessly into the empty sky. The chopper and Hannah were gone.

"Are you okay?" she asked, introducing herself as Jacqueline de Brunhof. "I am a *Chefin* for this walk. What happened?"

"I have no idea," Rick said. "My friend needs help."

"Yes," Jacqueline said. "We have called LAR. That is the Luxembourg Air Rescue service. They will be here in a few minutes. And of course the police and fire rescue units."

A scout working on Romain yelled, "He has a pulse."

"Burn wounds," another yelled. "Need plasma and stabilizing."

"We will do our best," Jacqueline said. "LAR has helicopters on standby—ready to leave within two minutes day or night. I don't know if they will dispatch a unit from Trier or from Dikierch or Luxembourg City, but a chopper will be here in the next ten minutes with a doctor on board."

Rick could only stand there and cry. Tears ran down his cheeks. He had been here before. Again he had failed. He had lost the battle with whatever or whoever was ruining his world and killing his buddies. This was too fucked for words, and he was helpless—that was the worst part.

Another leader or *chef*—a young man introducing himself as Martin Peralta—dark-haired, honey-skinned, mustache, beard shadow; totally competent take-charge attitude—came jogging. Like the rest, he wore an olive-drab campaign hat, clay-gray uniform shirt and trousers, and good hiking boots. Martin and Jacqueline tried to assist Rick to a sitting position on a fallen tree nearby, but Rick insisted on staying close to his friend.

"His wife lives in Luxembourg City," he told Jacqueline.

She made sympathetic eyes. "That will wait until we know what to tell her."

"Whether he lives or not," Martin said.

"Yes, of course," Rick said.

Distant Martin's Horn sirens could be heard, *ta-tooo, tah-tooo...*

"From Larochette and Echternach," Martin said. "And there is a Müllertal fire rescue unit."

Jacqueline said, "When we go on a camping trip or a hike, we always prepare to know where the emergency services are, in case we have to assist someone."

"You've done well," Rick said.

"There is the helicopter already," said one scout, pointing east.

That's awful fast, Rick thought. *Amazing how coordinated these people are.*

"Must be a German unit from Trier," Martin said. "They coordinate whatever they have available at the moment. The LAR service takes off within two minutes upon notification, and is positioned to be ten minutes or less from any point of emergency in the Grand Duchy."

Jacqueline said, "Mister—"

"Rick Buchan."

"Mr. Buchan, this is also a crime scene, which we are securing for the police. I don't imagine you are going anywhere."

"Oh god no, I'd fall on my face. I've been hiking through the Alps back there for several hours."

The helicopter was powerful, but flew with deceptive quietness—until it got close. As Rick would later learn, it was a U.S.-made McDonnell Douglas with two roaring Pratt & Whitney turbine engines, capable of thrusting the craft up to 260 kilometers per hour (near 160 mph).

One of the scouts, expertly raising and lowering a pair of flashlights, signaled with twin pillars of light to the pilot to bring the aircraft to a safe landing in the middle of the farm yard.

Again, the air filled with swirling dust. The noise was deafening.

A red, silver, and blue helicopter set down on skis. Piloting in the cockpit up front were two flight-suited figures in red helmets. Behind them was a compact but evidently sufficient stabilizing environment—an air ambulance. The doors opened, and two figures in flight suits jumped out and came running.

Both were women, one African looking, the other Asian. The African introduced herself as the emergency physician. She had a tight ball of kinky hair, bluish-black skin, and a stethoscope dangling around her neck. The other, also dangling a stethoscope, was a flight nurse from the former Portuguese colony of Macao, now the world gambling capital owned by China with the guidance of U.S. entrepreneurs from Las Vegas, and likely the earth's money laundering capital. Since China sanctimoniously did not permit gambling on the Communist (Capitalist) Chinese mainland, Macao would logically be a multi-purpose outlet and tax revenue source. The young R.N., taking a contrary tack, worked honestly for a living.

After a brief assessment, a half dozen scouts carried Romain on the stretcher to the helicopter. The pilots helped pull the stretcher on board and fasten it in place for the short flight. "We will go the trauma center in

Trier," the doctor informed Rick and the scout leaders. "He is very critical and may not live through the flight. I am ready to administer adrenalin directly to the heart if it stops." She and the nurse ran without further comment and jumped up into the chopper, with carried Romain aloft even as technicians pulled the doors shut.

At the same time, a row of police and fire emergency vehicles arrived to take over for the heroic scouts.

Rick thanked the young people profusely. A doctor, speaking French as a matter of routine but switching to English, asked Rick how he was doing. The doctor was a skinny young blond man with acne scars, wearing a short white lab coat and dark trousers. He had arrived in the fire-rescue ambulance that now stood nearby.

As darkness fell, the air around Rick was filled with flashing lights. "Are you okay?" the doctor asked. Two firemen took him by the elbows.

"You are looking pale. Are you dizzy?"

Rick nodded. Time for his medication. He held up a finger to keep them at bay. Lowering the backpack to the ground, he opened it and rummaged until he found the two brown pill bottles.

The doctor examined them with a flashlight. "U.S. Army. Very interesting. You are suffering from PTSD?"

"Yes."

"Are you still on active duty, Sergeant Buchan?"

"What, are you a fucking cop or a doctor? Right now, I feel like there are trucks driving through my torso. Give me my pills already."

"Of course," the doctor said. "I am also a Luxembourg Army captain, reserve duty. The police inspector from Echternach will be here in a few minutes, and we will appreciate if you and the good scouts here can explain what is going on here."

Meanwhile, a uniformed motorcycle policeman had both arms in Rick's backpack and said, "*Oh hoh!*" He produced the automatic that Romain had given to Rick.

There followed a torrent of conversations around Rick in several languages—German, French, and Letzebuergesch; possibly also in Flemish and Portuguese.

Rick weakened and staggered backward. Helping arms caught him before he could do a hard landing on his rear end. Where was that fallen tree when you needed it?

Nearby, a fire truck doused the burning car, which grew dimmer as the flames smothered and the air filled with a soapy, chemical smell. There were more twirling lights of various colors than on a Christmas tree.

Two girl scouts supported him as he sat on the tree. A Boy Scout handed him a plastic water bottle, while a nurse associated with the army captain doctor finally gave him his pills.

Rick said, "This is like being arrested in Times Square, New York for illegal possession of bubble gum as a deadly weapon."

Police and emergency officers took over, thanking the Scouts and Guides, who departed. As they left, they waved to Rick and wished him well. He smiled and waved his thanks after them. The last he saw of them was Jacqueline's blue eyes, tanned face, and beautiful white teeth.

"*Bonjour, monsieur,*" said a stern looking middle-aged man. "*Je suis l'Inspecteur Maurice Fischer de la Police Grand-Ducale. Comment allez vous?*" He had gray hair, smoothly ruddy skin, and an ash-colored brush-mustache under a prominent red nose. He wore a gray business suit, and had the large, raw hands of a boxer. *He's probably packing serious heat under that lounge jacket,* Rick thought.

Someone said, *Hien ass en Amerikaner. Am Beschten Dir schwätzt englesch matt him.*"He's an American. It's best to speak English with him."

"Ah," said the Inspector, switching to clear English with an undefined international intonation. "I am Inspector Maurice Fischer of the Grand Ducal Police. How are you doing here?"

"I'm all shook up," Rick said bitterly.

"Like in the song." Fischer was a match for anyone's biting tone.

"My girlfriend has been kidnapped. Or something. I have no idea what is going on." Rick thought fast. He could not tell anyone about this package thing; not just yet. But the events in Echternach were no secret.

He and the police inspector, who now had charge of the investigation, formed an island of conversation amid the organized chaos of a fire department action on the smoldering car, and a police investigation as patrol officers fanned out with flashlights in the deepening night.

The doctor showed the pill bottles to Fischer, who waved to a subordinate—also in civvies, thus probably a police honcho. That individual got on his cellphone and started blabbering like the Tower of Babel. *Very efficient, these people,* Rick thought. *Almost scary.*

"Help me, Monsieur. Don't let my patrol officers waste their time. What are we looking for?"

"I don't think you'll find any traces. She was involved with the Professor when he got clobbered at the post office."

"Oh that." Fischer brightened. "Can you tell me what that was all about?"

Oh god, Rick thought, *it's over for me. They'll turn me over to U.S. authorities at the U.S. Embassy in Luxembourg City.* That would probably mean the standard U.S. Marine Corps embassy guard unit. From there, he'd be transported by air to Kaiserslautern or possibly Mannheim or Frankfurt for processing and trial. Should he ask for his lawyer now?

Fischer said rather ominously, "The longer you stare at me that way, Mr. Buchan, the more suspicious I become that you are hiding something you don't want me to know about."

"Pardon me if I look at you strangely. I am a fucking nut. I am taking all sorts of pills for anxiety, depression, PTSD, you name it."

The doctor standing by interrupted, "Are you suicidal, Mr. Buchan?" As Rick gave him a calculating look, he continued, "If so, I can officially remand you to my care."

"I just have some questions," Fischer told the doctor aside, realizing the doctor could put a hold on his interrogation.

"I'm not suicidal, homicidal, or germicidal," Rick said. He thought to himself, *How long will it take for them to reach someone who knows about the search going on for me by the NATO forces?*

Rick glanced sidelong at Fischer's assistant, who was on the phone with someone, while nodding vehemently and waving his arms.

Oh my god, Rick thought. *If they arrest me on a NATO warrant, I'll spend the next five years stuck in paperwork and JAG proceedings. That's before I even go on trial for crimes I did not commit.*

"How are you feeling?" the doctor asked Rick while Inspector Fischer stood by, looking on the verge of apoplexy. "It is my legal obligation to ensure that you are fit for questioning before the police speak with you any further."

"I just have to pee so badly," Rick said, feigning tears.

"Here, I will accompany you out of sight," the doctor said.

"Thank you." Rick rose with effort, and hobbled around in a circle. "I think I am going to throw up."

"Take him in the ambulance," the doctor ordered.

The Inspector looked furious. "I will meet you at the hospital."

"You may be able to question him further in the emergency department."

"Very well."

Two uniformed police officers, wearing blue uniforms, blue jackets, and blue baseball-type caps (not the white kepis of traffic control officers) led Rick into the ambulance. Inside, they offered him a choice—either lie down on the stretcher, or sit between them on a bench along the window.

He climbed on board, holding the backpack with the money and the gun in it. They might be super-efficient, but they didn't apparently feel they had reasonable cause to search him. Laws and constitutions here in Europe tended to be more progressive than those back home, Rick had observed. Typically, children had rights not to be spanked, animals had personal rights like freedom from abuse, and marriages were a civil contract that was illegal for supernatural ministers or magicians to perform, at least not recognized as a valid legal contract. So he had the right to remain silent and hang on to his backpack undisturbed for the moment.

They haven't found out yet that I am wanted by NATO. Good so far.

"I'll just lie down here and rest," Rick said. He stretched out on the cool white sheets. "This is quite restful and comfortable."

"Good," said the doctor. "I'll stay with you. The officers can ride in front with the driver."

Last that Rick saw of the Inspector was his livid face, with pinprick eyes and a tiny o-mouth before the rear door of the ambulance closed.

"You have to let me know if you are feeling dizzy," the doctor said. "Did you take your medicine?"

"Yes. Thank you."

The ambulance began moving—over the bumpy farm yard, then crunching on the gravel driveway, and finally around the corner onto the smooth surface of CR118. The doctor produced a blood pressure cuff. "Roll up your sleeve for me, please."

Rick took off his jacket, offered a bare arm, and lay down. The doctor strapped the cuff around his upper arm pressed a button. An automatic process inflated the cuff and monitored the results, displaying the pressure and pulse rate on a little screen. As they waited, the doctor measured his oxyegen using a clip on one finger, looked into his ears, had him say *AHH...*, and looked up his nose.

"Your blood pressure is normal, and everything else is within limits. We'll do an EKG and a few other routine matters and release you to the joys of conversing with Inspector Fischer."

"I have much to say to him," Rick promised while rolling his sleeve down and putting his jacket on. As he did so, he rolled his eyes up and saw that there was only a small window from the front, overlooking the passenger side of the ambulance. He saw a blue police cap, but the man was engaged in chatty conversation and never looked back.

The doctor was putting away the blood pressure cuff and securing the rest of the equipment in the van.

In the frosted rear window, Rick saw a distant flash of blue and red lights. That meant that whatever escort was coming along was far behind. He had expected Fischer and other detectives to follow close behind, but there were no headlights in sight.

There was no time like now.

"I have to get my *flëgöstüshnistik*," Rick said in an imitation Luxemburgish-Mongolian accent, glancing at the backpack. It sat on the steel deck near the by the rear door.

"Your what?"

Rick leaned over, as if something had fallen on the floor. "Can you help me?"

The doctor turned and said helpfully, "Yes, what is it?"

Rick pointed to the floor. "There."

The doctor looked down. "I don't see—"

"Not a problem. Sorry about this." Rick rolled over, took him in a headlock with one hand over the man's mouth, and anchored him so that he cut off the blood supply in his neck. It was a tricky choke that could result in death, but he let off the moment he felt the doctor grow limp in his arms—unconscious within a minute.

"You'll feel better soon."

Rick twisted himself so that the man's body rolled over him and lay on the stretcher. He tossed a white sheet over him to make it look good. Then, keeping as low as possible, he duck-walked to the rear door, grabbed his backpack, and twisted the handle.

So far so good. No sign of consciousness in the cockpit either.

Now the really tricky part.

Already, the doctor was starting to make moaning sounds. In another minute or two he'd be groggy and starting to wake up.

Twisting the handle, Rick swung himself on the wide, steel rear bumper. Wind rushed around him in the free air. He pushed the door shut while dropping to the street and rolling.

For a moment, he thought he had miscalculated and was about to die.

As he rolled a few times too many, he stayed in a ball, avoided splattering on the road, and ended up topsy-turvy at the edge of a ditch by a farm house. The ambulance sped away, as the pursuit car quickly gained.

Rick dropped into the ditch, head over heels, just as the strong headlights swept over the spot where he had been. More headlights came—maybe three police cars following—and then the night was still and dark. It would take them a few more minutes at most to realize that their patient and passenger had disappeared.

I must improvise.

A motorcycle stood parked in the driveway. Rick pulled the backpack onto his back as he climbed from the ditch and ran to the red and silver bike—some teenager's Italian-made Ducati Monster 696 street bike, nothing complicated. The key was even in the ignition. There was even a black helmet on the seat. When Rick put it on, it smelled inside of cigarettes, peppermint, pizza, beer, and vomit. Quickly, he tossed it into a bush where it landed silently. *Gawd...yuuuuk!* He made a face. No wonder the kid left his keys and helmet on the bike—he'd barfed into his helmet on the way home from some biker *rendezvous* at a local pizzeria. Besides, who would steal a motorcycle here in the middle of nowhere? Careless, and very helpful. Rick had owned a Harley back home, and a friend had another model Ducati, so there was nothing strange here.

He clicked the stand back as quietly as he could, released the brake and, holding the handlebars, rolled the bike from the driveway into the street. There, he found there was a slight downward grade. He turned the key and ran the bike along the road until he could jump on it. When it was rolling, he hopped on board, stepped on the starter, and was happy to hear the roar and purr as the machine came to life. He switched on the headlights and drove at a typically European breakneck speed in the direction opposite from Echternach. Every second put more distance between him and that ambulance.

Now on to Wiltz before every cop in the Grand Duchy was looking for him. He had two things to go on. First, the Chinese man with Hannah apparently had a habit of visiting a sex club in Wiltz. Secondly, the helicopter taking Hannah away had flown into the setting sun—westward, in the general direction of Wiltz.

34. Wiltz—Kolibri

As he rode on dark roads through the night, Rick had to make some quick decisions. Should he stay on side roads, or risk a run on a major highway? Within about fifteen minutes on the CR118 he was in Mersch, the first large town along the way. By now, he had to figure that the police understood he had escaped. As fast as everyone worked here in Luxembourg, he'd have to assume police all over the country would have an all-points bulletin out within the next five minutes.

In his favor was the fact that nobody had any idea where he had come from, or where he was headed. They had some idea from his pills that he was a U.S. Army sergeant. They would soon know he was on the run. All that would take precious minutes. Maybe he had an hour or so before a serious manhunt got under way.

In Mersch, he stepped into a gas station and bought a cola from a clerk who never looked up at him. He asked the clerk to put the cola can into a bag. The clerk was reading a weight-lifting magazine with photos of proudly flexing women.

Next to him on the wall in the tiny, warm, crowded store was a wall map—just what he needed. Two or three minutes studying the routes— there wasn't much to the country—and he knew he had a ride of about forty minutes. He'd hop on the A7, which was a clean, fast ride on at least two well-marked lanes, on concrete roadways with steel guard rails on the outside. At this hour, there might only be some nighttime truck traffic, so it should be a clear shot.

Stepping outside, he tucked the cola in his backpack. The wind was driving him crazy. He put the paper bag over his head, leaving small eye holes. He had a scarf with him, which he wrapped and tightly tied around his head to prevent the bag from flying away. Thus equipped, he rode back out onto the highway.

Police would shortly start looking all over Luxembourg for him— probably in the capital first. Who would ever place him in Wiltz?

As he expected, it was a good ride. The motorcycle handled well, especially since he kept within speed limits to avoid getting nailed by any stray traffic checks. Luckily, there were no drunk driving patrols—because he had no papers. That would be sticky indeed—on some kid's stolen Ducati. Given his situation with the Army courts-martial system, he didn't even want to imagine the bureaucratic purgatory added with this theft. He might reach old age before the U.S. got him extradited from Luxembourg, or even the Hague, back to Germany for yet more processing. Rather than life sentences, could a person be condemned to decades of processing without possibility of parole or piss breaks?

The geographic center of Luxembourg seemed to lie between roughly Mersch and Ettelbrück. Apparently, this was also the Route du Nord (Northern Route) of Luxembourg. Around Ettelbrück, he ran into some traffic. The connections were a bit more big cityish, although a passing highway sign told him that it had a population of about 7,500 souls on a busy day. Soon he was in the open country again, roaring on the N15.

So far, so good. He did have a start as he approached Wiltz, when flashing emergency lights appeared behind him. He slowed down—but it was a fire truck passing him with no sirens, probably after fighting a fire.

The population of Wiltz was a stately not-quite 6,300 souls—which was a metropolis compared to Echternach at 5,400; Luxembourg City (the capital) at 107,000; or the whole nation at 563,000.

He passed the sixteenth-century Chateau de Wiltz as he rode on the Rue de la Grande-Duchesse Charlotte—a road named after the regally beautiful monarch who ruled 1919-1964 and guided the country, from exile in London, England and Montreal, Canada, through the dark times of World War Two. From there, she broadcast powerful resistance speeches against the Hitler regime, heard around the world on the BBC.

Following the Rue de Charlotte through some long, winding turns, he decided that his relationship with the Ducati must regrettably come to an end. He found a good spot outside the town's main cemetery. He left the bike parked off to the side, near a large auto repair shop with lots of other parked vehicles in the neighborhood. It might take a while before anyone noticed the bike, and wondered who had left it there—maybe some apprentice mechanic who only used it occasionally. By then, Rick was sure he would be onto other matters. So thinking, he hoisted himself over the cemetery wall in the dark of night. He found himself a nice, soft spot where he could rest with his head on his backpack and grab some sleep— because he was exhausted. It was now around ten p.m. As he hoped, nobody bothered him in the locked cemetery, and he slept almost as deeply as the other hotel guests around him.

He awoke in the gray morning light, after fighting to ignore the sounds of passing trucks on the Ramparts Street outside the cemetery. Apparently there had been some fortification walls here long ago. Workers opened the cemetery gates and drove in with a skip loader to dig a grave, presumably. The machine made a continuous, infernal beeping noise for warning as if constantly running backward. Rick stretched, rose, wiped wet dew from his hair and clothing, and hiked out of the cemetery as if nothing had happened.

He pulled the key and fob from his pocket and looked at the address again. The Klub Kolibri was on the northern edge of town on a small side street. He checked himself out in a store window—a bit haggard, unshaven, and rumpled. He would need a bath today. He'd figure that out. Maybe take a hotel room, but that got you into police attention here in Europe. By now, he was sure, the Grand-Ducal Police had a nationwide manhunt going. He had to figure they'd be in touch with U.S. Army authorities. He must act fast—no telling how long this brief window of freedom was open to him.

Klub Kolibri—a bar where men drank and slouched at a runway, while women danced before them nude or near-nude—was closed, dark, and silent at this hour. Its outside was a modest store front framed in glossy black tile, wedged between a hat shop and a video store. The club's one large plate glass window had been painted an opaque black as well, and plastered over with posters showing the photos and silhouettes of nude dancers. Above all, the logo Klub Kolibri in red neon letters graced the black tiles above the locked aluminum door. A picture of a humming bird (presumably male) sticking its beak into a blood-red (presumably female) flower graced the logo as well. The kolibri was a hummingbird. Now Rick got the picture. At least, he got one small corner of the picture. How did Hannah fit in? Who was her Chinese-looking escort or captor or ally? What were they to each other? Why did Romain need to be shot?

From a sign on the door, Rick gathered that the club opened at ten a.m. Until then, he had some other business to attend to. First, he should get rid of this jacket and find something less noticeable—and different, because Inspector Fischer had probably already broadcast a description of him.

One thing at a time.

He rolled up the jacket and pushed it into his backpack. Now he was a guy walking around in a white shirt.

In a pharmacy, he bought a disposable plastic razor, a plastic bottle of water, a pack of tampons, and some vaginal cream. He made the purchase without incident, and neither the heavy-set woman clerk nor the white-jacketed little bald pharmacist (who looked too harried to pay attention) seemed to pay much attention. There were lots of tourists in Luxembourg, so he was not unique. If anyone reported him, the discussion would be that he had bought some items for a wife or girlfriend. That could not be the missing American soldier.

He took a sip of water and put the bottle in his backpack. He dropped the tampons and vaginal cream in a public trash receptacle. Wrong trail, if they were looking for a couple.

In a dirty gas station bathroom, which smelled terribly—not sure if it was urine or week-old fish—Rick smeared his face with a mixture of water and hand soap. Letting water run in the dingy little corner sink, he shaved while regarding himself in a broken mirror on the wall. He washed the razor off, and pushed it into his backpack. He used toilet paper to pat his face dry. Much better already, he thought, looking at his reflection.

From the gas station, he strode down a long, achingly neat and clean-looking little street—how cool would it be to live your life here, in this little doll house country, with cute young women in abundance? He sensed an overwhelming need for safety and peace in his life.

Along the way as he strolled, he found a women's fashion shop. In the window he spied a kind of unisex sweater with several buttons up the front, and a wool belt that could be tied in a knot. It was a sort of brownish-gray mix of colors with dark red highlights. Nothing feminine. He stopped in and bought it cash, with a brief, friendly transaction with a pleasant, fortyish woman who seemed to think it was neat that he was buying his girlfriend or wife a present.

As he headed back toward the Kolibri, he reflected that he had now disguised himself—or at least toned down his appearance—to avoid being a billboard for his wanted poster.

His stomach rumbled, and his lightheadedness was returning. Time to eat. Along the way, he bought a bratwurst and coffee at a roach coach parked near a public park. He sat on a bench in the park, devouring his hot food. He watched children playing in the park, and pigeons strutting around looking for a bite to eat. He envied these people—even the birds, and a prowling cat, and a stray dog—their peace and happiness. They might have problems—everyone did, everywhere—but they didn't have to carry the weight around that he did.

He deposited his trash neatly in a steel basket attached to a tree. He wiped his mouth and fingers with a paper napkin, which he threw in there as well. Then, holding his paper coffee cup, he leisurely walked back uptown toward the Kolibri. The coffee steamed fragrantly in his hand, and he stopped several times to savor it. He tossed the empty cup into another steel basket attached to a light post, before crossing the bridge over the Woltz River, which originated near Bastogne and flowed into the Sûre River north of Echternach.

By the time he got back, the Kolibri's red neon logo was flashing. Music throbbed from inside, and the blacked out glass door stood open a few centimeters on a rubber doorstop.

Rick pushed inside, walking into a blast of rock music and a whirlwind of twirling lights. A glass sphere in the ceiling turned slowly, like a rainbow prism, throwing off stabs of multi-colored lights, along with a snowstorm of white light specks that raced around the otherwise comfortably gloomy hall.

On a hardwood island in the middle, near-nude young women pranced out of a back room to gyrate and make eyes at male guests. Rick counted a half dozen men, none of them Asian-looking. Three or four waitresses in white blouses and black skirts hustled about with round trays and order pads—leaning close to talk with customers.

Rick nodded to the bartender—a bearded man, wiping glasses in his domain of bottles and taps at the moment. The bartender gave him a friendly nod back.

Rick found the men's room, relieved himself against a wall and trough of white porcelain tiles on which a perpetual rain of water streamed—thus minimizing odors.

On the way out, he noticed a corridor off to one side. It ran behind the stage and deeper into the building. There, he saw what he had been looking for—mailboxes along several top rows, with larger locker compartments along the bottom row. He found number 39, and readily opened the small mail slot. He peered into the slot, and found several mail items. There appeared to be several invitations to join a similar club in Brussels, plus some advertising for escort services around Trier, and a folded porn magazine from a Thionville publisher. All the items were addressed to a Monsieur Chan, care of the Kolibri, no home address or other information. Disappointed and no wiser, Rick left the items as he'd found them, and closed the door. If this Chan guy was still alive and a member of this club—it had to be a man, not a woman—then he must return sometime. As an afterthought, Rick unlocked the small box again, took out a postal card, and closed the box. Everything was apparently very discreet here for members in this pounding, throbbing darkness full of hunger and lust.

Rick drifted over to the bar and ordered a cola drink. The bartender set a glass of Vichy water before him with a shot of bitters. He raised his hand when Rick offered to pay. Rick tipped him two Euro bills instead. That made the tall young man's bearded face light up. Rick asked, "Speak English?"

The young man's blue eyes sparkled, and his short, sandy hair seemed to stand up straighter. "I ought to, man. I'm from Dublin. Irish."

"I have a little of that in me too," Rick said.

"You're American?"

"Canadian. From Vancouver," Rick lied.

"Never been there," the fellow said while efficiently scrubbing and wiping a row of beer glasses on the soapy, sudsy brass counter. "I hear it's a nice area."

"You'd love it. Rains a bit more, but you'd be used to that."

"I'd prefer California or Mexico," he said. "Name's Roger Leary." He extended a pink, soggy hand.

Rick shook the hand. "Joe Gorman." He had no idea where that came from. He'd been in school with a freckled girl named Annie Gorman. He could be her long-lost brother Joseph. "Hey," he added, putting the post card on the bar. "Found this outside on the sidewalk."

Leary took the postal card and held it up to the light. "Oh, yes. Chan. He comes in about twice a week. I'll toss it in his box for him."

"He's one of the regulars?"

Leary shrugged, suddenly cautious. "We play our cards close to the chest. That's the discreet thing, you know? A lot of our guys are married and don't want the old lady to know they're out playing. Are you new in town?" He eyed the backpack. "Hiking the scenery?"

"Yes, hiking and enjoying the castles and all. Just visiting," Rick said.

"What line are you in, may I ask?"

Rick made up a story. "I own a small import-export business in California. I pick up a few little things here and there when I'm on vacation."

Leary digested that with a bit more nosiness than seemed healthy. "So you're just passing through then?"

"My wife has a sister in the capital. We're here on vacation, mainly in Germany, but we always drop in to say hello. I thought I'd stop by and cool my eyeballs for a while."

Leary laughed. "Plenty to cool your balls too, if you stick around." He was about to ask some more nosy questions, but a waitress called him to the service counter at the far end of the bar. She held an order slip for several drinks. "Excuse me." He walked away.

"No problem," Rick said. He was done with Leary for the moment. He'd learned what he needed to learn. Chan was a regular, that much was clear. Who was Chan? Why was he in the forest with Hannah yesterday? Was he the Asian-looking man who'd accompanied her to the helicopter?

Nothing to do now but wait. He took his cola and sat in a corner. The music pounded on around him. Slowly, the place filled up with men of all ages and statures in life, from laborers to workmen in blue overalls, and business types wearing suits. By now, at least four young women with spectacularly smooth, uniformly caramel skin and wonderful legs were taking turns gyrating and twirling around a steel pole in the middle of the runway. The air conditioning cut in, cooling the air and removing stinks of sweat and cigarette ash. The atmosphere remained dusky and alluring, with those wild lights bouncing around. Men ordered drinks, waitresses hustled, girls danced, the music throbbed, and business was being transacted in the form of credit, tips, and taxes. *Quite a racket*, Rick thought. In some form or other, this had been going on since ancient times. Maybe not with twirling lights and rock music, but certainly entertainment to suit the tastes of long ago and far away places.

By now two light-skinned Azorean bouncers had showed up and stood by the door, wearing tight pants and white muscle shirts to display their dark-muscled athletic prowess. You didn't want to mess with these guys, Rick thought. The last thing he needed was trouble.

A waitress stopped by and greeted him with the ubiquitous *Bonjour*. She waited, holding her round tray against her lap with both hands. She was kind of U.S.-diner cute, with a bouffant brown hairdo and acne scars covered by a coat of pancake makeup. She appeared to be mid-thirties, with a solid gold wedding band on the appropriate finger. Her name tag on the white, puffy blouse read Marie-Josephine.

"I'll have a Bofferding," he told the woman.

"Do you wish for anything to eat?"

"No thanks—I had something on the way. Say, have you seen McGillicuddy around?"

She scribbled on her pad. Her forehead wrinkled. "I have never heard of such a man."

"Oh, too bad. He was supposed to meet me here. What about our old friend Chan? Have you seen him around at all? Looks kind of Asian. Nice guy."

She made one of those European gestures with her shoulders, while exhaling in a dismissive way and shaking her head. It was what Rick called the European *Pouf*. It was the expression for anything you didn't understand or disagreed with. Like, why did dogs have black lips? *Pouf*—how should I know, much less care?

"Monsieur Chan comes in for a brandy or two, usually the same day and time. He sits in the same spot and watches the girls. He tips like an American."

"That's my old pal," Rick said. "I shared a drink and some stories when we were here last week."

"You know him well?"

"Sure. We went to different schools together." In the noise, she could not hear him well. As if launched from a carrier deck, she sailed away to attend to three different tables at the same time while giving Leary a hand-sign for one Bofferding.

Five minutes later, Leary came sauntering by. He wore his white apron, tied several times around his slender waist with a white cord, and stained from drinks and foods. He sat a foamy glass of Bofferding beer down. "What do you want with Chan?"

Rick looked up in surprise. "Conversation, maybe."

"The waitress says you were asking." Leary's demeanor had grown colder. "Be careful with some of the customers. They like their privacy. You're not a detective, are you?"

Rick laughed out loud. "No, hardly."

Leary shot a glance at Rick's head. "The haircut is kind of military."

"I grow it real long to save money, and get it cut short twice a year."

Leary stood with a languid, floating posture that signaled he didn't give much of a crap about anything. "Just saying, man. I've never seen you around here."

"I like my privacy too," Rick countered.

"Cool. I hear you, man." Leary rapped two knuckles on the table in a standard Germanic sort of gesture of comradeship. "Be good." He turned and walked back to his bar.

Rick considered himself warned, whatever that meant. He had clearly stepped on some sensitive toes. The Kolibri must offer a lot of services to its clients to guard their privacy so jealously. All he could think about was Hannah, alternating on the carousel of his anxieties with thoughts of JAG Major Kendra Walsh.

He half finished his beer, rose, and walked out of the club. Both Leary and Marie-Josephine noticed him from different ends of the room, and nodded goodbye. Leary was talking animatedly on a black wall phone, and held one hand over the receiver as he nodded to Rick—as if he subconsciously wanted to hide what he was talking about and with whom he was having the conversation.

Outside on the street, he counted the cars and took general note of their plates—all Luxemburgish, and local. A driveway between buildings led to a small rear parking lot with a dumpster in one corner and a willow tree hanging over the small pavement area. The lot was empty, and its floor was strewn with willow debris. The wet, yellowish-green leaves and twigs looked undisturbed, as if nobody much used this little lot. Satisfied that he had a handle on traffic around the Kolibri, he started thinking about calling his JAG contact in K-Town. He wasn't ready to turn himself in— especially not as long as he had some hope of tracking down Hannah and learning the truth about this mess. Also, he figured Kendra Walsh was working in his favor. Ethically, as the court-appointed military defense attorney, she must do everything possible to help him. She'd harangue and wheedle that he should come back—but he was not ready yet.

He spied a convenience store down the block. The sun was out, and the day was warming up. He wished he had a car to stash his backpack in. Nuisance carrying it around, and it did make him look a bit touristy. He walked down the block, and stopped into the small store run by a short, dark-skinned man and woman of Indian origin. "Good morning, Sir," said the man brightly.

"Top of the day to you," Rick said. If asked by the police, this couple would report him as having a slight Irish-sounding accent—not the U.S. deserter they were after. "I want to call my wife in the capital. Do you sell any sort of inexpensive telephone?"

"Oh yes, of course," the Indian said effusively, as if Rick should have anything he craved in this world—for a price. "Look here, Sir. We have a line of cheap, sturdy phones that come with up to twenty hours of pre-paid calling time. Have you ever used one before?"

"No, I have an expensive tablet phone, but I left it at the hotel."

He bought the phone for cash and walked out the door. Hopefully, he had not missed anything while in the store.

He walked back toward the Kolibri, slipping the burner into his backpack.

Same cars. Nothing had changed.

He stopped into a small grocery up the street, opposite from the Indian store. There, he bought two oranges and a water bottle. He carried these back to the Kolibri in a white plastic sack. He found a low wall in that empty back parking lot, and sat down on a dry spot exposed to sunlight. It was getting sunny by now, with the last night haze burning off. Funny, you didn't notice how gray and damp the air was until it cleared up a bit. It even smelled different. He hoped the day would warm up a bit. He hoped that Chan would drive in for some exotic distractions. Meanwhile, he sat and peeled an orange. It tasted sweet and tart at the same time, and was very juicy. He relished it, one slice at a time.

"Sergeant Buchan," said a dark, menacing voice.

Rick stopped in half-chew, with an orange slice on his lips, and looked up.

There stood Kendra Walsh's menacing boss, the Infantry colonel from K-Town, who had never made any secret of hating Rick. He was a huge, very dark man with graying kinky hair clipped short in a regulation U.S. Army cut. On one coffee-black cheek was an ugly scar from long ago, which had been softened by time and surgery, but still bore the after image of long-ago combat.

"Sergeant Buchan," the colonel repeated. Another figure even more menacing stepped beside him—a first lieutenant who was striving to get Rick put away for life at hard labor, at Fort Leavenworth, with reduction to private, forfeiture of pay, pension, and benefits; and lifelong disgrace.

Rick did not rise. He was in civvies in a foreign country. The two officers likewise wore sporty-looking sweat suits and jogging shoes, and looked incognito.

Rick chewed on the orange slowly, trying to guess if they were going to tackle him, shoot him, or try to nice-talk him. His run was over.

He flashed back to the scene as he was leaving Kolibri, Leary on the phone, cupping the receiver and looking as if he'd been interrupted doing something Rick must not know about; yeah, like calling whoever set him up with the Kolibri key. That had to have been a pure setup to draw him here. Why? Maybe to just get him out of the way—assuming they realized he didn't know anything.

This was where the rubber met the road. Hannah was history. This was about ten dead contractors and soldiers, and he was supposed to be the patsy.

35.   Kolibri-Busted

"Don't try to get cute," boomed Colonel Ivan Whitcomb while keeping his huge purplish fists loosely in the pockets of his maroon hoodie. Rick imagined there might well be a gun in one of those pockets. Whitcomb looked to be about six-four, with a broad, flat nose, large pinkish lips marred with old cuts, and that scar on his left cheek. He had the broad shoulders of a swimmer—and would resemble a torpedo in the water, no doubt.

"We have you covered," said Lieutenant Samuel Sherwin. The latter was thirty-something, compared with Whitcomb's fortyish. Sherwin was pale and freckled, with orange hair and calculating greenish eyes. He was leaner, smaller, and trimmer than the colonel—of a wiry construction, maybe barbed wire. Where the colonel already had nets of wrinkles around the corners of his eyes and mouth, Sherwin's skin was just beginning to show hints of decay in the making.

"I'm unarmed," Rick said. Nearby lay the backpack with a gun and spare rounds in it, along with items of clothing, documents, his medicines. He made no effort to sidle closer to the backpack. He'd wait and see what these two had in mind. No doubt they had backup with them. This was a business call.

"Stand up," Colonel Whitcomb said.

Rick rose, still holding one orange slice.

Sherwin roughly and efficiently patted him down. "He's empty."

"Good." Whitcomb's eyes roved to the backpack. "Check."

"Right." Sherwin lifted the sack, unzipped it at the top, and pawed around it. He extracted the gun, still in its holster. "Look here."

"Unarmed," Whitcomb said to Rick. He took the gun, wrapped it in Rick's white grocery bag to hide it, and threw the extra orange into the dumpster, where it landed with a dull thud. "You are a snake. Remind me never to take my eyes off you."

Rick pointed with his one remaining orange slice. "The cobra is this guy here. You're hating the wrong guy."

Not a cloud of doubt crossed the colonel's white eyes with their dark pupils. "We are going to take you to our car, Sergeant. You are under arrest. I'll show you the warrant at the car."

Rick shrugged. "Okay. I'm not going to resist." What hope was there?

Sherwin started to toss Rick's backpack into the dark-green, dented dumpster under the willow tree.

"Keep it," Whitcomb ordered.

"My medicines are in there," Ricks said.

"Put it in the car," Whitcomb told Sherwin, who made a fox-like face and knife-like eyes toward Rick—reading, *I'll get you when the right moment comes.*

Rick felt a shudder as he flashed back to that dark road far out in Huilongistan. Explosions rocked the ground, and he banged his head again inside the armored vehicle. He must have relived this scene a thousand times, he thought, and it still wrecked his day. He saw body parts, ripped steel, an oily half-axle sitting on the torn asphalt with the wheel ripped off. It was all very vivid, down to the little bolt holes in the plate on the half-axle where the rim had been attached.

"Buchan!" Colonel Whitcomb boomed. "Wake up."

"We have places to go," Sherwin said with icy sarcasm. "Like a nice dark stockade cell for you."

"What's with you?" Whitcomb said to Sherwin. "This is not personal."

"It is for me."

"Me three," Rick chimed in. "You killed us all," he said directly to Sherwin.

Whitcomb took the high ground. "This will not be personal. We have a mission to accomplish, and we have our prisoner. Now let's drive home to K-Town."

Sherwin gave Rick another raking glance, as if slashing him with broken glass.

They got into a silvery Mercedes sedan with German license plates—white, with black lettering that started with KL, indicating the car was registered in the Rheinland-Palatinate city of Kaiserslautern. This had long been the largest community of U.S. citizens outside the United States. At one time, late in the twentieth century, over a quarter million U.S. troops, dependents, and civil servants had lived and worked in K-Town, as G.I.s had dubbed the famously green and drizzly city with its predominantly sandstone buildings. Today, it housed barely 10,000 but was still the largest of the dwindling U.S. overseas colonies.

The car evidently was Whitcomb's personal one. He drove, while Sherwin sat in the rear to keep an eye on Rick. Before they drove out of the otherwise deserted little rear parking lot, Whitcomb dutifully showed Rick the U.S. Army SJA documents ordering his pursuit and arrest in a lot of fine print. Rick was cuffed with his hands behind him, and propped against the locked rear door behind Whitcomb.

With no more border checks, they would make Kaiserslautern in about two and a half hours if traffic was slow, Rick figured. Kiss Luxembourg goodbye. Kiss Hannah *au revoir.*

As his tortured gaze floated past tidy little houses on a narrow, quaint little street, Rick reflected, It's been nice. All good things must come to an end.

The only good thing was that now he was no longer running. He was about to encounter the fate he had been evading for weeks.

By tomorrow morning, Colonel Whitcomb would be in his normal working fatigues with black, subdued combat-type markings indicating his assignment to a Staff Judge Advocate slot high up in the chain of command. His background as an Infantry officer, with combat tours in several far-away wars, would serve him well in future promotions. His next step would potentially be brigadier general, at the convenience of the Army (as all things were).

Sherwin's status puzzled Rick. The guy was an Armor officer out of his element. As best Rick could figure it, Sherwin had been brought to K-Town because of injuries received in theater, separate from the IED explosion. They were keeping him on administrative duties, while awaiting Richard Buchan's trial, at which he would be the star witness—the only survivor of that night other than Rick, who was about to get flushed down the toilet for life. Rick's memory was still hazy, but he was pretty sure he had tried to protest being sent into that little town. Sherwin, then still a first lieutenant, had shouted all over him as if Rick were still a private in Basic Training. "Sergeant, are you a coward? Are you scared to go out there and lead those people? If so, I'll replace you and put you in custody as a frigging coward, a shirker, a traitor." *And so on.* Looking at Sherwin now, he could still see the crazed young incompetent acting like a mad dog to cover up his ineptitude. He was still getting away with it.

Whitcomb drove in a measured fashion. He and the large sedan seemed made for each other. His big hands floated around the nougat-white steering wheel. With an automatic transmission, there was no gear shift to constantly adjust. Sherwin sat holding the sack with the 9 mm gun in his lap. The gun was in the bag, where no casually peering local traffic cop could spot it. Rick could tell it was out of its holster and ready to be used—on himself.

Oddly, they appeared to be heading north toward Belgium—not toward Germany, which lay eastward. "Little detour, Colonel?"

"Actually, Buchan, we are going to deliver you to some people who will drive you back to Mannheim." That was the location of the stockade. "We have other things to do."

Rick felt the need for medicine coming on, but said nothing. He figured Sherwin would deny it to him, though Whitcomb seemed more of a stickler for legalities and would not deprive him of his prescriptions. Whitcomb, for all of his stony attitude and giant physical presence, seemed like the lesser of two evils. By contrast—how it all came back now, from having served in the same command with this guy—Sherwin was a red-haired serpent.

"You realize I know nothing about this whole mess," Rick said.

Whitcomb calmly looked into the rear view mirror with those large, white-rimmed eyeballs. "Oh yes, Buchan. But you see, this is a critical operation, and you are what is called a loose end."

Sherwin viciously laughed. "Like you were back in Huilongistan."

Whitcomb's shoulders sank noticeably. "Let's not make this too complicated."

Sherwin said, "It's all very convenient, that's all."

Rick said, "I wish I knew what you guys are talking about. Or maybe I'm glad I don't know."

"It won't matter," Whitcomb said in his deep voice. "You'll go back to Germany and you'll be busy dealing with what happened back in Huilongistan. With luck, you'll be alive and well in Kansas twenty or thirty years from now, mopping floors in the stockade and hoping they serve chocolate pudding for desert."

"Heads up," Sherwin said.

The two men suddenly ignored Rick and focused on the road ahead.

Whitcomb snapped his fingers over his shoulders. Sherwin reached under the front passenger seat and pulled out a leather satchel that looked like a woman's large hand bag. It was black, made of soft nappy leather, and had two carrying straps like the sort of satchel Europeans took to the grocery store to bring home vegetables and meats. Only whatever it was, Rick could bet there were no potatoes in there.

They drove on the CR329, another of those winding little two-lane country roads in Luxembourg.

They passed a road sign that read, *Aerodrome Civilien à Noertrange.*

With his basic and limited French, Rick understood this to mean there was a civil airfield nearby, probably in the vicinity of some town with that typically Luxemburgish or Walloon (French-Belgian) sounding name, a mix of Germanic and French patois.

They traveled through a lush, beautifully green landscape in the Ardennes foothills. Every few seconds, a car or truck passed with a *whoosh*, most of them out of Belgium which was not far away to the west.

The road wound through low hills, at an altitude of about 1500 above sea level, according to passing signs. They headed into the hamlet of Noertrange, which contained one of the country's oldest aerodromes. He caught sight of the call letters ELNT and remembered that had been part of the logo on the chopper taking Hannah away from the farm house yesterday.

His heart skipped a beat—Hannah. He must be closer to her now.

He must see her just once more before he died—just to know *why*.

He needed to understand why his life was on the line here.

"Coming up shortly," said Sherwin, who had been talking on his cell.

Whitcomb steered along the CR329, winding into the center of the tiny hamlet.

Rick squirmed uncomfortably as the handcuffs bit into his wrists.

"There he is," Whitcomb said.

The road made a curve in the little town's center. The visual focus was a plain little white church with a pointy black slate tower. To the left of the church was a stone bus stop, with a tiny street to its left, and the typical tidy little houses receding into the village.

The only figure on the street was a smallish, middle-aged man with white hair. He looked somehow all at once authoritative, cruel, and furtive. He wore steel-rimmed glasses behind which his gray eyes looked shifty— left and right—signaling to Rick that this meeting was not supposed to be taking place. The older man wore a clean, black sweat suit and blue track shoes. The pants looked a bit baggy as if he did a lot of running, and washed the pants often. The jacket was a hoodie type, with zipper front. He had his hands in his pockets, but took them out expectantly and stepped forward with a certain degree of desperate eagerness.

Rick did not have to wonder long what was in the bag that Sherwin held in the middle of the back seat. Sherwin reached in and grabbed a handful of Euro bills. So it was money—a lot of it. The bundle he grabbed must be ten thousand, Rick thought.

As Rick watched, the sociopathy in Sherwin came out as he tried to furtively slip the string-tied bundle into his own sweat jacket.

"Put it back," Whitcomb sharply said to Sherwin

Sherwin reluctantly threw the money back into the bag.

"Keep your hands out of there," Whitcomb commanded. "We don't want this to go wrong."

"I was going to split it with you."

"You really are a snake," Whitcomb said. He favored Rick with a brief flick of those white eyeballs that signaled hidden, unreadable emotions. Rick sensed conflict between the two and calculated desperately how he would save his own life. What he was seeing was some kind of a payoff— to whom and for what he had no idea, but clearly he was in the vortex of a really big frigging deal here. He felt shivery at the thought of the danger he was in.

Whitcomb drove past the man at the curb, who raised a hand—just a small gesture to signal the deal was on.

Whitcomb drove past a few hundred meters.

Then he did a U-turn in the middle of the CR329.

In the distance, a single-engine plane sailed in to a landing at the civilian aerodrome.

A moment later, another single-engine plane buzzed loudly as it soared aloft.

Busy little airport, Rick thought.

Whitcomb drove slowly back toward the church and bus stop. "Get ready to hand it off," he commanded. He was a man used to giving commands.

Sherwin rolled the window down, pulled the satchel to him, and pushed it out the window.

The man at the curb reached out, took the sack, and melted quickly away down the tiny side street.

Rick thought he saw several burly-looking men in sweat suits waiting there beside a dark green car. That looked unmistakably like a military staff car, Rick thought—with subdued or no markings.

Whitcomb speeded up the car in the direction of the airfield.

"Where are we headed?" asked Sherwin as he rolled the window up.

Whitcomb suddenly turned, holding a black NATO 9mm automatic on Sherwin. He pulled over with one hand on the wheel and the gun hand resting on the seat. "I need to take care of something."

"Easy," Sherwin said. His eyes were suddenly filled with fear.

"If you move, I shoot." Whitcomb stopped the car, pulled the emergency brake with his free hand, and got out. All the while brandishing the pistol, he walked around the front of the car.

Rick ducked as low as he could, all the while expecting a hail of big, nasty bullets to fill the air.

Whitcomb pulled open the back door and ordered, "Out."

"What the hell—?"

"Out," Whitcomb repeated. "Take the cuffs off this idiot."

"You must be crazy."

"I am out of patience. You say another word and I'll kill you. There just isn't time."

As Whitcomb spoke, he reached around the back of Sherwin's sweats and extracted the gun that Romain had given Rick. Sherwin had taken it from Rick at the little parking lot behind Kolibri, and apparently sneaked it into his own possession—for use against whom? *Probably Whitcomb.* What a worthless snake this Sherwin really was.

In the next two or three minutes, Rick found himself freed of the handcuffs, which Whitcomb ordered him to clap on Sherwin. Now it was Sherwin's turn to be the prisoner.

Whitcomb warned, "You're both under arrest. Don't either of you get any smart ideas." He told Sherwin, "I've been suspicious about you since you showed up. Taking that money was the last straw. Do you think I'm going to let a sneak like you sit in the back seat with a gun like that?"

Whitcomb took Sherwin's gun, removed the clip of bullets from the grip, and tossed the gun on the floor in the front. He put the clip in his own pocket. "These will be safely away from the gun. Buchan, you'll want to push it out of sight under the seat now."

Sherwin started to talk, but Rick took the opportunity to punch him hard—in the head. Sherwin staggered and fell into the back seat. "He had it coming."

"Careful," Whitcomb said. "I want you both alive. You're going back to K-Town, both of you. We'll sort this out."

Sherwin lay crumpled in a corner, with his mouth partly open.

"The two of us are going to K-Town," Rick said. It was a question. "Where are you going, and whose side are you on?"

"That's none of your business. You get in and drive. I'm going to sit behind you with a gun at your head." He pointed toward Sherwin. "This guy sits in the same spot as before, only with his hands safely behind his back. I don't trust you, but I trust him even less."

"What's the status with Kendra Walsh?" Rick asked.

Whitcomb glared at him. "She is trying to get you off the hook. She's been after you to come in, you idiot. She has a witness who may exonerate you."

"I did nothing wrong in Huilongistan. This guy was the lieutenant in charge that night."

"I understand," Whitcomb said.

"You do?"

"I'm starting to get the picture. You've been too out of it to remember."

"I remember now," Rick said. "We had intelligence that there was going to be an ambush. They were after a tribal leader we were going to transport to the capital to be on our side. He was in a separate car in our convoy. I tried to reason with this asshole lieutenant, but he threatened to court-martial me if I didn't go lead my people to certain death."

Whitcomb nodded. "You can tell it to the judge, Buchan. I don't have time. I half believe you by now. What you don't know is—we have Charley Hafford back."

"No. Charley was killed along with the others." Rick added, "One of my best friends ever."

"Well, he is alive and well, Rick. We thought we'd lost him, but the INA captured him along with the tribal chief."

"Oh my god."

"Yeah. Kendra has Charley Hafford waiting to testify. He was wounded, and we traded him for some INA prisoners. From what I gather, his story corroborates yours. Sherwin was the villain, not you."

Rick stood there, trembling at the thought of how his world seemed to be turning around, maybe righting itself. He felt like pissing his pants for sheer emotional chaos. Or was this another ploy, another in the series of shadow games, among forces here in Europe he could not fathom?

Whitcomb waved the gun. "Get in and start driving. I need you to do something for me."

Minutes later, the car was on the road—Rick driving, the massive presence of Whitcomb advertising itself behind him—and the hard steel muzzle of the gun pointed into his spine through the back of the seat.

Sherwin murmured as he came to, shaking his head.

Whitcomb glanced about—the whole car shifted under his weight. *I'd hate to tangle with this guy,* Rick thought.

"Hope nobody saw us waving guns," Whitcomb said, half to himself.

Rick shook his head. "What's your game, Whitcomb?"

"Just drive and be glad you're still among the living."

"Where to?"

"The airfield."

Rick studied the situation. Ahead, angling out from the town amid dark green woods broken up by green, wavy fields that would produce hay over the summer, was a long, single grassy air strip. It must be nearly a hundred years old, from the look of some of the buildings. This whole part of Belgium and Luxembourg had seen heavy combat during the Bulge during the freezing cold winter of 1944-5. This had really been Hitler's last, senseless gasp. Tens of thousands of troops had died for nothing, including many U.S. soldiers. As he drew closer along the long, narrow road, he saw vintage planes parked in a row along one side, including some with antique U.S. and German markings.

"The mission, Colonel?"

Whitcomb shifted conversationally. The gun never relented in Rick's back. "Sergeant, you are going to drive to K-Town with this prisoner. I am going to fly out of here because I have other things to do that are none of your business. Let's say I am going shopping in Brussels."

Was he joking, or did he have a woman there? Nothing made sense—less than ever.

"Drive onto the field."

Rick steered the car past a row of hangars and a control tower with the ELNT markings that were also on some of the little colorful private aircraft sitting with their wheels between wooden blocks.

"This is a civilian airport," he said conversationally.

"Yeah. Just keep driving down there by the wind sock, and stop. I am about to catch a plane."

As he spoke—sure enough—a twin engine cargo plane came drifting in. It looked dark, military, and ominous. Rick soon watched it roll past them with the propellers feathering as it braked to a halt.

The surface of the field was grassy, but it was kept mowed flat.

The car door opened behind Rick.

The car's center of gravity shifted, and Colonel Whitcomb stepped out.

At the same time, a side panel in the unmarked craft's cargo bay slid open, and three military figures in dark fatigues and berets waited for Whitcomb to climb in.

Rick rolled down the window as the colonel stepped close and spoke.

"You are on your own, Buchan." Whitcomb tucked the pistol into his own belt, and pulled his sweat jacket down over it. "If Sherwin gives you any trouble, put him in the trunk. He's got his hands behind him in cuffs, so I don't think he can do much. If he gives you any problems, you have my permission to pistol whip him." He looked fiercely at Sherwin, who sat in the back seat with his hands behind his back and his head against the window glass. "You hear that, Lieutenant? Keep your mouth shut and you may reach Kaiserslautern in one piece."

Sherwin mumbled some insults.

Whitcomb patted his palm on the driver's window sill in a parting gesture of good will. "Drive back on the CR329 until it runs into the CR319 back to Wiltz. There, you can pick up the highways—it's all clearly marked. The A62 will take you into Germany and K-Town in just over two hours. Pick up the A6 near Landstuhl and drive over to Ramstein Air Force Base. Turn yourself and the captain here in at the front gate. I'll call ahead and have the Air Force Security Police waiting for you. You know what to do?"

"Sounds straightforward, Sir."

"Good. Just two hours, and it's all over."

"Right."

Whitcomb poked a large, stubby finger in Rick's face. "Whatever you do, don't stop. Get out of this area while you can. It's a top-secret military test range, and you could get your nuts shot off by CEOC mercenaries guarding this place."

"Got it, Sir."

"Two hours. Get going."

Somehow, Rick wasn't prepared to believe everything would be so simple. Nothing ever was. Then again, he was still alive. That was a major benefit of being clueless but running faster than the other guy.

"Good luck, soldier. You have your orders. Carry out the mission."

"Yessir," Rick said from long habit. The reflex died hard. He knew of a guy who had served in Germany with him, who so much hated saying Sir to idiot lieutenants and other company-grade officers of questionable intellect (and morals), that when he'd returned to the Continental United States (CONUS), he made a point of calling everyone Sir—including small children, dogs, cats, and anything else that moved.

"Carry on." Whitcomb turned and ran for the plane. Helping hands pulled him onto the flight deck.

The sliding door closed, the propellers began to roar at flight pitch, and the plane rolled down the grassy strip. It made a few loopy left and right twists as the pilot wiggled its controls. Then it lifted into the air on its two powerful wing-mounted engines.

For a moment, Rick sat stunned.

He still had no idea where Hannah was, or what part she played in this kabuki theater.

"It's you and me now, Buchan."

"Shut up or I'll feed you some more knuckles."

"I'm an officer."

"You are a murdering asshole. Don't piss me off."

Sherwin sat sullenly. "You think you can make it all the way to K-Town with me in this car?"

Rick leaned over, picked up the useless gun, and threw it out the window.

"Watch me," he told Sherwin. He got the car turned around and rolled toward the small town.

He steered the car along the narrow road on which they had come.

Sherwin grew quiet in the back seat.

Rick thought about Hannah—and resigned himself. It was like death. Everyone had to die sometime. Everyone had to lose the love of his life. It was par for the course.

As he concentrated on driving, he thought about the medicine in his backpack. Was there water in there to wash the pills down? He felt a little woozy. That would mean either reaching over the back seat to get the backpack; or stopping the car and getting out to retrieve it that way.

He did not hear the subtle clicking of spare keys in back until the very last moment, when Sherwin freed himself and sprang forward to wrap the steel chain of the cuffs around Rick's throat.

From long martial arts training, Rick pulled his chin in and raised his shoulders to minimize the opportunity for Sherwin to get a purchase on his neck.

With split seconds to act—while Sherwin was struggling with the cuffs—Rick aimed the car at a massive tree and accelerated. He released his own safety belt.

Sherwin had time for a scream, cut short.

Rick stomped the brake, whipped the wheel left, and caused the car to drift sideways into the tree. It was like gliding sideways into a wall at about fifty miles an hour.

At the same time, Rick opened the door and shoved his way out. He would either die now, or get free.

The car wrapped itself around the tree, trapping Sherwin in a tangle of upholstery, broken glass, and twisted metal.

Rick found himself on all fours, dazed and shaken. He crawled on painful things—glass, tree roots, rocks, a door handle—and rolled onto his side to escape the sharp pain. He lay for a moment, smelling diesel fuel. Not likely the crate would explode. If it were gasoline, it would smell different and turn into a fire ball.

Sherwin was silent.

Rick debated. Get help? Whitcomb had warned him about mercenaries. What to do?

He looked into the rear of the car, and saw that Sherwin was covered in blood but still alive. "I'll see if I can find some help for you, asshole. Are you bleeding out?"

Sherwin moaned.

"Don't bleed, okay? I don't have time for this. If I see any Boy Scouts or Girl Guides, I'll send them your way."

Sherwin moaned strongly.

"You asked for this, you bloody idiot. So sit there and moan until I send some girl scouts for you. Or a passing Grand Ducal police patrol." Where was Inspector Martin whatsisface when you needed him? Probably still riding around in that ambulance, looking for his escaped prisoner.

Right now, the thought of Kendra Walsh and Kaiserslautern sounded like a great idea. In fact, it sounded like paradise. Maybe he could borrow a car or something.

He pulled his backpack out of the rear and started walking along the narrow country road. In his eagerness to get the gun out that morning, Sherwin had failed to notice the plastic-wrapped bundles of Euros amid Rick's knotted-up clothing.

Once again, he was on his own. It felt good—and as he walked, the stiffness from the rough landing during the crash began to soothe itself out. He had no broken bones—not even a sprain. How lucky could you get? Once in a while, you had to have a little luck.

That was when the shooting began.

36.   Dancing with Drones

For a moment, there in the middle of nowhere, amid all this restful beauty, Rick had no idea that someone was actually shooting at him.

He stood on the brow of a long ridge, with the road curving away from this gorgeous green valley that stretched out before him. To the left was a line of trees stretching two or three kilometers. To the right was another, higher ridge, overgrown with similar dark green tree crowns and dense bushes.

On the meadow, two or three small knots of cows stood grazing contentedly. They were white, with black spots, like in a painting. The meadow itself was nearly flat, forming a slight depression about a kilometer wide and curving out of sight about two kilometers ahead.

He was in no-man's-land, and the ground around him was going pock-pock-pock, stitched by bullets, while grit stung his face and rounds whined in the air.

"Holy shit," he yelled as he ran for cover near the first tree he saw.

He embraced the tree, which was about the width of a woman, as if he were dancing with it. As bullets continued to hammer the ground around him, he danced to the left and to the right, still holding the tree in both hands, until he was running around the tree. It would be funny if it wasn't so dangerous, he thought.

The shots were coming from above. He looked up, but there was no helicopter or aircraft in the sky.

Still the firing continued.

Now the shooting came from the direction in which he had been walking since leaving the wrecked car a klick behind. Could Sherwin be doing something? Not likely—the man was probably either dead by now, or struggling weakly to extricate himself—assuming he had no broken bones, and his spine was intact after the impact.

Seconds later, the shooting came from the opposite direction.

Rick threw himself off the roadside, rolling down an embankment into tall green grass, and landing in a shallow pond. "What the hell?"

Then he saw them: a swarm of drones, maybe six of them.

They streaked around like moths, sometimes spiraling around each other.

One drone, then the next, would emit a stream of machine gun fire.

He was momentarily out of sight and safe—but the drones had to have operators sitting somewhere behind consoles. The drones probably had sharp cameras and scopes to track their prey and observe their target closely.

Rick spotted a drainage culvert under the road and crawled rapidly in that direction.

The noise of his splashing, and the tossed whaling of water, came to the drones' attention.

He just managed to throw himself head-first into the dark, dank tunnel under the road as several traces of stitchery chattered in the water behind him. He could hear the weird hum of the bullets slowing to a stop as they hit the water and penetrated thick black mud.

From the darkness within—a smelly, dank, mossy place in which he was inches deep in liquid mud—he could see several drones swinging back and forth. For the first time, he was able to get a look at them. They were all cut from the same model, evidently. He wished he had binoculars. For the most part, the small aircraft swung rapidly from one place to another. Mostly they were a blur.

Gradually, as a few stopped and hovered, he made out their uniformly manta ray shape.

Could these be the type of unidentified flying killer machines that had murdered two Belgian air force pilots near Houffalize, a new kilometers from here? Maybe earlier models, he thought, because the mysterious UFO over Houffalize had been described as having glowing gold-like skin.

He remembered that the French aviation firm Dassault had long produced a line of saucer-shaped systems called the Neuron. Various Western NATO countries participated in the development effort, with variations in several countries. Generically, the craft looked like a very small version of the B-2 stealth bomber. Its dimensions were similar to those of a standard automobile roof. He had seen videos of these things as part of his combat training.

Of the many variants, this seemed to be a low-end model for close ground support, surveillance, and other tactical uses. These models seemed compact enough to carry high-resolution cameras and transmitters, as well as a chamber of (maybe, he guessed) 9 mm rounds like a hand gun but capable of automatic fire. That meant they would either run out of ammo soon, and have to return to base for reloading, or fly on empty and act as surveillance units.

He wished he had that hand gun now. He could shoot a few down and make a run for it.

They'd lost him for the moment.

He could not stay here in this cold, wet, smelly bath of lizards and god knew what other creepy-crawly things slithering up his trouser legs. This half-dome tunnel was just three feet high at the center, meaning he had to low-crawl to move through. Grimacing—*I'll be soaked and smelling like cow piss by the time I'm through*—he slithered through the frigid water and mud, into near total darkness, and then into light again as he emerged on the other side.

There, he saw the same beautiful, picturesque meadow of lush greenery stretching several kilometers out—a mirror image of the other side—and not a house in sight. Just unbroken, almost flat meadow.

Carefully, he slithered out far enough to look left and right along the road, which curved away in either direction. There was a sparse row of young trees on either side of the road, like the beech tree he had danced with, but not enough to furnish cover.

Could he make it if he ran across the meadow to the tree line?

He listened closely, with all his senses sharpened by life-and-death danger.

Water trickled steadily in the brook around him.

Frogs chirruped so that their sound echoed in the tunnel behind him.

The air was heavy with summer warmth at early afternoon.

Butterflies danced around on the meadow, looking for a dusting of yellow flowers.

Maybe they'll think they shot me, Rick thought. *But then they'd send out a patrol, which would be harder to avoid.*

Then he had a terrifying thought. What if they flew a drone into the tunnel? He'd be dead meat for sure. They'd spot him and shoot him from both tunnel entrances—no escaping if that happened.

No time to waste.

What to do?

As he lay in the tunnel entrance, propped up on both elbows, his lower half grew numb with cold from the water. He could not stay here like this.

Already, he was blubbering as his lips grew blue from cold.

Now two or three of the drones started to drift through the trees, over the road, and onto this side.

He pulled back, shivering and stuttering loudly. His lower half was numb.

The drones floated like a trio of nearly silent disks, like miniature B-2 stealth bombers.

Each was a dull field-gray color verging on smoky, dark camo. They carried only one marking in drab grayish blue, subdued and barely visible: FDLV-39. Must be the make and model.

Like manta rays. Or automobile roofs, a meter and a half across by a meter long, with two frightening-looking, hooded eye holes for cameras working in tandem, binocular style. Fitted and flattened into the foot-deep (maybe 300 cm) body was a command and control unit. Underneath were bulges—fuel pods, ammo pods, exhaust ports, and of course the phallic gun barrel that delivered death and destruction. He heard a plaintive whirring sound from their stealthy-silent engines.

As he watched, another three of the drones flew to this side of the road. All six hovered about now, in two flights of three apiece.

Then, leaving the first three to hang in the air looking at the road, the three newcomers sailed off together. They followed a straight course parallel to the road, ignoring the road's slight curvature, until they reached a point about half a kilometer away.

As he watched the distant drones, Rick began to make out some straight lines hidden amid trees and shrubbery. Then he saw a whip antenna rising straight up—too straight to be natural. And he made out the netted scoop of a dark, metallic satellite dish. They'd lost him for now, and recalled half their drones to refuel and rearm. Good to know.

It was just a matter of time now. They'd keep switching off three for three, until he had to surface. Meanwhile, a patrol must soon be on the way.

Whoever these jokers were...

Then it dawned on him. This must be the same high tech, stealthy tech development unit involved in the Intelligent Fuselage Skin (IFS) that Hannah had stolen from Wan. Whatever they had at stake, Rick was right near the heart of their operation.

Whitcomb had warned him: *get out of here as fast as you can.*

If that stupid Sherwin had not screwed up again, out of sheer malice and incompetence, they might be sailing into the comfort and security of a U.S. Air Force prison in Ramstein by now, en route to the U.S. Army stockade in Mannheim. At least, Sherwin would be going there—flattering himself, and assuming Whitcomb was not lying, Rick might be freed and restored to his proper military position—not that he had ever planned to make a career of it. Well, no time to think about any of that now.

The three nearby drones floated away again. Going to check out the other side of the road, looking for his corpse no doubt.

No time like now.

He pulled his numb legs out of the cold water, swung them around, and pushed himself as quietly as possible into a crouching position on his hands and knees. He crept out of the tunnel mouth, but stayed hiding in the tall, water-nourished reeds there.

That gave him an idea. The water flowing this way came from two directions. A beautiful, silvery little stream meandered across the meadow from the horizon, joining another stream that flowed along the base of the road. The road itself was built up about six meters above the meadow—for drainage, probably. That water flowed this way, joining the stream and going under the road through the tunnel. Where the road-side water flowed, the grass was a meter tall, with quite a few tall, corn-colored reeds sticking up. Using the reeds for cover, Rick low-crawled toward the command post. He almost bet he could surrender to them, if they'd just stop shooting, and if they could see he was unarmed and harmless. It was his only hope.

As he crawled slowly and effortfully, he heard a whirring sound behind him.

He froze.

The whirring sound was ear-piercing, though it was just at the edge of audible.

He waited, face down, to die.

They were still looking for him.

A shadow fled over him. *Oh god no, here it is.*

The device hovered blindly above him.

Evidently, it did not have good look-down visibility. It was made to look sideways. It could tilt slightly and look down at objects nearby, but not underneath. *Tell that to the design engineers*, he thought, *if I live long enough.*

What if they had motion sensors? What if they had heat sensors? What if fish could fly?

He turned and lay on his back. The hell with it.

And there, he was looking at the underbelly of a FDLV-39 drone whose machine gun muzzle swung gently left and right—looking for him, to kill him.

It was about two meters overhead.

On impulse, he grabbed a handful of mud in each hand and rose. He was stiff, but managed to move quickly. One by one, he lobbed the two handfuls—one at each eye hole camera.

The FDLV-39 backed away as if stung.

The operator in the command post must have recoiled as his visibility went dim.

Rick dashed and splashed as fast as he could, back to the safety of his tunnel.

A minute later, the other two drones whirred into view.

He watched as they eyeballed their blinded counterpart.

One of the two drones swung around and started searching—for him, no doubt.

The other two drones floated away toward the command post—the one leading the blind.

For the moment, Rick had only one drone to contend with. It was too high to somehow reach and maybe tip over. It was too hard to take down with stones. And now it was flying high enough to avoid getting mud in its face.

But with only one drone left, he might have a chance to run for it.

He ducked back into the tunnel, crawled as fast as he could on his elbows and knees, and emerged on the other side two minutes later.

Carefully, he peered out. No sign.

He clambered out of the tunnel and, with fast-beating heart, crawled up the embankment. He could see the drone, floating on the other side as it looked for the mud-slinger. The operators could not know what happened until they got the injured bird back. Only a human could have thrown that mud, probably. That would confirm he was still out there, alive and fighting. They'd send all the drones in.

His best hope—in the absence of any mercenary patrols—was that the drones would run low on fuel and ammo and return to base. Base appeared to be that well-camouflaged CP in the woods not too far away.

As he watched from his vantage point, he saw two drones returning. These looked different. It was easy to see they had rockets slung in pods under their fuselage, in addition to the machine gun. Each drone was capable of firing two respectable air-to-ground missiles that probably had a hell of a kick. With those, if you spotted a man, you could kill him even if you hit the ground five meters or so away. The concussion of a few pounds of explosive going off would be enough to stun the runner or render him utterly unconscious with blood coming from his ears.

He debated climbing on the road and waving his arms in surrender.

He decided just as quickly not to. They had not been fooling around when they stitched the ground around him with bullets that were meant to kill—no questions asked.

For the moment, they thought he was still on the other side.

Ducking low, he ran as fast as he could to get away from the culvert. That meant losing its protection. Maybe there would be another culvert or some other hidden spot up the road a bit.

Better than that—he came to an overpass. The road crossed over a wider stream here.

The overpass was concrete, with exposed steel trusses painted bright orange. The span was about six meters long, or about twenty feet, and wide as the road itself, again six meters. A stream a meter wide trickled through it over a bed of black mud and rounded rocks. Tall grass grew luxuriously in the cleft, offering some cover. During rainy weather, he imagined it might be water from one stony face to the other. Now it was just a little stream.

Carefully, Rick crossed back to the other side.

The CP was visible almost overhead now, just twenty meters (sixty feet or so) further on. It was an olive-drab trailer, with electronic transponder equipment on the roof. A field commel jeep sat parked nearby. Whoever was inside the air-conditioned safety inside that trailer evidently had no real supervision and did not believe in posting guards.

However, a wood and steel mobile platform extended out from the CP into the field about a car's length. The flatbed on which the platform had been trucked in sat parked not far away on the road shoulder, along with a row of three military vehicles.

On the platform, three young men in fatigues were busy working with their drones. Each wore a side arm in a holster strapped to a belt around his waist. Rick saw no rifles in sight.

Rick counted a total of six FDLV-39 units.

The three mercenaries kept recalling them and sending them out in rotations of two or three.

Rick started at the sound of a tremendous explosion in the direction from which he'd come.

The men on the platform shouted, pointed, and leaned over the railing in the direction where they must have blown up a wandering cow, poor thing.

"*Une vache,*" one of them roared, and they all laughed. Could be French, or Walloon Belgians.

These guys were losers, Rick decided. He'd never liked mercenaries. You could work with professionals, especially ex-U.S. military. You knew they made a hundred times in pay what you did, at the same risk to your life and limb. But an incompetent mercenary was a bum. And these guys seemed more like a cross between hooligans and computer hackers. They'd never been in combat, and had no respect for what they were doing, or whom they were trying to kill.

Still feeling bad for the dead cow, Rick hid and observed.

After about ten minutes, he had an idea.

The three goons made laughing noises as they entered the CP. Probably time for a beer or coffee break. That was one of the problems—a lot of these mercenaries did not have a command structure. The good ones had a professional system, with a boss. Some of the less professional ones were on a system of every man for himself.

Stealthily, Rick moved through the brush. As he neared the platform, he planned carefully.

Gauging the equipment on the roof and on the platform, he went for one piece of equipment that seemed obvious: a direction sensor.

It was a desperate shot, but he had nothing to lose.

At the moment, two of the drones were parked on their perches. Four other perches on the railings were empty as their units were out on patrol.

As he climbed silently onto the platform, he heard laughter inside. They were telling jokes in French or maybe Italian—he couldn't tell which.

He was on the platform no more than two minutes. In that time, he turned each of the direction-finding antennas askew by about ninety degrees. He hoped his plan would work because he had no backup. On a table lay several cheese sandwiches—the famous hot Luxemburgish *Kachkéis*, a kind of low-fat cream cheese that is eaten hot or cold slathered onto good farm bread. He daubed a fingertip of *Kachkéis* over each eye of the two parked drones.

Just as the door opened, he slid down into the darkness.

They missed seeing him by the bat of an eyelash.

He crawled into the darkest little hole he could find and waited.

Nothing. Good.

No guards, no dogs, no nothing. That meant utter confidence in their security. They were not on the perimeter of their operations, but somewhere close to the heart of it.

Two of the other drones now drifted home, and the young mercenaries leaned across the railings to intercept them manually for servicing. It was like holding out your hands for a hunting falcon to return, only these were multi-million Euro flying machines filled with sensitive electronics—and he had just messed with part of their communication network.

The young men appeared to be upset, because they made appropriate noises as if suddenly their day wasn't going so well anymore. The laughter stopped, although the babbling picked up in pitch.

All they had to do was climb down here, with those side arms, Rick thought, and shoot him.

But they were not professional enough. Hackers, yes. Tekkies, yes. But soldiers, no.

He gathered a handful of plum-sized stones and crept away about thirty meters in the safety of the reeds. As two drones drifted by overhead, he plunked each one with a rock. Then he ran like hell into the underpass and hid under a girder.

The drones came drifting into the shadows, looking for him. They turned this way and that.

One of them had a rocket underneath, ready to launch.

Each drone had evil looking eyes, and a phallic machine gun barrel.

As they entered the shadows, they also switched on bright headlights.

Rick ducked into cover as deeply as he could, rubbing his eyes. He saw brown floaters where his optic nerves had been torched. But the flare passed in a few minutes. The flying fish—they resembled sentient sea creatures—withdrew reluctantly and the headlights switched off.

And yet—the opportunity was too good to resist—they had to fly low to get under the road.

While they were still in the passageway, Rick darted forth with two handfuls of mud and let loose. They were quick, wild shots, but he must have at least partially blinded both machines.

They turned and unleashed torrents of machine gun fire.

Rick hid behind a pylon and held his aching ears. Even his eyes hurt with the fierceness of that sound.

Now, however, he had damaged four of the drones, at least temporarily until the technicians could clean their delicate optics. That might not be as easy as it sounded.

So there were two functional drones left now.

Those would be recalled any second now.

And here they came, flying carefully along the ground on this side. They were nose down, looking for him. Each had rockets strapped underneath.

Time for his gamble.

Two of the drones were inactive on the platform, and two were returning for cleaning and repair.

That left just these two in the field.

If drones could be pissed, he was sure these two were livid.

Pray to god he'd really screwed up their GPS and steering systems.

He filled his hands with rocks and ran out into the open field.

The drones at first did not see him, so intent were they on scouring the ditch alongside the road inch by inch.

A shout arose from the platform.

The mercs had spotted him. Several more came running, all with drawn pistols.

He heard the popping noises of shots being fired, but he was running, and he didn't expect they could hit him at this range with handguns. Rifles, yes—he prayed they didn't have any out on the platform yet.

The two functioning drones now swept across the grass toward him.

Their guns were firing steadily.

Rick threw himself into a hole in the field.

Bullets whizzed all around overhead. He curled into a ball in this deep wheel rut or whatever it was and waited. They had lost him again. When the looked up, the two drones were fifty meters further out.

Perfect.

They were out of ammo, by his reckoning and careful observation.

He rose and waved his arms. "Hey, you stupid bastards. Here I am. Come shoot me!"

As he yelled, he started running toward the CP.

The men on the platform started taking pot shots. Luckily, they were lousy shooters.

The two drones came sailing after him.

A few more sputters, and they were totally out of ammo.

Now all they had left were the two missiles.

Rick ran back and forth, throwing stones at the two flying machines.

The men had stopped shooting for fear of hitting them.

Rick could see them hanging on the railing, watching with ghoulish eyes.

The two drones floated on either side of him now—safely fifty meters away, and afraid to shoot him lest one drone take the other out.

So he ran toward the CP.

The drones were at his back.

The men were afraid to shoot, for fear of hitting their beloved machines.

Now came the moment of truth.

Do or die.

As he ran, first one drone, and then the other, unleashed its missile.

The two missiles streaked toward him but then, because their navigation systems relied on GPS rather than line of sight because of the speeds involved, the missiles curved and sailed directly into the CP.

The CP exploded violently in a noisy ball of red flames and black smoke. The platform rose in splinters, and with it the shattered bodies of the men who had just minutes ago been doing everything in their power to kill him.

This was not a type of combat he'd ever quite been in, but you learned to live by your wits.

The blast knocked him flat on the ground, and a hot wave passed over him.

But the drones were finished.

The CP, the wrecked platform, and the woods around it were engulfed in flames.

Fuel barrels exploded one by one in a small storage area, adding to the chaos.

Rick clambered up the embankment, away from the blazing inferno.

On the ground, he spotted a loaded 9 mm automatic one of the men had dropped.

He scooped it up while running and held it in both hands, marksman style. He kept it pointed ahead of him as he went up the slope with desperately superhuman energy. Leaves and grass and other debris flew around his feet. Burning bits of vegetation and papers swirled around him in the hot, smoky, oily air.

On the high ground near the road, he saw the intact vehicles parked.

Two men came running toward him, shooting.

He threw himself down.

Their shots were wild as they ran.

He took aim for a second and popped, popped, and dropped both of them.

This was combat, and he was back in Huilongistan, picking up where he'd left off. This time, his side was going to win.

In the silence, he tore open the door to a small, foreign-looking field vehicle. It was greenish inside, with simple instrumentation, like an old jeep. He tore the ignition wires and held them together while giving the gas pedal one pump. The vehicle stuttered and then bumbled into life. Shaking all over, it rattled and rolled until it was running smoothly.

Wheeling smartly about, he drove onto the road and took off in the direction of Germany.

After about ten minutes, he heard sirens. A stream of fire, police, and military vehicles passed him going the other way.

He kept driving, hoping nobody would come back after him.

As he drove, he became aware of an egg beater sound.

He drove on, with the pedal floored.

The sound got louder.

It was a helicopter with U.S. Air Force markings.

37. Chopper to Vianden

Must be NATO.

Had to be friendly—they weren't shooting at him. What a refreshing change.

The chopper circled around to land in front of him.

He could not outdrive it or outrun it. Should he try? Did he have no friends left in this world?

A loudspeaker voice carried over the road surface and lost itself in trees. "Sergeant Buchan…"

It was a woman's voice.

"Stop and stand down. We are here to help you. Stop the car."

It was the voice of Major Kendra Walsh, his JAG lawyer. She really went all out to help a guy.

He let off the pedal and let the vehicle coast to a long, long, slow stop.

He stepped outside and waited. It was over. He had no fight left, no running, no thinking. He was exhausted and close to tears of loss and frustration.

He waited as the chopper set down amid a whirl of wind.

In the distance, over the tree tops, he could see the spires of a town—Echternach, maybe.

The U.S. Air Force chopper set down on an open stretch of road without trees.

A moment later, the side panel slid open, and two women in dark-blue U.S. Air Force issue flight suits jumped down. The flight suits were unadorned with any markings of rank or unit, not even a shoulder patch.

One of the women was Kendra Walsh.

The other woman was Hannah Smith.

"I'm dreaming," Rick said quietly out loud to himself. "I've died and gone to heaven."

The two women ran toward him—Rick observed in a dream-like state—in that feminine way he'd often seen women run, with their forearms up and slightly spread, and their hips gyrating.

Both were laughing and squealing and happy to see him.

He stood with tears streaming down his face, finished, beaten, wanting to be rescued.

Hannah hit him so hard it was painful. Knocked the wind out of him. She sailed through the air and landed on him, wrapping her arms around him and crying for joy. "Baby, Honey, I have you back again—and this time I will never let you go."

Kendra Walsh—neat ball of kinky, shiny black hair, incredibly beautiful teeth and lips and nose, vivacious eyes full of intelligence and affection, hit him a moment later. They nearly knocked him on the ground, and he was never happier as he stood there holding the two women.

From the chopper emerged the Asian-looking man, named Shen, who had some 'splainin' to do, and behind him none other than Colonel Whitcomb.

As Whitcomb drew near, Rick said, "I thought you were off on a mission."

"I was," Whitcomb said with a row of grinning teeth, "but orders changed. Mission got turned around."

Hannah took her man in tow. "I'm not letting you out of my sight again."

"I don't understand," Rick said weakly.

"Of course you don't," Whitcomb boomed. "You're on the inside now. It will all be clear as soon as we get you where we are going." He added: "You apparently had a hell of a run-in with some of the mercenary drones they are testing near Wiltz. You know they shot down a Belgian air force plane not long ago. But with the Intelligent Fuselage Skin, you would never have stood a chance. The drones would have out-thought, out-maneuvered, and killed you. The IFS makes any aircraft into a smart machine that can process data a million times faster than a human pilot. It makes even our most modern aircraft into pterodactyl dinosaurs."

"Glad I got in ahead of the game," Rick said.

"You were one smart cookie though," Whitcomb said respectfully.

Hannah clung to Rick so hard she nearly bruised his ribs. Her hair was still short, but the dark was gone. Her hair color was back to blonde—and her lipstick had gone from deep chestnut brown, punk-slash, to a light, delicate girlie pink with a shine on it. "Oh sweetheart, I was worried sick about you."

He shook his head. "Now you tell me."

Together, they boarded the chopper, whose two U.S. Air Force pilots lifted off and headed in the direction Rick had come from.

"We have someone we need to pick up," Kendra said, as she sat on a bench facing the bench on which Rick and Hannah clung together.

The chopper set down near the wrecked car. It did not take long to track down Rick's nemesis, Sherwin, who was limping along the road but otherwise intact, making his way back to civilization.

Whitcomb took Sherwin prisoner at gunpoint. With Kendra's and Shen's help, Sherwin was cuffed and led to the chopper.

"You have a rendezvous at the stockade," Kendra told him.

The chopper lifted off, with Sherwin cuffed to the armrest of a bench.

"I didn't think I'd see you again," Rick told Hannah—their voices lost amid engine noise and wind.

She fairly purred, resting her blonde head against his chest. "Oh sweetheart, I was about to die without you."

"I'm still confused."

"I know," she said, "but Professor Sander and Kendra will explain soon enough. We are headed for Vianden, which is probably the most beautiful of the many castles here in the country. We still have a lot of work to do. It's a scary situation, but we are trying to turn it around—globally."

She added, "By the way, I have one piece of very good news. Romain is in a special burn hospital in Berlin, recovering from his injuries. He will have some scars and a limp, but much of that can be fixed. Mélu is with him as we speak. She said to thank you—and the Luxembourg Scouts and Guides—for saving him."

38.   Vianden Headquarters

Riding in the U.S. Air Force chopper over the green forests and meadows of Luxembourg were Rick Buchan; Hannah Smith (glued to his side, and clutching both of his hands in hers); Shen, the agent of mystery; Kendra Walsh, the young JAG officer wearing a plain dark-blue flight suit like Hannah; and a very imposing Colonel Whitcomb.

Strapped to a seat, facing away, with a jacket thrown over his head, was the creature who had tried to sell Rick down the plumbing to save his own ugly, sociopathic skin. Sherwin looked limp and beaten.

"Buchan," Whitcomb said with a strangely familiar grin creasing his features.

Rick looked at the colonel in confusion. Hannah noticed, and dug in his back pack for the medicines.

Whitcomb held up a sheet of paper. It was legal size, long, and covered with specks of black type set off by official looking seals and signatures. "This is the warrant for your arrest."

Rick felt a wave of shock pass through him.

Whitcomb ripped the warrant up with both hands and threw the pieces up so they floated in the air. "All done."

Kendra smiled in her wide, lovely manner. "You're off the hook, Sarge."

"It was Sherwin," Rick said simply. It all came back, flooding him with horrifying memories of that traumatic night. He let Hannah pour his pills into her hand and shove them into his mouth, followed by a long swallow as he accepted a plastic bottle of drinking water from her.

Whitcomb reached into a canvas satchel beside him on the seat. "Look here," he said above the engine noise. He took out the package vital to the Intelligent Fuselage Skin technology.

The flight to Vianden took only minutes.

Hannah had her arm wrapped around Rick's back. He felt her hand rubbing his side, and patted her hand. He took her hand lovingly and held it in his. She rested her cheek on his shoulder, took his free hand in hers on his lap, and kissed him on the neck.

Kendra and Shen looked on approvingly. Whitcomb winked.

The pilot spoke over the intercom: "Stand by. We are landing in Vianden."

"But we just took off, and now we're landing?" someone said.

The pilot replied, "The distance from Noertrange to Vianden, halfway across the country in the north, is about twenty-two klicks, just over thirteen miles."

Rick said, "That explains why we just flew five minutes, and already we are landing."

A patter of relieved laughter surrounded him in response.

Rick watched as a hill floated into view with a wide structure on top.

"That is Vianden," Kendra said. She pronounced it in the Luxemburgish manner, which sounds a bit like *FIE-yan-nun* with the accent on the first syllable. Rick thought it was a sort of a cool word—almost English-sounding—but then Luxemburgish, like Flemish and Dutch, is on the linguistic bridge between modern German and modern English.

Hannah squeezed his hands and shook them, almost tugging at him. "We're not on the run anymore, baby. We're on the inside."

"I'm still running inside."

She kept tugging at him. "I know, sweetheart, but we are the good guys now."

"I believe you," he said without entirely believing. He wanted to believe her, but he couldn't yet grasp what this was all about. His life had been a crazy quilt of death, danger, running, and betrayal since that night on the road in Huilongistan. Tears ran down his cheeks as he thought about his dead teammates and, yes, even the mercenaries who'd been along for a doomed mission set up by the lieutenant from hell. He felt sorry for Fincoff and anyone else who had been caught up in this meat grinder of insanity. Somewhere in the movie theater of his mind, far off, was a vision of walking on a quiet California beach, holding hands with Hannah. In his dream, the sun bloated into a great big orange ice cream scoop, a delicious ball of flavor and love melting over the Peaceful Ocean.

★★★ ▮▮ ▬ ▮▮ ▬ ≋ ★★★

The chopper flew over a valley, which Whitcomb explained was the Our River valley. The river is a small tributary to the Sûr or Sauer near which Romain had parked his car in Echternach. The Sauer in turn is tributary to the Mosel, which forms part of the border between Luxembourg and nearby Germany.

The small town (population 1,800) of Vianden flew past below. The chopper's shadow raced over the sparkling River Our, over the Victor Hugo museum, and other landmarks dating as far back as ancient Celtic and Roman times. Nestled on a hillside was one of the largest intact castles in Europe, restored since its ruination over centuries of warfare and neglect.

The chopper continued into a deep forest, and set down to a landing on a heliport, which itself was part of a sprawling modern complex of concrete and glass.

It was getting late in the day.

As the chopper's engines browsed down to a dull roar, a sort of sunny peacefulness overcame Rick. He was inwardly exhausted from all the terror and running and just surviving—not to mention his separation from Hannah, and his endless confusion about who was pushing the buttons and why.

Several young Luxembourg Army soldiers—men and women in fatigue uniforms, with combat boots and baseball caps—came to help take the prisoner off. Sherwin was led away, still in handcuffs and with his jacket draped over his head.

"We aren't going to have time for a vacation," Whitcomb informed them with an air of businesslike regret. "We are about to tackle the most important job of all."

Kendra told Rick, "You'll know everything shortly."

As the helicopter engine fell silent, Rick had a few moments to inhale fresh forest air. Above all, the silence was like medicine. It was a balmy summer evening under blue skies full of fluffy white cumulus clouds. Birds soared about, insects chirred in high grass on the surrounding meadow, and butterflies danced while cows looked on with cud-chewing indifference.

They entered a concrete building that seemed a cross between a castle, a bunker, and a modernist villa. The place was huge, and bore Luxembourg Grand-Ducal insignia around the doors.

An Italian-Luxemburgish captain in the Grand-Ducal Army met them at the door, escorted by two young male sergeants. She introduced herself—in near-perfect U.S. English—as Susanna Stefani, shaking hands with Kendra, Rick, Hannah, Shen, and Whitcomb in turn. Stefani was slender, dark-haired, olive-skinned, and pretty in a gamine way, with sympathetic dark eyes and wide, unadorned smile. She wore a dark green fatigue uniform with a black beret tucked through one shoulder lapel— quite jaunty. She also carried a no-nonsense black Glock 26 sub-compact automatic in a brown leather holster on a belt with spare clips.

"I lived in Connecticut for most of my teenage years," she informed them as she led Rick, Hannah, Shen, and Whitcomb into a cavernous entry that resembled a hotel lobby. There were, however, no obsequious civilian clerks. Instead, a military police sergeant and several lower enlisted ranks manned a duty desk and supervised several wide, double-winged doors leading into the major parts of the complex. "I went to school near New Haven, so I speak the language a bit."

"How did you happen to return to Luxembourg?" Kendra asked.

"My family have lived for generations in Luxembourg City. We originally came from Bari in southern Italy, but that is long ago in another age. I have dual U.S.-Luxembourgeois citizenship, and so also European Union citizenship."

"That is so cool," Hannah said. "Did you go to school in the U.S.?"

"I went to the University of Connecticut at Storrs," Stefani said with pride. "Majored in Foods and Nuts, what else? So now I became an intelligence officer with Luxembourg and NATO. Makes sense, huh?"

Rick shook his head. "I am studying to be a lawyer one day. Nothing makes sense." He was taking courses on and off with various overseas branches of major U.S. universities with military service contracts.

Hannah pulled him away from the knot of walkers, so they were out of earshot. She clung to his arm and muttered so only he could hear, "You're going to be a great lawyer. And I am going back to school to study business so I can hire you as my pitbull."

"Oh great," Rick said. "Do I have to wear a uniform?"

Hannah whispered in his ear: "You can be my general, and I'll be your majorette."

"That is not a military rank," he said tongue-in-cheek.

"I know. I want to twirl your baton."

"As soon as we are alone, we can start up the marching music."

"I'll play trombone in your band."

"What about that baton?"

"I think I already dropped it. I'm on that slide now, blowing into your trombone."

"And I'll bang your cymbals together."

"My ears are already ringing. Can you do that some more?"

"Wait until we are alone. I'll sing you a tune or two."

"I'll keep you on key."

Captain Stefani announced: "Here we are."

Back from distraction, Rick saw that they had come to an intersection amid wide, sunny corridors with marbled floors and many high, ogive windows in sturdy double glass to even out the seasonal temperature extremes. The carpet runners down the centers of the halls were dark red. Overhead in a series of small vaults hung dark iron chandeliers with glowing yellowish lights—more for décor than illumination. Rick noticed wall sconces—plain, round frosted disks—that would probably throw enough soft, indirect light to brighten the halls without glaring.

"This is where you will stay while you are with us." She led them through a double door into an inner, carpeted hall with locked rooms resembling a hotel. "These are the guest quarters. I'll let Professor Sander know you have arrived. He has been a guest here for several days."

Last Rick had seen of Sander, he lay in the doorway of the Echternach post office, bleeding from the head, and Hannah had the package in hand, running for her life.

"Why don't we all meet in the dining area in twenty minutes," Susanna Stefani said. "The professor will be anxious to meet you."

Kendra thanked Stefani with a firm handshake. "Peace," she said.

Stefani gave a conspiratorial wink. "*Pax vobiscum.*"

"I'll let you sort yourselves out," Susanna Stefani told them. "You'll find your keys inside. The rooms are unlocked until you take possession."

Rick observed that Whitcomb took one room across the hall, Shen another for himself, and Kendra a third for herself. Hannah towed him into a room, saying: "I'm gonna eat your ice cream, friend. Get in here."

Rick let her lead him into the room. He pushed the door shut.

Alone at last, they slammed together in a hard embrace. She lifted off the ground, supporting herself with both arms around his neck, while he cradled her rear end—ah god, that softness, so dear—in his hands. They sucked face in a violent, hungry sharing to make loss, sorrow, and hunger go away.

"I missed you so," she whimpered while stroking his eye brows.

He nibbled on her upper lip, playfully, letting it snap away pink and soft. "I thought you dumped me."

"Oh no, baby, I wanted you to be safe. I didn't have time to explain."

"I saw you run with the package."

"I would have given anything to take you along, but you might have gotten hurt."

"But you're here in one piece."

"I'm lucky. So are you."

"I was attacked by UFOs."

"I believe you."

"You know about the drones?"

She nodded.

"And why—?" he started to ask, but she stuck her tongue in to his mouth and ground her face against his. Then she said, "Let's go—talk—get it over with—and then we will have our marching band."

Since they had no baggage, it was a matter of washing up. The hostel service provided white towels and cloths, as well as perfunctory soap and shampoo, pretty much like a luxury hotel without the hoopla.

They found their plastic room key and locked the door as they entered the corridor. Their companions were in the hall, walking in a small herd toward a well-lighted room near the end of the hall. They came to a plain, rectangular room with a long table and a dozen wooden chairs with high backs. Young army privates hustled about, holding chairs for the ladies, bringing coffee in several white porcelain services on silvery trays.

"I smell dinner," Whitcomb boomed in satisfaction.

"I'm starving," Kendra said. "It's been a busy day."

Susanna Stefani entered, with Professor Sander close behind. The Professor looked rested, wearing a pale wheat summer suit of Italian make, along with an open short in light cranberry that displayed white chest hair. He looked tanned and recovered. His face had that same authoritative, stern but warm demeanor with an aquiline nose, fierce grayish eyes under bushy brows, and a smallish mouth in a long face. He still wore a white, square patch over his bald spot, with wild fluffs of white hair sailing in the air around it.

"You all know Professor Sander either from news articles or meeting him," Susanna said, standing by her chair, while a sergeant pulled the chair out for Sander to sit. The professor acknowledged the service but waved it politely away, showing that he preferred simplicity and equality.

"*Bonjour*," Professor Sander said. He joked for a moment, "You are wondering who clobbered me on the head. The truth is simple. I was so anxious to hand the package to Miss Smith, to avoid Wan's agents from seizing it at the post office, that I ran into the door and fell down half unconscious."

"I actually told the postal people to call an ambulance for him," Hannah said, "while I intercepted a Hail Mary pass from Professor Sander and ran for my life with the package."

"I still have a decent throwing arm," Sander said, "from my old football days."

Captain Stefani signaled for her soldiers to seal the room. "We are going to have a top-secret meeting," she announced. "There are no recording devices and there will be no witnesses except when the servers bring our dinners. I am sure you are all as hungry as I am. Dinner is..." She consulted a menu sheet. "...*Rouladen* in cognac sauce, mashed local potatoes in butter and parsley, Belgian asparagus, and farm bread. We serve water, white Moselle wine or a nice red Chianti from Toscano, or you may drink soda or Mousel beer. Those are the choices." She beamed.

"There will be nobody complaining," Kendra assured her. It was sort of evident to Rick that Kendra was the de facto hostess on his side, while Stefani represented whoever the other side was.

"While we are waiting," Professor Sander said, "I would like to bring you all on board with the latest information and news."

Kendra said, "Richard will appreciate the information. If you explain for him, everyone else will be up to speed."

Sander regarded Rick in a paternal, comradely manner. "Excellent." He reached a long arm out, and Rick shook his soft but strong hand. Sander continued, "How do I explain this in an easy manner? As you may know, I am a widower, and a few months ago I suffered the tragedy of losing my only child—my son Pierre, who was gunned down in London by the people I am making it my life's work to oppose in every way that I can." He spoke quietly and evenly, but with strength and conviction. "What this is all about—that is what you want to know..." *(*Endnotes #10)*

..."Here we are today, on the verge of a very important vote that will probably determine the future of this corporate world. On the one hand, we have the Chinese oligarch Wan, who is running for president of the Corporate Executive Officers Confederation, or CEOC. He leads a faction who want to end democracy as we have known it, reduce workers to serfs without any rights, and move the clock back centuries to the middle ages.

"On the other hand, we have a resistance movement of which I am a leading exponent, called PAX, which stands for Progressive Alliance for Peace. It's from the Latin Pax, from where the modern English world peace comes.

"And, Mr. Buchan, if you have followed all this so far, the technology Wan's criminals stole from my son is the key to convincing more of these oligarchs that the correct road for them is to follow him. He wants to end democracy as we have known it, and have a small clique of CEOC rule the world as if we were back in the middle ages.

"My son developed the Intelligent Fuselage technology for the benefit of mankind, not to give more power to a megalomaniac like Wan. We developed all the test data here at the international research and development facilities near Wiltz, where you, Mr. Buchan, ran afoul of the conservative element of CEOC—those opposed to democracy, opposed to worker and middle class rights, and totally in favor of corporate dictatorship.

"Key to understanding the technology were the intricate chemical and electronic data from several years of rigorous testing. Without those data, the fuselage material and its avionics are worthless. When I saw that CEOC was out to grab that technology, I sent the data to my son Pierre, who was teaching at university in London. Wan's agents stole the data, and then murdered my son so nobody else could duplicate the research.

"Unfortunately for Mr. Wan, just as he was about to start convincing his oligarchic friends that he held the future in his hands, Hannah Smith freed herself from his disgraceful ownership of her, and took the data package with her.

"Mélu, who was working in Shanghai at the time, prevailed upon Hannah to free herself, and to help PAX. Mélu never anticipated the coup when Hannah stole the data. Hannah tried to put the package in PAX hands in Paris, but as you know, that ended in an attempt by a grimy middle man, Fincoff, to bribe PAX or sell the package to the highest bidder—which would have been Wan and the hard core of CEOC.

"Mr. Buchan, you and Hannah managed to evade Wan's tracking systems and get all the way to Luxembourg. Hannah mailed the package to herself at the Gare post office in Luxembourg City. Her plan was to pick it up and walk with it to Mélu and Romain's house in Belair. When she realized she was being followed, she panicked and mailed it to me in Echternach."

Hannah cut in: "I understand now—I thought Shen was working for CEOC."

Shen said, "I am actually with the U.S. Central Intelligence Agency. Everyone in the U.S. these days, following the corporate take-over and the poverty, is split between two camps. There are those who still believe all the pseudo-patriotic and pseudo-religious lies told by False News organizations and demagogues, who blindly support the corporations. They are willing to take that one last vote to weaken the government and thereby make the corporations stronger—which no longer matters, because the country is effectively ruled by foreigners now. I have been tracking your progress since Paris, Mr. Buchan and Miss Smith, trying to get you to safety and the package into the hands of Professor Sander."

Rick looked at Whitcomb and said, "So, Colonel—what about your sudden change of orders?"

Whitcomb held his coffee cup in two big hands and said, "I am an officer in the United States Army. I'm serving with the last NATO command, and I'd like to see democracy restored in the United States. I don't want to go backward to blind nationalism, manipulated by oil companies and health denial and big pharma and the war industry. I also don't want any sort of totalitarianism—I am looking for balance. A balance of powers, a separation, like the Constitution calls for. We need to take the Constitution away from the liars who have said they are saving us from ourselves while they sell our jobs and our houses and our economy to foreigners for a short profit and then run. So I, and Major Walsh here, are part of a resistance movement called PAXUS that works with PAXEUR and global, straight vanilla PAX, to achieve a peaceful and prosperous resolution for everyone. I have been working as a double agent with CEOC—and I'll let the professor explain what that is all about."

Whitcomb continued: "I meant it when I wanted you to drive Sherwin back to Germany. I had just handed a huge bribe package to General Mendé of NATO and CEOC, and was supposed to return to my liaison job in Brussels. Then we received word that a crisis was at hand here in Luxembourg, and my orders were to pick you up along with Sherwin and Miss Smith and bring you, along with the IFS package, here to the Vianden corporate reserve. Major Walsh, you are the PAXUS sponsor here. Maybe you'd care to add your two cents."

Kendra nodded. "Sure. I am, like Colonel Whitcomb, an active proponent of restoring democracy and balance. None of us are against corporations, free markets, or rule of law. Quite the contrary. We want good business, healthy economics, but also democracy—which means workers and artisans (the middle class) possess the rights of liberty, happiness, equality, and property ownership. The conservative, laissez-faire wing of CEOC is on the verge of taking the world to a new level of tyranny. Professor Sander has not yet mentioned the use that Wan's faction wants to make of this technology."

"Right," Sander said, "here is what it all boils down to. I am known and respected by a lot of corporate leaders. They understand that the universities produce technology for them so they can compete. To have universities, the common people have to have access to good health, education, jobs, and so forth. To have that, we need democracy where every individual can compete on a free and equal basis. I'll call to your attention that, in the United States for example, university education was not open to the average worker until after World War Two, when President Truman created the G.I. Bill for returning military personnel of all ranks, regardless of whether their father was a billionaire or worked with a pick and shovel in a ditch. Democracy wasn't really all there until that time period. You can read the history of the age on your own. I'm not teaching classes tonight. And yes, I am grieving for the loss of my dear son, and prepared personally to die in this cause."

He rose to his feet and spoke animatedly, with his hands over the table and his fingertips doing pushups on the linen. "There is an all-important CEOC plenary session scheduled this week in the Valley of Seven Castles, right here in Luxembourg. Some people are calling it the next Schengen, referring to the town in Luxembourg where the Europeans set aside their borders, their history of wars and hatred, and decided to become one single economic union. That's been through a lot of challenges. Some are calling today's situation the New EU, or NEU, which is German for 'new'.

"There are two factions in CEOC. One group, led by Wan, what to return t the middle ages, end democracies, and create a new age of ignorance and poverty. It's an appealing idea for ruthless people who don't care about anyone or anything but their own money and power. Miss Smith here had a taste of this when she was bought and sold like a slave. I apologize for mentioning it, Hannah, but you were a victim and I join you in fighting to prevent others from being victims of human slave trading. It's fashionable among the young and gullible to trade a few years of personal liberty for supposedly having a lot of fun overseas, seeming really cool to their friends, and retiring for life with a large pension. The truth is that most of these young people end up as sex slaves, and either die from disease, from abuse, or simply disappear—because nobody wants to give them that pension. That would mean they have rights, and the people like Wan do not believe in human rights. In many cases they come from cultures that are centuries behind the West, and ridicule the idea that their untouchables should have any rights. That is what we are up against.

"We can turn it around. We can take control of the media back from corporations so they can't monopolize the truth and turn it into a night and day carnival of lies, propaganda, advertising, and corporate disinformation.

"More importantly, let me explain to you the importance of the upcoming vote. Wan's faction wants to get the complete IFS data and offer their CEO members a new level of power.

"One of the top NATO generals is General Gaston Mendé of Sweden, who is in the process of creating the first corporate military forces. He is simply building upon a century of private intelligence corporations and mercenaries. With the IFS technology, General Mendé can offer the CEOC hardliners the ability to field their own armies and air forces. No existing national government, including the now very weak United States, will be able to resist this technology. From there, he wants to use university resources around the world to build ultra-smart ships, tanks, and other military and police technologies. They already are masters of surveillance and eavesdropping, so totalitarian corporate control is right around the corner—unless we can stop them.

"The good news is that we managed to grab the IFS data package back from them. It would take them several years to regain that lead, in which time the national governments of the United States, the EU, China, India, Brazil, and others can develop parallel technologies.

"Again, I am a proponent of corporations in a legal framework. They must not be above the law. They must not control the media and the information and raise millions of uninformed people to overthrow democracy and replace it with the simpler, stupider emotionalism and tyranny of demagogues. I have accepted the nomination of the PAX faction of CEOC—the moderates—to run for presidency of the CEOC this week in the Valley of the Seven Castles. Without the IFS package, Wan cannot intimidate anyone into fearing for their corporate survival. In fact, I am sure they will welcome the opportunity to vote against Wan and General Mendé and reject a new middle ages for the entire world.

"We are standing up to some very brutal people. They murderd my son. As long as we keep them from having technological power, Wan cannot make the case to his right-wing cronies that they can bully the rest of us. And so we'll win. There will be a separation of powers again, freedom of the press, informed and responsible voters, and end to demagoguery, and a real free market for everyone, not just the top one thousand families.

"I want to thank you for your support, especially Miss Hannah Smith and Mr. Richard Buchan in outwitting and outrunning the CEOC gangsters of Mr. Wan, including his Triad soldiers from Macao, his Mafia and Yakuza and Narco and other gangsters from around the world. I will go so far in this private meeting to tell you that General Mendé represents a legal form of gangsterism at the top of the social stratum, along with out-of-control corporations. Colonel Whitcomb, you are developing some information along those lines."

Sander sat down. Whitcomb spoke up: "Yes. I can't reveal the details yet, but we have some other important intelligence that will cripple the CEOC conservatives at VOSC this week. We do need you to make a strong run for office, Professor Sander."

"I will do my best," Sander promised.

Someone knocked on the glass door leading into the room. Outside, Rick saw a group of chefs in white jackets and tall white hats, pushing wagons loaded with dinner, dessert, and drinks as promised. Captain Susanna Stefani rose to open the door.

"Dinner is ready," said a senior chef as she led the procession into the room, to the sound of clapping and cheering.

"All that political talk gets my stomach growling," Rick told Hannah.

"We'll eat now, and then rest. Tomorrow is a big day as we get ready to fly out. Get a good night's sleep, everyone," Kendra said as they prepared to feast.

39. Alone: Rick & Hannah

When Rick and Hannah closed the door, locking themselves into their room, they stood and looked at each other with serious, almost overwhelmed eyes and emotions.

"Is it real at last?" Rick said as he reached for her.

She nodded. "I never lied to you, Rick. I am bowled over by you. I just didn't have time to tell you to get out, to leave—because I was afraid you'd be killed if you got into this mess any deeper."

"And I nearly got killed anyway."

They drifted into each other's arms. Holding her, he rocked her gently, while his hands explored the hills and valleys of her geography.

"I am all yours," she said, "if you want me."

"I want you," he murmured, nibbling at her ear lobe. "Just think. I can have this ear forever. What a lovely ear. And you have another little ear on the other side." He imitated a lion roar, and went *row-wow-wow* around her neck as if she were a child. She laughed. "That tickles."

Playfully, they undressed each other, pausing often to lick this or bite that.

"You are my ice cream," he said softly.

"I am melting down there," she agreed. "Feel me."

He did. "Juicy."

"Yours," she said in a dreamy tone while writhing her arms like an exotic dancer on either side of his head.

"I will savor your berries."

"I love when you bite my berries."

"I will savor them—*right now!*"

With that, as she squealed happily, he lifted her in the air, so she rode backward on the saddle of his flat abdomen, as he ran toward the bed. Her legs rocked behind him, as he glimpsed him and her in the mirror. "You have the cutest feet," he said. Everything about her was perfect. "I can't believe how lucky I am," he said as they bounced on the bed together and started a leisurely embrace.

"I am the bun," she said, "and you are the bunny."

"Oh, let me hop into your patch."

"Hop on over, and come all you want."

"Hop, hop, hop," he said, nuzzling her neck. "I want to forget all that crap. The McGuffin, the terror, the running, the yelling..."

"I know, me too." She wrapped her arms around him and pulled his head down so she could nibble on his nose and lips. "Nice bunny." He felt one bare leg rise around him, one bare foot hooking him close. She gave a few pulls, with her heel on his buttocks, to get him rocking.

"Fuck like bunnies." He enveloped her in his muscular, smooth, rippling grip and snuggled so close that his carrot found her patch. A bunny hand helped the carrot slide into the wetness.

She rolled her eyes up, and closed them. "Mmm."

Rick felt waves of pleasure and joy as they started to rock and roll to their very own heavenly rhythm.

40.   Morning in Vianden

Rick and Hannah lay entwined naked and warm in the comfort of their love. Gray morning light flooded into the room from the foggy woods and meadows all around.

They could hear Kendra banging on doors up and down the hall. "Rise and shine."

"I want to get out of the military," Rick murmured into the privacy of her armpit.

She laughed and rolled on top of him. "I can't wait to get rank on you."

"You mean pull rank, you bad girl." He gently paddled her deliciously soft bottom, making slappy noises that echoed through the simple room with its bed, desk, and closet.

She blew into his ear. "I want to yank your crank."

He blew on her neck, which made a farting noise. "I want to thank your flank."

"Silly guy." She looked down on him with wide, vulnerable, adoring eyes.

He gripped her slender waist in his hands and returned her gaze. "All mine."

"All yours," she said. "Oh baby…"

"All mine," he said, rocking her from side to side in his embrace.

"Weigh me," she said.

He rolled over on top.

"Lay me."

He slid in easily and started rocking. She gripped him fiercely to her and rocked even harder, so that the headboard banged continuously and roughly against the wall.

"We're gonna break the bed," he gasped, breathlessly.

"We'll buy them another one." She nearly strangled him, wrapping her forearms around his neck. "Take me, Richard, take me." He did, and she urged him on, "Do me. Every minute you fuck me, it makes the bad go away. You make me clean again, take the dirt away…"

He reached down with both arms, cupped his hands around her buttocks, and pulled—while they rocked together with soft, wet, squishing sounds that made her delirious. "Yes," she cried in a long, broken wail of pleasure as he drilled into her. He was overcome with passion, throwing her legs over his shoulder and pounding away so that the room filled with slapping sounds. She responded with cries for *more, harder, do me, take me...*

★★★ ▮▮ ═ ▮▮ ▬ ▓▓ ★★★

She laughed, a bit later. "I am so sore I think I'll be limping all day."

They stood stark naked in the tile shower, testing the water for just the right temperature.

"I think I'll be limp for a week," he said.

"No, I know how to inflate your blimp."

"Oh god, I think I'm hard again. It's like having a clothes pin stuck on your crank. Ouch."

She laughed. "I can kiss it and make the owie go away."

They stood in a long, tender embrace, skin against skin, eyes gazing into eyes.

The glass booth filled with warmth and steam as water pummeled and caressed them. He was blinded by the water jet, and tossed his head back to get the mop of soggy hair out of his eyes.

"You look so cute when you are all wet," he said.

"And you—I could mistake you for a dolphin."

He tried to think of dolphin jokes, but nothing rose to mind. So he got on his knees in the delightful torrent. He sudsed her all over with a washcloth and some frothy Belgian soap that smelled faintly of chamomile and honey. "Do you mind if I do this for a really long time?"

She giggled. "I am going to be a very, very clean woman."

She screamed as he blew into the valley behind her Venus hill, making a trumpet sound.

"I will get you back for that," she said, and went down to her knees. "Stand up and take your punishment."

He stood up, and took it while bracing himself against the shower wall with both palms. It was his turn to roll his eyes up as she noisily vented the full fury of her hunger and passion. Totally unrestrained, she pawed and sucked and licked him, slapping his skin as she grabbed him this way or that way to take her pleasure. She gave new meaning to the term man-handling. Like a wild animal, she savaged his sensitive areas while he stood with his legs apart, and she lay twisted and splattered this way and that under him to get at him from every direction. When he began to gasp and then groan in spurting spasms, she uttered a violent shriek, slammed her palms against the steel of his thighs, and took him full in her mouth. She cupped his rear in both hands as he exhausted his sea foam into her mouth. She accepted him into her arms and held him while he rested in utter satisfaction against the wonderful fullness of her young breasts with their puffy pink nipples that screamed desire, ringed with hungry, bumpy aureoles while shower water fell around them like a warm rain storm. He watched water roiling in circles on the tile floor, under her healthy, firm thighs, and under her soaked bottom.

When he mumbled weakly, she leaned down and said to the man who lay cradled in her arms and across her lap, "What, darling?" She stroked his hair gently and lovingly.

He repeated so she could just barely hear, "You still have soap suds in your bunny hair."

She hugged him to her. "Well, baby, I guess that means we just have to keep showering."

Closing her eyes, she rocked him from side to side, pressing her lips on his temple in an unending kiss. She squeezed him and whispered, "I just cannot stop kissing you."

He whispered: "Let's just stay here in the shower. We can order in three times a day."

She laughed. "And like the mermaid Melusina, we can grow fins and floss around."

"Yeah."

So saying, they flopped and slid around, laughing and squealing on the slippery, soapy shower floor.

41.   Savia & Yoichi Alas

By eight thirty, the group were all assembled in the dining room. It smelled heavenly of fresh coffee and bread. A wonderful spread of jellies, slices of meats, and butter sat on the table.

Kendra had flown back to Kaiserslautern with two MP escorts to take Sherwin in for trial and hopefully a lifetime of hard labor at Fort Leavenworth.

Rick and the remaining crew ate with Professor Sander and Captain Stefani.

"Today we fly to Ansembourg," said Sander. "That's in the Valley of Seven Castles. A Japanese cult there has agreed to host the CEOC world conference for a tidy sum."

"And this valley is—?" Hannah asked.

Stefani explained, "You have zigzagged across the Grand Duchy. Now you are going south to Mersch, and then to Ansembourg, which is north-northwest of the capital. PAX will provide security under the aegis of the Grand Ducal army special forces. There will be a mix of Belgian, Luxemburgish, French, German, and U.S. special forces troops on our side. CEOC understands this."

Whitcomb added, "General Mendé and his headquarters have tacitly agreed to a truce. He would prefer that Professor Sander has an unfortunate accident. Then Wan can become world president of CEOC, and he will be the new field marshal of all corporate mercenary militias."

Rick asked: "So if they have a one-world corporate government, who would this military fight?"

Whitcomb smiled coldly. "Each other. Don't you see? It's more of a Franz Kafka police force to prevent any corporation or group of corporations from banding together against the others. This is why a lot of the CEOC chiefs are scared of Wan and really want to vote for Sander."

Sander nodded. "We'll help them. I'm doing this for my son Pierre, and for all the young people in the world struggling to raise a family, buy a little house, have a decent job with real health care and benefits and safety in the workplace—all the things corporations don't want, because they are purely after profit."

Stefani agreed. "I have studied business enough to know that the corporation has only one mandate: to increase the wealth of the share holders by any means possible. They have enough lawyers to stretch the law any way they want, especially when they buy and sell politicians—like the corporate republican party in the United States—and get to appoint the Supreme Court justices. So the corporations have to be put on a leash. The professor is right."

Sander said as he ate, "Corporations are big, beautiful dogs. We absolutely need them. But if we let them loose, like they have been since Reagan's time, they will eat all the other pets and children in the neighborhood. They get bigger and bigger and start eating houses and then entire towns—so to speak. The ancient Romans had it right, and the Framing Fathers in 1787 created a strong, centralized federal republic based on the Roman model—with safeguards hopefully that it wouldn't die a sad death like the Roman republic did by the time of Julius Caesar. I'm afraid we are well along that path. It's a scary road—past nationalism, past world wars and senseless border disputes."

"The whole world as a sort of European Union," Shen echoed. "I'm almost sure you can persuade most countries to go that route. We just need to leverage CEOC away from becoming a one-world nation, and break it up into a confederacy of many little parts, a separation of units kind of like the E.U.—so no one group or person can ever become supreme leader or chief demagogue again—like Hitler, Mussolini, Milosevic, Pol Pot, and similar rabble rousers; including a few U.S. makes and models of late."

"Okay," Stefani said, rising in response to a wave from a uniformed orderly outside in the hall. "We are ready to fly. We can be in Ansembourg in ten minutes by helicopter."

She handed a plain, old leather briefcase to the Professor. He thanked her, and hefted its grip in his hand.

Whitcomb whispered, "That's the package. He's going to personally carry it to Ansembourg for his presentation and put Wan and General Mendé to shame."

Sander dusted himself off. "This is the big one. This is the decisive round coming up. By the end of this week, we'll know which way the world is going to turn—toward democracy, or toward totalitarianism. Let's wish ourselves luck."

On a full stomach, well rested, and informed to the max, the group marched down the halls toward the helipad outside.

Hannah and Rick, wearing unadorned khaki flight overalls, walked along holding hands. Ahead of them walked Professor Sander, carrying the briefcase. With him walked Captain Stefani, Colonel Whitcomb, and CIA operative Shen.

Only Stefani was in uniform this morning—fatigues with subdued markings. Several armed Luxembourg soldiers accompanied them—five tough looking men and two women, all wearing berets and sporting Uzi-type automatic weapons held at ready. They all wore civilian clothing—all but Sander in stripped down flight overalls that the Vianden center here seemed to keep in generous supply.

Rick started to get an unholy feeling. *Where there is smoke there is fire,* he thought.

"What's the matter?" Hannah asked him, sidling close to whisper the question.

"Keep an eye out."

"You're scaring me."

"Is everything all right?" Stefani asked, marching slightly ahead. She had heard Rick's tone.

Rick gave a sullen shrug.

They came to the main portal of the facility. Two of the accompanying guards opened the doors and held them thus while keeping their assault rifles at ready. The other three men and the two women marched out ahead with their weapons raised.

Sander and his entourage walked out into the crisp, sunny morning air.

The heliport was empty. Its concrete surface, with a landing target marked in white paint, was dotted with wind-blown puddles from the night's drizzle and fog.

Clouds hung in the surrounding forests like kites that had run aground. Shreds of fog drifted among the tree tops.

"There—I see the helicopter," said Stefani.

Whitcomb frowned.

Rick pulled Hannah back a bit.

He heard a rattling sound behind him and looked.

A group of guards inside the building were locking the doors. Was that standard procedure?

The chopper rattled in to a landing. It was a larger one, with two engines powering longer blades.

"Something looks wrong here," Whitcomb said as he pulled out a handgun.

Stefani had her Glock 26 in hand. "Around the Professor!" she shouted.

The chopper roared in close, setting down nearer the group than Rick had expected. The target was over there, and the chopper was over here.

The side doors slid open, and two faces peered out from behind foreign-looking assault rifles.

Rick recognized them. "Savia! Yoichi! It's an ambush." Why the hell had he not been given a weapon? Control, he supposed as he whirled and covered Hannah with his body, facing away from the blast of air from the rotors.

"Guard Sander!" Stefani yelled. "Get back to the doors."

"Can't," Rick shouted—"people have locked them."

"CEOC faction," Shen yelled miserably as he waved a hand gun.

At that moment, two of the male guards snatched the briefcase, knocked Sander to the ground, and bolted like hell for the chopper.

The two women soldiers opened fire.

A rattle of answering fire came from the chopper.

One of the women soldiers was killed with a gruesome head wound.

Whitcomb took Sander by the coat and yanked him backward. At the same time, he stepped in front of Sander. In that same motion, he took a bullet from Savia or Yoichi, who were laying down covering fire from the chopper. Another soldier went down.

Rick swept Hannah off her feet and threw himself on top of her—hard. She looked dazed. He hugged her and hunched over her, trying to shield her as much as possible.

Stefani ran forward of the chopper, firing her Glock 26 until it ran out of ammo.

She took a bullet and crumpled to the concrete.

One of the runners went down, shot from behind by the surviving Luxembourg female soldier.

Shen scrambled after the chopper with a gun in each hand, blazing away until they were both empty. The surviving traitor and the briefcase were on the chopper, which was already out of range of small arms fire. Shen picked up the dead woman's assault rifle and emptied it into the sky to no avail.

"They are gone," Sander said, sitting on the concrete holding Whitcomb by the arm. "So is my dear friend here."

Rick rose and ran to see what he could do. Whitcomb was gone. A soldier was checking him for a pulse, but shook his head. Whitcomb's eyes were open, staring into eternity while a trickle of blood ran from his mouth and a puddle formed on the concrete under his chest. His overalls were red and wet near his heart.

There was a burst of gunfire at the door, and two more of the CEOC troops, who had locked the doors to prevent backward flight, lay dead. Loyal soldiers came pounding out on combat boots, with rifles at the ready.

"Too late," Sander said. "They killed our good people here, and got away with my son's work." He looked destroyed as his anguished face and eyes tracked the by now mosquito-sized chopper clapping away into distant clouds.

A man helped Stefani limp back toward Sander. She looked devastated as well. She had taken a round through a leg and another through the side—probably a flesh wound. She hopped along, holding a hand over her bloody, leaking side and raising her injured leg at the knee.

Just then another chopper clattered in close. This one had Luxemburgish army markings—including the Grand Duchy's state emblem with a red lion snarling as it climbed up a field of blue and white stripes. "This one is legit," Sander said as he jumped up with more energy than Rick would have thought possible. He dusted himself off. "Where were they?"

Stefani sat down beside Whitcomb and grimaced in both pain and grief, laying a hand on the dead man's massive chest.

"He took a bullet for me," Sander said. "A young man with his whole life still ahead of him."

Rick clapped a hand on Sander's shoulder. "For him, and all of us, we need you to become the next president of CEOC. He died for that. Let's not make it be for nothing."

"You are right," Sander said, obviously in shock. "So did my son Pierre. I need to get to Ansembourg—safely. Not for me but the cause."

The chopper landed and a burly colonel of infantry with Luxembourg insignia on his fatigues hopped out. He was followed by several armed soldiers. He demanded: "What happened here?"

Stefani started to explain, and then fainted, falling backward. Several medical personnel carrying stretchers came running from inside the building. A female medical officer with them began triaging. Whitcomb was gone. The female soldier had just died in a puddle of blood on the concrete. Stefani was unconscious from loss of blood, but six medical people worked on her in an efficient, grim manner. "She will live," the doctor said. "We have a tourniquet on the leg, and a patch on her side wound."

By then, a red and silver LAR flight ambulance came screaming in from the north, leaving a white, pencil-thin contrail over the hazy forest air. Rick recognized it as one of those aircraft that can switch between hover mode and jet mode. It set down on the concrete apron not far from the NATO aircraft. EMT staff in white civilian overalls came running from the LAR plane.

The Luxembourg colonel named Gaston Pierrot took charge. He was a slender, gray man with glasses, who looked more like a bureaucrat than a warrior. "What do we have? Stefani being airlifted to the capital. Two dead. Sander okay—anyone else hurt?"

Shen put his gun away and stepped forth, shaking his head. "By a miracle, that's it."

The survivors teamed up to be close together and share their sense of grief and shock.

Hannah said, "We lost the package."

Rick told Colonel Pierrot: "Your mission now is to getting Sander to Ansembourg safely."

"Into the Valley of Seven Castles," a NATO officer nearby said.

Pierrot looked him over and nodded. "You're right." He turned to Sander. "I am concerned for your safety. Do you have to go right now?"

Sander extended his hands out plaintively. "I have to get there for the vote. I have speeches to make, or Wan will be elected."

"I'm not sure what all that means," Pierrot said. A label over his left chest pocket read *Luxembourg*, while the label over his right pocket read *Pierrot*. The colonel ordered in good English, "This is what we do. Professor Sander, your trip to Ansembourg will be delayed a few hours or whatever is necessary until the Grand Ducal military can provide a safe escort. I will contact my superiors in Luxembourg City for orders. In the meantime, I ask that you all retreat to the safety of the building." He made a herding motion, extending his arms out, and walking them back to the concrete and glass building. "Our people have secured the area."

Hannah began crying softly. "Poor Whitcomb. He seemed like such a nice man. And the soldier."

Rick put his arm around her shoulder. "I know. I've been through this before." He thought of his combat experiences. "It is always fresh, shocking, and awful. I'll always remember Whitcomb, maybe in ways that nobody else will. He was a soldier and a hero." He felt his own eyes growing salty and stinging. He wiped a sleeve over them, while keeping the other arm around Hannah.

"This is such a bitch, the whole thing," she said.

"I know." He gave her a squeeze. It was all he could offer.

She put her arm around his torso roughly. "I have you."

"We have each other." He muttered further, "Let's get you and me out of this mess as soon as we wrap up business. You did your part—stole the McGuffin and set most of this in motion."

Sander came alongside and extended a hand to stop Rick. "Mr. Buchan, you and Miss Smith will need to help us out."

Rick and Hannah regarded him with stricken eyes.

"Only you two would recognize the people on the chopper who shot our friends. Who were they?"

"Savia and Yoichi."

Shen added, "I know the names, but not the faces, from when I tracked you guys from Paris to Luxembourg. I'm afraid the Prof is right. We need you to come along to the conference in case they try to sneak in and do any more damage—like try to hurt or kill Sander."

Sander pressed a finger against Rick's chest. "Buchan, let's make a deal. You're a soldier. This young woman isn't. Let's send her safely home to California. You can join her soon enough when all this is over."

Rick was ready to agree, but Hannah wrapped herself around him like steel cable. "Where he goes, I go."

And that, as they all swept back into the safety of the regional military command, was that. But Rick told the professor: "You remember Colonel Whitcomb said he was developing some information against General Mendé?"

Sander stopped in the lobby, hands jammed in his pockets, shoulders slouched in misery. His face had a look like *what next?*

"Who has he been working with?" Rick asked. "Who would know?"

Sander shook his head slowly, looking dazed. "I am baffled."

A phone rang in Rick's pocket.

Amazed, Rick pawed himself, until he remembered he had purchased a burner from the Indian guy near the Kolibri in Wiltz. He'd intended to call Kendra again for status. He took the phone out and said, "Yes?"

"Rick, this is Kendra Walsh."

"You're kidding."

"We have more ways of tracking people than you realize. I don't know where you got that phone, but we managed to track you down. 'We' meaning Army and Air Force in the Ramstein area with all the technology we've got. What the hell just happened there?"

"We were ambushed. Wan's goons grabbed the package."

"Sad, but not surprising," Kendra said. "We—PAXUS elements sympathetic with PAX and PAXEUR—are in the minority. Most of our troops and our people are innocent victims and bystanders. But we have to expect that every group will have divided loyalties—even the tiny Luxembourg army. So be on your guard."

He also told her that Whitcomb was dead, along with two Luxembourg commandos, and Stefani had been airlifted with injuries.

"I'm coming back there right now," Kendra said. "What's the plan?"

"We are supposed to stay here until Luxembourg can arrange safe escort for Sander."

"Stay put, and guard him with your life."

"Okay." He said it reluctantly, but knew it was true—it would be his mission until this affair was over. One way or another. He rang off and pocketed the phone. What if Sander lost? What if CEOC turned fully Kafka and put Wan and General Mendé in charge of the whole corporate planet? The thought was too scary to contemplate.

"We must win," said Pierrot in his stolid, rock-like manner.

"We will," Rick said.

Pierrot, who appeared to know more than he let on, said, "You know, Sergeant Buchan, that this package alone will not make or break the hard-liners. They have more up their sleeve."

Rick nodded. "That'swhat I think. What will tip the scales?"

Sander cut in, "Fear. That's what it's all about. Intimidation. My son's technology will give them air superiority and I'm sure they can adapt it to fit armor as well. Maybe even smart ammunition. They don't want to reason with their fellow CEOs. They want to terrify them into voting for Wan. Whoever isn't with them is against them, and they will make that very clear. As Susanna was saying this morning, they have only one law, and that is to maximize the wealth of their shareholders. If they don't do that, they are violating the contract whereby the investors handed their money over. The corporation can be sued and may be destroyed in court. A lot of those CEOs aren't going to risk it. It's a wolf pack, like all else. They'll run with the leader—Wan, and his capo, General Mendé."

42. Valley of Seven Castles

Colonel Pierrot, followed by several young men in commando gear, took charge in the lobby. He ordered the front doors locked and guarded. He strode around, talking into two field phones—one at each ear—and gave orders for the complex to be secured and guarded by soldiers called in from headquarters in Diekirch.

The huge lobby echoed with voices and running boots as the troops followed orders. There was a metallic chatter of guns being checked.

Pierrot held out his arms as if to encircle Rick, Hannah, and Sander. "I am consulting with the government in Luxembourg City," Pierrot said. "We are thinking of sending you by bus later today. Please go either to your rooms or to the dining hall." He introduced a sharp looking young *chef-sergeant* (three chevrons, just a grade under Rick who had recently made staff sergeant in the U.S. Army). "This is Sergeant Gaston Corneille. He is a professional soldier in one of our NATO rifle companies, and he will be my assistant in place of Captain Stefani—who by the way is doing well at the hospital in Luxembourg City. She will be on recuperative leave for at least three months, so we will have to do without her. So again, I ask you to relax, eat if you wish, have coffee, or stay in your rooms until we organize a safe expedition to the Valley of Seven Castles."

Sergeant Corneille shook hands all around. He was a thin, handsome young man with short-clipped blond hair, brown eyes, and a lightly freckled Frisian-looking face—pale, Germanic, although his name was French.

Hannah put her arm around Rick. He rejoiced inwardly, giving her a quick little kiss. Arm in arm, they strolled to the dining room.

During this stroll, Rick overheard something that made his skin crawl, his spine tingle, his nerves jangle.

He overheard a very different, nasty-sounding Pierrot telling a younger fellow officer some instructions in a low voice. The tall, thin brown-haired captain nodded darkly. Rick overheard the words "Plan B" spoken in a tone that suggested Plan B, whatever it was, might not be a good thing—even sinister.

As far as Rick could tell, in this tiny nation, the distance from Vianden to Ansembourg in the Valley of Seven Castles was something on the order of forty klicks by surface road, or 24 miles—by air, a flight of minutes; by land, a drive of forty minutes to an hour depending on traffic, weather, and circumstances. He recalled Kendra's orders to guard Sander.

"Professor, why don't you stay in the dining area with us? We'll be safer together."

"Capital idea," said the Professor, looking less ruffled now despite the horror they had all just endured. "We don't want any more death and destruction. That is what Wan and his people relish—terror, disaster, the four horsemen."

Hannah put her arm around Sander. "We want peace."

Sander put his arm around her shoulder and hugged her to him briefly in a fatherly manner. "That's right. We hang together, or we hang separately, as Ben Franklin said."

Shen, joining them, added: "That was independence from kings. This is from corporations."

"We will restore democracy," Sander said. "Everyone will have a voice again, and nobody will be powerful or wealthy enough to be above the law—like offshoring their billions so they don't have to pay taxes, and denying ordinary citizens health care while they enjoy hot and cold running doctors and nurses on tap as they need them for a broken fingernail or whatever."

Rick laughed. "Good speeche. Tell them that in Ansembourg."

They all drifted into the dining room, with its long table. Orderlies served coffee and pastries, which in Luxembourg are first class. Sander said proudly, while chomping on an éclair, "In my opinion, when it comes to sweet stuff, we are tied with Vienna, which makes the best in Europe. My vote is for Belgium in second place, followed by the rest of the pack all running and baking together and trying to keep up."

Sergeant Corneille, walking alongside, grinned ruefully and said, "I'm Belgian on my mother's side, and I do think the Belgians make some of the best chocolate. I'd place them tied with Vienna on that note."

"I have to concede your point," Sander said.

As the minutes and hours wore on, and the sun rolled around in the sky outside the huge picture windows overlooking the valley, the mood in the dining room became lighter and more surreal. They were surrounded by danger and death, and on a mission to save the world from tyranny— but it all seemed somehow distant and unreal. Hannah went to the room for a nap. Rick accompanied her, and made sure she was safely locked in with the key under her pillow before he returned to the dining room. It was the only time he ventured away from Sander' side.

Where was Kendra?

What was Plan B?

He asked Corneille, "Sergeant, have any more U.S. Army personnel arrived?"

Corneille shook his head and said, "Not that I know. Why would more of your troops be arriving?"

Rick shrugged. "The more the merrier."

Pierrot stopped in. "It is confirmed. We will have a military convoy leaving in an hour. We leave at two in the afternoon, and expect to be in Ansembourg by three. Grand Ducal police will keep the route open for us all the way, and we expect to have air cover from the Luftwaffe." He clapped Sander on the shoulder, speaking heartily and switching to their common *Letzebuergesch* halfway: "We will guard you with our lives, *Häer Professer*."

"*Villemol merci*," Sander replied with familiarity. *Many thanks.*

Rick spoke quietly with Corneille. "Can you furnish me a side arm?"

"I'll see what I can do."

Rick, Shen, Hannah, and Sander stayed sitting at the table. Corneille left to speak with someone—Pierrot, Rick assumed. Maybe they didn't want to have any loose cannons on deck, so to speak. Maybe it was all about control. He had a feeling it would be difficult for anyone but the authorized military and police escort under Pierrot's command to carry weapons.

At that moment, Colonel Pierrot entered the room. "It's arranged. We are ready. Let's go to Ansembourg." He swung his hands, clapping them together, as if herding geese.

"Thank god," Sander said. "Let's get this show on the road."

43.   Kendra Surprise

Hannah was exhausted from the emotional rollercoaster of the last day especially. She'd been overjoyed to be reunited with her beloved Rick, a guy who had rescued her and whom she adored. She lay in bed, quiet and alone, with her hands prayered between her knees, just thinking about him. She shivered with pleasure—and her bunny trembled wetly and warmly with her—at the memories of making love with her sweetheart again.

Seeing Whitcomb killed was a downer of the first magnitude. She tried to push the memory away, but it was something that stayed with you for life. She did not have the combat experience Richard did, but she imagined even a seasoned soldier took a body blow each time he experienced killing or maiming in the field—so senseless, so sudden, so final. She almost started to cry, but forced herself to think about Rick. She was sorry for the pretty young soldier who had lain dead on the concrete, and for the injured Susanna Stefani. She even felt a pang of sadness about the dead CEOC sympathizers—they had lived lives also. They had maybe believed in their cause, or gotten paid well—probably mercenaries who'd infiltrated the Luxembourg uniformed services, tiny as those were, but people were people everywhere. That was PAX's central theme—everyone should have a chance at life and happiness. And, as in all past wars, good people died for that cause. Good people died on both sides, while some of the leaders were horrible people, and others were good leaders.

As she drifted off into an exhausted, thirsty sleep—she had to pee also, but didn't have the energy to get up—she thought she heard a muffled pounding.

Try as she might to ignore it, the pounding continued. She could have drifted off to sleep but her plumbing was telephoning—*hello, Hannah, your bladder calling, need to go potty...*

Finally, grumbling "Oh drooling dementia," she swung out of bed.

Outside, the light was starting its long decline. A glance at the wall clock told her it was close to five p.m. In June, when the days were longest, daylight faded only after eleven p.m. Evenings lasted long, with a kind of sad, melancholy golden light mixing with mist among the trees.

Wearing only panties and a bra, she stumbled on long legs to the bathroom. Half asleep, she barged through the door, which swung open and crashed against the shower in the tiny bathroom. She pulled her panties down to her knees, swung her rear around, and sat on the cold plastic seat.

Next to her, someone or something was pounding on the wall.

What?

Oh for god's sake, she thought, hopping lightly up and down on her thighs on the seat. *Tinkle already so I can go back to bed.*

There was the pounding again: slow, heavy, and systematic.

Was that someone yelling?

She managed a few squirts before her bladder got all tight and nervous. Wiping herself, she pulled her panties up and started back to bed.

The pounding resumed.

And a voice—in trouble. Someone was yelling in anguish.

Hannah stood in the bathroom, frozen—listening.

More pounding.

"All right, that does it."

She wrapped herself in a large towel that hung over her shoulders like a white terry cape, down almost to her knees.

Barefoot, she padded to the door. She made sure she had her plastic room key. She peeked out into the hallway. She didn't want to be seen in her semi-nude condition.

Then she padded as fast as she could to the room next door.

She knocked on the closed door.

No answer.

She tried the door handle.

Locked.

She knocked on the door again. "Hello? Is someone in there?"

The door made a clicking sound, and a tiny green light blinked.

The door had unlocked itself.

She pushed it open.

"Hello? Anyone here?'

The room was semi-dark, because it did not have an exterior window like the one she and Rick had. She reached around, and flicked on a light.

One the floor at her feet lay a human body.

She shrieked and jumped aside, holding her hands up defensively. She looked down in horror.

It was a man—a young man, in military uniform—tied up with his hands behind his back. His ankles were tied in a thick bundle of rope so he could not move. He had a gag in his mouth and looked up at her with terrified, pleading eyes.

Nearby, she was startled to hear loud pounding and splintering noises. A woman's voice yelled, "Hey! Over here!"

The soldier on the floor nodded. He looked toward a closet in the room.

Hannah stepped over him, holding her towel close with both hands, and peered though a half-open closet door. The closet adjoined her bathroom in the room next door.

In the closet, also bound hand and foot, with a gag that had slipped from her mouth down around her neck, was Major Kendra Walsh, Rick's friend the JAG officer.

"Hannah, get me out of here."

"Oh my god," Hannah said. She rushed into the closet and pawed at Kendra's bonds.

"We've got to reach Sander," Kendra said. Her lovely features looked frantic and shadowy. Her hair as always made a resilient ball of neatly trimmed, kinky curls. "Get the box cutter."

Whoever had tied the two up had left the cutting tool, with which they'd cut the ropes from a coil of industrial plastic cord that lay in the corner on its side.

Hannah sliced away at Kendra's bonds until she had her hands free. Kendra took the box cutter and freed her ankles. "Let's get Andy Jones over there free. Sergeant Jones was my escort on the way back here from K-Town."

"What happened?"

The two women worked at the young soldier's bonds. Kendra said, "I heard about the ambush this morning on the helipad. I spoke with Rick and told him I was on my way back here. I have unfinished business that poor Whitcomb died trying to complete."

They got Andy Jones standing on his feet. He was an average healthy looking U.S. soldier from some heartland state—Minnesota, it turned out—and he was just serving a three year tour hoping to get some benefits and attend college, which was nearly impossible otherwise these days.

"Thank you," Andy said, rubbing large, raw-knuckled hands over his bony features. He was a skinny guy—not an ounce of fat on his lean body. His short hair made a brown, uneven cascade past his ears. He wore dark green camo fatigues and combat boots—no hat, no side arm—those must have been knocked aside or taken from him. "We were landing on the chopper deck. The flight was—" he looked at Kendra.

She confirmed: "—ten minutes. It was over in such a short time. Then these guys came out and took us into custody."

"Yeah," Andy said. "We were so surprised we didn't think to put up a fight."

"I was still dumfounded from hearing about the ambush earlier. You can't just figure on attacking everyone you see."

"They got us before we could suspect they were bad guys," Andy seconded.

"Luckily the soldiers took us here and tied us up rather than killing us."

Andy said, "But they probably aim to kill this professor who is so important."

"Go get dressed," Kendra said. "We'll go together."

Hannah ran as fast as she could—into her room, where she hopped and jumped as she pulled the flight coveralls around her and zipped up. She sat on the bed and pulled on her green socks, followed by the dark blue track shoes she'd been wearing since Paris. She grabbed her small purse—what else?—that was about all—and joined Andy and Kendra in the hallway.

Together, they walked cautiously but quickly toward the doors of the hostel.

"They are all in the dining room," Hannah said. "Colonel Pierrot told us to stick together where he and his people could guard us."

"Right," Kendra said. "Pierrot is known to be a close adjutant of General Mendé."

"Oh no."

"Yeah, the wrong side have got us."

They left the hostel and entered the main hall of the dormitory wing. Nobody stopped them—not even two female medical orderlies chatting girl-stuff as they walked by, wearing white tops and stethoscopes over dark green NATO fatigue uniforms.

Kendra took the lead as they burst into the dining room. "Oh no!"

The room empty.

Hannah and Andy piled into Kendra from behind as Kendra held the wide door open.

Several young workers were cleaning the table off, putting dishes on a bussing cart. They looked up with surprised features—all very innocent and friendly.

Kendra said sharply, "Professor Sander and his group—where are they?"

A young orderly pulling the linen tablecloth off the bare table said pleasantly, "Colonel Pierrot and the Professor's group have all left for the Valley of Seven Castles."

"Yes," said another, "they should be there already."

"Which castle?" Kendra demanded.

"Ansembourg, the new castle," said one of the orderlies.

Kendra whirled—a shapely figure in her fatigue uniform and boots— and hurried back down the hall. Hannah and Andy tagged along.

Kendra came to a wall phone. "They took our phones. Maybe I can call out." She picked up an old-fashioned receiver and clicked the yoke repeatedly. "Hello? Hello?"

She slammed the phone down. "Nothing. It's dead. They might have cut off phone service."

"They?" Hannah echoed.

"CEOC symps," Kendra said as she strode down the hall toward the main lobby. "They would prefer for Sander to have an unfortunate accident on his way to Ansembourg. That way, Wan will have a clear path to becoming CEOC president. He's got a lot of backing from the conservative wing in the military and politics. Whitcomb briefed me just this morning before I left to take Sherwin back to K-Town for bind-over and trial."

Kendra slowed down and spread her arms for Andy and Hannah behind her to put the brakes on.

The lobby was filled with dark uniforms and suits.

"Too late," Kendra said.

Several troopers in helmets and body armor, like dark knights, brandished automatic weapons. They wore French flag shoulder patches.

"French army commandos," Kendra guessed.

"'*Allo? Qu'est que vous faites ici?*" shouted a senior NCO brandishing a black side arm. Hello? What are you people doing here?

"U.S. Army officer," Kendra said, waving her wallet to display I.D.

A sharp-looking young officer of Asian extraction stepped up and took charge. "We are serving with a French army unit in Lorraine. We airlifted from our garrison near Thionville to assist the Luxembourgeois."

"We need to find Professor Sander," Kendra told him.

"An important Luxemburgish intellectual was kidnapped here in the past two hours by an unknown faction."

"Are you PAXEUR?"

The man looked at her sharply. His eyes betrayed fear. If he was, and he admitted it, he could be endangering his several dozen troops. If he wasn't, he would already be ordering Kendra and her two friends to be arrested.

She and the French officer evaluated each other in a split second.

These days, you never knew who was friend or foe. The situation was like holding a live electrical wire over an open barrel of gasoline—one wrong move, and more people died.

But, Kendra reasoned, you had to say or do something. You couldn't just stand there holding your tit. So she made the first move. "We are PAXUS," Kendra told him. "There is no time for games."

He nodded. He understood. Two other officers rushed in to conference with their U.S. Army counterpart. The French troops looked totally professional, ready—and confused. In the chaos of events, they had been flown in at a moment's notice from some exercise at a French army post— then told to await orders here in the lobby of this concrete hotel slash intelligence post in a foreign country.

"I thought you were our liaison for orders," the French officer said.

"I'm just glad you're not CEOC," Kendra said.

One of the other French officers said, "Those are on the way to the Valley of Seven Castles with their prisoners. It does not look like a good outcome."

44.   Valley—Rick

Colonel Pierrot and Chief Sergeant Corneille led the group from the dining room, out of the main hostel area, and into the main lobby of the building. They were accompanied by at least ten armed commandos in dark blue camouflage uniforms, a color Rick had previously seen associated with navy or air force personnel in various countries. It occurred to him, as he puzzled over this, yes, also with police or gendarmerie. These guys were shaven headed and tough looking with black berets—the real, traditional ones with the thin black ribbon hanging down the rear. They seemed tight-lipped, dedicated, and very focused. Each cradled a NATO-issue machine gun in both arms, in addition to web gear loaded with gun, spares, a canteen, medical kit, and—yes, now he noticed—plastic handcuff ties. Must be a special forces unit to protect Sander, Rick supposed.

They emerged in an underground garage—a sterile, concrete world coldly illumined by overly bright fluorescent tubes in the ceilings. An air exchange blew noisily.

A convoy of five armored vehicles stood waiting. Their engines ran quietly, with bluish-black exhaust fumes drifting out but quickly absorbed upward into massive, galvanized-steel air exchange ducting.

Pierrot spoke quietly to his lieutenants, and to Sergeant Corneille, who all took their stations. Corneille held the door of the middle vehicle open for Rick, Sander, and Shen to board. Corneille climbed up, pulled the door shut, and locked it. The four men settled into a spacious utility chamber that could be used for a CP, or evacuation of wounded, or communications. A cockpit up front served a driver and an armed guard.

Two vehicles rode ahead, and two behind as they rolled out of the garage.

"We will be in Ansembourg in about an hour," Corneille assured them. "It will still be getting dark now. It will be night by the time we arrive."

"This is Plan B?" Rick said conversationally. He and Sander sat on a bench, with Corneille and Shen facing them on the opposite bench.

Corneille gave him an odd look. "Where did you hear that?"

Rick shrugged. "Just making conversation." Suddenly, he wasn't sure about this. It was an instinct.

Corneille looked away—perhaps bored, perhaps contemplating. The look on his features changed somehow, subtly.

Corneille had not provided him with a side arm, and now Rick did not want to press the point by asking again. It seemed like a discourtesy—or did Plan B require something else, like being unarmed?

Rick thought of Hannah and hoped she was sleeping sweetly. He hoped they would feed her well. He wished he'd had a chance to say goodbye for now, but Sander required his presence every moment.

"How did you get with the CIA?" Rick asked Shen.

The man smiled at memories of home. "I grew up in New Jersey."

"I knew it. You look like a New Jersey guy."

"Yeah right. More like Chinatown in New York or San Francisco."

They both laughed.

Shen said, "I did my trick in the army. Got an ROTC commission out of Princeton."

Rick whistled. "Ivy League guy."

Shen shrugged. "I was a high school track star, got good grades, and stayed out of trouble. My parents are second generation—their grandparents came from somewhere near Shandong, near as we can tell, so the study hard, work hard, keep nose clean ethic was alive and well."

"And impress the neighbors. Keep up with the Hongs," Rick said.

"And the Kongs," Shen joked back. "Anyway, ROTC, commission as a Military Intelligence officer, made captain, got out, didn't like selling insurance, and went to work for Uncle Semolean. Here I am. And you?"

Rick sat with his shoulders hunched slightly, as he punched his palms idly from one hand to the other. "Small-town USA. My dad owns a gas station and my mom is a librarian. My brothers and sisters finished college and have real jobs. I was the black sheep. I ended up in Huilongistan, feeding fifties and eating goat cheese." By fifties he meant a large caliber machine gun, often mounted on trucks or field vehicles.

Sander said, "You have such a large country, and so many paths of opportunity. Rick, I have taught classes at Heidelberg and Bitburg to many U.S. military people. You should finish your college."

"I plan to," Rick said.

"Got a girl back home?" Shen asked.

Rick smiled dreamily, thinking of Hannah. "Yeah, I am planning to ask her to marry me when I get back home."

"She will be waiting for you when this is over," Sander said gently, radiating kindness and well-wishes. He knew they were a couple.

Rick nodded. "I'm totally set. We are going to do it, and then I am going to get serious about cracking the books."

"What are you interested in?" asked the professor.

"I want to be an engineer. My dad owns a garage. He's a mechanic. He always drummed this into us—be more than I am. I hold the wrench—you go design wrenches and be a bigger man."

"But not a better man," Sander said. "That is your wonderful tradition of equality and opportunity."

"That's right," Shen said. "I have a wife and two kids back in Ohio."

"Not New Jersey?" Rick asked.

Shen grinned. "We move around like gypsies."

"You can do that," Sander said. "Luxembourg is so tiny that if you move in any direction, you fall over the border and are in a foreign land."

Rick asked Corneille: "What about you?"

The man shrugged. "I was born and raised in Ettelbrück. That is in the southwest, near Belgium. My wife is Belgian in fact, from the Province of Luxembourg in Belgium."

45.   En Route, Not Yet Knowing

As they bantered about, the column of vehicles moved steadily on small but good surface roads. Through the elongated portholes of bullet-proof glass, Rick glanced at the passing countryside with its small, white-washed villages, interspaced with meadows on which black and white cows grazed, and forests that were already becoming enveloped in evening fog. Although there might only be a few hours of night at this latitude in June, the weather often made it seem darker and gloomier than need be.

"Looks chilly out there," Rick said in the general direction of Corneille.

"It may start drizzling also," Corneille said.

The vehicle ground to a halt.

"What now?" Sander said.

Corneille looked as if he knew something but wasn't telling.

Someone rapped sharply on the door.

Corneille said, "Excuse me a few minutes. I'll be back." He opened the door, clambered outside onto the gritty surface of a country road, and slammed the door shut.

Other doors could be heard banging open and shut. Rick heard voices—no laughter; no banter, unusual for young troops; just business.

In a minute or two, the vehicles all started moving again.

With a lurch, their own vehicle rolled forward.

Shen, Rick, and Sander regarded each other with puzzled looks.

Shortly, Rick's phone warbled. He'd forgotten he had it in his pocket. "Yes?"

"Rick, this is Kendra. Is it safe to talk?"

"Wha—?"

"Listen. You are all in deadly danger. You've been kidnapped by General Mendé's forces allied with Wan and the CEOC hardliners. They've got Sander, that is the important thing. They'll probably kill you all or at least keep you prisoner. What is your status?"

Rick turned to look outside. "I see a sign going by. It's a place called Mersch."

"You are at the beginning of the Valley of Seven Castles. By car, it's about ten clicks or a fifteen-minute drive."

"Our Luxembourg army commando guide just bailed out."

"That is a sign something is going to happen any second."

"Oh shit."

"Right."

"Any ideas?"

"Wish I were there."

"Having a great time, wish you were here."

"Rick, stop joking."

He told Shen and Sander: "We are being kidnapped. These are the wrong guys. We're about to die."

"Rick, are you taking your medicines?"

"Oh yeah. Now I need a few beers to wash them down."

"I can get a commando group to you in ten minutes. I have about twenty French commandos here, with their choppers feathering on the pad. The Luftwaffe is patrolling the air."

"I want the navy here," Rick said. "Submarines."

"I am going to strangle you with my own hands."

"You gotta catch me first."

Sander said, "Rick, I am getting scared. Not for me, but for PAX."

Shen said, "Dude, get serious."

"I am serious, you fucking Bozo. Hey listen, Kendra, no time to talk now. If you intercept this convoy, we're dead."

"What are you going to do?"

"Stand by. I'll call you." He added: "Don't call us, we'll call you. But wait—there's more." With that, he hung up.

"Shen are you armed?"

Shen shook his head. "I turned in my sidearm like they told me."

"Bad," Rick said. "I never got mine. Sander, can you run? Jog a little?"

"I have perfectly strong bones and healthy muscles."

"Good. We're going to need them."

So saying, Rick turned the door handle. *Locked.*

Those sons of bitches.

But hey—there was a release latch on the inside. He pulled the lever—and the door gave. He opened it a crack and did a quick assessment. He heard the soft whine of deeply mufflered engines ahead. In back, due to the Doppler Effect, the sound was even quieter.

He saw the road fleeting past.

"Any minute, they'll stop and we'll have an unfortunate accident," Rick said.

Shen crossed the deck and squatted under the window. "There's another hatch under the window here, on the right side."

"See if you can open it," Rick said. He pulled the main hatch shut. There was no reasonable way to bail out, land on the road, survive the impact, and not be noticed by the two drivers behind. Especially with an elderly man along. These vehicles were made for loading on all sides, as well as bailing out under combat conditions.

"Got it loose," Shen said. He pulled up a steel panel, exposing daylight. "Looks like a ditch out there."

"Sander, can you do an elegant swan dive?"

"I can try." The older man peeled off his coat, leaving him in cream trousers, light cranberry shirt open at the collar, and a merlot sleeveless vest. He rolled up his sleeves, revealing pale, sparsely hairy arms.

"You go first," Rick told Sander. "Help me," he added to Shen.

The two younger men squatted on either side of the professor as he awkwardly prepared to go head first into the unknown. As he propped himself against the open hole, and the flashing street underneath, wind whipped his white hair. The air smelled fresh and damp and grassy.

"Ready?" Rick said.

The professor courageously launched himself into space.

"Ouch," Shen said, grimacing. "I hope he landed rolling."

"Any way you figure, we're going to die," Rick said. "Go."

Shen rolled himself in to a ball and let gravity take over.

Rick went right behind him.

For a terrifying moment, he thought he was dead. He hit the ground rolling, and felt grit ripping at his skin. His neck and face felt like they were on fire. His shoulders felt as if he'd just played two hours of touch football with a team of linebackers. In that same blinding moment, he felt a spray of gravel, and saw the black rubber teeth of huge combat-ready tires go whirling past at merciless speed. They were probably going slower than it seemed, but at this angle—with his legs over his head, and his arms joined over his chest as gravity rolled him over and over toward unconsciousness—it looked as if those toothy wheels were out to kill him.

Seconds later, the vehicles were gone, all but for a lingering stench of half-burned kerosene.

46.   Machine Guns

Rick let gravity give him one more wrenching spin, until he landed in ice cold water in a ditch.

Been there, done that. Am I alive?

He emerged sputtering and shivering. "You guys okay?"

"All in one piece, sore but intact," Shen said. He'd landed about three meters further back.

Another four or five meters behind him sprawled the lifeless form of Professor Sander.

"Oh my god," Shen said, scrambling on all fours, rising on his way.

Rick followed. They examined the body.

Professor Sander, sprawled on his back with all four limbs out straight in a big X, opened his eyes and grinned. "I have made my decision. I will not take up sky diving."

Laughing and hugging, they all rose and dusted themselves off.

Rick pulled out the phone and called Kendra. "Hey."

"Rick, are you okay? We are tracking you on GPS. You are standing still."

"Right. And the assholes are rolling."

"I never know if you are kidding or not."

"Women never do. I'm a sphinx that way."

"Okay, Mr. Comedian. Are you on the road?"

"We are soaking wet and ice cold in a ditch, but alive and ready to duck for cover."

"You can't stay there. If they discover you got away, they will come back. Or they may have patrols coming after. Motor cycles. Who knows."

"Right, Kendra. I know all that. Stop jacking me around and tell me when and where you are going to rescue us."

Shen shoved him roughly. "The assholes are coming back."

"Oh *Schissi*. Gotta run."

He stuffed the phone in his shirt pocket.

He and Shen took Sander by the elbows and ran for cover in some bushes in a meadow ten meters away from the road.

Seconds later, the five armored vehicles came flying past.

Three of them had their hatches open, and each had a helmeted machine gunner manning a heavy salad maker.

Just then, one of the gunners opened up, with a deafening series of echoing explosions, as heavy machine gun rounds cut into the bushes on the other side of the road. They were fifties or even sixties, Rick thought.

An instant later, another M2HB type started banging away at the bushes and trees on Rick's side. He, Sander, and Shen ducked low and prayed.

The column streaked past, raking their surroundings with deadly fire that threw up debris.

They left a mixed stink of diesel smoke and stinging cordite—a bit like sneezing powder but far deadlier.

"They'll be back," Sander said.

Shen pointed to a nearby range of hills. "If we can run that way, we can take cover behind them."

"Let's go," Rick said, starting to run through sometimes knee-high grass. No sense having a conversation and wasting precious seconds and fractions of seconds.

With Sander gamely hobbling between them, Shen and Rick made for the ridge. The way the hills lay, one folded before the other, offering a line of cover if you got between them. He figured that it would take the assholes minutes to turn around and come back. That might with luck just barely be enough time.

Mostly what Rick heard was the sound of their labored, desperate breathing, aside from their trouser legs being lashed by tall grass, and innocent birds twittering while hidden frogs *burrup*-ed.

Sander wheezed.

"You okay?" Shen asked.

"Never felt better. I'll race you to that hill."

Rick added: "If I have a heart attack, don't bother picking me up."

With a growing sense of hope and relief, they made it to the ridge line and ducked leftward, where a rille deepened between gently sloping grassy hills.

Rick's phone barbled. "Yeah?"

"You sound breathless."

"I'm doing pushups."

"You dodo. Any news?"

"Yeah. Running."

"The German pilots say they are seeing machine gun fire."

"That's the assholes going by."

"Okay. We are tracking you. They have GPS also. Stay off the phone unless I call."

He rang off and kept running.

"There is a ridge of trees ahead," Sander wheezed.

"Go for it," Shen said.

They helped Sander along, almost lifting him by the elbows.

Rick heard a new sound and looked behind him.

"Oh no," Shen said.

A big, unmarked, subdued-olive military helicopter—you could tell because of the rocket pods and machine gun bubbles—was flying back and forth along the roadside, stabbing down with a powerful search light.

"We're getting some ground fog," Rick said, regarding a bluish-gray mist rolling in like smoke, low over the fields. "That should help us."

For a minute or two they must have been visible as they clambered out of the rift, up a bare shoulder of grassy hillside, and then disappeared into the dense forest, which was swathed inside with roiling fog. Rich golden evening sunlight, tinged with red and orange, made the fog look magical, as if it were on fire. Rick hoped he'd live to tell Hannah about it.

Their path through the woods took them slightly uphill.

Whatever lay on the other side of that rise was unknowable from here.

"Oh god," Shen said. "Look." He pointed back where they'd come from.

A skirmish line of infantry were coming down the road, and fanning out into the meadow. There must be a hundred of them—a whole company. No way of telling the nationality. They could only be the CEOC forces loyal to General Mendé and Colonel Pierrot and their hardliners.

"The Fourth Reich," Rick joked, "and those are the next-generation SS."

"You are so right," Sander said.

They came to the top of the rise.

What lay beyond was breathtaking.

A castle lay in the valley spread like a vast bowl around them.

They were now truly in the Valley of Seven Castles.

47.   Castle Schoenfels

"Which castle is that?" Rick said.

Sander squinted in the weakening light. "I'm not sure. I do know there is a hiking path connecting all seven castles from Mersch down to Koerich. We have no choice. Let's walk down to the path and follow the signs."

Rick nodded. "Come on, guys. I have an idea."

Within ten minutes they had hiked downhill through heavy forest, which gave good cover.

They came to a flat, nicely graded gravel path.

"That is it," Sander said. "At least here, we can let someone know to find us."

Shen said, "I was a Boy Scout. One of the rules is—if you're lost, stay put. That way the people searching for you don't go in circles, you don't go in circles, and you rest rather than get disoriented."

"Sounds like good advice, except when half of NATO is hunting you and wants to kill you," Rick said. "But Sander is right. We are running out of time and out of options. Let's hike."

"South," Sander said. "Ansembourg is somewhere south of here along the Eisch River. We are on the right path. It's just that, once we get near Ansembourg, we want PAX troops to find us, not CEOC like Pierrot and his crowd."

Rick called Kendra.

"Yes?"

"We are on the path through the Valley of Seven Castles."

"Where?"

"No idea. North of Ansembourg somewhere. The assholes have rangers out beating the brush for us, helicopters with rockets, and anything else you can imagine. Just not the IFS yet, thank god."

"I make you just a kilometer north of Schoenfels. That's the second of the castles. The name means, literally, Pretty Cliff. You missed the little pink one in Mersch that serves as their town hall."

"I don't like pink castles."

"Rick."

"I know. I am a shmoe. Look, I have an idea. The other side can track us by GPS. I'll leave the phone here on the path. You can guesstimate where we'll be. If they waste time looking for the phone, that buys us a few more minutes."

"We'll do our best to get people in there for you. It's just hard to tell who is who. Friend or foe."

"Send the U.S. Army. Send the Marines. You know who they are."

"I'll do what I can. I have the French guys here. The Belgians are right across the border. There are PAXEUR Luxembourg police and army units—I don't know how to sort them out. Leave the phone and go. Good luck."

"Thanks." He set the phone down carefully on a boulder off the path, where it was sheltered from view by a tall patch of reeds.

"Let's go," he told Sander and Shen.

Soon, they came to a large wooden sign on two massive posts. On the sign was a very detailed, overly busy map for hikers, with a lot of small print. Luckily, the major highlights were indicated for idiots, like an image of a castle that resembled a rook from a chess set. You could be from Siberia, Rick thought, or Papua New Guinea, and figure out the icon.

Not far away, along the twisting trail, was Schoenfels castle—or what was left of it after centuries of war and neglect, plus a goodly amount of rebuilding in modern tourist times. This one was a large square building with Disneyland turrets, towering five or six stories and terminating in a pitched roof.

Sander said, "According to the map back there, we are about four miles from Hollenfels, the next castle if we walk across country in a straight line. That's maybe six kilometers. We can make that in an hour."

"Let's get zipping," Shen said.

They marched westward across meadows and hills, sometimes within sight of an isolated farm house roof, but usually in open country with dense forests alternating with open land.

At times, they spotted a distant hovering shadow—a clattering helicopter, shedding its searchlight below. "So far, so good," Rick said.

"I just hope we don't have any bad surprises," Shen said.

Sander said, "We are in the hands of the Divine."

They came to a small but definite river.

"The Eisch," said Professor Sander. "It is a modest little river, which defines the Valley of Seven Castles. You can imagine all the warfare over thousands of years. Roman soldiers marched through these hills while Jesus Christ was still alive. Celtic warriors hunted and fought here. Druids worked their magic. And Stone Age men hunted animals that are now extinct."

They followed the river through lush countryside.

"We must be getting close to Hollenfels," Sander said. "From there, it is only about three kilometers or so to Ansembourg. Then we get back into mortal danger, the closer we get."

They were going up a rise, in echoing forest, when Rick frowned. "Listen."

They stopped and looked at the sky all around.

"Hear that?" Rick said.

"Voices," Shen said.

"Lots of voices," Rick said.

"What are they doing?" Shen said.

"I hear laughing," Rick said.

Sander suddenly got a bright expression. "Let's go. I know what that is."

Rick and Shen followed Sander, who suddenly strode ahead like a youngster.

They came to the top of a hill, and there lay another valley spread out like a green, foresty bowl.

Sticking up from amid trees, on a cliff, was a castle. This one was bigger than the last, and had round towers rather than the single tall, square edifice of Schoenfels an hour back.

Sprawling across a meadow in the valley below were at least a hundred tents.

48.   Hollenfels & Scouts

"This is Hollenfels," Sander said. "The name means Hollow Cliff. Like so many names around the region, it originated in the Middle Ages. There really are hollowed out cliffs, in some cases prehistoric like in the Müllertal area."

Rick was overwhelmed to see at last a thousand figures moving around on the meadows below the gray castle walls.

Flags and pennants waved as in a medieval military camp. Rick remembered the scouts who had rescued Romain, and maintained a high regard for these young people.

Somewhere, a bugle posted a plaintive, haunting melody that echoed among the hills.

"What on earth is this?" Shen said.

Rick had an idea—and almost laughed out loud.

"I was here as a teenager long ago," Sander said. "I had quite forgotten. You see, Hollenfels is a major youth hostel in Luxembourg. It is especially popular for Boy Scout and Girl Guide jamborees with kids coming from all over the world."

They stood and looked out over the vast encampment below.

"There must be a thousand of them," Shen said.

Rick said, "Do you think they will help us cross the road?"

Sander nudged Rick. "You aren't old enough, Joker."

Rick remembered the Boy Scouts and Girl Guides who had rescued Romain. "I think we are going to be in good hands."

"We can lose ourselves in the crowd," Sander said jovially. "Maybe some of those young people are students of mine."

They hiked down the hillside, and approached the encampment. A line of string, on wooden stakes, delineated the safe area for the youngsters, some of whom included *Wellefcher* (Little Wolves), the Luxembourg equivalent of Cub Scouts.

A group of adults, wearing campaign hats of the 19th Century style, gathered to meet them. Professor Sander spoke with them in Letzebuergesch, and they had immediate, deep respect for him. Some knew him from news stories. He was something of a social, political hero to working and middle class people in this part of Europe.

Sander turned and explained to Rick and Shen: "They know who I am and what I represent. I don't know if they are all friends, or if some belong more to the corporate model of politics. I trust that PAX will outweigh CEOC here by a thousand to one. We are going to be safe here. There is an underground area by the castle, where they will escort us because they don't want to endanger any of the kids by having us here."

"That's fair," Rick said.

"More than fair," Shen agreed.

Soon, the three of them hiked through the camp. In one direction were the Girl Guides. Along a separate row of alleys and streets were the Boy Scouts. They passed a huge, blazing bonfire along the way, where the Little Wolves were just then having a story telling session—laughing, clapping, waving their arms in all innocence, a sea of dark blue uniforms with little caps and neck-kerchiefs.

Shen pointed upward. A field gray helicopter with Maltese Cross markings rattled by overhead, nose slightly down as the Luftwaffe pilots scanned the area with binoculars. On its flanks were painted the black, yellow, and red colors of the Federal Republic of Germany.

"About time they found us," Sander said. "Don't wave."

"I hope Kendra has the situation in hand," Rick said. He spoke with an older Scout master (who wore German insignia like those on the chopper) walking beside them. "Say, can I borrow your phone?"

The man looked puzzled.

Sander explained: "*Er fragt ob er ihr Telefon benutzen darf.*"

The German regarded Rick. "Of course. Why didn't you say so?"

"It's my accent," Rick said. "We speak terrible English in California."

"You should try Jersey," Shen quipped.

"Or take English lessons in school like I did." The German handed over a phone, and Rick dialed Kendra's number in K-Town, which rerouted to the installation near Vianden.

"Yes?"

"It's Rick."

"Oh my god. Are you okay?"

"We've been taken prisoner by about a thousand Cub Scouts."

"Any sign of the bad guys?"

"Nope. In fact, we just had a fly-over by the Luftwaffe."

"Can you stay put? Where are you?"

"We're at a Scout Jamboree at Hollenfels Castle."

"I should have realized," she said. "We had a bulletin about that. I will have the Germans pick you up in the next five minutes. Where will you be?"

"Tell them to look for a huge bonfire with a lot of little round caps around it. Cub Scouts."

"Oh how cute."

"Is Hannah okay?"

"She is fine, and worried sick about you."

"Tell her I love her."

"I will. And you know how much she loves you."

"She's kept me going. And so have you."

"Awwww."

"Yeah. Lucky guy, whoever gets in your life."

She made a warm voice like *we've said enough now*. "Rick, thanks for taking care of the Professor. We'll get you home soon."

"I can't wait."

Ten minutes later, a larger Luftwaffe helicopter rattled in low over the Scout camp, causing much excitement, arm waving, jumping, and running in packs. Male and female scout leaders herded their young charges away from a clearing near the camp fire. The Cub Scout story, whatever it was, had grown silent on the storyteller's tongue, and would probably not rise again to the same level of excitement.

Sander said to Rick and Shen, as they waited for the machine to land, "I just have a feeling that most people in the world, who are working people and pay taxes, are going to take our side. The CEOs at Ansembourg have to know that. I suddenly have this feeling that Wan and his cronies can spread all the False News lies and propaganda they want, but people with common sense will see through it. We'll have a corporate world, but with the big dogs on the leash under law and key."

Two more Luftwaffe helicopters hovered in the air not far away as the middle chopper set down on the flat, grassy field. This was a large machine with heavy black tires, not a little toy on skids. It had rockets and Gatling guns on board and looked like it meant business.

From an open bay on one side, a rope net fell down. Luftwaffe aviators in overalls and white helmets leaned out and reached down to help the three on board.

"If we're not safe now," Sander said, "we never will be."

Rick and Shen clambered up the thick ropes and collapsed on the rippled steel flight deck, exhausted in spirit and body.

With hundreds of Scouts and Guides waving and cheering, the net pulled in and the chopper lifted off on powerful rotors, leaving a blast of wind and noise.

A warrant officer named Luepfing introduced himself and said, "We will be at Ansembourg in five minutes. Your forces will take you in safely there." He was a small, trim man with a bit of paunch and graying hair around neatly trimmed temples. He looked a bit like a bowling pin in his flight suit.

"I love you," Sander said sincerely—glad to be alive and in one piece. His white hair blew in the wind.

Luepfing walked away, shaking his head and laughing, as if to say *what all I don't have to do in this job*.

Sander clapped Rick on the back. "I have learned from you that crazy humor is the best remedy for a scary day."

"Works every time," Rick said.

Shen added, "Especially when all else fails."

Luepfing returned and said in English, "The pilot asks you to come up front." He pointed to Rick.

Rick followed him up a steel staircase between walls of equipment. He came into the cockpit area, where two pilots in white helmets and flight suits operated a maze of blinking, winking equipment.

The co-pilot handed Rick a pair of earphones.

Rick put them over his ears. "Hello?" he said, feeling silly.

"Richard?" It was Hannah.

"Oh baby." He nearly cried, as a melting sensation swept over him from top to bottom.

"Honey, I love you so much."

"And you called the Luftwaffe so you could tell me."

"It was better than shooting rockets after you."

"I'll see you soon, gorgeous. We'll shoot some rockets in the air, baby."

"Get here safely."

"Where are you?"

"Ansembourg. Here, talk to Kendra. And get ready. Pucker your lips up—I'm going to be all over your face soon, like an octopus on a boat's bottom."

A moment later, he had Kendra in his ear. "Rick?"

"Yes. Hi, Kendra. Thanks."

"We have fifty French paratroopers guarding us—in full gear; lean, mean, armed, and ready to hunt bear. They look so cute with green and black camo grease all over their faces. Nobody's going to mess with us."

"Hallelujah."

"Amen. I've got Hannah here. She wants to hug you."

"We already talked about that."

"I'm so happy for you two."

"You are an angel yourself."

"Awwwww."

49. New Ansembourg Castle

The three heavily armed, field-gray Luftwaffe helicopters rattled over forests, over hills and dales, and came to a magnificent park-like property with a huge castle at its heart.

Sander explained: "This one is the *Burg* or castle of the Ansen, originally place name, and from that a family. There are two castles in this tiny village of forty people. One is the old castle, which dates back to the Dark Ages and is now privately owned by the Counts of Ansembourg, an ancient lineage. The New Castle is where we are headed. That is a beautifully rebuilt property belonging to a Japanese religious cult. Don't ask me about them—I don't know. They are called Sukyo Mahikari and obviously have lots of money. They claim to have a million followers in over one hundred countries. No matter—CEOC rented their facilities for a month. The castle and township will be home to about a thousand visitors representing the CEOC parliament."

"The whole Mafia is here?" Rick asked. "Wow, a single large bomb would change the balance of power on Earth."

Sander regarded him brightly. "I am reading your mind. They are not that stupid. Many of the CEOC chiefs around the world are dialed in by Internet. They are participating via laptop screen from their secure facilities around the world. Or yes, someone would take them out. They know that. These are the world's modern kings, dukes, and aristocrats. They got into power through a mix of brutality and sly, secret deals—and they know the next rat can take their cheese away just as easily. Read Macbeth or Hamlet. Shakespeare had it all figured out, and he got his information from Boccaccio in Renaissance Italy, who learned from even earlier literature. Nothing ever changes. It's the Human Condition."

Shen clapped him on the back. "Always making a speech. We love you, Professor."

"Someone has to do it," Sander said.

Two escort choppers hovered in the air, while the middle chopper set down on a rolling lawn in the middle of the New Ansembourg Castle estate.

"There is probably nothing like this anywhere in the world," Sander said. "I have only been here two or three times, mostly driving past. The Sukyo Mahikari are a strange mix of secretive and public. They recruit huge numbers of people to come here for their lectures and meditations, most of whom drop out after spending the money. But look what they have done here. They have restored the entire estate from near ruin to something like a strange, other-worldly fairy land."

Theestate was as strange as it was opulent. *(*Endnotes #11)*

Rick, Sander, and Shen climbed down from the chopper on a green meadow surrounded by tall hedges. The grounds consisted of several areas separated by foliage, almost like a labyrinth, and with a phantasmagoric drift—less of purpose or function, and more of dream or fantasy. The effect was enchanting and to Rick's eye a bit dark and moody, almost crazy in a way. He found it more ominous than peaceful. *Or do I need my medicines again,* he wondered.

A row of damaged statues coated in moss and lichen lined a path.

Lily pads floated on one of several rectangular ponds. An angel with gilded wings poured a stream of water into a green fountain. Massive old stone-block walls guarded the shadows from themselves. Sun-blazing portals opened in the walls to take you from one park to another. Bearded mythological faces stared at you—their eyes almost seemed to follow you around. At the lower end of the gently sloping property was indeed a small hedge-maze, with a black-roofed turret-like garden house beside it.

The property was surrounded by mansion-like walls, a miniature fortress of ideas and dreams, with an ornate entrance archway. Cars could drive in through the archway from the narrow, two-lane road, and enter a parking lot worthy of a large manor. Here was the front of an extensive, remodeled structure—modern in some aspects, but still a castle.

From various vantage points, it looked one moment like a tender cloister from the medieval period, the next moment like a solemn chapel where knights might go to meditate through the night, the next moment like a romantic bower out of Romeo and Juliet.

Rick felt the added magic of seeing Hannah again. She ran toward him across a lawn of grass that was almost too lush and green. She flew into his arms, and they made circles, hugging each other. Kendra walked closer with a smile that suggested she was sincerely happy for them. Professor Sander was surrounded by a group of senior male and female advisors wearing business clothing and serious faces.

Shen met a few intelligence cronies and walked off to talk quietly in a corner among gargoyles and wind-ruffled ivy.

Kendra put her arm through Rick's and gave him a friendly tug. "You saved the day."

"Shen helped," Rick said modestly.

She let out a peal of laughter. "You're going to be on late night TV as a clown."

"I won't let him," Hannah said, holding his other arm. "He's going to be in bed with me, watching that TV."

Kendra said, "Seriously, we've checked and check-mated Wan at every turn. He's going to put up his pitch to the CEOC parliament, but it's going to be a tough sell. They've got too many popular movements going against them, and they know it. PAX, PAXEUR, PAXUS, you name it."

"I'm glad," Rick said. "I'm tired of all this. Can I go home soon?"

"We can get you released with an Honorable Discharge, a couple of medals, a lot of benefits, and maybe a commission in the Reserves if you want it. You'll have to work on a degree—you're certainly cut out for it. I'd serve with you any day."

"You already have."

They bumped fists. "Partners," she said, and he echoed the same word.

50.   Casematten

Rick spent a blissful night with Hannah.

In the morning, he woke to a call from Kendra. "Rick, I need you. It's very important."

He kissed Hannah on her soft pink cheek, and tucked her in so she could continue sleeping. She snuggled and smiled in her sleep, and sank away under the covers so only tatters of blonde hair were visible. He shaved, showered, and otherwise did his morning plumbing duties, and dressed to venture forth.

There was some dark ice berg of power at work in the parliament of corporations. This was, after all, a de facto world government. Most of the world's wealth was represented in the thousand families who either sent their duke or prince, or kept a digital presence for their own safety and convenience. The annual electorate conference of CEOC was not advertised. A private army of mercenaries were scattered around the area for protection of the delegates—from the outside world, and from each other.

In that spirit, the two rival factions—PAX and CEOC conservatives— stayed in secure hotels off the property. The delegates and their entourages occupied every spare room in the castle. The Japanese cultists were nowhere to be found.

Rick waited for Kendra in the entrance hall by the main doors. This was in the middle wing of the palace, a sort of neutral ground.

That was where Rick had his one and only meeting with Wan, the man who had raped and abused Hannah among his other concubines and sex slaves. Wan happened to be passing with an escort of Asian men— probably Triad toughs on their way to some committee meeting or a breakfast.

Wan orbited dangerously close to Rick. While carrying a briefcase in hand, he favored Rick with an expression of cold triumph and malignant loathing in his smirking face. "Mr. Buchan. My associates informed me that you might be on your way to a military prison for your crimes and incompetence."

Rick stared at this caricature of a human being, as he saw him—a creature who was not really a man, but a sociopath, a hollow shell of greed and infantile narcissism grown into a kind of walking tumor that infected everyone around him with its disease.

Of course he has had me followed, and knows a lot about me. Rick said, "For a guy who pays lots of money to stupid people to collect false data, and to murder people for sleazy profit, you don't know much."

Wan shifted the briefcase and nudged the air between them with his chin. The smirk grew ever more mean-spirited. "I have the stolen data here, Rick. How is Hannah? I trust she is better in bed with you than my boys found her to be."

"You don't insult me with that kind of talk. You just make yourself look like the human crap that you are." Rick turned and walked away.

He heard a gloating laugh behind him as Wan and his entourage of goons walked on.

One day, I will kill you, Rick thought. *If you don't kill me first. That's how it works in your primitive jungle world. That's why we need to defeat you and your type. The world deserves to be run by real people.*

He remembered something an older friend had once told him about staying upset over the evil of shallow people. "It's like being mad at the weather. Nothing you can do. Let it go."

He thought to himself: *I am so lucky to have her. She is so precious, and everything you touch turns to death and foulness.*

He was jolted out of his dark thoughts by Kendra, who looked bright and pretty as she came sailing into the crowded foyer and found him. "Hey, good morning."

"Morning."

"What's with you?"

"I just ran into Wan."

"Oh." Her sympathetic stare said it all.

"I'm trying to flush him down the toilet of circumstance so I can forget ever meeting him."

"He is human garbage." Kendra wrapped an arm around him. She squeezed while towing him away. "Come on. We have important stuff to do."

"I'm all ears."

"We'll take it a bit at a time," she said, looking mysterious.

They stepped outside and down the front steps of the chateau. From this perspective, the place was not a castle in the medieval sense, but a modern chateau of wealth and privilege in the Industrial Revolution.

"We are going to fly to Germany," Kendra told him.

"Oh? I was hoping—"

She grinned. "No, silly, it's not about you. It's about your old nemesis, Shipwreck."

"You mean Sherwin."

"That guy. You are going to love this."

"Next to Wan, even Sherwin would seem like a ray of light among dark clouds."

"I thought you'd feel that way. We are flying to Mannheim, where Shipwreck sits in the army stockade, waiting for his trial and conviction and then years of hell to pay."

"So Kendra, on the day that Sander and Wan are going to start giving their speeches and rebuttals, why is this more important? Why are you dragging me away from the action?"

As they spoke, he saw a helicopter parked in a meadow on the edge of the estate. The rotors were turning, the wings feathering, and the engines warming up.

"We have some drama coming up that we hope will ruin Wan's day. One of them you'll learn about when we get back—which I hope will be this evening. I don't want to miss the circus here either. But this is the other thing."

"Huh?"

"Rick, one of the things we are going to throw at Wan—or let Sander and his spokesmen throw—is this cool information we are about to get from Sherwin. You see, he realizes his number is up. He could face the death penalty for what he did in Huilongistan, with you and the other NCO as surviving victims testifying to his attempts to cover up. In fact, the cover-up will probably go worse for him than his gross negligence and inattention to duty, resulting in combat casualties and mission failure."

"Sounds serious."

"It is, Rick. No jokes now."

"It's the only way I can keep from breaking down in tears."

"I know, my friend. Hang in there. You have Hannah, and a whole new life ahead of you with money and benefits. You'll be taken care of."

As they walked to the helicopter, she explained: "Sherwin has asked for a plea bargain. In return for leniency—which could mean just five to ten years at hard labor, revocation of commission, forfeiture of pay and benefits, he has indicated he is going to drop a couple of dimes on Wan and on General Mendé. You see?"

Rick felt a thrill in his gut. He whistled. "That would be awesome. We could help Sander drive nails into Wan's career coffin. I like that."

She said, "I thought you would," as they climbed up the steel steps into the chopper.

The flight to Mannheim would take maybe thirty minutes.

Rick did not relish seeing Shipwreck. It would bring back too many horrible memories.

As they buckled in, she said, "He asked to see you because he wants to make a personal apology."

"He's always serving his own best interests," Rick said. "He has no soul and no remorse."

"I know," she said. "He's like Wan. That's why them hit it off."

"They know each other?"

She smiled. "Shipwreck was assigned to the R&D detachment from USAREUR after being sent to Germany to participate in the witch hunt he created over you, to cover his tracks. Don't worry, the judges are seasoned colonels and generals who see a coward and coyote like him coming from a mile away."

"So what is this information Shipwreck is about to tell us?"

She gave him a mysterious grin. "Let's go to Mannheim and find out."

51.　Morning at New Ansembourg Castle

Hannah and Shen attended the first session in a small auditorium that must once have been a ballroom. The hall was packed with spectators as Sander and other dignitaries from the moderate and hard line wings of CEOC sat along the wall of the stage.

At the podium stood a small woman with wire-rimmed glasses and tousled, graying hair. She wore a dowdy suit and never smiled. "Good morning. My name is Caroline Forscher. I am a member of the organizing committee of CEOC for this annual participants' meeting and the parliament where we will select our new leadership this week." She held the podium with both hands as she looked around the hall. "Welcome. As you all know, this is a very influential and powerful organization. The days of nation-states and their wars and greed are over. There will be no more world wars, no more Napoleons or demagogues, as long as the new evolution of democracy takes root and grows, nurtured by our care and attention." She paused again and looked dramatically around.

Shen whispered to Hannah, "Interesting how they spin the facts. They've all but destroyed popular democracies in the U.S. and Europe, and prevented progress in the rest of the world."

Madame Forscher said, "Today, we will hear opening remarks from Mr. Wan, the head of Wan Industries and a leader in the globalization of economics and politics. We will also hear opening remarks from Professor Sander, a Luxemburgish intellectual and political-economic scholar of history, who represents a somewhat different view than Mr. Wan's. In a few minutes, I will ask Mr. Wan to come up here and begin his presentation. In the meantime, I will entertain you with the history of CEOC and its development over the last quarter century..."

As the woman spoke, Hannah heard a faint buzzing sound.

Shen had his cellphone in his lap and surreptitiously read a text message. He rose, indicated for Hannah to follow, and sidled among the crowded seats until they were outside the hall. Hannah relished the leg room. "What's up?"

"That was Rick. He texted me to meet him at the chopper port."

"Why?"

"No idea. We have somewhere to go. He made a point of telling me to leave you here, where you will be safe and sound."

Hannah was instantly anxious. "I want to be with him."

"Hannah, no. You'd be a distraction. Sorry, my dear. Do this for Rick."

"He won't get hurt, will he?"

Shen shook his head. "That boy lands on his feet every time."

She gave him a wistful look. "I have to stay and listen to all this blather. I know everything they are going to say. Sander is going to say we need to put a leash on the corporations.."

She continued: "And Wan is going to get up there and tell the people who really matter that they are the only ones who matter. Why share the wealth with a bunch of drones and artisans who are nothing but wage slaves? He's going to roll out General Mendé and explain that he wants to build a world peace keeping force with General Mendé as its field marshal and as the world's police chief. He's going to show videos of the IFS in action, shooting down that Belgian military jet. The IFS will make the national forces of yesterday obsolete. And blah blah blah. Tell me something new."

Shen gripped her upper arms and shook her in a brotherly fashion. "Be brave, Hannah. Be strong. Sit through the blather and keep the seat warm for Rick. Catch up on your sleep and dream of a day walking on the beach, just you and Rick."

Hannah said, "Well, now that you put it that way…"

52.   Rick & Kendra

They sat in a Spartan meeting room at the U.S. Army prison in Mannheim, Germany: Rick, Kendra, Sherwin, and four burly U.S. Military Police in Army uniforms, with white saucer caps and white leather, including holsters for their heavy black automatics. They wore traditional white arm bands marked *MP* in large black lettering. A white-haired NCO acted as sergeant of the guard.

At a desk to one side sat a German civilian with excellent language skills, who typed away at a transcription machine. She was the court reporter, making a permanent legal record of the meeting.

Sherwin looked small and insignificant in his orange jumpsuit with the words PRISONER printed in large letters on front and back. Underneath that, smaller lettering cautioned in German, *Vorsicht—Gefangener*. Sherwin was handcuffed to a steel ring in the wall as he sat in a plastic chair, reeking of cigarette smoke. He looked old, devious, and desperate. The sergeant of the guard had let him smoke, but made him extinguish the cigarette before Rick and Kendra entered the interrogation room.

"I want to sincerely apologize to Sergeant Richard Buchan..." he began.

Rick's eyes glazed over as he sat through the charade. When it was over, he did not bother respecting Sherwin with a direct look in the eyes— just a glance of contempt. Rick said simply: "I will never see you again, and this is once too many for my taste."

Kendra jammed him in the ribs. She'd warned him not to get personal. He bit his tongue.

"I am Major Kendra Walsh of the Staff Judge Advocate's office for the regional U. S. Army court martial jurisdiction. I have been requested by Lieutenant Sherwin to meet with him, as I am doing now in the presence of Sergeant Buchan, to hear Lieutenant Sherwin's proposal for a plea bargain. Are we here to receive a request for plea bargain from you, Lieutenant Sherwin?" She sat straight upright and was all business, Rick thought. She knew what she was doing.

"Yes, ma'am," the prisoner said.

"You are facing up to forty years to life in a federal military prison, significant portion of which likely at hard labor; that and the usual penalties, like reduction in rank, forfeiture of commission, loss of pension and benefits as well as pay, and so forth. Do you understand, Lieutenant Sherwin?"

"Yes, Ma'am."

The transcriptionist typed away in great concentration. The session was also being video-recorded.

"What information do you propose to give me today, without reservation or restriction, that would make me wish to propose to the court a plea bargain on your behalf?"

"I know some things about Wan and General Mendé."

"Do you propose to reveal those alleged things to me without reservation, under oath, today?"

"Yes, ma'am."

"Is that all, Lieutenant Sherwin? You said there was something else."

He got a crafty look. "Yes, ma'am. I can tell you where they are keeping the R&D model that shot down the Belgian air force plane." He stared at her with a look of greed—calculating how many years off his sentence he could buy for himself with that information..

"I am here to listen to your story," Kendra said. "Sergeant Buchan will remain in the room as a witness."

Sherwin's face underwent a series of changes, from arrogant disdain for Rick to defeat, and finally resignation. He seemed to become a prisoner in truth, right then and there, a beaten man, like a dog rolling over when told to do so, in return for a biscuit.

Rick took no pleasure in it. Just the information. And then he wanted to leave this room and never see this stinking creature again.

53.   Semper Paratus

"I thought we could use an extra hand," Kendra told Rick as the unmarked chopper set down amid a gust of prop wash on the lawn near the Ansembourg Chateau in Luxembourg. It was mid-afternoon. This had taken a total of four hours in total: in the air, in the U.S. Army stockade at Mannheim, and now on the return trip.

"I imagine they are making their speeches at the chateau," Rick said.

"I imagine so," Kendra echoed. "Good thing we missed all the chat."

As the chopper set down on big black inflated tires, Shen climbed on board. He wore a beige flight suit, blue baseball cap—all without markings—and combat boots.

Another man climbed on board. Rick barely recognized him, but the man introduced himself first, extending a rough paw. "Inspector Maurice Fischer of the Police Grand-Ducale, situated in Echternach. We met when your friend Romain Poncelet was badly burned at the farm house."

"Oh yes, I remember."

The Inspector, who wore a dark suit, white shirt, and nondescript merlot necktie, strapped himself into the doughnut bench in the chopper. "Someday, you will have to entertain me with a story about how you escaped from a locked, moving police ambulance on a road at night."

Rick felt a bit uneasy. "Necessity is the mother of invention."

"Of course." Fischer betrayed no emotion. "For now, we must concentrate on the task at hand."

The chopper lifted off into the long, lingering sunlight of evening and headed south toward the nation's capital. They would arrive in about fifteen minutes.

"I have notified the police in the capital. They are sending undercover units to the scene in case we run into complications."

"*Semper paratus*," Shen advised.

"Ample apparatus?" Rick said. It was not a question. He knew the answer.

"Boy Scout motto," Shen said. "Always Prepared."

"*Stets bereit*," Fischer said in German, looking pleased at some memory of his teen years long ago. "*Emmer parat*."

54.   Mélu: Revelations

Hannah was praying the speeches would soon be over. Seeing Wan in the same room made her stomach turn. After what he had done to her, and the other women and some young men as well—it was hideous to see such a criminal presenting himself as the savior of the human race. She wanted to vomit.

An important-looking lady had taken Shen's place beside her, and they struck up a conversation during one of the fifteen-minute breaks, when coffee and pastry were served. One thing about the Luxemburgers, Hannah thought: they know how to enjoy their coffee and sweets.

"I hear that there is an important speech coming up," said the woman. "You are Hannah Smith?"

Hannah nodded, startled. "How did you know?"

"Madame Forscher told me. I am Genevieve Grau from Geneva of the Human Rights Commission. Please do stay, Hannah. You will be very interested in the proceedings this afternoon."

"Oh?"

"You know a woman named Mélu?"

Hannah was further startled. "Yes?"

"Mélu will be making a speech from Berlin. It will be on the big screen." She leaned close and whispered: "She will ruin the day for Mr. Wan and General Mendé—you'll see."

"Oh?"

"You'll want to stick around for this."

Shortly, Wan took the podium for the second time that day. "Good afternoon, my friends," he said. He wore a pair of horn-rimmed glasses that he did not need, Hannah knew, but he must think they made him look intellectual.

Wan said, "I have made my presentation, Professor Sander has made his, we have engaged in debate and rebuttals, and now we are here to sum up. Professor Sander will shortly make a speech in which he will once again express his desire to take from the wealthy that which they have legitimately earned through their intelligence and ambition, and turn that wealth over to the general population. I shudder to think how these forms of communism and socialism will dilute the ambitions of the masses to be more productive, to study, to train, and to work diligently. Today, with honor and integrity—"

(Hannah nearly barfed)

"—I offer you an alternative. Strength though science, and joy through hard work by all. I do not advocate a class society. Far from it. I advocate a merit system whereby those who work the smartest and hardest are rewarded. Professor Sander wants to take from us, the wealthy, and give to the poor and the indolent. I propose, above all, to turn a new corner in history by weakening national governments to a point that they can no longer start and wage wars in which millions of innocent victims perish for the greed of a Hitler, a Milosevic, a Mussolini, a Stalin, a Mao, a Pol Pot, a Napoleon, or a Kim Jong Il. The list of despots is long, and the list of their victims is immeasurable. We propose to institute a one-world police force. It will be a military so powerful that no national government can ever prevail against it. To that end, I now present to you my minister for defense, General Mendé of Denmark."

A ripple of applause rolled through the crowd—mostly the wives and associates of oligarchs, Hannah observed. Not a class society, eh? These were the dukes and barons of the new order. They looked regal, they behaved like snobs, and they thought only of themselves and their positions, she thought.

The General was a short, fat man with wire rim glasses, a round bald head, and a pink fleshy face. Despite the pudge he looked hard around the edges, merciless around the eyes, grim around the mouth. He gave a short, no-nonsense speech about how he and Wan would create a world order of peace through power.

When he was done, Madame Forscher introduced Professor Sander once again, who began to speak. "Ladies and Gentlemen, I have made my position clear, and Mr. Wan has offered his. The real test in an age of false news and fools' news is whether the truth lives up to the words. I will have a few concluding remarks shortly about my proposed program of liberty, equality, happiness, and security for all—especially universal health care. On the matter of universal health care—not only can we afford it, but we must have it. What we cannot afford is tens of thousands of innocent men, women, children, and infants sentenced to death each year in an ongoing holocaust of mass murder at the hands of a health denial industry, laughingly called health insurance, which delivers nothing but only withholds medical care and pharmacy, while stealing a trillion dollars a year from the economy. On top of that, they bankrupt hundreds of thousands of families if a member gets sick, and before denying care they take away everything those people have worked all their lives for. I am offering you an example from one great nation's tragic history to illustrate what happens when a nation is in the grip of uncontrolled capitalism at the expense of law, order, equality, and common sense. When the control the media, the message is always that god loves the oligarchs (who also control the churches and temples), while anything that is good for common working people or the artisan middle class is evil—like health care, work place safety, minimum wages, and the like—and must be abolished. You like to quote Jesus. Well, let me quote Jesus. *By their fruits you shall know them.* Let me illustrate to you the fruits of Mr. Wan and his privileged class who increasingly, year by year, increase their wealth and power at the expense of everyone else. To illustrate this, I will now introduce to you a young lady from Luxembourg, who has been part of an international effort to document what happens when corporations rise above the law, and their owners become the owners of the rest of us as their slaves and serfs."

He stepped aside as a large screen appeared on the wall behind the stage. Hannah gasped as she recognized the face of Mélu, her friend, the wife of Romain who still lay recovering in a Berlin specialty burn hospital.

"Good afternoon," Mélu said. She looked plain, serious, and courageous. She wore round glasses and had her hair parted in the middle. It hung loosely to the sides in a limp and demure but ageless cut. *Bonjour,*" she said, and added: *E schëenen Nometteg.* "Good day—and a nice afternoon."

She cleared her throat and looked down at some papers she held in her hands. She read from them, pausing sometimes to look up at the video camera in Berlin, as if gazing directly into the eyes of her audience. *Meng léef Letzebuerger, a Biirger vun der ganze Welt...* She began with the famous words spoken by the exiled Grand Duchess Charlotte from London during World War II as she began her patriotic speeches: "My beloved Luxemburgers..." Mélu added: "...And citizens of the world."

She spoke in a steady, firm voice showing little intonation or emotion. Hannah and the audience listened with electrified concentration. "You are about to decide between a man of intellect and honor—Professor Sander—who speaks truth and wishes us all well—versus a man whose every word is a selfish lie designed to increase his wealth and power, not to mention his bestial appetites at the expense of innocent victims. Mr. Wan and his cronies, in particular but not only General Mendé, are living examples of why we cannot afford to live in a world described by Franz Kafka, inhabited by Winston Smith and Julia of George Orwell's *1984*, and ruled by the secretive cliques described by G. K. Chesterton in *The Man Who Was Thursday*."

As she continued to speak in her level, emotionless tone in words freighted with feeling, her image was frequently replaced by a series of video clips. It was clear that PAX, PAXEUR, and PAXUS intelligence services had been working very hard to expose the secret dealings of Wan's class.

As she explained, one of the greatest heroes had been the late Colonel Whitcomb, U.S. Army, who had worked undercover as a purported CEOC hardliner close to General Mendé. In several videos secretly made by Whitcomb, General Mendé could be seen accepting large amounts of cash bribes for throwing contracts to his cronies, among other crimes. One of these videos had been outside a bus station in Wiltz.

Rick had been in the car with the late Colonel Whitcomb at Wiltz during this transaction. He would be able to add his testimony.

In other videos, Wan could be seen consorting with Macao and Las Vegas based known gangsters, including Mafia, Chinese Triads, Japanese Yakuza, and South American narco-terrorists, not to mention a few U.S. tycoons.

"The amount of intelligence we have legally compiled on Mr. Wan and his cronies should make you aware that you must not continue voting to put these people in office, or to support their tyrannical, opportunistic power play this week."

She rattled her papers, in a transition. "I have other evidence to reveal from our intelligence operations, conducted across many nations in the world. It is true that sometimes government is not the solution but the problem. It is also true that sometimes big business is the problem, not the solution. It is also true that all of us require leadership and consensus, or democracy turns into rule by the rabble, always manipulated and led by the wealthy and powerful behind the screen of demagogues with seductive personalities and hideous plans.

"The real solution is that which the ancient Romans came up with more than 25 centuries ago when they founded their republic in 509 BCE, which lasted successfully for almost five hundred years, and was the model for the first great modern democracy, that of the United States. When the United States founding fathers became the framing fathers at Philadelphia in 1787, there had not been a major democracy in the world since ancient Rome before the five hundred year tyranny of the Caesars replaced the democratic republic of ancient Rome. The key lies in separating powers so that no one person can ever seize power again—and eliminating an oligarchy in which the few own everything, and the many are serfs or slaves on their own land to serve the few. Rome's republic evolved over time because of the intelligent design of Rome's founding fathers. The Framers of 1787 in the United States were acutely aware of Roman history, and learned from it—which is why the United States is a republic, from the ancient Latin words meaning 'the people's business.'"

She looked directly into the camera, and Hannah felt as if Mélu were speaking directly to her. "Mr. Wan and his class have furthered the idea, among the impoverished masses of our depressed economy, that it is smart to sell yourself into indentured servitude for a period of three to seven years. For that time, you sacrifice your freedom and individual rights— even your sexual integrity—for the pleasure of these leering, wanton slave owners. I am speaking up on behalf of all the abused and trafficked men, women, and children of the world. Do not be ashamed to come forward and accuse those who have abused you. Stop them from continuing that abuse with other victims. Join together, like the labor unions who seek a just wage and just working conditions for all working people. Join together and force the law makers, judges, and executives of the world to end this horrific practice. Be brave, and speak to the press or to our intelligence services and expose the cruelty and unfeelingness of Mr. Wan and his ilk."

Hannah knew she was speaking directly to her—and realized she must offer a deposition before returning to her real life in California.

Mélu rattled her papers again, turning pages to read further. "I wish to reveal one more fact today. This regards the murder of those innocent Belgian air force pilots by agents of Wan Industries and General Mendé. It just as well implicates the same individuals in the murder in London of Mr. Pierre Sander, the only child of Professor Sander, who developed a revolutionary Intelligent Fuselage Technology to improve the human condition for all people. Pierre was murdered by Mr. Wan's agents in London so that Mr. Wan, who had stolen the technology, could prevent anyone else from duplicating it.

"Two fine young Belgian pilots died in a surprise attack by General Mendé's R&D model of the IFS technology."

In the audience, a man rose to his feet—a close associate of Wan— waved his fist, and shouted, "That is an outright lie! There never was such a model. There was no mockup. The Belgians died in an unfortunate accident due to sloppy maintenance at the hangar."

Mélu must have heard the outburst, maybe expected it, because she looked directly into the video camera and said in a more emotional tone: "Like everything else I have stated, I can prove what I have said."

55.   Casematten Killers

The helicopter containing Rick, Inspector Fischer of the Grand Ducal Police, Shen of the CIA, and Kendra of the U.S. Army Judge Advocate Corps stuttered through blue skies and light haze under a wan sun. The towers and turrets, ramparts and Adolphe Bridge of the capital city came into view.

The chopper rattled toward the old city, or high city—*Haute Ville*, in previous centuries Europe's so-called Gibraltar of the North. *(*Endnotes #12)*.

Today, for the most part, the tunnels—known as *Casematten*—are closed up and under padlock—open only for guided tours by experienced leaders who will not lose themselves in the cold, damp, drippy tunnels. Of the word origin for *Casematten*, a number of theories exist. *(*Endnotes #13)*

The helicopter roared in to a landing at the Boulevard Royal as it overlooks the Petrusse Valley by the Pont Adolphe. By arrangement of Inspector Fischer, city police briefly stopped traffic as the four climbed out. Just as soon, the chopper hauled off to the Findel Airport northeast of the city. Police barricades came down, and traffic resumed its normal flow.

But all was not normal. Black police vans and dark green military trucks quietly arrived from all directions. There were no lights or sirens. Rick estimated that, within a half hour, at least 200 uniforms surrounded the rim of the Petrusse on the north side, where the national cathedral, the Grand Ducal palace, and the Place Guillaume lay. It was the area where Hannah and Rick had taken a long, dreamy walk after their night of *amour* in Belair at the home of Romain and Mélu.

Fischer received updates from a mobile police command post—a black, squat vehicle borrowed from earlier army usage—that was parked near the Cathedral and pilgrimage shrine of Our Lady, Consoler of the Afflicted. From here, it was a ten-minute walk to the Grand Ducal palace near the oldest part of the city. "We are not taking any chances," Fischer said. "We have police and commandos on every one of the Casematten entrances, including the bridges and viaducts leading across the Petrusse. We will be ready in a half hour to open the doors and send armed parties in."

Fischer stepped closer to Rick and his U.S. companions. "Mr. Buchan, I apologize for mistaking your situation the other day. It grieves me that we were not more helpful."

"It's okay," Rick said. "It was sort of fun."

"I should have known you are a fun guy," Fischer said drily.

"Fun guys recognize each other."

"Rick," Kendra warned.

"Dude," Shen said.

Fischer said, "We have a strong national interest in concluding this operation successfully. I am glad you are here to provide moral support and witness."

"We're with you," Kendra said.

During the systematic preparation to penetrate the miles of the underground mazes, Rick excused himself and wandered off to find a public toilet. This was near the rim of the Petrusse, where the pavements, streets, and balustrades on top overlook the deep green valley, the bridges, the rooftops, and the tiny, winding silver ribbon of the Petrusse stream below. As he emerged from the facility, Rick sauntered over to the balustrade. Putting his hands on it, he glanced right and left, and then down—and looked upon two familiar figures.

One was the Cuban woman Savia, whom he had seen shooting Fincoff in a Bagnolet, Paris alley. The other was Wan's favorite martial artist, bodyguard, and when necessary, killer Yoichi. They had not seen him, and he snapped away from the balustrade. From a safe distance, he observed them as they stood on an incline path halfway down the valley.

Savia was a compact, athletically solid woman with an exotically, brutally attractive face. She had a wide jaw, slash mouth, sharply drawn nose, and dark, almost almond eyes under high, dark eye brows. She wore a maroon coat, charcoal pants, and a yellow silk kerchief, along with petite dark brown Doc Marten designer hiking and kicking boots. She stood in the lee of a huge old pine tree, watching intently as the police closed in all around. Nearby was Yoichi, wearing a black beret, black crew-neck sweater, and black jeans with similar dark brown boots as Savia's.

What to do?

Already, Savia and Yoichi walked slowly, hands in pockets in a show of nonconcern, toward a steel door in the cliff face. This was one entrance to the *Casematten* that the police had not yet closed in on.

Kendra was unarmed and not trained for this.

Rick gave Shen the high sign.

Shen trotted over to him.

Fischer was instructing a semi-circle of detectives and uniformed police on procedure, and could not be reached with a hand signal.

Rick put a finger over his lips.

Shen jogged closer. "What is it?"

"I just spotted Savia and Yoichi. I saw them head into the tunnels."

"We have to tell Fischer."

"I don't want to lose them. Give me your gun."

Shen handed over his Glock 26 subcompact and a spare clip.

"Go tell Fischer, okay? I'll need backup."

Shen gave him a pat on the upper arm and ran back to the Inspector.

Rick hoisted himself over the railing and jumped and slid down three meters of grass, dirt, and sandstone to land on his feet amid crumbling red gravel. In the cliff face, a steel door stood half open. Cautiously, Rick approached.

He heard water dripping inside, but no voices.

The light in the Casematten was low and steady—the yellowish glow of old-fashioned light bulbs. If the name of these tunnels was any testimonial, Casematten truly were houses of darkness.

And dread.

He advanced slowly, keeping the gun ready before him in both hands.

As he moved stealthily, he focused on taking one silent step at a time while listening intently.

Each time he came to a crossing, where shafts made a T or an X intersection, he paused and looked with extra caution in all directions.

The walls still had some niches cut out for torch sconces. Must have been dangerous down here with fire and gun powder. In fact, during the 1600s up top, a siege bombardment by over 50,000 cannon shots had leveled much of the medieval city—why most of the high city was rebuilt in subsequent centuries.

Water leaking through natural fissures and capillaries in the stone made an uneaven tattoo on the roughly cut but flat tunnel floors..

There.

He froze and listened.

Was that creaking sound behind or in front?

Echoes.

Where were Shen, Fischer, and the gendarmes?

Rick took out his phone, opened the back, and removed the battery so Fischer or Hannah could not call and give his presence away if the phone warbled. He couldn't see well enough in the dark to struggle with putting in on airport or silent mode.

Rick took another step, and another, and another…

At times, he squeezed his eyes shut in the dim light, as if that let him listen better.

He pressed forward.

There were miles and miles of this labyrinth. In some places, corridors led away into pitch black off the common tourist path. Most of the tunnels are rarely explored.

Hearing footsteps, Rick ducked quickly into a dark side tunnel.

He waited with pounding heart and gun at ready.

A squad of men passed no more than five meters away. They carried lanterns that cast a hard bluish-white light in contrast with the purposely weak electric bulbs in this section. The troops of General Mendé were well armed, and clad in the bluish fatigues with black boots and dark caps he had seen before. They were also well armed and looked thoroughly trained.

As glaring light stabbed this way and that, Rick flattened himself against the cave walls as best he could.

The boot steps passed, and the light dimmed but did not completely go back to *matte*.

Now he heard an odd, distant whirring sound.

The sound grew more intense. It echoed in the miles of caverns.

Rick raised one shoulder to protect his ear, while pressing the other side of his head to the cold, damp wall that smelled of water and underground lichens.

As he hid in the side corridor, Rick watched in amazement as a new, golden glow filled the intersection from where he'd come, and where the CEOC troops had just passed.

The golden light grew brighter.

Rick held a hand before his face, and stared curiously between his fingers.

In the intersection ahead floated a large drone.

This one was not dark, nor was it shaped like a hooded car's roof like those at Noertringen.

This drone appeared almost alive, pulsating intelligently—more like a swimming manta ray in the ocean than a hovering saucer. It was large enough to fill the corridor as it floated past with lazily undulating edges. For a moment, Rick thought he saw large white eyes with black pupils, like those of a giant undersea squid. But of course—the top-secret NATO R&D people around Houffalize and Wiltz had borrowed on nature's own best technologies to create a fearsome weapon of the next century.

Rick was instantly certain that he was staring at a small scale version of Pierre Sander' IFS—a craft that was robotic pilot and android flyer all at once. It was capable of ultra-fast maneuvering, fast flight, and self-guiding tactics. No wonder this very machine, or one just like it, had outflown and killed two highly trained NATO fighter pilots from Belgium. This was the future of aviation from air into space. Even artillery shells would become intelligent and able to hover for hours before streaking at many times the speed of sound to kill their target in space, in the air, or on land.

Rick hesitated to shoot at it, for fear it could retaliate in self-defense.

He breathed as softly as he could, and stayed hidden in shadow with his back pressed to the wall.

The IFS craft, whirring softly, floated past in the direction the soldiers had gone. The corridors echoed with that fearsome sound that pulsed in an ear-piercing tone barely in hearing range.

One more lantern passed—held by Yoichi.

With him was the warrior woman Savia holding an assault rifle.

As soon as they passed, Rick ducked further down into the dark side corridor. In the dimmest of lighting, from far away, he fumbled and put his phone back together.

He called, and Kendra answered: "They are bringing the IFS model out. Be careful. I think it may be armed."

"Okay—can you stay put?"

"Yes. I think they are going to try and fly it out of their hiding place here."

"We'll do our best to intercept it."

"Good luck."

When his ears stopped ringing, and his heart stopped pounding in his neck, Rick carefully walked back toward the light. He waited, but no more opposition troops passed by. Hopefully they had all gone now. With his gun held high, ahead of him, in both hands, Rick advanced as quickly as he dared back to the Casematten entrance in the middle of the cliff face where he'd entered.

He saw daylight far ahead. A knot of figures undulated like underwater shadows.

His phone warbled softly in the echoing corridor.

"It's Rick."

"It's Kendra. Stay in the tunnels. We're about to have a major battle in the air."

Rick rang off and jogged forward at a careful crouch.

Ahead of him, two of the blue-clad soldiers turned and ran back into the tunnels.

When they saw him, they started firing their compact assault rifles.

Rick threw himself down in a sailing dive while emptying his hand gun.

One of his assailants crumpled.

The other ran a few steps forward.

Both he and Rick were totally out of ammo.

The man jumped over Rick and kept running back into the caves.

Rick scrambled forward.

He picked up the dead man's weapon—a French-made FAMAS Type F1—along with a replacement clip from the man's belt. This was the standard French infantry weapon. He'd handled it before at NATO arms ranges. Its short stock and light weight fit neatly into the crook of his arm as he made his way forward.

He was just in time to see several things happening all at once.

The squad of General Mendé's troops lay face down with their hands behind their necks.

Above, Inspector Fischer and a Luxembourg army colonel barked orders to surrender and stay lying down.

A squad of Luxembourg and Belgian assault commandos in black armor came cautiously, in single file, and rapidly down the concrete path. They moved as one body, with their assault rifles pointing before them. Several NCOs in similar battle dress, brandishing side arms, move in tandem alongside.

Rick caught sight of Yoichi and Savia running down in the stone culvert of the Petrusse River. They were too far for him to bother trying to shoot after them. A brief rattle of gunfire sounded on the parapets above, and gun smoke drifted away in nasty, peppery tatters, but the shooters gave up. Snipers could have taken the two out, but this was all impromptu and improv.

In the center of the Petrusse—in mid-air—hovered a golden, glowing IFS drone.

For a second, Pierre's design hovered gloriously at the center of attention as if daring anyone to strike it.

The next second, three smaller machines, similar but glowing silver, streaked down at a 45 degree angle spitting bullets of light energy—so fast the Rick's eye could barely keep up.

It was over in a moment.

The golden drone was crippled and began to dim.

It drifted slowly sideways.

A trickle of black smoke started to pour from underneath.

The three silver drones—probably a later model, Rick imagined, in the hands of legitimate government forces loyal to their people rather than corporate owners—circled like predatory falcons around the dying killer drone.

As the craft floated toward the cliff walls, heavy smoke suddenly poured out from the engines at its core. In one or two seconds, a torrent of bluish-white-red liquid fire (the national colors, ironically) brightened the black smoke trail. A second later, the device exploded in a rather anticlimactic fashion—with a final whirring noise revving up into an explosive bang, followed by a shattering sound like glass breaking as shards of it flew all about. The main piece fell dead to the ground below.

The three silver sentinels streaked away, following the wide concrete flood canal of the tiny Petrusse stream, which was now just a shiny ribbon drifting slowly in a bottom trough that a man could comfortably hop over.

Savia and Yoichi were gone—somehow, they had gotten away.

Kendra called. "Rick?"

"I'm good."

"It's safe. Come on up. But tune in to Radio Luxembourg."

Rick walked up the concrete ramp, past commandos who were cuffing the CEOC mercenaries. Up top, the Grand Ducal police and army units waited to take them into custody.

Rick tuned his phone to Web broadcast. That was Mélu's voice speaking…

56.   Shame vs. Honor

Hannah listened with a new sense of passion as Mélu's face and voice, from a secure location in Berlin, guarded by German commandos loyal to the Bundestag, were broadcast in Chateau Ansembourg and to billions of screens around the world.

"People everywhere," Mélu spoke in a firm voice of leadership and conviction. "Now is not the time for radical action or violence. That would play into the hands of men like the industrialist Wan and his intended warlord, General Mendé.

"Our democratic institutions, which have been undermined and in extreme cases have been taken over by global corporations who infiltrated while the media and corporate party were controlled by international money and propaganda lies. Such democratic institutions can be revitalized and restored simply by a new democratic, progressive, social vote at the ballot box. Do not follow the traditional path by which greedy and ruthless families send your children into horrible and worthless wars, while their own children avoid service and taxes, and become the privileged princes of a new global aristocracy. Do not let them profit from chaos and war. Make peace, not war.

"I call on the progressive leaders of labor, business, and even religious orders of all persuasions to demand fresh elections around the world. We are not against corporations or investment. We simply call for a balance of interests in which everyone gets their fair share in liberty, equality, and unity for all.

"We do not call for a new world order, but for a restoration of the old democratic principles that guided our forefathers. Thank you, and may god bless you and the world."

With that, Mélu's voice fell silent. For a moment, her haggard, unadorned features looked at the world with luminous, beseeching eyes and a passionate expression made all the more eloquent by its silence. Then the screen went blank.

The hall in the chateau erupted in waves of clapping that rose in power until even the most hardened corporate chiefs were whistling, applauding, and stomping their feet.

The lady beside Hannah said gently, "We have at least three dozen young victims like yourself, including a few young men, who were trafficked by Wan and his fellow oligarchs. Will you make a statement and go on record about the mistake you made signing that contract, and the savagery with which they trafficked you?"

Hannah nodded. She was all cried out. "I will do it for my mother. I sold myself, thinking it was to save her, but they raped me and left her to die. I will do it for all the people in my country who are left to die by the corporations who steal a trillion dollars a year from us for a worthless joke called health insurance."

The lady patted Hannah's shoulder gently. "You have many supporters and admirers."

"That's funny," Hannah said dreamily. "I felt a deep sense of shame, but now I'm not even angry anymore. We have won, and we're going to take the world back. I have something very special."

The lady looked puzzled. "You do?"

Hannah nodded. "It's called love. I have a man who wants me, no matter what I've done or what was done to me. He loves me, and I have faith again."

Just then her phone rang. She took it from her pocket. "Yes?"

"Honey, it's Rick. I'm coming to pick you up. We are going home, baby, and I will get on my knees and beg you to marry me."

"Oh, yes," she said dreamily. "I will be waiting here at the chateau. I have some new friends, and I'll be doing some good things. You can help me."

"I love you forever, and I'll help you whatever you decide to do."

"I'll also make sure you take your medicine."

"I may not need much of that anymore. I think once I get back to the Pacific coast, and do a lot of surfing and running, without all the yelling and shooting and sheer terror every minute, I'll be just fine."

"Come home to me, baby."

"Oh god I love you so much. I'm on the way."

With that, Rick rang off and Hannah followed her new friend to a room in which dozens of women and girls gathered to kiss Wan's new world order goodbye.

Sanders Elected CEOC President

ANN (Europe)—Our correspondents in Luxembourg, Brussels, Paris, Berlin, and Rome report that Professor Sander has been elected president of a new and moderate CEOC organization by a large majority of the world's corporate leaders, who say they are happy to be free from the coercion of a greedy and violent minority of ruthless executives.

Professor Sander, the new president of CEOC, will be inaugurated at a gala event in New York City two weeks from now, and the Empire State is readying red carpets, fireworks, and the biggest, happiest rock and roll concert the impoverished nation has seen in many years since the most recent corporate great depression has shattered its power, sovereignty, and economic muscle.

As quoted by New York City's current mayor: "In the words of the great U.S. President Abraham Lincoln at his second inaugural in 1865—only a few weeks before he was murdered by corporate extremists fanatically supporting the slave owner oligarchy—the incoming democratic leadership of CEOC promises to level the playing field in fairness and truthfulness *...with charity for all, and malice toward none...*"

CEOC Chief Sander pledges to meet with world leaders to make common cause for a new program of revitalization that will benefit workers and business leaders alike. He asks that the leaders look to the German model of cooperation between unions and management going back generations. It is a model in which management and labor manage their separate interests but realize that we are all in the game together—if the company benefits, so do the workers if they are not merely serfs or temporary employees.

Germany was also the world's first nation to institute universal health care—in 1884, under Chancellor Otto von Bismarck and Kaiser Wilhelm I. It is a system of health care run not by government, though refereed by government on behalf of all citizens—and not a robber baron, murderous mafia run by predatory insurance companies—but a universal human right, administered by nonprofit corporations. The German model is economical, affordable, highly effective, and leaves nobody a victim of health care denial, nor has anyone ever lost their entire life's work due to illness.

"We have a lot of work to do," Sander declared before a crowd of cheering supporters after his acceptance and victory speech at Chateau Ansembourg in Luxembourg.

58.   ANN News 2

General Mendé Deceased

ANN (Europe)—Word has reached ANN's Copenhagen bureau that the body of General Mendé, the former associate and security chief of industrialist Wan, has been found at his beach villa on the Baltic Sea. It appears the General Mendé shot himself in the head with his service revolver when he realized that his dreams and ambitions of being the next Attila the Hun or Napoleon Bonaparte were not going to happen.

Wan Pledges Future Re-Try

ANN (China)—This morning, an eager press corps awaited the arrival of the losing CEOC candidate, Mr. Wan. The zillionaire industrialist retains control over roughly five per cent of the world's steel, fossil fuels, and electronic industries. At latest update, he has emerged waving and smiling in the fuselage door of his private jet liner, atop a flight of mobile debarkation stairs, to put the best face on his loss in the CEOC election.

He has pledged to return for another try at the CEOC presidency next year when the organization meets in its plenary session in Singapore.

However, analysts tell us his goal is all but impossible. They say the impetus and momentum of Professor Sander' movement is global and so powerful it will guide democratic labor and popular voter movements for generations to come.

Sanders To British Union: Progress

ANN (Europe)—Professor Sander, looking forward to his inauguration in New York City, has attended a luncheon hosted by the seven British Economic Union leaders at the National Independence Hall in Cardiff, Wales—this year's rotating presidency among independent Union members, including the Neutral Territory of Ulster and several historically important islands. Professor Sander remarked that he finds it ironic that now the world does have a responsible, coherent corporate leadership—minus the medieval tyranny of bloody war lords in the mold of the Borgias and the Macbeths of Shakespearean drama, and the corporate war lords who turned the Industrial Revolution into seas of human blood during new forms of Industrial Warfare. Doctor Sander has pledged to teach the world that it is possible to have good, constructive leadership—as long as time-honored principles of democracy and segmented government powers are maintained.

New U.S. Administration Progressive

ANN (USA)—In Washington, D.C., a newly elected U.S. government pledges to roll back the corporate globalist legislation and Supreme Court decisions that weakened the U.S. in recent generations as jobs and industries were sold off by corporate Republican operatives to the highest bidders around the world. Incoming House and Senate leaders—both being women, one of color—declare new initiatives toward universal tolerance and integration. They pledge to work with the new female president and her cabinet to insure universal health care as a human right, not to be denied any citizen. "We can afford it, and everyone will have it," the incoming U.S. president declared at a breakfast meeting with the nation's new nonprofit healthcare corporations. "We have been lied to and victimized for too many generations." She was roundly applauded by the nearly one hundred executives attending, including many real health care providers—doctors and nurses, rather than insurance salesmen and CEOs—representing hospitals and medical workers' unions in all the states and territories.

59.   ANN News 3

New Luxembourg Memorial

ANN (Luxembourg)—The Grand Duchy has officially announced plans to rename a public square in the city as Place Pierre Sander, in honor of CEOC President Dr. Hilaire Sander' murdered son. The late Dr. Pierre Sander will also be honored with a martyr's statue in the square, to be dedicated in a ceremony including Professor Sander and His Royal Highness, the Grand Duke, along with top members of the national government, and representatives from at least thirty nations or confederations, including China, India, the E.U. including its newest member Russia, and the United States.

Pierre Sander Memorial

ANN (Luxembourg)—This network will broadcast live the ceremonies at the new Place Pierre Sander, along with special honors at the Grand Ducal palace, in which HRH the Grand Duke will confer national honors upon Professor Sander, recognizing the contribution of Pierre and Hilaire Sander. Hundreds of millions of workers around the globe will benefit from new guarantees of participation in pensions, health care, and work place safety regulations.

Professor Sander has recommended that particular lessons may be learned from post-World War Two social innovations in modern Germany, including strong management-labor union relations across most industries, and a corporate, nonprofit health care system that eliminates what Dr. Sander has long called "the dead hand of thieving and murderous health denial mafias, laughingly called health insurance companies, who provide absolutely nothing, but kill over 45,000 U.S. citizens a year through denial, and bankrupt hundreds of thousands of families through unreasonable and unjustifiable extortion during health care crises."

Dr. Sander points out that, ironically, it was imperial Germany's Chancellor Otto von Bismarck, under Kaiser Wilhelm I in the 1880s, who innovatively created a series of programs that may be considered the world's first universal health insurance programs.

New: Collective NATO Neutrality

ANN (Brussels)—A news bulletin from Brussels affirms that the new IFS technology, named the Pierre Sander Initiative in honor of Professor Sanders' murdered son, will be officially turned over to the collective military leadership of NATO. That alliance today networks with peaceful defensive unions around the world including East Asia, Southern Asia, and the former Middle East or West Asia, as well as Africa, the Pacific Cooperation Zone, and the Americas. The commanding general of NATO has pledged that IFS will be shared across global militaries, thus assuring its neutrality. I will be used exclusively for peaceful purposes.

60.   California Dreaming

Hannah and Rick walked hand in hand on a beach in San Diego after making long, passionate, and glorious love in their new condo in a high rise building on Pacific Coast Highway. They'd been husband and wife now for several months. It was all the medicine he needed, and he'd left his pills aside. Hannah would keep a close eye on him, and they would take good care of each other forever.

The Pacific Ocean curled in sweeping, lazy waves along Torrey Pines State Park. The sky glowed in flawless shades of blue. There were just a few hints of white, moist clouds on the horizon. Tall Mexican fan palms swayed from side to side and their fanned crowns rustled like a gentle song. The delicate mist of an early marine layer was just starting to make the city skyline to the south look hazy and majestic.

Gulls wheeled and cawed nearby over the thundering surf.

In Europe, Kendra Walsh had gone to work as an international human rights lawyer, reporting to a nonprofit sponsored by Professor Sander's progressive CEOC confederacy.

In a small town in Kansas, in a grassy little park near the Baptist Church, stood a windblown little stone monument commemorating the heroism and sacrifice of a local son and church deacon—Colonel Whitcomb, U.S. Army, fallen in the line of duty. His ashes rested at Arlington National Cemetery with those of other veterans. Gentle winds, and prevailing silence, were more eloquent than words in educating future generations filled with verification, trust, hope—and charity, rather than malice, for all.

Rick and Hannah wore bathing suits as they sauntered along that peaceful, secure sand warmed by sunlight. Her bikini, showing off a lithe, tanned figure with small but growing breasts and a pert behind on long, thin legs, was a cute little happy citron combo with fine red and green quadrille hatchings. As Rick told her while nuzzling her ear with his nose, "You look good enough to eat."

"You can have my ice cream; both scoops."

He swung his hand and hers between them. "I want you to play my trombone in our band. You have such good slide technique as you march along with that cute little butt."

"You can bang my cymbals until we shout for joy together," she said.

He pointed to the sea. "More importantly at the moment, we could go for a swim." It was a question.

"Why not?" she said brightly as she pulled him to the water—down the beach, past sun bathers on towels looking like perched sea birds. "I had an EGS from Mélu," she told her husband, referring to the latest chatterbox fad as old as it was new, the Emergency Gossip Shout. "She says that Romain is now fully back to health. He's had surgery and looks like new, and he says hello as he runs ten miles a day."

"In the Haute Ville?" Rick wondered out loud. He remembered the cobblestone squares, the narrow alleys, the flower and vegetable markets. Standing at attention before the monument to a past Grand Duke on his horse, a military band banged out a snappy tattoo (*Den Hemmelsmarsch*, or The Lambs' March). All the while, the cathedral's carillon tinkled in a silvery hymn of good will to all.

The world was at peace. How long it would last depended on how well coming generations remembered history and relived the best, while avoiding the inevitable worst every generation must work against.

Eternal vigilance is the price of liberty.

Hannah's face lit up with a glow of memory. "Oh Rick, just remember Belair, the Petrusse, the Boulevard Royal. I remember it as so beautiful, when I just blank out all the stress and struggle at the time."

Rick said, "We have all our lives ahead of us. We can do it all, without the running and shouting and shooting and constant sheer terror. It will be refreshing."

She rubbed her growing belly. "There'll be three when we fly to visit Mélu and Romain next year."

Rick added: "We'll visit Paris again also, if we just avoid night clubs in Bagnolet."

She gave his hand a tug. "Silly. You never know what kind of nice person you might meet in a place like that."

Fin

Appendix: Thrillerology
(Continued from Opening Pages)

1. Welcome to a Luxembourg Thriller

Welcome to my novel, which is not only a Luxembourg Thriller, but also the world's first Progressive Thriller. It is a love story (of course: all literature is the love story). And it is written as a fast-paced suspense novel that covers much mileage really fast, both on the ground (danger) and in the head (ideas).

WARNING: Plot Spoilers occur in this *Thrillerology*, so don't let your suspense be spoiled. You may want to read *Valley of Seven Castles* first, and then come back to the Thrillerology.

In this Thrillerology, I have a lot to tell: the background of this novel, not only as a novel of ideas and as a first-class romp across Europe amid danger and romance—but structurally and technically, a carefully built engine of storytelling that draws upon some amazing secret sauce I uncovered while tracking down the secrets of some top thrillers of the past century. The really amazing thing is that I found what I call The Final Secret of Alfred Hitchcock (more on that shortly, but lesser things first).

For the North American or other foreign reader, this novel should be a sort of fast-paced, colorful, sometimes gritty tour of one of the world's smallest nations (Luxembourg, 999 square miles of sovereign nation, with the same seating in the United Nations as the United States and other world powers.

Like the 2002 suspense thriller film *The Bourne Identity*, starring Matt Damon and Franka Potente, this novel takes my two heroes (Rick Buchan and Hannah Smith) on a desperate and dangerous ramble through the heart of Europe. The core of my novel starts in Paris and ends in Luxembourg City. They're running from ruthless and deadly enemies, but they're also running toward a Luxembourg solution to the world's problems, in the form of Professor Hilaire Sander. Sander's son invented a key military technology (the Intelligent Fuselage Skin for aircraft, or IFS), but Pierre Sander was murdered in London by the Chinese zillionaire (Wan) of Shanghai who happens to also be Hannah's boss, or owner, in a terrifying new world of the near future.

For Luxemburgers, and their neighbors, I hope this will be an entertaining 'make you proud' tour of their scenic and fascinating region. If you love a rousing adventure, a passionate love story, and a novel of ideas, I have a *Sachertorte* of books for you. Of course, I am the chef, so I would think so.

In this Thrillerology, I am going to touch upon a number of important themes. You may ask: What is a Thrillerology, and why write one? The answer is: initially, I had no idea about writing such a thing. I was simply intoxicated and infatuated with my young characters, with the wonderful landscapes of Europe and specifically Luxembourg (where I lived as a child, still speak the language, and have cousins living there today).

Driven by my study of history, as well as my concern with U.S. politics, I was impassioned to write a progressive thriller. The thriller is a favorite form of mine. I felt that the time is overdue to lay aside all the stale material from the last century, and instead present timely, relevant new food for current thought. Writing this novel was a love affair on several levels, and I plan to write more of these Progressive Thrillers, many of them anchored in Luxembourg and greater Europe. I've written other novels, including a few thrillers, and I never felt moved to write an '-ology' (from Hellenic logos, meaning word, speaking about, knowledge, etc.). There is a first time for everything.

2. World's First Progressive Thriller

This novel is, as far as I know, the world's first Progressive Thriller, at least specifically so named. Readers should know that the novel is set slightly in the future, in case they feel puzzled while moving through its darker passages. The setting of my novel is a Europe of tomorrow, where global corporations and zillionaires are making national governments obsolete. Whatever progress the West (outside the U.S. corporate feudalism) has achieved is in danger as the oligarchs begin to take over, as they are doing in this novel.

This novel is, at heart, a romp across Europe (in suspenseful thriller mode) but it's as much a U.S. as a European story. It's a story for the world. And of course it celebrates the beautiful history, culture, and landscape of my other country, Luxembourg. As I move through this Thrillerology, explaining the literary and technical background of the story (plot structure, antecedents, etc.), it is important to begin by identifying the progressive urgency underlying the fast pacing and romantic struggle of Rick and Hannah.

The two young heroes, on the run for their lives and on a mission of great importance, are a U.S. pair from California. They are Hannah Smith and Rick Buchan, both 25. Each is separately trapped by dark circumstances in Europe and, as in any good love story, they join forces to bring the McGuffin (Alfred Hitchcock's pet name for "what is the story about?") to Luxemburgish Professor Hilaire Sander in a small Luxemburgish town near Echternach. So the characters are both European and U.S., united in a common struggle.

I wrote this novel primarily with the entertaining story in mind. This is a European story, a universal story, but also a U.S. story. I try to avoid specifics, to not get mired in exposition and lectures, except for the obvious exposure of corporate health care denial in the U.S. (laughingly called 'health insurance') in a nation where over 45,000 citizens are murdered every year because of health care denial, documented in a landmark 2009 Harvard Medical School, Harvard University, and Cambridge MA Health Services study). Also, millions of families have been bankrupted over many years, because the corporations steal over $1,000,000,000,000 (that's *trillion*) every year from our economy while robbing and killing vast numbers of citizens, who usually don't know that their dark fate in life doesn't have to be this way, as proven in every other industrialized, modern nation around the world where they all have universal health care.

Since I wrote the novel, the United States has gone into a life and death struggle (orange mullet, etc.) that seems baffling to many, but not at all to me. Rather than spend this Thrillerology time going into that tragic saga, I'll discuss it in a separate venue (book series and website) titled *Explanation*

Nation, or *EX-NAX* for short. The first EX-NAX book is already published, with more to follow. See print link at left, e-book link at right. That is all I want to say about political and economic progressivism in this Thrillerology. A new, dedicated website (*Explanation Nation*) will launch soon, so stay tuned if you are interested. In the meantime, let's get back to having fun with our Thrillerology.

My core position is for moderation, cooperation, tolerance—and a revolution at the ballot box in keeping with the U.S. Constitution. It's time to take our world back from the sixty-three billionaires who own more than half of the world's wealth. Already, much of the U.S. has been outsourced with the help of corporate-republican political actors in all three branches of U.S. government—executive, legislative, and judicial. Similar stealthy destruction has been wreaked across other Western nations in a world increasingly run by political tyrants working hand in hand with demagogues and those religio-corporate tyrants who use simple people's faith to deliver those devastating, suicidal votes for their worst enemies (e.g., Trump, Putin, Assad, Milosevic).

My premise in developing *Valley of Seven Castles* has been that the action themes of previous thriller generations served well to entertain readers in the previous century. The Cold War is over, World War II is ancient history, and the evil government is a canard of the corporate-owned press to support crimes like preventing U.S. citizens from having universal health care while stealing up to a trillion dollars a year from the U.S. GDP; trashing the union movement through false propaganda; and denying climate change while the earth and its creatures undergo a manmade extinction.

3. Thrillerology Historical Sketch (to 1900)

Some Long Ago Masters. If we search for a starting point of the thriller, we won't find one. We can go back as far as we wish, for example as Gilgamesh and Enkidu journey into the great howling forest of darkness in search of the giant monster Huwawa; I still get chills just thinking about it. That's no different from early Roman writers describing the perceived horrors of their own dark forest (*Silva Cimina*) to the north, or impenetrable Pomptine Marshes (*Pomptinae Paludes*) to their south. To me, the horrors of these Roman nightmares seem congruent with those of the great forest of Huwawa thousands of years earlier, or thousands of years later, the terrifying island on which Robinson Crusoe finds himself in Daniel Defoe's 1719 thriller (not a Walt Disney fuzzy-bunnies cartoon for children, as too many people think, who have not read the real novel, which interestingly is a sectarian, gloomy religious rant, so talk about purposed thrillers!). In a word, thrillers are timeless.

More Recent Masters. Our journey in search of thrillerology brings us into the 19th Century (1800s), and into the dark spaces of Edgar Allan Poe, Arthur Conan Doyle, H. G. Wells, and many a Penny Dreadful. Why is the 19th Century particularly significant? Because it marks the rise of urbanization, greater literacy, and many other factors concomitant with the Industrial Revolution—above all, a population explosion signaling recovery from the devastating plagues and pandemics of earlier centuries. Cholera in the urban setting of London is eradicated by identifying the mixed curse of public water pumps and poor sanitation, and creating a new sewer system (inhabited, to be sure, by new monsters and phantoms to ruffle our thriller hackles). Suffice it to say that these three masters are but a few of the thriller-spillers of their time. Think of Mary Shelley (*Frankenstein*) and Dr. John Polidori (*The Vampyre*) meeting with Lord Byron at his Villa Diodati on the shore of Lake Geneva in Switzerland—that was in 1816, a 'year with no summer' around the world owing to a volcanic winter spewed up by the massive, Plinian explosion of Mt. Tambora on the other side of the globe in 1815. Tambora is a stratovolcano in Indonesia; its explosion, the largest in nearly 2,000 years, made church bells in London ring at an odd hour that nobody for a long time could explain. In that darkness, that chill and drizzle, the English group gathered for a night's thrilling story-telling frightened themselves out of their wits and ran out of the house together, to clutch each other in panic on the lawn until their hearts resumed normal tempos. There is much more to tell about that incident alone, but that story must keep for another day and time. I promise to tell it, and you will again be amazed; but I digress...

Charles Dickens created human monsters in his poverty-wracked new industrial mega-city of London—where 'rookeries' prefigured modern ghettos, and phantoms from Springheeled Jack to Jack the Ripper (1888) plied their bloody trade by lamplight. The first gas lamp in London is credited to about 1816 (coincidentally, during that ominous year without a summer). From Polidori's 1816 Vampyre to Bram Stoker's 1897 Dracula was but a dream and a scream away. Ultimately, the 19th Century is so laden with suspense and thriller fare that a list becomes unwieldy. We leave the century of Willkie Collins' 1860 *The Woman in White* and Victor Hugo's *The Hunchback of Notre Dame* and Edgar Allan Poe's 1838 *Ligeia* (to pick but a few out of thousands), as we migrate into the more recent century.

Suspense and the faster-paced thrillers have been with us since time immemorial, when Paleolithic hunters came home with lunch, and entertained their spell-bound clan members with tales of (well, the fish was actually *thiiiiiis* big, farther than I can spread my arms) and we can imagine the listeners' mouths hanging open, and firelight dancing in their wide eyes. Certain types of stories (archetypes) go back eons, and beg to be retold. The background of *Valley of Seven Castles, a Luxembourg Thriller* lies with an early 20th Century thriller, an archetype, published in 1915 by British writer John Buchan. Let's get into the 20th Century next.

4. Thrillerology Historical Sketch (since 1900)

Twentieth Century. The world had never before contained more human beings than by 1900, and never saw more of them pointlessly killed in the ensuing world wars, human-caused famines, concentration camps, and other disasters. To give nature her due, the Great Influenza pandemic of 1918 brought World War I to a swifter end. In less than three years (1918-1920), this influenza plague killed an estimated hundred million souls, or one in twenty of all humans alive on earth. In a bizarre twist, it did not kill the weak (very young and very old) but targeted men and women (often parents) in their most vigorous years from the late teens through middle age.

Humans gave nature a run for her money. A safe bet is that, during the Twentieth Century, half a billion souls perished in such nightmares (to name just a few) as two industrial-scale world wars, plus Lenin's mass-murder agricultural purges, and the German efforts at world conquest that cost tens of millions of lives, and worst of all, Mao's great leap back into the Stone Ages that may have cost as many as a quarter billion lives—making Mao history's worst mass murderer, followed by Stalin at about 150 million, and Hitler at somewhere near 100 million (such numbers can only be approximated).

At the start of that apocalyptic century of horror—whose inhumanity and bloodshed (usually with stirring music, fluttering penants, and fancy uniforms) beggar the darkest imagination—we may pick the point where Erskine Childers published his 1903 *The Riddle of the Sands: A Record of Secret Service*. It's not the first or the last thriller, but it is as good a starting point as any for the 20th Century. Oh yes, and barely twenty years later, Childers was executed by firing squad in Dublin as an Irish nationalist.

Stepping forward from the enormous list of 19th Century suspense and thriller fiction (including vampires, phantoms, and other monsters both human and not quite human), let's begin in the early Twentieth Century with a handful of reasonably modern exemplars. These predate World War I and include Erskine Childers' *The Riddle of the Sands* (1903), Joseph Conrad's *The Heart of Darkness* (1903), and John Buchan's *The Thirty-Nine Steps* (1915).

The range of imaginative fiction is vast; our purpose here is to pick a narrow path winding among literary giants, to reach our destination in the 21st Century (*Valley of Seven Castles, a Luxembourg Thriller*).

We'll sidestep a considerable number of masterworks, including for example Joseph Conrad's 1904 *Nostromo* and more. In particular, I reluctantly avoid discussing Leslie Charteris, creator of The Saint, and Ian Fleming, creator of James Bond (this is a Ciceronian trick of oratory; "I will not begin to tell you of Catiline's evil thoughts and deeds…" and then the great orator and contemporary of Julius Caesar goes on at length to detail them). In terms of atmospherics and suspense, Charteris and Fleming were prime movers in setting the pace for suspense thrillers like the 21st Century's (2002) film *The Bourne Identity*.

* * * *

My Thrillerology, as a personal story, starts tracking with John Buchan's 1915 novel *The Thirty-Nine Steps*. It is not just a classic, but an archetype—a story instantly so mythological that it begs to be retold at least once in each generation. For the most part, the remakes of Buchan's novel in the 20th and 21st Centuries have been films. I purposely used Buchan's plot line to craft *Valley of Seven Castles, a Luxembourg Thriller*.

As already mentioned, I drew inspiration for my pacing from the 2002 film *The Bourne Identity* (based on Robert Ludlum's 1980 eponymous novel). In the 2002 film, the characters played by Franka Potente and Matt Damon go on a frantic run from the Mediterranean to Paris at top thriller speed. In my novel, the heroes race from Paris to Luxembourg, carrying a Hitchcockesque

McGuffin (the IFS or Intelligent Fuselage Skin technology). Hannah's Chinese zillionaire owner, Wan, acquired it by having Professor Hilaire Sander's son murdered in London. *Owner?* Hannah is a BAN (Butlers And Nannies) a near-future fad, whereby you sell yourself into something between indentured servitude and slavery for five years, hoping for a nice fat, early retirement pension. As with most fads, reality turns out to be a horrific opposite of what was promised.

Hannah sold herself to pay for her mother's murderous hospital bills in the U.S. corporate health denial industry, which let the mother die anyway when her money ran out, including Hannah's desperate payments. I discuss those sorts of real-life U.S. nightmares in my series *Explanation Nation* (website and nonfiction book series).

Early on, Hannah takes charge of her life, steals the IFS from Wan in Paris, and goes on a deadly run toward Luxembourg to meet up with the young technical writer Mèlu and her husband Romain (secretly part of a social-progressive spy network called PAX, with Prof. Sander of Echternach as a leader). Along the way, she picks up a U.S. Army deserter (Rick Buchan, falsely accused of a war crime, while suffering from severe PTSD as well). Pursued by Wan'ss powerful and deadly assassins, the two make their way from Paris to Luxembourg, first the capital of Luxembourg City and later the Valley of Seven Castles. That's just a quick plot rundown.

I derived my ten-part plot structure from John Buchan's 1915 novel. From there, the history tracks with interesting consequences until we arrive at a true story involving Alfred Hitchcock, who had similar ideas—and created one of history's most iconic movies. I'm calling that bombshell Alfred Hitchcock's Final Secret.

You may notice in *Valley of Seven Castles* that my hero is Richard Buchan (strong male lead) and his love interest (strong female lead) is Hannah Smith. Yes, I took the hero of John Buchan's first novel (Richard Hannay) and created from his name the male and female leads. The two meet at the scene of a brutal murder outside a Paris bar in Bagnolet called The 39th Step. That's about as blatant as hints can be, but the real shocker (as I see it) lies in the string of thrillers built from John Buchan's novel.

5. Bombshell Revelation for Thriller Lovers

My path to *Valley of Seven Castles, a Luxembourg Thriller* was in some ways accidental. I am referring primarily to the technical, structural, plotting aspects and therefore the models and antecedents on which this structure is built.

I have already mentioned my debt (primarily on atmospherics and pacing) to Robert Ludlum and the film makers of *The Bourne Identity*. The tense and dangerous run of Hannah Smith and Rick Buchan from Paris, across France, and into Luxembourg will remind readers of the cross-European odyssey in that 2002 film, one of my favorites. As my Thrilleroloy progresses, I will mention other favorites in the thriller genre—none more so than Alfred Hitchcock's 1959 classic *North By Northwest*.

I have been writing novels for half a century (over forty books to date) and have long been an avid student of plotting and structure, out of necessity in striving to deliver the best story possible. In the technical substructure of story telling (fiction, plays, and film), we endlessly dissect and analyze such issues as the three-act, four-act, or five-act structure.

I have made a particular point of studying the theories of the romance category, as expounded by Romance Writers of America and many writers in that field. I even wrote an RWA-sty le romance novel of the so-called 'clean' subcategory, titled *Nice Cry* that has been well received. In my youth, while stationed with the U.S. Army in West Germany, I wrote a novel of a romantic affair set in a New England college town, titled *On Saint Ronan Street*.

As you'll see in my dissection of John Buchan's archetypal 1915 classic (*The Thirty-Nine Steps*), I found a ready builder's model for *Valley of Seven Castles*—and a deep secret about Alfred Hitchcock's *oeuvre*.

* * * *

A number of pieces floated together to shape January 2016's *Valley of Seven Castles*. The following pieces are not necessarily in chronological order.

Piece #1: Years ago, my wife and I enjoyed watching a very nice film, a remake of John Buchan's 1915 thriller novel *The Thirty-Nine Steps*. This story has been remade so many times, and I felt such an immediate strong affinity for it, that I realized it must be an archetype. It stayed in my memory for years until I finally found my own vehicle (*Valley of Seven Castles*) to express the same basic plot idea. In other words: while I was studying all sorts of plot structures (three, four, five acts, etc.) it never really occurred to me to delve into what made Buchan's novel such a magnet—it is still getting film remakes into the 21st Century (some better than others, but it's an archetype of plot structure for sure).

Piece #2: Somewhere along the line over the years, I enjoyed watching a rather ancient black and white movie made in 1935 by Alfred Hitchcock, titled *The 39 Steps*. Yes, it was based on the 1915 John Buchan thriller. Note the slight difference in spelling the title. I figured that, if Hitch thought it was a great story, it really must be a great story. So far, so good.

Piece #3: Somewhere along the line, after 2000, I came across a cheap, plain Dover Edition of John Buchan's 1915 novel *The Thirty-Nine Steps*. I bought it and stashed it among my stacks and piles of books at home. I think I read it at some point, but retained only a general impression. All along, something nagged at me: what made this story so enduring?

Pieces #4: Over the years, I not only read thrillers, but wrote my first real thriller (*CON2: The Generals of October*) around 1992. As already mentioned, I wrote the first draft in three weeks, but spent a decade rewriting. It was my first really long, mainstream novel.

Pieces #5+... I had long studied the evolution of thrillers (as described in the previous section called *Thrillerology*). I have been passionate about political and social causes for many years, and my dissatisfaction with the corporate-republican rise from 1980 forward finally pushed me to the point where I wanted to capture my thoughts and feelings in a big novel that would serve as something of a parable. I was ready to write *Valley of Seven Castles*.

To understand where I am driving, we need to take my key influences one by one, starting with John Buchan's 1915 novel, and then Alfred Hitchcock's 1935 film based on Buchan's novel. The real surprise in all this is what comes next. Hint: it's another Alfred Hitchcock film.

* * * *

The 1915 story is a classic novel in ten relatively simply chapters or parts. I will indicate them in lower case for a reason. The story begins with a murder in the first chapter. The hero is framed for this crime, which he did not commit.

The hero goes on the run across the very green and scenic English countryside. He runs from both the bad guys and the authorities separately, hoping to discover the solution to the mystery (what Hitchcock typically termed "the McGuffin"—what are they after? What is the movie about?). He needs to all at once solve the mystery, save the nation, and clear his name.

In chapter six, the hero (Richard Hannay) is buzzed by a low-flying 'aeroplane,' a canvas-and-wood job from the early days of aviation, before World War I.

In chapter seven, the hero stumbles by chance upon a professor in an isolated cabin, who reveals much knowledge to him (the Wise Elder, I think Joseph Campbell called this persona).

Starting in chapter six, Hannay flips from being an outsider to becoming an insider. He is now privy to the central plot, and becomes a pivotal figure in solving it. He stops being on the run from authorities in chapter six, but is still on the outs with the bad guys right until the bitter end in chapter ten. The eponymous thirty-nine steps turn out to be exactly that many steps at a seaside villa, where the Kaiser's spies land on English soil.

One more note: the 1915 novel was an Edwardian fiction, written by a man of Victorian origins, and women did not figure in such fiction. We might point out exceptions like Wilkie Collins' *The Lady in White*, but generally women were hardly seen and not at all heard—even when you consider A. Conan Doyle's *A Scandal in Bohemia* (1891), in which the fictional actress Irene Adler has a prominent if shadowy role ("To Sherlock Holmes she is always *the* woman…").

* * * *

Go forward twenty years, past the Great War. In 1935, Alfred Hitchcock recognized the powerful nature of Buchan's story, and made a movie of it. Hitchcock made the McGuffin something other than a seaside mansion of thirty-nine steps. The title in 1935 refers ambivalently to the name of a 1914ish German spy organization in England, and to the steps leading up to the Big Ben bell inside London's Westminster Tower.

Hitchcock does place two women in the film, one of whom he kills off early, and the other who becomes sort of a ditzy, attractive prop (Madelaine Carroll) for hero Richard Hannay (Robert Donat).

By the way, Hitchcock had a fascination with clocktowers. Besides Westminster in *The 39 Steps*, there is one in his 1934 *The Man Who Knew Too*

Much, and another (Mission San Juan Bautista near San Francisco) in 1958's *Vertigo*.

Like the novel, the film is about a man framed for a crime he didn't commit. Now look for the same generic chapter/section structure here as in Buchan's novel. You could call it episodic (lurching from one action scene to the next).

Richard Hannay runs from the good guys and the bad guys, with a nuisance or complication being the reluctant inclusion of a female interest who is not developed very deeply.

In the sixth part (get the picture?) Hannay is buzzed by a plane. Hitchcock is said to have borrowed the first helicopter—a gyroplane or autogyro—for that scene.

In the seventh part, the hero stumbles on the professor in the cabin, and so forth to the ending.

You'd think that the Buchan plot structure faded away in 1935. But lo and behold, what did I discover?

6. The Final Secret of Alfred Hitchcock

Here at last is the big reveal:

It happens that my all-time favorite suspense film is Alfred Hitchcock's 1959 *North By Northwest*. Guess what? Around 1959, Hitch was turning sixty years old and having a midlife crisis. So he turns to a leading Hollywood screenwriter named Ernest Lehman, and says (we can surmise from the known facts) "Hey, Ernie—I want to be young again and make a thriller like I used to make as a struggling youth. Can you help me out?"

"Sure," Ernie says, "glad to oblige. Any ideas?"

"Oh, I dunno," says Hitch, "why don't you begin by sifting through my old screenplays and see what you can find?"

So Ernest Lehman goes off and does just that. The resulting screenplay and world-class thriller movie in 1959 was *North By Northwest*.

Ta-dahhh!

But wait, I'll prove it. Look at the ten-part structure.

As the movie opens, Roger Thornhill (Cary Grant) is framed for a crime he didn't commit, and goes on the run for his life from both the authorities and the criminals. That's exactly how Richard Hannay's story unfolds in John Buchan's 1915 *The Thirty-Nine Steps*.

The McGuffin in Hitch's movie is a stolen microfilm containing U.S. government secrets, which the Soviet agents want to smuggle out of the country. In Buchan's story, it's a mystery about someone, something, or somewhere involving thirty-nine steps; and of course a Berlin plot to undermine London's empire on home turf.

Thornhill takes a train, on which is his love interest Eve Kendall (Eva Marie Saint) who also happens to be a spy. Or is she? Actually, she is a double agent working for the good guys.

After several chapters or parts in *North by Northwest* (think chapters two through five in Buchan's novel), the sixth segment or chapter is one of the most famous scenes in movie history. This is the aeroplane (1915) and the gyrocopter (1915) equivalent. In the 1959 scene, Thornhill is chased through a Kansas cornfield by a crop duster airplane. The airplane (i.e., aeroplane; gyroplane) trope, and the frame-up in the first part, are two dead giveaways that Lehman borrowed the structure from the 1935 screenplay (based on the 1915 novel) to write a new plot for the 1959 film. The parallels continue.

Still on the run, Thornhill is so desperate that he tries to get himself arrested by acting goofy at an art auction attended by the bad guys. When he is arrested, the next incident is a reprise of the mysterious professor in the cabin (Buchan's chapter seven). In section seven, there is once again a total turn-around or flip. I nicknamed it my Cosmo Topper Reveal while I was developing *Valley of Seven Castles*, because in the 1959 film, the professor turns out to be Professor (Unnamed, literally), an FBI or CIA chief. Leo G. Carroll, who played the Professor in *North By Northwest*, later played Cosmo Topper in a famous TV comedy series called *Topper*, involving two ghosts (George and Marian).

So—in this Cosmo Topper segment in *North By Northwest*, Thornhill like Hannay flips from outsider to insider. Once again, we have a clear congruency with Buchan's 1915 novel and Hitchcock's 1935 film.

By 1959, however, the lead character has a real love interest. Cary Grant plays the lover in his inimitable style that is at once endearing, goofy, engaging, and smart. The penultimate scene on Mount Rushmore is another of film history's most dramatic and famous. The ultimate scene, in which the train rushes into a tunnel, is the kind of erotic innuendo inserted during an age of extreme censorship, signifying that Thornhill and Kendall chugged their way to HEA-ven with whistles screeching and steam flying by. Train inserted into the tunnel... phallic... into...? We get it.

So there you have it. I don't know that anyone has ever really picked these three works apart and seen their congruencies. I based the structure of *Valley of Seven Castles* closely and deliberately on this episodic structure, but with a strong love story between equally strong male and female leads (Richard Buchan and Hannah Smith).

* * * *

As in the 2002 movie *The Bourne Identity,* where Matt Damon's and Franka Potente's characters work together, so also in *Valley of Seven Castles*, I have two leads operating separately at first, who come together in the second chapter. WARNING: Spoilers.

Remember that my novel is set in a frightening near future. Female hero Hannah is a BAN, a contractual slave owned by a Chinese billionaire. She has been raped and abused, and ultimately betrayed. She signed up as a BAN (Butlers And Nannies, a marketing term for what amounts to sexual and inhumane battery in the horrible new corporate medieval world of our global near future)...

...In Shanghai, Hannah meets Mélusine (Mélu) Poncelet, who rescues her from some gang members. Mélu tells her about a secret technology (IFS) that Wan has stolen while murdering Pierre Sander in London. Not long after, in Paris, Hannah sees the opportunity to escape from Wan—and takes the IFS (McGuffin) with her. Now she is on the run, wanted by Wan's gangsters, and by the authorities on trumped up charges. I had no intention of making the Chinese into tomorrow's bad guys; far from it; so I inserted a good-guy

Chinese agent named Shen who works with Professor Hilaire Sander and his PAX resistance against global oligarchs like Wan.

The male hero of my novel, Rick Buchan, is on the run as well. He is a young U.S. Army sergeant, accused of a crime he did not commit while in a combat zone in the Middle East. He is severely shell-shocked (PTSD we call it today), and needs rescuing—which the courageous Hannah will do. They will rescue each other from their terrible pasts, and emerge stronger both as individuals and as a couple.

Rick and Hannah meet in a Bagnolet, Paris bar called The 39th Step (okay, obvious, but fun). From there, they flee across France and into Luxembourg on a mission to get the IFS package (the McGuffin in this story) into the hands of Pierre Sander's father, Professor Hilaire Sander.

As in the three previously mentioned thrillers, Rick and Hannah undergo a series of episodic adventures leading up to (of course) their separation at the Wolf Gorge in Luxembourg—so now Rick is not only dealing with this military problem back in Germany, but with the IFS package that must not fall into the wrong hands, plus he is searching for his lost Hannah.

Notes: (a) I added a chapter (Shanghai Ramble) at the beginning, so the sixth chapter became the seventh—but the structure remains true to Buchan's model; (b) to avoid misunderstanding: I didn't just numbly trudge along with his model; I followed it vigorously, with relish and joy, because it was there to be emulated, *ars gratia artis*.

In Chapter Seven (#6 in Buchan), he is assailed on a northern Luxembourg meadow by several ultra-modern stealth drones (whose eerie, spooky attacks remind me as much of the hooded alien spaceships in Tom Cruise's 2005 *War of the Worlds* movie as anything else). That's my version of the aeroplane-gyrocopter-crop duster; now we add the killer drones.

In Chapter Eight (#7 in Buchan), Rick does the Cosmo Topper flip and becomes an insider. He is still desperately searching for Hannah, the love of his life. From there we cruise on to a climax in the Valley of Seven Castles, with a secondary climax in the Petrusse Valley in downtown Luxembourg that is actually a war of drones...and HEA. What more could we ask?

So that is the secret of the *Valley of Seven Castles*: a plot structure from *The Thirty-Nine Steps*—hatched 101 years earlier by an English writer on the eve of World War I, developed into the film *The 39 Steps* by Alfred Hitchcock in 1935, revisited later in life by a still vigorous Hitchcock in his 1959 *North By Northwest*, and discovered by me to form the plot skeleton of my 2016 *Valley of Seven Castles, a Luxembourg Thriller* that kicks off the Progressive Thriller Series.

By total coincidence, in 1959 London-based Rank Organization produced a color remake of 1935 Hitchcock film *The 39 Steps*, loosely borrowing John Buchan's 1915 novel *The Thirty-Nine Steps*, in no way connected with Los Angeles-based MGM's *North By Northwest*.

I have made a particular point of studying the theories of the romance category, as expounded by Romance Writers of America and many writers in that field. I even wrote an RWA-style romance novel of the so-called 'clean' subcategory, titled *Stop By: He's Red Hot, She's True Blue* that has been well received.

I have always liked writing fiction with a strong male and a strong female lead involved in a love story. For me it's the most personal, natural, and powerful way to write fiction. I have come to believe that all literature is essentially about the love story of the young (20ish) man and woman at the height of their powers, seeking to mate and procreate the human race. It's evolutionary and biological.

Start with Gilgamesh and Shamhat; visit Achilles and Briseis; or Odysseus on his quest for Penelope; the tragic story of Aeneas and Dido; and wend your way through world literature; the quest is usually by the male seeking his female mirror image to complete the marriage of morning and evening or the sun and moon upon a bed of the four elements.

As I will show, this is a critical element in *Valley of Seven Castles* and in the development of Progressive Thrillers as I envision them.

* * * *

A number of pieces floated together to shape January 2016's *Valley of Seven Castles*. The following pieces are not necessarily in chronological order.

Piece #1: Years ago, my wife and I enjoyed watching a very nice film, a remake of John Buchan's 1915 thriller novel *The Thirty-Nine Steps*. This story has been remade so many times, and I felt such an immediate strong affinity for it, that I realized it must be an archetype. It stayed in my memory for years until I finally found my own vehicle (*Valley of Seven Castles*) to express the same basic plot idea. In other words: while I was studying all sorts of plot structures (three, four, five acts, etc.) it never really occurred to me to delve into what made Buchan's novel such a magnet—it is still getting film remakes into the 21st Century (some better than others, but it's an archetype of plot structure for sure).

Piece #2: Somewhere along the line over the years, I enjoyed watching a rather ancient black and white movie made in 1935 by Alfred Hitchcock, titled *The 39 Steps*. Yes, it was based on the 1915 John Buchan thriller. Note the slight difference in spelling the title. I figured that, if Hitch thought it was a great story, it really must be a great story. So far, so good.

Piece #3: Somewhere along the line, after 2000, I came across a cheap, plain Dover Edition of John Buchan's 1915 novel *The Thirty-Nine Steps.* I bought it and stashed it among my stacks and piles of books at home. I think I read it at some point, but retained only a general impression. All along, something nagged at me: what made this story so enduring?

Pieces #4: Over the years, I not only read thrillers, but wrote my first real thriller (*CON2: The Generals of October*) around 1992. As already mentioned, I wrote the first draft in three weeks, but spent a decade rewriting. It was my first really long, mainstream novel.

Pieces #5+... I had long studied the evolution of thrillers (as described in the previous section called *Thrillerology*). I have been passionate about political and social causes for many years, and my dissatisfaction with the corporate-republican rise from 1980 forward finally pushed me to the point where I wanted to capture my thoughts and feelings in a big novel that would serve as something of a parable. I was ready to write *Valley of Seven Castles.*

To understand where I am driving, we need to take my key influences one by one, starting with John Buchan's 1915 novel, and then Alfred Hitchcock's 1935 film based on Buchan's novel. The real surprise in all this is what comes next. Hint: it's another Alfred Hitchcock film.

* * * *

The 1915 story is a classic novel in ten relatively simply chapters or parts. I will indicate them in lower case for a reason. The story begins with a murder in the first chapter. The hero is framed for this crime, which he did not commit.

The hero goes on the run across the very green and scenic English countryside. He runs from both the bad guys and the authorities separately, hoping to discover the solution to the mystery (what Hitchcock typically termed "the McGuffin"—what are they after? What is the movie about?). He needs to all at once solve the mystery, save the nation, and clear his name.

In chapter six, the hero (Richard Hannay) is buzzed by a low-flying 'aeroplane,' a canvas-and-wood job from the early days of aviation, before World War I.

In chapter seven, the hero stumbles by chance upon a professor in an isolated cabin, who reveals much knowledge to him (the Wise Elder, I think Joseph Campbell called this persona).

Starting in chapter six, Hannay flips from being an outsider to becoming an insider. He is now privy to the central plot, and becomes a pivotal figure in solving it. He stops being on the run from authorities in chapter six, but is still on the outs with the bad guys right until the bitter end in chapter ten. The eponymous thirty-nine steps turn out to be exactly that many steps at a seaside villa, where the Kaiser's spies land on English soil.

One more note: the 1915 novel was an Edwardian fiction, written by a man of Victorian origins, and women did not figure in such fiction. We might point out exceptions like Wilkie Collins' *The Lady in White*, but generally women were hardly seen and not at all heard—even when you consider A. Conan Doyle's *A Scandal in Bohemia* (1891), in which the fictional actress Irene Adler has a prominent if shadowy role ("To Sherlock Holmes she is always *the* woman...").

* * * *

Go forward twenty years, past the Great War. In 1935, Alfred Hitchcock recognized the powerful nature of Buchan's story, and made a movie of it. Hitchcock made the McGuffin something other than a seaside mansion of thirty-nine steps. The title in 1935 refers ambivalently to the name of a 1914ish German spy organization in England, and to the steps leading up to the Big Ben bell inside London's Westminster Tower.

Hitchcock does place two women in the film, one of whom he kills off early, and the other who becomes sort of a ditzy, attractive prop (Madelaine Carroll) for hero Richard Hannay (Robert Donat).

By the way, Hitchcock had a fascination with clocktowers. Besides Westminster in *The 39 Steps*, there is one in his 1934 *The Man Who Knew Too*

Much, and another (Mission San Juan Bautista near San Francisco) in 1958's *Vertigo.*

Like the novel, the film is about a man framed for a crime he didn't commit. Now look for the same generic chapter/section structure here as in Buchan's novel. You could call it episodic (lurching from one action scene to the next).

Richard Hannay runs from the good guys and the bad guys, with a nuisance or complication being the reluctant inclusion of a female interest who is not developed very deeply.

In the sixth part (get the picture?) Hannay is buzzed by a plane. Hitchcock is said to have borrowed the first helicopter—a gyroplane or autogyro—for that scene.

In the seventh part, the hero stumbles on the professor in the cabin, and so forth to the ending.

You'd think that the Buchan plot structure faded away in 1935. But lo and behold, what did I discover?

6. The Final Secret of Alfred Hitchcock

Here at last is the big reveal:

It happens that my all-time favorite suspense film is Alfred Hitchcock's 1959 *North By Northwest.* Guess what? Around 1959, Hitch was turning sixty years old and having a midlife crisis. So he turns to a leading Hollywood screenwriter named Ernest Lehman, and says (we can surmise from the known facts) "Hey, Ernie—I want to be young again and make a thriller like I used to make as a struggling youth. Can you help me out?"

"Sure," Ernie says, "glad to oblige. Any ideas?"

"Oh, I dunno," says Hitch, "why don't you begin by sifting through my old screenplays and see what you can find?"

So Ernest Lehman goes off and does just that. The resulting screenplay and world-class thriller movie was *North by Northwest.*

Ta-dahhh!

But wait, I'll prove it.

In this movie, Roger Thornhill (Cary Grant) is framed for a crime he didn't commit, and goes on the run for his life from both the authorities and the criminals.

The McGuffin in this case is a stolen microfilm containing U.S. government secrets, which the Soviet agents want to smuggle out of the country.

Thornhill takes a train, on which is his love interest Eve Kendall (Eva Marie Saint) who also happens to be a spy. Or is she? Actually, she is a double agent working for the good guys.

After several chapters or parts (think chapters two through five in Buchan's novel), the sixth segment or chapter is one of the most famous scenes in movie history. This is the aeroplane-gyrocopter equivalent. In this scene, Thornhill is chased through a Kansas cornfield by a crop duster airplane. The airplane (i.e., aeroplane; gyroplane) trope, and the frame-up in the first part, are two dead giveaways that Lehman borrowed the structure from the 1935 screenplay to write a new story for the 1959 film. But there is more.

Still on the run, Thornhill is so desperate that he tries to get himself arrested by acting goofy at an art auction attended by the bad guys. When he is arrested, the next incident is a reprise of the mysterious professor in the cabin (Buchan's chapter seven). In section seven, there is once again a total turn-around or flip. I nicknamed it my Cosmo Topper Reveal while I was developing *Valley of Seven Castles*, because in the 1959 film, the professor turns out to be Professor (Unnamed, literally), an FBI chief. Leo G. Carroll, who played the Professor in *North by Northwest*, later played Cosmo Topper in a famous TV comedy series called *Topper*, involving two ghosts (George and Marian).

So—in this Cosmo Topper segment in *North by Northwest*, Thornhill like Hannay flips from outsider to insider. Once again, we have a clear congruency with Buchan's 1915 novel and Hitchcock's 1935 film.

By 1959, the lead character has a real love interest. Cary Grant plays lover in his inimitable style that was at once endearing, goofy, engaging, and smart. The penultimate scene on Mount Rushmore is another of film history's most dramatic and famous. The ultimate scene, in which the train rushes into a tunnel, was the kind of erotic innuendo inserted during an age of extreme censorship, signifying that Thornhill and Kendall chugged their way to HEA-ven with whistles screeching and steam flying by. Train inserted into the tunnel... phallic...into...☺? We get it.

So there you have it. I don't know that anyone has ever really picked these three works apart and seen their congruencies. I based the structure of *Valley of Seven Castles* closely and deliberately on this episodic structure, but with a strong love story between equally strong male and female leads (Richard Buchan and Hannah Smith).

* * * *

In *Valley of Seven Castles*, I have two leads operating separately at first, who come together in the second chapter.

Female hero Hannah is a BAN, a contractual slave owned by a Chinese billionaire. She has been raped and abused, and ultimately betrayed. She signed up as a BAN (Butlers And Nannies, a marketing term for what amounts to sexual and inhumane battery in the horrible new corporate medieval world of our global near future)...

...In Shanghai, Hannah meets Mélusine (Mélu) Poncelet, who rescues her from some gang members. Mélu tells her about a secret technology (IFS) that Wan has stolen while murdering Pierre Sander in London. Not long after, in Paris, Hannah sees the opportunity to escape from Wan—and takes the IFS (McGuffin) with her. Now she is on the run, wanted by Wan's gangsters, and by the authorities on trumped up charges.

The other hero, Rick Buchan is on the run as well. He is a U.S. Army sergeant, accused of a crime he did not commit while in a combat zone in the Middle East.

Rick and Hannah meet in a Bagnolet, Paris bar called The 39th Step. From there, they flee across France and into Luxembourg on a mission to get the IFS package (the McGuffin in this story) into the hands of Pierre Sander's father, Professor Hilaire Sander.

As in the three previously mentioned thrillers, Rick and Hannah undergo a series of episodic adventures leading up to (of course) their separation at the

Wolf Gorge in Luxembourg—so now Rick is not only dealing with this military problem back in Germany, but with the IFS package that must not fall into the wrong hands, plus he is searching for Hannah.

Notes: (a) I added a chapter at the beginning, so the sixth chapter became the seventh—but the structure remains true to Buchan's model; (b) to avoid misunderstanding: I didn't slavishly follow his model; I did so with relish and joy, because it was there to be emulated, *ars gratia artis*.

In Chapter Seven (#6 in Buchan), he is assailed on a northern Luxembourg meadow by several ultra-modern stealth drones (whose eerie, spooky attacks remind me more of the hooded alien spaceships in Tom Cruise's 2005 *War of the Worlds* movie than anything else). That's my version of the aeroplane-gyrocopter-crop duster.

In Chapter Eight (#7 in Buchan), Rick does the Cosmo Topper flip and becomes an insider. He is still desperately searching for Hannah, the love of his life. From there we cruise on to a climax in the Valley of Seven Castles, with a secondary climax in the Petrusse Valley in downtown Luxembourg that is actually a war of drones…and HEA. What more could we ask?

So that is the secret of the *Valley of Seven Castles*: a plot structure from *The Thirty-Nine Steps*—hatched 101 years earlier by an English writer on the eve of World War I, developed into the film *The 39 Steps* by Alfred Hitchcock in 1935, revisited later in life by a still vigorous Hitchcock in his 1959 *North by Northwest*, and discovered by me to form the plot skeleton of my 2016 *Valley of Seven Castles, a Luxembourg Thriller* that kicks off the Progressive Thriller Series.

By total coincidence, in 1959 London-based Rank Organization produced a color remake of 1935 Hitchcock film *The 39 Steps*, loosely borrowing John Buchan's 1915 novel *The Thirty-Nine Steps*, in no way connected with Los Angeles-based MGM's *North by Northwest*.

7. Gender Equality & Plot Structures A Century After Buchan

I'm a passionate promoter of progressive causes, including gender equality. Author John Buchan, in his archetypal 1915 thriller The Thirty-Nine Steps, author John Buchan (essentially still an Edwardian if not Victorian writer) introduces the hero Richard Hannay, but there is no real female protagonist. In his 1935 movie The 39 Steps, based on the Buchan novel, Alfred Hitchcock makes some changes; e.g., he introduces the Westminster clocktower, with its Big Ben clock, as the destination. He introduces two women, one of whom is a villain and gets killed off, while the other is a fairly pale sort of love interest (hand holding at best).

I believe I have discovered dynamite. In 1959, an aging Alfred Hitchcock told his leading screenwriter, Ernest Lehman, that he wanted to make some robust thrillers like in his early years. Based on the outcome, I am 100% certain of what Lehman did. The outcome was one of movie history's most iconic films (one of my favorites): North by Northwest. The plot structure fits perfectly. Lehman obviously referred back to Hitch's earlier movies, and picked the archetypal ten-chapter structure of John Buchan's 1915 novel. Each evolutionary story, over the next century of remakes, has that sixth-chapter airplane terror, which becomes the iconic 1959 cropduster scene with Cary Grant. In North by Northwest, we have Cary Grant in a plausible (if light) romantic tangle with a solid female actress, Eva Marie Saint. The romantic subplot starts somewhere, does something, and goes somewhere—ending with a passionate thrust into the phallic metaphor of a train rushing into a tunnel with a shrill whistle and lots of steam.

In time-honored literary fashion, I was thrilled to discover the *North by Northwest* connection, even as I was already laying out my ten-part plot with a drone aircraft battle in the sixth (or seventh) part, followed by the spy or the man on the run coming in from the cold (to a Wise Elder in a shack in the woods, so to speak), and then becoming a vital part of the solution in the final chapters. I very consciously took the lone male hero (Richard Hannay) in John Buchan's novel, and split him into a gender-equal male-female duo working on equal terms: Rick (Richard) and Hannah (from Hannay). I've said elsewhere that the thin potboilers of the early to mid 1900s always included a female prop called simply "the girl." I've noticed that in Michael Crichton's early novels, for example. I call it "wallpaper." If "the girl" is "wallpaper," then by definition "the guy" becomes "wallpaper" as well—shallow.

I've always preferred working with a strong female lead and a strong male lead. For example, in my first mainstream novel—begun 1992: The *CON2: The Generals of October* (also *Autumn of the Republic, title of a 20th anniversary edition*)—I dramatize and analyze what would or will happen when an unhappy USA finally has a Second Constitutional Convention or CON2. My male lead in *CON2: The Generals of October* is a young, handsome US Army Captain named David Gordon, working for a secret intel unit disguised as an Inspector General office. He pairs off with Lieutenant Victoria "Tory" Breen, a highly competent and courageous Military Police officer also assigned to protect or shadow the enormous encampment of CON2 with its delegates and protective military units in Washington, D.C.

Together, David and Tory stop the menace, save the nation, and fall in love happily ever after (HEA).

This seems to be the most sensible and the optimal author practice. Keeping things simple, which usually makes ideas strongest, we have:

Story Arc: Call the essential story skeleton its story arc, which is comprised of two interdependent trajectories:

—Plot Arc: the plot arc (what happens)

and

—Character Arc: the character arc (who does it and why).

Having worked in this mode for a long time, I find it comfortable and extremely powerful. You have to flush "the girl" down the pipes of history, and treat your characters with total and equal respect regardless of gender and other tags.

You can (almost paradoxically) then use their powerful gender differences to optimal effect because, as I like to point out, all literature is the love story. It's a biological imperative that drives why we need stories in the first place.

That's my theory. I haven't seen a better one yet. I'm already working on the next novel with exactly those ingredients to make my story sizzle.

About Clocktower Books

Clocktower Books, a pioneering Internet, e-book, and San Diego small press publisher, launched in April 1996 by publishing the world's first entire (not partial) proprietary (not public domain) novels (long works, industry standard) for reading online in HTML format (not for reading on portable media like CD-ROM, floppies, or other intermediary media). Some reviewers are confused and think Gutenberg did this first, but they specialize in public domain. We were the first (John Argo: Neon Blue, This Shoal of Space, Pioneers; John T. Cullen: The Generals of October) to publish proprietary novels as noted. Gutenberg strictly releases pre-published public domain material.

www.clocktowerbooks.com

Clocktower Books Museum Site

You will find at the Museum Pages on our website a detailed (and still developing) history of our pioneering publishing house starting from 1996—including references and documentation (ever a work in progress).

museum.clocktowerbooks.com

From 1998 to 2007, Clocktower Books also published what was, during its decade-long run, the world's first professional Web-only (online) magazine of speculative and dark fiction (or SFFH). We published new authors as well as officers and top names of the Science Fiction Writers of America (SFWA); more on our pioneering work at the Science Fiction Encyclopedia online (look under Far Sector).

Our magazine's major names over the years included Deep Outside SFFH and Far Sector SFFH. We published many nominees or later awardees of the Hugo, Nebula, Sturgeon, and other global awards including British, Canadian, and Australian. The leading SF magazine historian Mike Ashley (Liverpool University Press) has stated he will recognize our pioneering magazine in the final volume of his authoritative SF magazine histories. We are mentioned in the SF Encyclopedia.

About the Author

John T. Cullen is a pseudonym of Jean-Thomas Cullen, born 1949 in Nürnberg, West Germany, to a U.S. Army soldier father and an ex-pat Luxemburgish mother. By law, Mr. Cullen was born a U.S. citizen as if born on U.S. soil—one of about a million such U.S. citizens born in occupied and later allied Germany to U.S. military and diplomatic personnel. As an Army brat, he lived his first ten years mostly in France, Luxembourg, and West Germany. Upon his father's retirement in 1960, the family moved to New Haven, Connecticut (his father's home city), where the author spent his teenage years.

He began writing as a child, wrote his first small (10,000 words book) at eleven, and was a published poet at 18. He began his professional writing career in 1967 at age 17 as a summer intern newspaper reporter on *The New Haven Journal-Courier* (three summers). He finished his first novel, a SF story titled *Star Mate: Cosmopolis-City of the Universe*, in 1969 at age 19, having started it at 15 and rewritten it numerous times. First edition due from Clocktower Books: July 2017.

After graduating with a B. A. in English from the University of Connecticut at Storrs, he lived two years in New Haven as a starving artist (fiction and poetry). At 23, he typed up a final collection of his poetry, the last of which he would later write at the mythological age of 27 when rock stars die and lyric poets fade to write prose or find other lives to lead. Soon after moving to San Diego, he enlisted in the U.S. Army, to see Europe again, and because he was not ready to settle down. He spent five years in West Germany, worked hard, traveled extensively, wrote novels and poetry, and returned home to San Diego with an honorable discharge plus medals for outstanding service. He married and divorced in that time.

He left the Army in 1980, remarried at age 37 and remained happy ever after with a wonderful former Peace Corps volunteer (India) and RN named Carolyn. They have a son named Andrew who seemed destined to become the Next Great Guy. Through thick & thin, Mr. Cullen continues writing fiction and nonfiction with great passion.

In 1996, while working at a small software firm in San Diego, he and a friend—Brian Callahan—launched what was probably the first true publisher of digital fiction to be read online in HTML format (no portable media like floppies or CD-ROM). More on this history to follow in the section about Clocktower Books. You can also read about the history of Clocktower Books (www.clocktowerbooks.com) at the official publisher website. There is also a Museum Site at museum.clocktowerbooks.com.

He has written books (fiction, nonfiction) and shorter work (stories, articles) under several pseudonyms. Readers can search online at Amazon.com for his three author pages:

Writing as John T. Cullen

As John T. Cullen, he has written several papers and a nonfiction book titled *A Walk in Ancient Rome* (a virtual tour through every district of the ancient imperial capital, with attention to its history and monuments according to the best modern scholarship in tandem with the ancient Regionary Catalogs). The latter book is due for its first authorized, official publication in 2016-2017. His papers include a plausible, scholarly explanation of the ancient Sator Arepo enigma (due out mid to late 2016).

He has written several major historical and spy suspense thrillers: *The Spy's Daughter, Doctor Night*, the bestselling *Lethal Journey: Legendary 1892 Gaslight Mystery: True Crime & Ghost Story at the Hotel del Coronado near San Diego* (1892 noir period piece based on a true crime/ghost story at the Hotel del Coronado near San Diego). His nonfictional historical analysis *Dead Move: Kate Morgan and the Haunting Mystery of Coronado* remains the only and most plausible solution to the 1892 crime and ghost story—actually, a woman's terrible tragedy, which comes to life in the form of a true Victorian 'Fallen Angel' story by gaslight (the novel Lethal Journey).

In 1992, John T. Cullen began work on a political thriller titled *CON2: The Generals of October* (also *Autumn of the Republic*). The premise concerns a Second Constitutional Convention, which turns into a military and political nightmare leading to a coup d'etat as dark forces including mercenary generals seize power. The author was quite cognizant of the famous 1962 political thriller *Seven Days in May*, and other classic thrillers like like *Three Days of the Condor* and *The Parallax View*.

In 2016, he launched a new type of thriller—the Progressive Thriller—starting with *Valley of Seven Castles, a Luxembourg Thriller*. He suggests that the political themes and outcomes of *CON2* and *Doctor Night* fit well within the purview of his political and social parables.

Writing as Jean-Thomas Cullen

Under his real name (Jean-Thomas Cullen), he has written a number of novels, including a sentimental romance (*Stop By*) and the love story *On Saint Ronan Street*, written as a young U.S. Army soldier in a Hitler-era U.S. Army barracks in West Germany). The latter two are among his most personally treasured books, special in a way that no others could be. Also under his real birth name: Cymbalist Poems, a selection of early poetry. He was a published poet and professionally employed author by age 17.

Writing as John Argo

This is the pseudonym he picked in the heady early days of Internet publishing. As the first person ever to publish one or more complete proprietary novels online in HTML format (to be read online, not carried or downloaded on portable media like floppies), he celebrated the wonder of the new digital medium by choosing a historical name—that of the ship of wonder, Argo, that carried Jason and the Argonauts ("Argo-sailors") around the Aegean some 3,000 years ago on a set of mind-bending adventures that set the imagination on fire back then, and has led to many modern movies as well. It's a perfect example of archetypal stories—so universal that they beg to be constantly remade, like the 4,000 year old (more more) tale of Romeo and Juliet (originally Babylonian, if we take a hint from Ovid's choices of locale in the tale of Pyramus and Thisbe, 2,000 years ago).

As John Argo, the author has written dozens of novels and short stories. Most of the novels are science fiction, dark fantasy, or horror, with a few suspense stories thrown in.

His stand-alone SF novels are the DarkSF Series, which include titles like *Robinson Crusoe 1,000,000 A.D.* and *Nebula Express* and *Monopol City*. They also include one science-horror novel, *Doom Spore*. In 2015, after gathering dust for over twenty years, the John Argo novel *Streamliners* was published by Clocktower Books.

John Argo's *future history, the Empire of Time mega-series*, which he launched in the 1960s with *City of the Universe*, contains a growing number of titles including *Mars the Divine*, *Lantern Road*, and *Moon Berry Wine* among others. Look for more titles by this author in this series.

His one historical fantasy as of 2016 is *The Sibyl's Urn*, a romp back in time through history and mythology in search of a lost parchment, in which a modern professor named Darwin, plus an unnamed second-person hero or heroine ("you"), and a strange creature part goddess and part cricket.

* * * *

Here are some samples of the author's work.

Most or all are available in print and e-book editions online. Check the author's website (www.johntcullen.com) for details.

Sample Books by the Author
John T. Cullen: CON2: Autumn of the Republic

Note: 20th Anniversary Edition; original: The Generals of October or CON2

CON2: Autumn of the Republic is the most important and relevant political thriller you will read in your lifetime—after Valley of Seven Castles. The stakes cannot be higher. In CON2, the 1787 Constitution is about to go in the trash, replaced by a document from hell, if enough followers send a dangerous demagogue to the White House.

This was (and still is) the first and only novel to tackle the premise of a second Constitutional Convention. Cullen thinks it through step by step without bogging down in needless detail that would break the story spell. The author lets the story of CON2 tell itself as a vast background scrim, while the drama of David, Tory, and supporting characters like Ib Shoob, Jet, and Rocky Devereaux plays out in the foreground.

Any year now, we will have a Second Constitutional Convention (CON2), the first such assembly of the states since the Founding Fathers of 1776 became the Framing Fathers of 1787 at the Constitutional Convention in Philadelphia. It will be the worst mistake we ever make.

The author wrote his classic political thriller in 1992 as a silver bullet to kill this werewolf before it ever shows its teeth. CON2 must be killed dead before it can ever happen. Calls for such a convention from the cesspool of corporate-republican politics are frequent and shrill; as are calls for secession, laws banning LGBTO citizens from civil rights, bills punishing women for exercising their Constitutional right to reproductive choice, and various other attempts to dismantle the United States.

Article V is a ticking time bomb embedded in the U.S. Constitution. Article V lets us change our Constitution one amendment at a time, or rewrite it, or just totally scrap it and go for broke with something utterly new and crazy. This is the big What If. A CON2 has been convened, and the nation is on the brink of civil war.

Two young U.S. Army officers, serving in differing intelligence units in Washington, D.C. as CON2 begins, join forces in a puzzling murder investigation. Captain David Gordon and Lieutenant Victoria (Tory) Breen are on the trail of a missing Coast Guard computer genius. The trail takes them to a virtual world of digital commerce (presciently envisioned years ago, and still vibrantly original). The hidden worlds of the CloudMaster network take them to a conspiracy involving the vice president (murdered by domestic terrorists a year ago) and from there to a cabal of generals, admirals, and others determined to save us from ourselves, scrap all that evil liberal and godless nonsense in the Constitution, and hand us a new, improved scriptural tyranny to make Oliver Cromwell, Savanarola, or Cotton Mather envious.

The author' tells a gripping suspense thriller with a solid romantic story line, leaving the enormous story of CON2 sufficiently but not overwhelmingly displayed as a backdrop. It's a love story, a murder mystery, a conspiracy thriller, and above all a good read. It's not a history of the universe or a road map for galactic hitchhikers, but a good solid story that keeps its feet on the ground and its head low while the world explodes all around it.

If you love intense, brainy thrillers like *Seven Days in May*, *Three Days of the Condor*, *The Parallax View*, or *The Lost Constitution*, here is a powerful companion story. New Author Preface contains fascinating background details and fascinating info.

John Argo and Clocktower Books Present

Stunning and poetic far-future history by John Argo in the tradition of Cordwainer Smith's Classic Norstrilia and other tales of the Instrumentality. Part of the Empire of Time series.

Jean-Thomas Cullen and Clocktower Books Present

A sentimental, clean romantic story set in contemporary Connecticut. A young war widow has become a Sleeping Beauty, stung by the loss of her soldier husband, and works as a librarian in the tiny town of Emery. One hot summer day, just looking for a cool spot while his car is fixed, Prince Charming stops by in the form of a young millionaire who has suffered a painful divorce and isn't really looking for love. Neither is she. But old Cupid shoots them both with his arrows, and the ground moves beneath their feet...

By John Argo: YANAPOP

Here's a thriller unlike anything you've ever read (unless you've been a lifelong fan of Thomas Pynchon's iconic 1965 *The Crying of Lot 49*); or consider the dark comedy movie *After Hours* (Martin Scorsese, all-star cast), one of the funniest (and brainiest) films ever made. We agree. Think of Linda Fiorentino in *The Last Seduction*, Jack Lemmon in *The Out-of-Towners*, and a very tiny, select number of other such irony-rich *Odysseys*. YANAPOP (Young Adult, New Adult, Participating Older Persons) is the name of a vast (fictional) entertainment corporation in Los Angeles, with tentacles around the world. From its strange gardens grows the love story of Martin Brown and Chloë Setreal, in which Martin became Odysseus in his insane and dangerous journey to reach his Penelope.

Nonfiction by John T. Cullen: Dead Move

John T. Cullen, a San Diego author and scholar (BA, BBA, MS) applies his journalistic and historical expertise to solve a long-standing true crime. During Thanksgiving Week 1892, a stylish young woman (about 24) officially called The Beautiful Stranger by the Hotel del Coronado near San Diego, checked in under a false name and died a violent, mysterious death a few days later. Her case became a national sensation full of notoriety overnight because of allegations of affairs with men in high places.

It was a Victorian scandal of epic proportions, resulting in the famous ghost legend at the hotel. John T. Cullen, basing his research entirely on true history (no ghosts were harmed), provides the first ever plausible explanation of what really happened—including a coverup of global proportions. See also Lethal Journey, the noir gaslight mystery thriller he wrote to dramatize *Dead Move*, on which the novel (dramatization) *Lethal Journey* is closely based.

Thriller by John T. Cullen: Lethal Journey
Closely based on his nonfictional scholarly analysis of the 1892 true crime (*Dead Move*) here is a dramatization treated as a gaslight era noir suspense thriller.

Ray Bradbury Loved This One:

Ray Bradbury wrote a personal fan mail note to John T. Cullen in January 2008, praising this little gem, a novel that is a tribute both to Charles Dickens' classic *A Christmas Carol*, and to Ray Bradbury's dark but playful fantasies.

By Jean-Thomas Cullen—On Saint Ronan Street

This romantic coming of age novel tells of the passionate love affair between a 23-year-old idealistic, talented poet and a beautiful, neglected young married woman in a New England college town set in 1973. Written by a young soldier in 1976 Cold War West Germany and forgotten for forty years, it glows as fresh today as it was when I composed it in Paris and Heidelberg and other European cities where I traveled in my old orange VW as a single, adventuresome young man.

This book is a streamlined edition containing only the novel, not the companion volume of poetry—ostensibly written by the young hero's alter ego, the fictional poet Charles Egeny. The two books are twins, separated at birth, and finally reunited in 2016 as a double e-book (*27duet*). The *Cymbalist Poems* can be found in separate editions (ebook or print), or together in the double titled *27duet*.

The author says: "The star of this duet is my 'year 27 coming of age novel', written nights among moths and ghosts in an old Hitler-era army barracks to strains of Mozart. I was a young U.S. Army soldier, stationed in 1970s West Germany during the Cold War. *On Saint Ronan Street* was a nostalgic retrospective on my lost past in New Haven, wellspring of my poetic art; and its women, my first loves.

"Long titled cryptically just *Jon+Merile* in manuscript, it gathered dust for 40 years until I published it in 2016. In the novel, talented, aspiring 23 year old poet Jon Harney graduated from a small college, and is now mowing lawns and doing other odd jobs around Yale University while showing his verse portfolio to New York City publishers. He meets a lonely young woman, Merile Doherty. She explains to Jon that her name is pronounced like Merrill, but she has softened and feminized it so it looks different than it seems—an apt metaphor for her life. Her husband Bill is an archeologist on faculty at Yale University. Bill is older and colder, vacant at affection, always gone, never quite there for her. He is Absent Without Emotional Leave—AWEL (or Ah Well?).

"When Merile meets Jon Harney, she's been alone again for a time. Bill is far off in Australia digging for bones, while also digging chicks in Sydney. He phones to tell her that he has fallen in love with an Australian woman, and is going to leave Merile. That's before he calls to tell her he isn't. That's how it goes. Merile is vulnerable and Jon Harney is smitten. Their chemistry is incendiary. Like hungry wolves, they cannot get enough of each other. Their mad, passionate love affair is as glorious as it is doomed.

"I wrote backwards, into an idealized past, while stationed in Europe in such an enviable and idyllic situation. The Army does get in your eyes and you may get tangled in the camouflage netting instead of seeing the big picture. I was single, healthy, and educated. I worked hard, and the Army provided three hots and a cot. I owned a cool orange VW van in which my buddies and I drove around Europe in our free time. Great places like Heidelberg, Paris, Brussels, or Luxembourg were a few hours' drive away. My job (junior enlisted, first tour) was largely 9-5, aside from the usual Army rigamarole of alerts and duties. I always had poetry and stories percolating in my head, whether in the Quartier Latin in Paris, or the castle at Heidelberg, or a Palatinate wine festival. I had a stable base from which to cruise every weekend—or stay in the barracks, go the office alone, and type novels. On Saint Ronan Street was a cry from the heart—yearning, passionate, actually pretty desperate.

At 27, I did not die at 27 like Jim Morrison, Janis Joplin, Jimi Hendrix, Kurt Cobain, Amy Winehouse, and other meteoric talents who flamed out at that scary age. I carried my poetic candle on to writing decades of carefully and lovingly wrought prose. I have authored many books (including history-nonfiction). My fiction was long still imbued with an intoxicating, lyric wine (poetry) grown richer and mellower with time but not any more passionate and song-filled than under Lili Marlene's lantern by my barracks in Rheinland-Pfalz. If you like a story where the language is music, and the characters draw you in, this is for you.

www.ingramcontent.com/pod-product-compliance
Lightning Source LLC
Chambersburg PA
CBHW031154020726
47499CB00002B/361